NEBULA AWARDS
SHOWCASE
2013

NEBULA AWARDS
SHOWCASE

2013

STORIES AND EXCERPTS BY

CONNIE WILLIS, JO WALTON, KIJ JOHNSON, GEOFF RYMAN, JOHN
CLUTE, CAROLYN IVES GILMAN, FERRETT STEINMETZ, KEN LIU,
NANCY FULDA, DELIA SHERMAN, AMAL. EL-MOHTAR,
C. S. E. COONEY, DAVID W. GOLDMAN, AND KATHERINE SPARROW,
E. LILY YU, AND BRAD R. TORGERSEN

THE YEAR'S BEST SCIENCE FICTION AND FANTASY

Selected by the Science Fiction and Fantasy Writers of America

EDITED BY
CATHERINE ASARO

an imprint of **Prometheus Books**
Amherst, NY

Nebula Awards showcase 2013 / edited by Catherine Asaro.
ISBN 978–1–61614–783-9 (pbk.)
ISBN 978–1–61614–784-6 (ebook)

Printed in the United States of America

To Eleanor Wood,
who has given so much to the field of speculative fiction.

PERMISSIONS

CONTENTS

CONTENTS

Introduction

A HARMONY OF THOUGHTS

Catherine Asaro

Drawing is not what you see, but what you must make others see.
—Edgar Degas, *The Shop-Talk of Edgar Degas*,
edited by R. H. Ives Gammell

When I was a child, my parents gave me several framed prints of ballerinas by painter Edgar Degas. To this day, they remain in my old bedroom, on the wall above the ballet barre where I was supposed to practice but almost never did. Although I loved to dance, doing it alone in my room held little appeal when the alternative was to join my friends, the other dancers at the studios where I trained. Those Degas paintings, however, remain a part of the creative landscape in my mind, whether I am writing, dancing, composing music, or solving the partial differential equations of quantum scattering theory.

The conventional assumption in our culture is that artistic endeavors are distinct from analytic pursuits such as science and math. On one side lies the lush realm of emotion; on the other, we find the straight lines of logic. That separation is reflected in how we view works of speculative fiction. Although the division is most prominent in comparisons between fantasy and hard science fiction, it comes into play for all the speculative subgenres.

I protest this idea that emotion and logic are two mutually exclusive lands separated by a wall of our perceptions, that these realms must be disparate, one ruled by passion, the other by logic. In my experience, the analytic and artistic threads of human endeavor are so thoroughly entangled, it is impossible to separate them. In reading the stories on the ballot this year, I was struck by how well they illustrate that idea.

I wish I could have included every nominated story in this anthology.

Unfortunately, that would have resulted in a book that cost more than would fit between two covers, while giving the contributors little more than the proverbial penny for their thoughts. However, the full ballot appears in this anthology, and I recommend all the stories.

> Music was my refuge. I could crawl into the space between the notes and curl my back to loneliness.
> —Maya Angelou, *Gather Together in My Name*

David W. Goldman's short story "The Axiom of Choice" is an ingenious play on a famous (some might say infamous) mathematical axiom. The axiom of choice seems simple at first glance. What it says is essentially this: given any collection of buckets, each holding at least one object, it is possible to choose exactly one object from each bucket. If every bucket contained a pair of shoes, for example, we could specify "the left shoe." Then we've picked out one shoe from each bucket. Easy, right? But what if each bucket contains the same pair of identical socks? How do we specify one sock or the other when every choice is the same? The axiom of choice claims it is always possible to make that choice even if we don't see how.

In his story, Goldman has the reader choose the plotline, making the story an interactive experience. As he weaves the tale of a guitarist who suffered a debilitating accident, the reader determines the plot. Or do we? The plot unfolds as a series of choices, forming an allegory for the axiom, which itself is a metaphor for the emotional journey taken by the musician.

Math and music are inextricably tangled together. The mathematics of music is one of the most beautiful areas of physics. Goldman's story, with its structure of branches and numbered sections, is reminiscent of both a musical composition and a mathematical proof. So it seems only appropriate that he uses the axiom as the framing device.

In math, the axiom of choice is fundamental to the Banach-Tarski paradox, which says we can cut a solid ball into a finite number of pieces, even as few as five, and reassemble those pieces into two solid balls, each the same size and shape as the original; in fact, we could cut up a pea and reassemble it into a ball the size of our sun.[1] *Say what?* Such wild projects don't work in real life because we would need to cut the balls into such convoluted pieces, they wouldn't have a physically defined volume. They exist only in theory. And so Goldman plays with the choices made by his protagonist—or those that, in theory, he could have made. The musician's choices, real or theoretical, become the space he curls into, seeking refuge between the notes he can no longer play. The story is an exquisite blending of mathematics and emotion, tangling the analytical with the human heart.

> Origami, like music, permits both composition and performance as expressions of the art.
> —Robert J. Lang, origami artist and physicist,
> www.langorigami.com

> I wished to fold the laws of nature, the dignity of life, and the expression of affection into my work.
> —Akira Yoshizawa, origami grandmaster,
> *Inochi Yutaka na Origami (Origami Full of Life)*,
> quote translated by Kondo Kanato

> Describe, with proof, what fractions p/q can be obtained as areas of squares folded from a single unit square . . .
> —2006 American Regional Mathematics League,
> *The Power of Origami*

Origami is the art of paper folding, where the artist uses an intricate series of folds to transform a flat sheet of paper into a sculpture. Not only is it a visually exquisite art form, it has also defined an entire branch of mathematics and appears in questions on internationally renowned programs such as the American Regional Mathematics League.

In his story, "The Paper Menagerie," Ken Liu explores the complex relationship between a young man of mixed heritage born in the United States and his mother, who was a mail-order bride from China, through the medium of her origami creations, which, in his childhood, she magically brought to life for him. The duality of origami—a pursuit that deeply embodies both artistic and analytic properties—becomes an inspired frame for Liu's tale. The geometrical nature of origami is never described in the story, but for me as a reader, the complexity and multilayered tension felt by the son toward his mother is aptly symbolized by the tension that so many people perceive between art and the math therein, especially the three-dimensional complexity embodied by origami. That both of those aspects simultaneously exist in the same work despite their apparent contradictory nature offers an apt paradigm for love and its denial in this heartbreaking relationship between a son and his mother.

> Dance is the hidden language of the soul.
> —Martha Graham, *New York Times*, 1985

In her story, titled "Movement," Nancy Fulda writes about an autistic prodigy who excels at ballet. Autism is a neural disorder that impacts how the brain interprets information, making it difficult for those affected to communicate with others. A small percentage of autistics are savants, particularly with music, memory, math, and, in this case, dance. Fulda uses the protagonist's relationship with ballet to explore the ramifications behind a potential treatment for her autism.

As a former dancer in both ballet and jazz, I was struck by how well Fulda brought to life that sense of timelessness—meditation, even—that comes when you immerse yourself in the movement. It is a fitting device for the story, which centers on a narrator who experiences time differently than most people; it can take her hours, days, or even longer to answer a question. But that answer—when it finally comes—is a brilliantly choreographed piece of writing.

> A work of art is a world in itself, reflecting senses and emotions
> of the artist's world.
> —Hans Hoffman, *Search for the Real*
> *and Other Essays*

> As the builders say, the larger stones do not lie well without the
> lesser.
> —Plato, *Laws*, Book 10,
> translated by Benjamin Jowett

Plato's words could apply equally well to the construction of a building, a bridge—or a science fiction novella. In "The Man Who Bridged the Mist," Kij Johnson uses the creation of a bridge to construct the story of the man who raises that remarkable span. The bridge becomes a metaphor for his life and his world.

We often think of a bridge as an engineering feat, a triumph of physics and math, but the relationship of architects to their creations is much like that of artists to their art. As so aptly described by Plato, every piece of that bridge, whether the largest stone or the smallest cube, is necessary to its creation. It is fitting that Plato's quote comes from his work *Laws*, in that laws—whether they are created by our judicial systems or are natural laws that we have discovered—are highly analytical yet achieve results that tangle intricately with the emotional well-being (or lack thereof) of those who live by them.

"The Man Who Bridged the Mist" reminds me of the lithograph "Hand with a Reflecting Sphere" by M. C. Escher. Just as Escher's creation is an image of himself holding a sphere that reflects both his image and world, so the process of building a bridge across the mist reflects the architect in the story and his remarkable world. Escher evokes the scene in his lithograph with careful detail, using simple objects to tell us about himself; so the details of how the builder constructs his bridge tell us about his hopes, his history, and the people who impact his life.

Escher's image achieves a dramatic effect with no explosion of color and action; it is done in gray and white and is all the more powerful for that choice. Johnson is similarly subtle with "The Man Who Bridged the Mist." It is a story in colors of fog and stone. We learn of "fish" living within the mist, shadowy creatures considered small at six feet in length. The legendary "Big Ones" hidden in the depths are an ever-present threat. Johnson could have taken the easy path and thrown in an action-adventure scene, where such monsters explode from the gorge and go about canonical havoc-wreaking activities. She chooses a far more nuanced approach that, in the context of her story, is eminently more effective, providing a metaphor for the half-hidden events that shape and so subtly shatter the lives of the characters. She leaves the reader with a question: Are the submerged "Big Ones" hidden beneath our emotional landscape as great as we fear? It is a fascinating novella with new layers that emerge every time I reread the story.

> Art is a staple of mankind ... urgent, so utterly linked with the pulse of feeling that it becomes the singular sign of life when every other aspect of civilization fails.
> —Jamake Highwater, *The Language of Vision: Meditations on Myth and Metaphor*

In "The Ice Owl," Carolyn Ives Gilman tells the story of Thorn, a bright and edgy young woman. She centers the story on the girl's interactions with her tutor, an elderly collector who repatriates artwork stolen during a war that took place more than a hundred forty years prior. The loss and return of such works offers an effective allegory in the novella for the price exacted by wars on the people who survive them.

Throughout the novella, Gilman makes explicit connections between art and math or science and, in doing so, creates allegorical gems for the reader. A central aspect of the story derives from an ingenious blending of art and math used by certain artists. If they apply a certain algorithm to their media, each artist can create a work of art that looks dramatically different depending on how a person views the image. It is a clever play on holographic images in our real world that are visible only at certain angles, such as those that appear on many driver's licenses. That artwork is a fitting theme for Thorn, who must learn to face the ways that "truth" can change depending on how she views her world. In another instance, Gilman uses the aromatic chemistry of benzene-based compounds to define a combination lock formed from the ornamentation on a box, itself a piece of art, which may or may not contain yet more secrets. The layering of puzzles on puzzles is an effective metaphor for the layered design of this inspired novella.

Gilman uses the word *Holocide* to describe a war that—like a holograph—encompassed every dimension of its world and was viewed from all sides by an interstellar civilization. Its similarity to the word *Holocaust* is telling. During World War II, the Nazis confiscated hundreds of thousands of artworks, and to this day the repatriation of those stolen pieces continues. In Gilman's able hands, repatriation becomes a symbol of the impact war has on our humanity. The theme had a particular resonance for me in that I was writing this introduction when I read that Anton Dobrolski, the oldest known survivor of Auschwitz, had died at age 108. As the last survivors from the concentration camps of World War II pass away, their oral histories fade into a few sentences in history texts. If we forget, will that allow the atrocities to happen again? In Gilman's novella, where relativistic spaceflight allows people to jump into the future every time they travel, the memories of the survivors stretch out for centuries and spread across the stars.

> Crying, whistling, calling, they skimmed the placid sea and left the shore. Make haste, make speed, hurry and begone; yet where, and to what purpose? The restless urge of autumn, unsatisfying, sad, had put a spell upon them and they must flock, and wheel, and cry; they must spill themselves of motion before winter came.
> —Daphne du Maurier, *The Birds & Other Stories*

In "The Migratory Pattern of Dancers," Katherine Sparrow writes about men who are genetically engineered with the DNA of birds, which have become extinct. Although the men remain essentially human, twice a year they are driven to travel the routes that birds once flew during their migrations. As part of their journey, the men make periodic stops to perform dances in places such as Yellowstone National Park, choreographing works that draw on the traits of those vanished birds—and that also make millions of dollars for the avaricious backers who sponsor their shows. The performances evoke the avian multitudes that once soared through our skies in the freedom of flight, yet that very evocation of freedom becomes a form of prison for the dancers.

Audiences come to the shows to be entertained, amused, and, yes, to see what fate might befall those dancers who dare to seek the closest that humans can come to unaided flight. As such, the story explores the ramifications of the human fascination with death as entertainment. Sparrow hints at an insidious end to humanity; will we become so inured to the loss of life through our entertainment that we participate in our own demise? Rather than a dramatic apocalypse, the story suggests that human extinction may come from within, prodded by the same instincts that led the characters in the story to reduce the once-great species of birds that flew our skies to an echo found only in human dances.

> Science and literature are not two things, but two sides of one thing.
> —Thomas Huxley, *Science and Culture:*
> *And Other Essays*, volume 3

Jo Walton turns around the idea of combining science and the arts in her metafictional novel *Among Others*. Here the art is writing; the book is told through the narrator's love of literature, in particular, science fiction. As such, the novel invokes many of our great speculative writers, specifically those from the science fiction canon of several decades ago. Literature plays a role in Walton's novel similar to the role played by art, music, or dance for other works in this anthology. But the art that Walton uses to frame her story is *our* art, the literature of the fantastic, as illustrated, for example, by this anthology. The *Nebula Awards Showcase 2013* doesn't dance, sing, paint, strum, or drum—but it becomes a recursive loop, one constructed out of its stories, which use other arts to frame the literary works so that the anthology becomes the art that frames itself.

Metafiction is a story that refers to literature and its conventions as part of the story. In other words, the tale is self-referential. The idea is that it exposes the illusions created by a work of fiction, blurring the line between the "real" world of the reader and the imagined world of the story. Walton employs this technique to good effect in her novel, using speculative fiction to frame a story of fantasy, even prodding the reader to ask if the magical aspects to the story are "real" within the context of the narrator's tale or a fiction within a fiction masquerading as reality for the fictional characters.

In analogy with the self-referential loop that arises from the description of this anthology as an art that frames itself, it could be said that Walton's book leaves out one important novel in the works she referenced—*Among Others*, by Jo Walton. What a satisfying creation of fractal metafiction that would be; the book refers to the book that refers to the book that refers to . . . well, you get the idea. It could be a recursive triumph worthy of Mandelbrot, the mathematician who created the gorgeous fractal known as the Mandelbrot set, which repeats itself the mesmerizing structure of its images at ever-finer and finer detail. For me, *Among Others* felt close to a literary version of the online video that shows the Mandelbrot fractal at greater and greater magnification, offering a musical glimpse into the ultimate representation of self-referential art.[2]

> But Marlow was not typical (if his propensity to spin yarns be excepted), and to him the meaning of an episode was not inside like a kernel but outside, enveloping the tale which brought it out only as a glow brings out a haze . . .
> —Joseph Conrad, *The Heart of Darkness*

The Club Story has a long tradition in science fiction. Such a tale consists of two parts: a frame that describes a club or other place where the narrator is relating his story within a story, and the tale itself, which the narrator often claims involved him. In the words of John Clute, "A club story is a tale told by one person to others in a place where the story can be related safely, either a collection featuring one teller with many tales or several storytellers taking turns." Clute, one of our two Solstice Award winners this year, offers here an essay on the Club Story adapted from his article in the online *Encyclopedia of Science Fiction*. Not only does it form a compelling entry in the discussion of fiction as art form, but the essay itself is a form of art in its construction for an online audience, illustrating how the electronic age is changing the way we present literature. For the paper copy of this anthology, we can't give the hyperlinks that allow readers to click on words and phrases from the essay to find connected entries in the encyclopedia, creating a hypertext document. However, you can enjoy the essay in its original electronic form in the *Encyclopedia of Science Fiction* at www.sf-encyclopedia.com/entry/club_story.

> I am trusted with a muzzle and enfranchised with a clog;
> therefore I have decreed not to sing in my cage. If I had my
> mouth, I would bite; if I had my liberty, I would do my liking: in
> the meantime let me be that I am and seek not to alter me.
> —Don John, in William Shakespeare's
> *Much Ado about Nothing*

> Censorship ends in logical completeness when nobody is allowed
> to read any books except the books that nobody can read.
> —George Bernard Shaw, "Literary Censorship
> in England," *Current Opinion*

In her all-too-short story "Ado," Connie Willis uses the art of literature in a satire that, beneath its lighthearted comedy, gives a satisfying smack to censorship. The "world" she creates lies in the not-so-distant future where the constraints on what teachers may teach is stringently limited for fear of offending someone. *Anyone.* For all that it is amusing, the story also offers a sobering look at what could happen to our children and their futures if we allow censors to eviscerate the literature they read. In the world of "Ado," I've already written too much—

> Some painters transform the sun into a yellow spot. Others trans-
> form a yellow spot into the sun.
> —widely attributed to Pablo Picasso

Another theme that struck me about the stories on this year's ballot is the diversity in the portrayal of both real cultures on Earth and those formed in the imaginations of the writers. At its best, speculative fiction can evoke astonishing universes. We paint prose pictures of other places, other worlds, other suns. Ironically, in earlier days of science fiction, the "alien" worlds depicted in many of our works were sometimes less alien than other cultures on our own planet. The current ballot illustrates the maturing of the genre. It is a cornucopia of world building, not only for imagined places, but also in exploring the people, ways of life, and ideas on our own planet that come from other cultures besides the West.

> Imagination will often carry us to worlds that never were. But without it, we go nowhere.
> —Carl Sagan, *Cosmos*

When I was a child, about age eight or nine, I remember being at my grandparent's Spanish-style home in Escondido, California, not the endless metropolis that area has become now, but back in the days when it was a sleepy little town among the avocado farms. With nothing to do on a day baking beneath a relentless summer sun, I wandered down to the local library and sat in the air-conditioned reading room absorbed in a book about bees. I don't remember the title or the author, but I will never forget how much I loved its tale of great bee adventure.

I remembered that book when I read E. Lily Yu's story "The Cartographer Wasps and the Anarchist Bees." Yu extrapolates the behavior of bees and wasps as known to modern science into a tale set in the village of Yiwei, which in Mandarin Chinese roughly translates as "to suppose." It is an apt name for the opening locale of a story that concerns map-making wasps and their conflicts with bees both revolutionary and not. The societies of these remarkable insects are portrayed with depth and a gentle humor. Their cultures serve as a foil for the other culture in the story, that of the humans. The tale offers an unusual twist on science fiction stories of first contact and a salient commentary on human political systems of Earth.

> Painting is silent poetry, and poetry is painting that speaks.
> —Simonides of Ceos, in "On the Glory of the Athenians," by Plutarch, in *The Moralia*, Book 4

Amal El-Mohtar's poem "Peach-Creamed Honey" gives bees a very different look. They are among the many images she invokes with her sensual poem that won the 2011 Rhysling Award in the short form category. The sheer beauty of the writing is a pleasure to read, like a song. As I write this, it inspires my mind to compose melodies, edgily sweet, a haunting fusion of Western and Near Eastern music with a mesmerizing drumbeat, all conjured by these lines from the poem:

"And I know she'll let me tell her how the peaches lost their way
how they fell out of a wagon on a sweaty summer's day,
how the buzz got all around that there was sugar to be had,
and the bees came singing, and the bees came glad."

C. S. E. Cooney, the 2011 Rhysling Award winner in the long form category, also treats the reader to gratifyingly evocative language in "The Sea King's Second Bride." Her lyrical word pictures evoke a fantastic land in the deep sea. At turns graceful and irreverent, the poem is a sequel to the traditional Scandinavian ballad "Agnete and the Merman." Cooney offers the ill-behaved merman a second chance for happiness, though at first he refuses to notice. The clever contrasts between the conventions of traditional folktales and the sensibility of a modern woman make for a delicious mix in this poem.

> Pouring forth its seas everywhere, then, the ocean envelops the
> earth and fills its deeper chasms.
> —Nicolaus Copernicus, On the Revolutions
> of the Heavenly Spheres

Brad R. Torgersen offers a science fiction take on the deep sea in his story "Ray of Light." Although the world he evokes with such careful detail is here on Earth, it is as alien to most of us as another planet. "Ray of Light" centers on the confinement of Earth's last humans in undersea settlements after the surface has become unlivable. Torgersen uses the milieu to frame a teenager's alienation, not only her rebellion against her father, but also against her environment. The setting exerts a literary pressure on the characters analogous to the pressure of the deep sea that dominates their lives. It didn't surprise me that the means by which the young people came together in secret to plan was through a music club. Although music played a relatively small part compared to the arts in other stories in this anthology, I found it a satisfying accent for the tale of a father's struggles to accept his child's transition into adulthood.

> Sauerkraut is tolerant, for it seems to be a well of contradictions. Not that it would preach a gastronomic neutrality that would endure all heresies. It rejects dogmatism and approves of individual tastes.
> —Julien Freund, director of the Institute of Sociology
> in Strasbourg, *Les Saisons d'Alsace*

Ferrett Steinmetz sweeps us off to another sort of world in his novelette "Sauerkraut Station." The story is set on a space habitat that offers medical aid and refits ships with supplies. Those supplies include their specialty, sauerkraut, which most of their visitors hold in far too low esteem, at least in the view of Lizzie, the narrator. The setting is brought alive by the author's careful detail and serves as a foil for the political background of the universe Steinmetz builds. The tale is both stark and reaffirming, the story of a remarkable young woman.

When I first read "Sauerkraut Station," I assumed it had appeared in *Analog*. It has that feel for me in part because of the well described life in a space station, including what happens if we lose amenities we take for granted, such as light and gravity. I was intrigued to learn that it came from the online zine *GigaNotoSaurus*. In fact, two works in this book first appeared in *GigaNotoSaurus*, the other being "The Migratory Patterns of Dancers." They offer telling examples of the sea changes in publishing we've experienced over the last decade. In the past, when the outlets for short fiction were limited to hardcopy markets, the expense of producing and distributing such publications drastically constrained the number of markets, which meant many good stories went unpublished or appeared in hard-to-find places. Now, with the advent of so many online markets, more top-notch stories than ever are seeing print. This is the first I've seen of *GigaNotoSaurus*, but I will definitely be looking up more of their issues.

> You can't remake the world
> Without remaking yourself.
> —Ben Okri, *Mental Fight*

Geoff Ryman's carefully rendered novelette "What We Found" takes place in Nigeria. On one level, it centers on the attempts of Terhemba, a Nigerian scientist, to reconcile his research with the ravages suffered by his family; the two converge when he discovers evidence that parents can pass the effects of traumas they have endured to their children. The narrator writes, "What we found is that 1966 can reach into your head and into your balls and stain your children red. You pass war on. . . . We live our grandfathers' lives." In telling Terhemba's story, Ryman writes vividly of a Nigeria that is in turns severe and beautiful.

On another level, "What We Found" draws on a phenomenon observed by psychologists, in particular John Schooler, that their research showed a "decline effect," where attempts to duplicate a well-documented result become less and less successful over time even if many scientists initially replicate the work. The decline may derive from psychological effects, that the experimenters expect the result and so are subconsciously predisposed toward work that verifies their expectation. The decline is then the reassertion of the scientific method over time. However, even that theory doesn't seem to fully account for the effect. In "What We Found," Ryman extrapolates the idea to a fascinatingly eerie extreme. What if *all* scientific results disappeared over time?

To motivate the idea, Ryman draws on quantum theory, specifically the result that the act of observing a system changes that system, collapsing it from a mixture of possible states to the one observed. As a physicist, I've calculated linear superpositions of quantum states to describe the behavior of atoms and molecules. Mathematically, it simply means that more than one state exists for the particles in a collection, and we don't know which applies to a particular particle until we look at it. In popular culture, it has become famous as the "Schrödinger's cat" paradox, which essentially says, "The cat in the box is neither dead nor alive, but is a mixture of those states—until we look."

Ryman takes the idea a wonderfully fanciful step further. Suppose the act of observation changed *everything* scientists observed, including on a macroscopic level, so that the more they attempted to replicate previous results, the less they succeeded? All our scientific laws, including those we've known for centuries, even millennia, would eventually cease to be true. Ryman uses the idea to frame one man's attempt to understand himself, his family, and his future.

> The golden age of science fiction is twelve.
> —Peter Graham, *Void*

The two novels excerpted in this anthology both have vivid resonances for me. As with many science fiction readers, I related to the protagonist in the book *Among Others*. Like her, I was an outcast during my elementary school years, and I too found a refuge in science fiction, practically inhaling every book I could lay hands on. But my world had another aspect: ballet. I began training as a small child and never stopped regardless of the obstacles, including a body shape better suited to jazz than classical dance. When I hit puberty, the unexpected happened. Those many years of dance classes after school and on weekends, those mornings I got up early and went running in the park to let my feet pound away my frustrations—they paid off in a manner I had no idea would happen. Until then, I had known only that when I danced, I could let free a part of myself that had no other outlet. I never realized all that training was also turning me from the proverbial ugly duckling into if not a swan, then at least a graceful duck.

By the time I hit middle school, I was deep within the cognitive dissonance of going from the least popular kid in school to being liked and accepted as a dancer, knowing all the time that inside, I was the same person my peers had bullied only two years before. To me, nothing had changed except my exterior. It was a sobering wake-up call to the effects of bias and stereotype. For many, twelve is the "golden age" of science fiction, that age when they find the genre and community that speaks to them. For me, twelve was the end of my (first) science fiction age. Struggling with the confusion of a puberty that hit me like an express train slamming into a brick wall, I could no longer ignore the sexism in the science fiction stories I had devoured for so many years, nor the fact that those stories were targeted at my male peers. The books were about their dreams, their confusion, and their adventures, and I didn't fit in anywhere.

I went to John F. Kennedy High School in Richmond, California, which was known at that time for its innovative academic programs. In those days, the Richmond Voluntary Integration Plan was at its height, bringing in students from all over the region. As a result, I attended a school noted for its diversity, a student body that was about one-half African American and the rest a mix of other races, mostly Caucasian, also Asian and Hispanic. That had a marked effect on my new preferences in literature, though I didn't realize it until years later. I read what my friends and classmates were reading, authors like Martin Luther King Jr. and discussions about the music of Miles Davis. At that point in my life, Ralph Ellison's *The Invisible Man*, the story of a young black man dealing with the invisibility conferred by racism, spoke to me far more than H. G. Wells's science fiction novella "The Invisible Man."

> Rest at pale evening . . .
> A tall slim tree . . .
> Night coming tenderly
> Black like me
> —Langston Hughes, "Dream Variations"

Another work that stands out in my mind from that time is a book by John Howard Griffin, an American journalist who wrote about racial inequality. In 1959, Griffin darkened his light skin and traveled through the American Deep South as an African American. He took the title of his book about his experiences, *Black Like Me*, from the poem "Dream Variations" by Langston Hughes. The narrative of a white man experiencing the full force of racism against black Americans left an indelible impression on my young mind.

Echoes of Griffin's book came to me when I read the excerpt printed here from Delia Sherman's Norton Award–winning novel, *The Freedom Maze*. The three chapters concern a young woman sent from 1960s Louisiana back to 1860. The girl, a descendant of the plantation owners who built her ancestral home, is taken for a slave, the by-blow of a white man with a black woman. Not only must she confront the crushing racism of that time, which she comes to realize has survived in more subtle forms into her future world, but she must also live under its weight.

Sherman's narrator offers a different viewpoint than is usually seen in works of social commentary; this is the story of a teenaged girl, traditionally one of the most misrepresented groups in literary canons. It is ironic that as a sign of our more enlightened times, we can now read stories where the main character undergoing such grueling experiences is a young woman. Is that progress? I would say yes, because it is a statement that the experiences of women are as valuable to our social conscience as those of men.

> Every great work of art has two faces, one toward its own time and one toward the future, toward eternity.
> —Daniel Barenboim, *Parallels and Paradoxes: Explorations in Music and Society*

In graduate school, I began reading science fiction again to relax from the rigors of my doctoral program. This time around, my selections included many authors I hadn't known before, among them Ursula Le Guin, Marion Zimmer Bradley, Joan D. Vinge, and Anne McCaffrey. I also found new stories by the authors I had read as a child and discovered I could enjoy them again. I was left with the best of speculative fiction, a genre that dares to ask what could be different. Our literature has two faces: one that looks toward the beloved past I knew as a child, but also the face that looks forward, that asks challenging questions and pushes the envelope in almost any way we can imagine, whether it is scientific, fantastic, sociological, cultural, political, or artistic. Most of all, it became the genre of my intellect and of my heart.

I heard the universe as an oratorio sung by a master choir of stars, accompanied by the orchestra of the planets and the percussion of satellites and moons. The aria they performed was a song to break the heart, full of tragic dissonance and deferred hope, and yet somewhere beneath it all was a piercing refrain of glory, glory, glory.

—R. J. Anderson, *Ultraviolet*

1. Editor's note: After I wrote this introduction, some of my early readers had questions about the Banach-Tarski paradox and the axiom of choice. I did a web search and found a number of sites that talk about the concepts. The one I liked best was an essay in the blog *Good Math, Bad Math*, written by Mark Chu-Carroll. If you'd like a look, see tinyurl.com/AxiomChoiceBlog.

2. For the video of the Mandelbrot fractal, see "Mandelbrot Zoom," YouTube video, 1:18, posted on July 8, 2009, by "Kevin O'Toole," www.youtube.com/watch?v=rajXu9E_Ry0 (accessed March 11, 2013).

THE PAPER MENAGERIE

Ken Liu

One of my earliest memories starts with me sobbing. I refused to be soothed no matter what Mom and Dad tried.

Dad gave up and left the bedroom, but Mom took me into the kitchen and sat me down at the breakfast table.

"*Kan, kan,*" she said, as she pulled a sheet of wrapping paper from on top of the fridge. For years, Mom carefully sliced open the wrappings around Christmas gifts and saved them on top of the fridge in a thick stack.

She set the paper down, plain side facing up, and began to fold it. I stopped crying and watched her, curious.

She turned the paper over and folded it again. She pleated, packed, tucked, rolled, and twisted until the paper disappeared between her cupped hands. Then she lifted the folded-up paper packet to her mouth and blew into it, like a balloon.

"*Kan,*" she said. "*Laohu.*" She put her hands down on the table and let go.

A little paper tiger stood on the table, the size of two fists placed together. The skin of the tiger was the pattern on the wrapping paper, white background with red candy canes and green Christmas trees.

I reached out to Mom's creation. Its tail twitched, and it pounced playfully at my finger. "*Rawrr-sa,*" it growled, the sound somewhere between a cat and rustling newspapers.

I laughed, startled, and stroked its back with an index finger. The paper tiger vibrated under my finger, purring.

"*Zhe jiao zhezhi,*" Mom said. *This is called origami.*

I didn't know this at the time, but Mom's kind was special. She breathed into them so that they shared her breath, and thus moved with her life. This was her magic.

*　　*　　*

Dad had picked Mom out of a catalog.

One time, when I was in high school, I asked Dad about the details. He was trying to get me to speak to Mom again.

He had signed up for the introduction service back in the spring of 1973. Flipping through the pages steadily, he had spent no more than a few seconds on each page until he saw the picture of Mom.

I've never seen this picture. Dad described it: Mom was sitting in a chair, her side to the camera, wearing a tight green silk cheongsam. Her head was turned to the camera so that her long black hair was draped artfully over her chest and shoulder. She looked out at him with the eyes of a calm child.

"That was the last page of the catalog I saw," he said.

The catalog said she was eighteen, loved to dance, and spoke good English because she was from Hong Kong. None of these facts turned out to be true.

He wrote to her, and the company passed their messages back and forth. Finally, he flew to Hong Kong to meet her.

"The people at the company had been writing her responses. She didn't know any English other than 'hello' and 'goodbye.'"

What kind of woman puts herself into a catalog so that she can be bought? The high school me thought I knew so much about everything. Contempt felt good, like wine.

Instead of storming into the office to demand his money back, he paid a waitress at the hotel restaurant to translate for them.

"She would look at me, her eyes halfway between scared and hopeful, while I spoke. And when the girl began translating what I said, she'd start to smile slowly."

He flew back to Connecticut and began to apply for the papers for her to come to him. I was born a year later, in the Year of the Tiger.

*　　*　　*

At my request, Mom also made a goat, a deer, and a water buffalo out of wrapping paper. They would run around the living room while Laohu chased after them, growling. When he caught them he would press down until the air went out of them and they became just flat, folded-up pieces of paper. I would then have to blow into them to re-inflate them so they could run around some more.

Sometimes, the animals got into trouble. Once, the water buffalo jumped into a dish of soy sauce on the table at dinner. (He wanted to wallow, like a real water buffalo.) I picked him out quickly but the capillary action had already pulled the dark liquid high up into his legs. The sauce-softened legs would not hold him up, and he collapsed onto the table. I dried him out in the sun, but his legs became crooked after that, and he ran around with a limp. Mom eventually wrapped his legs in saran wrap so that he could wallow to his heart's content (just not in soy sauce).

Also, Laohu liked to pounce at sparrows when he and I played in the back-yard. But one time, a cornered bird struck back in desperation and tore his ear. He whimpered and winced as I held him and Mom patched his ear together with tape. He avoided birds after that.

And then one day, I saw a TV documentary about sharks and asked Mom for one of my own. She made the shark, but he flapped about on the table unhappily. I filled the sink with water, and put him in. He swam around and around happily. However, after a while he became soggy and translucent, and slowly sank to the bottom, the folds coming undone. I reached in to rescue him, and all I ended up with was a wet piece of paper.

Laohu put his front paws together at the edge of the sink and rested his head on them. Ears drooping, he made a low growl in his throat that made me feel guilty.

Mom made a new shark for me, this time out of tin foil. The shark lived happily in a large goldfish bowl. Laohu and I liked to sit next to the bowl to watch the tin foil shark chasing the goldfish, Laohu sticking his face up against the bowl on the other side so that I saw his eyes, magnified to the size of coffee cups, staring at me from across the bowl.

*   *   *

When I was ten, we moved to a new house across town. Two of the women neighbors came by to welcome us. Dad served them drinks and then apologized for having to run off to the utility company to straighten out the prior owner's bills. "Make yourselves at home. My wife doesn't speak much English, so don't think she's being rude for not talking to you."

While I read in the dining room, Mom unpacked in the kitchen. The neighbors conversed in the living room, not trying to be particularly quiet.

"He seems like a normal enough man. Why did he do that?"

"Something about the mixing never seems right. The child looks unfinished. Slanty eyes, white face. A little monster."

"Do you think *he* can speak English?"

The women hushed. After a while they came into the dining room.

"Hello there! What's your name?"

"Jack," I said.

"That doesn't sound very Chinesey."

Mom came into the dining room then. She smiled at the women. The three of them stood in a triangle around me, smiling and nodding at each other, with nothing to say, until Dad came back.

*   *   *

Mark, one of the neighborhood boys, came over with his Star Wars action figures. Obi-Wan Kenobi's lightsaber lit up and he could swing his arms and say, in a tinny voice, "Use the Force!" I didn't think the figure looked much like the real Obi-Wan at all.

Together, we watched him repeat this performance five times on the coffee table. "Can he do anything else?" I asked.

Mark was annoyed by my question. "Look at all the details," he said.

I looked at the details. I wasn't sure what I was supposed to say.

Mark was disappointed by my response. "Show me your toys."

I didn't have any toys except my paper menagerie. I brought Laohu out from my bedroom. By then he was very worn, patched all over with tape and glue, evidence of the years of repairs Mom and I had done on him. He was no longer as nimble and sure-footed as before. I sat him down on the coffee table. I could hear the skittering steps of the other animals behind in the hallway, timidly peeking into the living room.

"*Xiao laohu*," I said, and stopped. I switched to English. "This is Tiger." Cautiously, Laohu strode up and purred at Mark, sniffing his hands.

Mark examined the Christmas-wrap pattern of Laohu's skin. "That doesn't look like a tiger at all. Your Mom makes toys for you from trash?"

I had never thought of Laohu as *trash*. But looking at him now, he was really just a piece of wrapping paper.

Mark pushed Obi-Wan's head again. The lightsaber flashed; he moved his arms up and down. "Use the Force!"

Laohu turned and pounced, knocking the plastic figure off the table. It hit the floor and broke, and Obi-Wan's head rolled under the couch. "*Rawwww*," Laohu laughed. I joined him.

Mark punched me, hard. "This was very expensive! You can't even find it in the stores now. It probably cost more than what your dad paid for your mom!"

I stumbled and fell to the floor. Laohu growled and leapt at Mark's face.

Mark screamed, more out of fear and surprise than pain. Laohu was only made of paper, after all.

Mark grabbed Laohu and his snarl was choked off as Mark crumpled him in his hand and tore him in half. He balled up the two pieces of paper and threw them at me. "Here's your stupid cheap Chinese garbage."

After Mark left, I spent a long time trying, without success, to tape together the pieces, smooth out the paper, and follow the creases to refold Laohu. Slowly, the other animals came into the living room and gathered around us, me and the torn wrapping paper that used to be Laohu.

* * *

My fight with Mark didn't end there. Mark was popular at school. I never want to think again about the two weeks that followed.

I came home that Friday at the end of the two weeks. "*Xuexiao hao ma?*" Mom asked. I said nothing and went to the bathroom. I looked into the mirror. *I look nothing like her, nothing.*

At dinner I asked Dad, "Do I have a chink face?"

Dad put down his chopsticks. Even though I had never told him what happened in school, he seemed to understand. He closed his eyes and rubbed the bridge of his nose. "No, you don't."

Mom looked at Dad, not understanding. She looked back at me. "*Sha jiao* chink?*"

"English," I said. "Speak English."

She tried. "What happen?"

I pushed the chopsticks and the bowl before me away: stir-fried green peppers with five-spice beef. "We should eat American food."

Dad tried to reason. "A lot of families cook Chinese sometimes."

"We are not other families." I looked at him. *Other families don't have moms who don't belong.*

He looked away. And then he put a hand on Mom's shoulder. "I'll get you a cookbook."

Mom turned to me. "*Bu haochi?*"

"English," I said, raising my voice. "Speak English."

Mom reached out to touch my forehead, feeling for my temperature. "*Fashao la?*"

I brushed her hand away. "I'm fine. Speak English!" I was shouting.

"Speak English to him," Dad said to Mom. "You knew this was going to happen some day. What did you expect?"

Mom dropped her hands to her side. She sat, looking from Dad to me, and back to Dad again. She tried to speak, stopped, and tried again, and stopped again.

"You have to," Dad said. "I've been too easy on you. Jack needs to fit in."

Mom looked at him. "If I say 'love,' I feel here." She pointed to her lips. "If I say '*ai*,' I feel here." She put her hand over her heart.

Dad shook his head. "You are in America."

Mom hunched down in her seat, looking like the water buffalo when Laohu used to pounce on him and squeeze the air of life out of him.

"And I want some real toys."

*   *   *

Dad bought me a full set of Star Wars action figures. I gave the Obi-Wan Kenobi to Mark.

I packed the paper menagerie in a large shoebox and put it under the bed.

The next morning, the animals had escaped and took over their old favorite spots in my room. I caught them all and put them back into the shoebox, taping the lid shut. But the animals made so much noise in the box that I finally shoved it into the corner of the attic as far away from my room as possible.

If Mom spoke to me in Chinese, I refused to answer her. After a while, she tried to use more English. But her accent and broken sentences embarrassed me. I tried to correct her. Eventually, she stopped speaking altogether if I were around.

Mom began to mime things if she needed to let me know something. She tried to hug me the way she saw American mothers did on TV. I thought her movements exaggerated, uncertain, ridiculous, graceless. She saw that I was annoyed, and stopped.

"You shouldn't treat your mother that way," Dad said. But he couldn't look me in the eyes as he said it. Deep in his heart, he must have realized that it was a mistake to have tried to take a Chinese peasant girl and expect her to fit in the suburbs of Connecticut.

Mom learned to cook American style. I played video games and studied French.

Every once in a while, I would see her at the kitchen table studying the plain side of a sheet of wrapping paper. Later a new paper animal would appear on my nightstand and try to cuddle up to me. I caught them, squeezed them until the air went out of them, and then stuffed them away in the box in the attic.

Mom finally stopped making the animals when I was in high school. By then her English was much better, but I was already at that age when I wasn't interested in what she had to say whatever language she used.

Sometimes, when I came home and saw her tiny body busily moving about in the kitchen, singing a song in Chinese to herself, it was hard for me to believe that she gave birth to me. We had nothing in common. She might as well be from the moon. I would hurry on to my room, where I could continue my all-American pursuit of happiness.

*   *   *

Dad and I stood, one on each side of Mom, lying on the hospital bed. She was not yet even forty, but she looked much older.

For years she had refused to go to the doctor for the pain inside her that she said was no big deal. By the time an ambulance finally carried her in, the cancer had spread far beyond the limits of surgery.

My mind was not in the room. It was the middle of the on-campus recruiting season, and I was focused on resumes, transcripts, and strategically constructed interview schedules. I schemed about how to lie to the corporate recruiters most effectively so that they'll offer to buy me. I understood intellectually that it was terrible to think about this while your mother lay dying. But that understanding didn't mean I could change how I felt.

She was conscious. Dad held her left hand with both of his own. He leaned down to kiss her forehead. He seemed weak and old in a way that startled me. I realized that I knew almost as little about Dad as I did about Mom.

Mom smiled at him. "I'm fine."

She turned to me, still smiling. "I know you have to go back to school." Her voice was very weak and it was difficult to hear her over the hum of the machines hooked up to her. "Go. Don't worry about me. This is not a big deal. Just do well in school."

I reached out to touch her hand, because I thought that was what I was supposed to do. I was relieved. I was already thinking about the flight back, and the bright California sunshine.

She whispered something to Dad. He nodded and left the room.

"Jack, if—" she was caught up in a fit of coughing, and could not speak for some time. "If I don't make it, don't be too sad and hurt your health. Focus on your life. Just keep that box you have in the attic with you, and every year, at *Qingming*, just take it out and think about me. I'll be with you always."

Qingming was the Chinese Festival for the Dead. When I was very young, Mom used to write a letter on *Qingming* to her dead parents back in China, telling them the good news about the past year of her life in America. She would read the letter out loud to me, and if I made a comment about something, she would write it down in the letter too. Then she would fold the letter into a paper crane, and release it, facing west. We would then watch, as the crane flapped its crisp wings on its long journey west, towards the Pacific, towards China, towards the graves of Mom's family.

It had been many years since I last did that with her.

"I don't know anything about the Chinese calendar," I said. "Just rest, Mom."

"Just keep the box with you and open it once in a while. Just open—" she began to cough again.

"It's okay, Mom." I stroked her arm awkwardly.

"*Haizi, mama ai ni—*" Her cough took over again. An image from years ago flashed into my memory: Mom saying *ai* and then putting her hand over her heart.

"Alright, Mom. Stop talking."

Dad came back, and I said that I needed to get to the airport early because I didn't want to miss my flight.

She died when my plane was somewhere over Nevada.

*   *   *

Dad aged rapidly after Mom died. The house was too big for him and had to be sold. My girlfriend Susan and I went to help him pack and clean the place.

Susan found the shoebox in the attic. The paper menagerie, hidden in the uninsulated darkness of the attic for so long, had become brittle and the bright wrapping paper patterns had faded.

"I've never seen origami like this," Susan said. "Your Mom was an amazing artist."

The paper animals did not move. Perhaps whatever magic had animated them stopped when Mom died. Or perhaps I had only imagined that these paper constructions were once alive. The memory of children could not be trusted.

* * *

It was the first weekend in April, two years after Mom's death. Susan was out of town on one of her endless trips as a management consultant and I was home, lazily flipping through the TV channels.

I paused at a documentary about sharks. Suddenly I saw, in my mind, Mom's hands, as they folded and refolded tin foil to make a shark for me, while Laohu and I watched.

A rustle. I looked up and saw that a ball of wrapping paper and torn tape was on the floor next to the bookshelf. I walked over to pick it up for the trash.

The ball of paper shifted, unfurled itself, and I saw that it was Laohu, who I hadn't thought about in a very long time. "*Rawrr-sa.*" Mom must have put him back together after I had given up.

He was smaller than I remembered. Or maybe it was just that back then my fists were smaller.

Susan had put the paper animals around our apartment as decoration. She probably left Laohu in a pretty hidden corner because he looked so shabby.

I sat down on the floor, and reached out a finger. Laohu's tail twitched, and he pounced playfully. I laughed, stroking his back. Laohu purred under my hand.

"How've you been, old buddy?"

Laohu stopped playing. He got up, jumped with feline grace into my lap, and proceeded to unfold himself.

In my lap was a square of creased wrapping paper, the plain side up. It was filled with dense Chinese characters. I had never learned to read Chinese, but I knew the characters for *son*, and they were at the top, where you'd expect them in a letter addressed to you, written in Mom's awkward, childish handwriting.

I went to the computer to check the Internet. Today was *Qingming*.

* * *

I took the letter with me downtown, where I knew the Chinese tour buses stopped. I stopped every tourist, asking, "*Nin hui du zhongwen ma?*" Can you *read Chinese?* I hadn't spoken Chinese in so long that I wasn't sure if they understood.

A young woman agreed to help. We sat down on a bench together, and she read the letter to me aloud. The language that I had tried to forget for years came back, and I felt the words sinking into me, through my skin, through my bones, until they squeezed tight around my heart.

*   *   *

Son,

We haven't talked in a long time. You are so angry when I try to touch you that I'm afraid. And I think maybe this pain I feel all the time now is something serious.

So I decided to write to you. I'm going to write in the paper animals I made for you that you used to like so much.

The animals will stop moving when I stop breathing. But if I write to you with all my heart, I'll leave a little of myself behind on this paper, in these words. Then, if you think of me on Qingming, *when the spirits of the departed are allowed to visit their families, you'll make the parts of myself I leave behind come alive too. The creatures I made for you will again leap and run and pounce, and maybe you'll get to see these words then.*

Because I have to write with all my heart, I need to write to you in Chinese.

All this time I still haven't told you the story of my life. When you were little, I always thought I'd tell you the story when you were older, so you could understand. But somehow that chance never came up.

I was born in 1957, in Sigulu Village, Hebei Province. Your grandparents were both from very poor peasant families with few relatives. Only a few years after I was born, the Great Famines struck China, during which thirty million people died. The first memory I have was waking up to see my mother eating dirt so that she could fill her belly and leave the last bit of flour for me.

Things got better after that. Sigulu is famous for its zhezhi *papercraft, and my mother taught me how to make paper animals and give them life. This was practical magic in the life of the village. We made paper birds to chase grasshoppers away from the fields, and paper tigers to keep away the mice. For Chinese New Year my friends and*

I made red paper dragons. I'll never forget the sight of all those little dragons zooming across the sky overhead, holding up strings of exploding firecrackers to scare away all the bad memories of the past year. You would have loved it.

Then came the Cultural Revolution in 1966. Neighbor turned on neighbor, and brother against brother. Someone remembered that my mother's brother, my uncle, had left for Hong Kong back in 1946, and became a merchant there. Having a relative in Hong Kong meant we were spies and enemies of the people, and we had to be struggled against in every way. Your poor grandmother—she couldn't take the abuse and threw herself down a well. Then some boys with hunting muskets dragged your grandfather away one day into the woods, and he never came back.

There I was, a ten-year-old orphan. The only relative I had in the world was my uncle in Hong Kong. I snuck away one night and climbed onto a freight train going south.

Down in Guangdong Province a few days later, some men caught me stealing food from a field. When they heard that I was trying to get to Hong Kong, they laughed. "It's your lucky day. Our trade is to bring girls to Hong Kong."

They hid me in the bottom of a truck along with other girls, and smuggled us across the border.

We were taken to a basement and told to stand up and look healthy and intelligent for the buyers. Families paid the warehouse a fee and came by to look us over and select one of us to "adopt."

The Chin family picked me to take care of their two boys. I got up every morning at four to prepare breakfast. I fed and bathed the boys. I shopped for food. I did the laundry and swept the floors. I followed the boys around and did their bidding. At night I was locked into a cupboard in the kitchen to sleep. If I was slow or did anything wrong I was beaten. If the boys did anything wrong I was beaten. If I was caught trying to learn English I was beaten.

"Why do you want to learn English?" Mr. Chin asked. "You want to go to the police? We'll tell the police that you are a mainlander illegally in Hong Kong. They'd love to have you in their prison."

Six years I lived like this. One day, an old woman who sold fish to me in the morning market pulled me aside.

"I know girls like you. How old are you now, sixteen? One day, the man who owns

you will get drunk, and he'll look at you and pull you to him and you can't stop him. The wife will find out, and then you will think you really have gone to hell. You have to get out of this life. I know someone who can help."

She told me about American men who wanted Asian wives. If I can cook, clean, and take care of my American husband, he'll give me a good life. It was the only hope I had. And that was how I got into the catalog with all those lies and met your father. It is not a very romantic story, but it is my story.

In the suburbs of Connecticut, I was lonely. Your father was kind and gentle with me, and I was very grateful to him. But no one understood me, and I understood nothing.

But then you were born! I was so happy when I looked into your face and saw shades of my mother, my father, and myself. I had lost my entire family, all of Sigulu, everything I ever knew and loved. But there you were, and your face was proof that they were real. I hadn't made them up.

Now I had someone to talk to. I would teach you my language, and we could together remake a small piece of everything that I loved and lost. When you said your first words to me, in Chinese that had the same accent as my mother and me, I cried for hours. When I made the first zhezhi animals for you, and you laughed, I felt there were no worries in the world.

You grew up a little, and now you could even help your father and I talk to each other. I was really at home now. I finally found a good life. I wished my parents could be here, so that I could cook for them, and give them a good life too. But my parents were no longer around. You know what the Chinese think is the saddest feeling in the world? It's for a child to finally grow the desire to take care of his parents, only to realize that they were long gone.

Son, I know that you do not like your Chinese eyes, which are my eyes. I know that you do not like your Chinese hair, which is my hair. But can you understand how much joy your very existence brought to me? And can you understand how it felt when you stopped talking to me and won't let me talk to you in Chinese? I felt I was losing everything all over again.

Why won't you talk to me, son? The pain makes it hard to write.

*   *   *

The young woman handed the paper back to me. I could not bear to look into her face.

Without looking up, I asked for her help in tracing out the character for *ai* on the paper below Mom's letter. I wrote the character again and again on the paper, intertwining my pen strokes with her words.

The young woman reached out and put a hand on my shoulder. Then she got up and left, leaving me alone with my mother.

Following the creases, I refolded the paper back into Laohu. I cradled him in the crook of my arm, and as he purred, we began the walk home.

THE ICE OWL

Carolyn Ives Gilman

Twice a day, stillness settled over the iron city of Glory to God as the citizens turned west and waited for the world to ring. For a few moments the motionless red sun on the horizon, half-concealed by the western mountains, lit every face in the city: the just-born and the dying, the prisoners and the veiled, the devout and the profane. The sound started so low it could only be heard by the bones; but as the moments passed the metal city itself began to ring in sympathetic harmony, till the sound resolved into a note—The Note, priests said, sung by the heart of God to set creation going. Its vibratory mathematics embodied all structure; its pitch implied all scales and chords; its beauty was the ovum of all devotion and all faithlessness. Nothing more than a note was needed to extrapolate the universe.

The Note came regular as clockwork, the only timebound thing in a city of perpetual sunset.

On a ledge outside a window in the rustiest part of town, crouched one of the ominous cast-iron gargoyles fancied by the architects of Glory to God—or so it seemed until it moved. Then it resolved into an adolescent girl dressed all in black. Her face was turned west, her eyes closed in a look of private exaltation as The Note reverberated through her. It was a face that had just recently lost the chubbiness of childhood, so that the clean-boned adult was beginning to show through. Her name, also a recent development, was Thorn. She had chosen it because it evoked suffering and redemption.

As the bell tones whispered away, Thorn opened her eyes. The city before her was a composition in red and black: red of the sun and the dust-plain outside the girders of the dome; black of the shadows and the works of mankind. Glory to God was built against the cliff of an old crater and rose in stair steps of fluted pillars and wrought arches till the towers of the Protectorate grazed the underside of the dome where it met the cliff face.

Behind the distant, glowing windows of the palaces, twined with iron ivy, the priest-magistrates and executives lived unimaginable lives—though Thorn still pictured them looking down on all the rest of the city, on the smelteries and temples, the warring neighborhoods ruled by militias, the veiled women, and at the very bottom, befitting its status, the Waster enclave where unrepentent immigrants like Thorn and her mother lived, sunk in a bath of sin. The Waste was not truly of the city, except as a perennial itch in its flesh. The Godly said it was the sin, not the oxygen, that rusted everything in the Waste. A man who came home with a red smudge on his clothes might as well have been branded with the address.

Thorn's objection to her neighborhood lay not in its sin, which did not live up to its reputation, but its inauthenticity. From her rooftop perch she looked down on its twisted warrens full of coffee shops, underground publishers, money launderers, embassies, tattoo parlors, and art galleries. This was the ninth planet she had lived on in her short life, but in truth she had never left her native culture, for on every planet the Waster enclaves were the same. They were always a mother lode of contraband ideas. Everywhere, the expatriate intellectuals of the Waste were regarded as exotic and dangerous, the vectors of infectious transgalactic ideas—but lately, Thorn had begun to find them pretentious and phony. They were rooted nowhere, pieces of cultural bricolage. Nothing reached to the core; it was all veneer, just like the rust.

Outside, now—she looked past the spiked gates into Glory to God proper—there lay dark desires and age-old hatreds, belief so unexamined it permeated every tissue like a marinade. The natives had not chosen their beliefs; they had inherited them, breathed them in with the iron dust in their first breath. Their struggles were authentic ones.

Her eyes narrowed as she spotted movement near the gate. She was, after all, on lookout duty. There seemed to be more than the usual traffic this afternote, and the cluster of young men by the gate did not look furtive enough to belong. She studied them through her pocket binoculars and saw a telltale flash of white beneath one long coat. White, the color of the uncorrupted.

She slipped back through the gable window into her attic room, then down the iron spiral staircase at the core of the vertical tower apartment. Past the fifth-floor closets and the fourth-floor bedrooms she went, to the third-floor offices. There she knocked sharply on one of the molded sheet-iron doors. Within, there was a thump, and in a moment Maya cracked it open enough to show one eye.

"There's a troop of Incorruptibles by the gate," Thorn said.

Inside the office, a woman's voice gave a frightened exclamation. Thorn's mother turned and said in her fractured version of the local tongue, "Worry not yourself. We make safely go." She then said to Thorn, "Make sure the bottom door is locked. If they come, stall them."

Thorn spun down the stair like a black tornado, past the living rooms to the kitchen on street level. The door was locked, but she unlocked it to peer out. The alarm was spreading down the street. She watched signs being snatched from windows, awnings rolled up, and metal grills rumbling down across storefronts. The crowds that always pressed from curb to curb this time of day had vanished. Soon the stillness of impending storm settled over the street. Then Thorn heard the faraway chanting, like premonitory thunder. She closed and locked the door.

Maya showed up, looking rumpled, her lovely honey-gold hair in ringlets. Thorn said, "Did you get her out?" Maya nodded. One of the main appeals of this apartment had been the hidden escape route for smuggling out Maya's clients in emergencies like this.

On this planet, as on the eight before, Maya earned her living in the risky profession of providing reproductive services. Every planet was different, it seemed, except that on all of them women wanted something that was forbidden. What they wanted varied: here, it was babies. Maya did a brisk business in contraband semen and embryos for women who needed to become pregnant without their infertile husbands guessing how it had been accomplished.

The chanting grew louder, harsh male voices in unison. They watched together out the small kitchen window. Soon they could see the approaching wall of men dressed in white, marching in lockstep. The army of righteousness came even with the door, then passed by. Thorn and Maya exchanged a look of mutual congratulation and locked little fingers in their secret handshake. Once again, they had escaped.

Thorn opened the door and looked after the army. An assortment of children was tagging after them, so Maya said, "Go see what they're up to."

The Incorruptibles had passed half a dozen potential targets by now: the bank, the musical instrument store, the news service, the sex shop. They didn't pause until they came to the small park that lay in the center of an intersection. Then the phalanx lined up opposite the school. With military precision, some of them broke the bottom windows and others lit incendiary bombs and tossed them in. They waited to make sure the blaze was started, then gave a simultaneous shout and marched away, taking a different route back to the gate.

They had barely left when the Protectorate fire service came roaring down the street to put out the blaze. This was not, Thorn knew, out of respect for the school or for the Waste, which could have gone up in flame wholesale for all the authorities cared; it was simply that in a domed city, a fire anywhere was a fire everywhere. Even the palaces would have to smell the smoke and clean up soot if it were not doused quickly. Setting a fire was as much a defiance of the Protectorate as of the Wasters.

Thorn watched long enough to know that the conflagration would not spread, and then walked back home. When she arrived, three women were sitting with Maya at the kitchen table. Two of them Thorn knew: Clarity and Bick, interstellar wanderers whose paths had crossed Thorn's and Maya's on two previous planets. The first time, they had been feckless coeds; the second time, seasoned adventurers. They were past middle age now, and had become the most sensible people Thorn had ever met. She had seen them face insurrection and exile with genial good humor and a canister of tea.

Right now their teapot was filling the kitchen with a smoky aroma, so Thorn fished a mug out of the sink to help herself. Maya said, "So what were the Incorruptibles doing?"

"Burning the school," Thorn said in a seen-it-all-before tone. She glanced at the third visitor, a stranger. The woman had a look of timeshock that gave her away as a recent arrival in Glory to God via lightbeam from another planet. She was still suffering from the temporal whiplash of waking up ten or twenty years from the time she had last drawn breath.

"Annick, this is Thorn, Maya's daughter," Clarity said. She was the talkative, energetic one of the pair; Bick was the silent, steady one.

"Hi," Thorn said. "Welcome to the site of Creation."

"Why were they burning the school?" Annick said, clearly distressed by the idea. She had pale eyes and a soft, gentle face. Thorn made a snap judgment: Annick was not going to last long here.

"Because it's a vector of degeneracy," Thorn said. She had learned the phrase from Maya's current boyfriend, Hunter.

"What has happened to this planet?" Annick said. "When I set out it was isolated, but not regressive."

They all made sympathetic noises, because everyone at the table had experienced something similar. Lightbeam travel was as fast as the universe allowed, but even the speed of light had a limit. Planets inevitably changed during transit, not always for the better. "Waster's luck," Maya said fatalistically.

Clarity said, "The Incorruptibles are actually a pretty new movement. It started among the conservative academics and their students, but they have a large following now. They stand against the graft and nepotism of the Protectorate. People in the city are really fed up with being harrassed by policemen looking for bribes, and corrupt officials who make up new fees for everything. So they support a movement that promises to kick the grafters out and give them a little harsh justice. Only it's bad news for us."

"Why?" Annick said. "Wouldn't an honest government benefit everyone?"

"You'd think so. But honest governments are always more intrusive. You can buy toleration and personal freedom from a corrupt government. The Protectorate leaves this Waster enclave alone because it brings them profit. If the Incorruptibles came into power, they'd have to bow to public opinion and exile us, or make us conform. The general populace is pretty isolationist. They think our sin industry is helping keep the Protectorate in power. They're right, actually."

"What a Devil's bargain," Annick said.

They all nodded. Waster life was full of irony.

"What's Thorn going to do for schooling now?" Clarity asked Maya.

Maya clearly hadn't thought about it. "They'll figure something out," she said vaguely.

Just then Thorn heard Hunter's footsteps on the iron stairs, and she said to annoy him, "I could help Hunter."

"Help me do what?" Hunter said as he descended into the kitchen. He was a lean and angle-faced man with square glasses and a small goatee. He always dressed in black and could not speak without sounding sarcastic. Thorn thought he was a poser.

"Help you find Gmintas, of course," Thorn said. "That's what you do."

He went over to the Turkish coffee machine to brew some of the bitter, hyper-stimulant liquid he was addicted to. "Why can't you go to school?" he said.

"They burned it down."

"Who did?"

"The Incorruptibles. Didn't you hear them chanting?"

"I was in my office."

He was always in his office. It was a mystery to Thorn how he was going to locate any Gminta criminals when he disdained going out and mingling with people. She had once asked Maya, "Has he ever actually caught a Gminta?" and Maya had answered, "I hope not."

All in all, though, he was an improvement over Maya's last boyfriend, who had absconded with every penny of savings they had. Hunter at least had money, though where it came from was a mystery.

"I could be your field agent," Thorn said.

"You need an education, Thorn," Clarity said.

"Yes," Hunter agreed. "If you knew something, you might be a little less annoying."

"People like you give education a bad name," Thorn retorted.

"Stop being a brat, Tuppence," Maya said.

"That's not my name anymore!"

"If you act like a baby, I'll call you by your baby name."

"You always take his side."

"You could find her a tutor," Clarity said. She was not going to give up.

"Right," Hunter said, sipping inky liquid from a tiny cup. "Why don't you ask one of those old fellows who play chess in the park?"

"They're probably all pedophiles!" Thorn said in disgust.

"On second thought, maybe it's better to keep her ignorant," Hunter said, heading up the stairs again.

"I'll ask around and see who's doing tutoring," Clarity offered.

"Sure, okay," Maya said noncommittally.

Thorn got up, glowering at their lack of respect for her independence and self-determination. "I am captain of my own destiny," she announced, then made a strategic withdrawal to her room.

*   *   *

The next forenote Thorn came down from her room in the face-masking veil that women of Glory to God all wore, outside the Waste. When Maya saw her, she said, "Where are you going in that getup?"

"Out," Thorn said.

In a tone diluted with real worry, Maya said, "I don't want you going into the city, Tup."

Thorn was icily silent till Maya said, "Sorry—Thorn. But I still don't want you going into the city."

"I won't," Thorn said.

"Then what are you wearing that veil for? It's a symbol of bondage."

"Bondage to God," Thorn said loftily.

"You don't believe in God."

Right then Thorn decided that she would.

When she left the house and turned toward the park, the triviality of her home and family fell away like lint. After a block, she felt transformed. Putting on the veil had started as a simple act of rebellion, but out in the street it became far more. Catching her reflection in a shop window, she felt disguised in mystery. The veil intensified the imagined face it concealed, while exoticizing the eyes it revealed. She had become something shadowy, hidden. The Wasters all around her were obsessed with their own surfaces, with manipulating what they *seemed* to be. All depth, all that was earnest, withered in the acid of their inauthenticity. But with the veil on, Thorn *had* no surface, so she was immune. What lay behind the veil was negotiated, contingent, rendered deep by suggestion.

In the tiny triangular park in front of the blackened shell of the school, life went on as if nothing had changed. The tower fans turned lazily, creating a pleasant breeze tinged a little with soot. Under their strutwork shadows, two people walked little dogs on leashes, and the old men bent over their chessboards. Thorn scanned the scene through the slit in her veil, then walked toward a bench where an old man sat reading from an electronic slate.

She sat down on the bench. The old man did not acknowledge her presence, though a watchful twitch of his eyebrow told her he knew she was there. She had often seen him in the park, dressed impeccably in threadbare suits of a style long gone. He had an oblong, drooping face and big hands that looked as if they might once have done clever things. Thorn sat considering what to say.

"Well?" the old man said without looking up from his book. "What is it you want?"

Thorn could think of nothing intelligent to say, so she said, "Are you a historian?"

He lowered the slate. "Only in the sense that we all are, us Wasters. Why do you want to know?"

"My school burned down," Thorn said. "I need to find a tutor."

"I don't teach children," the old man said, turning back to his book.

"I'm not a child!" Thorn said, offended.

He didn't look up. "Really? I thought that's what you were trying to hide, behind that veil."

She took it off. At first he paid no attention. Then at last he glanced up indifferently, but saw something that made him frown. "You are the child that lives with the Gminta hunter."

His cold tone made her feel defensive on Hunter's behalf. "He doesn't hunt all Gmintas," she said, "just the wicked ones who committed the Holocide. The ones who deserve to be hunted."

"What do you know about the Gmintan Holocide?" the old man said with withering dismissal.

Thorn smiled triumphantly. "I was there."

He stopped pretending to read and looked at her with bristly disapproval. "How could you have been there?" he said. "It happened 141 years ago."

"I'm 145 years old, sequential time," Thorn said. "I was 37 when I was five, and 98 when I was seven, and 126 when I was twelve." She enjoyed shocking people with this litany.

"Why have you moved so much?"

"My mother got pregnant without my father's consent, and when she refused to have an abortion he sued her for copyright infringement. She'd made unauthorized use of his genes, you see. So she ducked out to avoid paying royalties, and we've been on the lam ever since. If he ever caught us, I could be arrested for having bootleg genes."

"Who told you that story?" he said, obviously skeptical.

"Maya did. It sounds like something one of her boyfriends would do. She has really bad taste in men. That's another reason we have to move so much."

Shaking his head slightly, he said, "I should think you would get cognitive dysplasia."

"I'm used to it," Thorn said.

"Do you like it?"

No one had ever asked her that before, as if she was capable of deciding for herself. In fact, she had known for a while that she *didn't* like it much. With every jump between planets she had grown more and more reluctant to leave sequential time behind. She said, "The worst thing is, there's no way of going back. Once you leave, the place you've stepped out of is gone forever. When I was eight I learned about pepcies, that you can use them to communicate instantaneously, and I asked Maya if we could call up my best friend on the last planet, and Maya said, 'She'll be middle-aged by now.' Everyone else had changed, and I hadn't. For a while I had dreams that the world was dissolving behind my back whenever I looked away."

The old man was listening thoughtfully, studying her. "How did you get away from Gmintagad?" he asked.

"We had Capellan passports," Thorn said. "I don't remember much about it; I was just four years old. I remember drooping cypress trees and rushing to get out. I didn't understand what was happening."

He was staring into the distance, focused on something invisible. Suddenly, he got up as if something had bitten him and started to walk away.

"Wait!" Thorn called. "What's the matter?"

He stopped, his whole body tense, then turned back. "Meet me here at four hours forenote tomorrow, if you want lessons," he said. "Bring a slate. I won't wait for you." He turned away again.

"Stop!" Thorn said. "What's your name?"

With a forbidding frown, he said, "Soren Pregaldin. You may call me Magister."

"Yes, Magister," Thorn said, trying not to let her glee show. She could hardly wait to tell Hunter that she had followed his advice, and succeeded.

What she wouldn't tell him, she decided as she watched Magister Pregaldin stalk away across the park, was her suspicion that this man knew something about the Holocide. Otherwise, how would he have known it was exactly 141 years ago? Another person would have said 140, or something else vague. She would not mention her suspicion to Hunter until she was sure. She would investigate carefully, like a competent field agent should. Thinking about it, a thrill ran through her. What if she were able to catch a Gminta? How impressed Hunter would be! The truth was, she wanted to impress Hunter. For all his mordant manner, he was by far the smartest boyfriend Maya had taken up with, the only one with a profession Thorn had ever been able to admire.

She fastened the veil over her face again before going home, so no one would see her grinning.

*   *   *

Magister Pregaldin turned out to be the most demanding teacher Thorn had ever known. Always before, she had coasted through school, easily able to stay ahead of the indigenous students around her, always waiting in boredom for them to catch up. With Magister Pregaldin there was no one else to wait for, and he pushed her mercilessly to the edge of her abilities. For the first time in her life, she wondered if she were smart enough.

He was an exacting drillmaster in mathematics. Once, when she complained at how useless it was, he pointed out beyond the iron gridwork of the dome to a round black hill that was conspicuous on the red plain of the crater bed. "Tell me how far away the Creeping Ingot is."

The Creeping Ingot had first come across the horizon almost a hundred years before, slowly moving toward Glory to God. It was a near-pure lump of iron the size of a small mountain. In the Waste, the reigning theory was that it was molten underneath, and moving like a drop of water skitters across a hot frying pan. In the city above them, it was regarded as a sign of divine wrath: a visible, unstoppable Armageddon. Religious tourists came from all over the planet to see it, and its ever-shrinking distance was posted on the public sites. Thorn turned to her slate to look it up, but Magister Pregaldin made her put it down. "No," he said, "I want you to figure it out."

"How can I?" she said. "They bounce lasers off it or something to find out where it is."

"There is an easier way, using tools you already have."

"The *easiest* way is to look it up!"

"No, that is the lazy way." His face looked severe. "Relying too much on free information makes you as vulnerable as relying too much on technology. You should always know how to figure it out yourself, because information can be falsified, or taken away. You should never trust it."

So he was some sort of information survivalist. "Next you'll want me to use flint to make fire," she grumbled.

"Thinking for yourself is not obsolete. Now, how are you going to find out? I will give you a hint: you don't have enough information right now. Where are you going to get it?"

She thought a while. It had to use mathematics, because that was what they had been talking about. At last she said, "I'll need a tape measure."

"Right."

"And a protractor."

"Good. Now go do it."

It took her the rest of forenote to assemble her tools, and the first part of afternote to observe the ingot from two spots on opposite ends of the park. Then she got one of the refuse-picker children to help her measure the distance between her observation posts. Armed with two angles and a length, the trigonometry was simple. When Magister Pregaldin let her check her answer, it was more accurate than she had expected.

He didn't let on, but she could tell that he was, if anything, even more pleased with her success than she was herself. "Good," he said. "Now, if you measured more carefully and still got an answer different from the official one, you would have to ask yourself whether the Protectorate had a reason for falsifying the Ingot's distance."

She could see now what he meant.

"That old Vind must be a wizard," Hunter said when he found Thorn toiling over a math problem at the kitchen table. "He's figured out some way of motivating you."

"Why do you think he's a Vind?" Thorn said.

Hunter gave a caustic laugh. "Just look at him."

She silently added that to her mental dossier on her tutor. Not a Gminta, then. A Vind—one of the secretive race of aristocrat intellectuals who could be found in government, finance, and academic posts on almost every one of the Twenty Planets. All her life Thorn had heard whispers about a Vind conspiracy to infiltrate positions of power under the guise of public service. She had heard about the secret Vind sodality of interplanetary financiers who siphoned off the wealth of whole planets to fund their hegemony. She knew Maya scoffed at all of it. Certainly, if Magister Pregaldin was an example, the Vind conspiracy was not working very well. He seemed as penniless as any other Waster.

But being Vind did not rule out his involvement in the Holocide—it just meant he was more likely to have been a refugee than a perpetrator. Like most planets, Gmintagad had had a small, elite Vind community, regarded with suspicion by the indigenes. The massacres had targeted the Vinds as well as the Alloes. People didn't talk as much about the Vinds, perhaps because the Vinds didn't talk about it themselves.

Inevitably, Thorn's daily lessons in the park drew attention. One day they were conducting experiments in aerodynamics with paper airplanes when a man approached them. He had a braided beard strung with ceramic beads that clacked as he walked. Magister Pregaldin saw him first, and his face went blank and inscrutable.

The clatter of beads came to rest against the visitor's silk kameez. He cleared his throat. Thorn's tutor stood and touched his earlobes in respect, as people did on this planet. "Your worship's presence makes my body glad," he said formally.

The man made no effort to be courteous in return. "Do you have a license for this activity?"

"Which activity, your worship?"

"Teaching in a public place."

Magister Pregaldin hesitated. "I had no idea my conversations could be construed as teaching."

It was the wrong answer. Even Thorn, watching silently, could see that the proper response would have been to ask how much a license cost. The man was obviously fishing for a bribe. His face grew stern. "Our blessed Protectorate levies just fines on those who flout its laws."

"I obey all the laws, honorable sir. I will cease to give offense immediately."

The magister picked up his battered old electronic slate and, without a glance at Thorn, walked away. The man from the Protectorate considered Thorn, but evidently concluded he couldn't extract anything from her, and so he left.

Thorn waited till the official couldn't see her anymore, then sprinted after Magister Pregaldin. He had disappeared into Weezer Alley, a crooked passageway that Thorn ordinarily avoided because it was the epicenter of depravity in the Waste. She plunged into it now, searching for the tall, patrician silhouette of her tutor. It was still forenote, and the denizens of Weezer Alley were just beginning to rise from catering to the debaucheries of yesternote's customers. Thorn hurried past a shop where the owner was beginning to lay out an array of embarrassingly explicit sex toys; she tried not to look. A little beyond, she squeamishly skirted a spot where a shopkeeper was scattering red dirt on a half-dried pool of vomit. Several dogleg turns into the heart of the sin warren, she came to the infamous Garden of Delights, where live musicians were said to perform. No one from the Protectorate cared much about prostitution, since that was mentioned in their holy book; but music was absolutely forbidden.

The gate into the Garden of Delights was twined about with iron snakes. On either side of it stood a pedestal where dancers gyrated during open hours. Now a sleepy she-man lounged on one of them, stark naked except for a bikini that didn't hide much. Hisher smooth skin was almost completely covered with the vinelike and paisley patterns of the decorative skin fungus *mycochromoderm*. Once injected, it was impossible to remove. It grew as long as its host lived, in bright scrolls and branching patterns. It had been a Waster fad once.

The dancer regarded Thorn from lizardlike eye slits in a face forested over with green and red tendrils. "You looking for the professor?" heshe asked.

Thorn was a little shocked that her cultivated tutor was known to such an exhibitionist creature as this, but she nodded. The she-man gestured languidly at a second-story window across the street. "Tell him to come visit me," heshe said, and bared startlingly white teeth.

Thorn found the narrow doorway almost hidden behind an awning and climbed the staircase past peeling tin panels that once had shown houris carrying a huge feather fan. When she knocked on the door at the top, there was no response at first, so she called out, "Magister?"

The door flew open and Magister Pregaldin took her by the arm and yanked her in, looking to make sure she had not been followed. "What are you doing here?" he demanded.

"No one saw me," she said. "Well, except for that . . . that. . . ." She gestured across the street.

Magister Pregaldin went to the window and looked out. "Oh, Ginko," he said.

"Why do you live here?" Thorn said. "There are lots better places."

The magister gave a brief, grim little smile. "Early warning system," he said. "As long as the Garden is allowed to stay in business, no one is going to care about the likes of me." He frowned sternly. "Unless you get me in trouble."

"Why didn't you bribe him? He would have gone away."

"I have to save my bribes for better causes," he said. "One can't become known to the bottom-feeders, or they get greedy." He glanced out the window again. "You have to leave now."

"Why?" she said. "All he said was you need a license to teach in public. He didn't say anything about teaching in private."

Magister Pregaldin regarded her with a complex expression, as if he were trying to quantify the risk she represented. At last he gave a nervous shrug. "You must promise not to tell anyone. I am serious. This is not a game."

"I promise," Thorn said.

She had a chance then to look around. Up to now, her impression had been of a place so cluttered that only narrow lanes were left to move about the room. Now she saw that the teetering stacks all around her were constructed of wondrous things. There were crystal globes on ormolu stands, hand-knotted silk rugs piled ten high, clocks with malachite cases stacked atop towers of leather-and-gilt books. There was a copper orrery of nested bands and onyx horses rearing on their back legs, and a theremin in a case of brushed aluminum. A cloisonné ewer as tall as Thorn occupied one corner. In the middle hung a chandelier that dripped topaz swags and bangles, positioned so that Magister Pregaldin had to duck whenever he crossed the room.

"Is all this stuff yours?" Thorn said, dazzled with so much wonder.

"Temporarily," he said. "I am an art dealer. I make sure things of beauty get from those who do not appreciate them to those who do. I am a matchmaker, in a way." As he spoke, his fingers lightly caressed a sculpture made from an ammonite fossil with a human face emerging from the shell. It was a delicate gesture, full of reverence, even love. Thorn had a sudden, vivid feeling that this was where Magister Pregaldin's soul rested—with his things of beauty.

"If you are to come here, you must never break anything," he said.

"I won't touch," Thorn said.

"No, that's not what I meant. One *must* touch things, and hold them, and work them. Mere looking is never enough. But touch them as they wish to be touched." He handed her the ammonite fossil. Its curve fit perfectly in her hand. The face looked surprised when she held it up before her, and she laughed.

Most of the walls were as crowded as the floor, with paintings hung against overlapping tapestries and guidons. But one wall was empty except for a painting that hung alone, as if in a place of honor. As Thorn walked toward it, it seemed to shift and change colors with every change of angle. It showed a young girl with long black hair and a serious expression, about Thorn's age but far more beautiful and fragile.

Seeing where she was looking, Magister Pregaldin said, "The portrait is made of butterfly wings. It is a type of artwork from Vindahar."

"Is that the home world of the Vind?"

"Yes."

"Do you know who she is?"

"Yes," he said hesitantly. "But it would mean nothing to you. She died a long time ago."

There was something in his voice—was it pain? No, Thorn decided, something less acute, like the memory of pain. It lay in the air after he stopped speaking, till even he heard it.

"That is enough art history for today," he said briskly. "We were speaking of airplanes."

*　　*　　*

That afternote, Hunter was out on one of his inscrutable errands. Thorn waited till Maya was talking to one of her friends and crept up to Hunter's office. He had a better library than anyone she had ever met, a necessary thing on this planet where there were almost no public sources of knowledge. Thorn was quite certain she had seen some art books in his collection. She scanned the shelves of disks and finally took down one that looked like an art encyclopedia. She inserted it into the reader and typed in "butterfly" and "Vindahar."

There was a short article from which she learned that the art of butterfly-wing painting had been highly admired, but was no longer practiced because the butterflies had gone extinct. She went on to the illustrations—and there it was. The very same painting she had seen earlier that day, except lit differently, so that the colors were far brighter and the girl's expression even sadder than it had seemed.

Portrait of Jemma Diwali, the caption said. *An acknowledged masterpiece of technique, this painting was lost in GM 862, when it was looted from one of the homes of the Diwali family. According to Almasy, the representational formalism of the subject is subtly circumvented by the transformational perspective, which creates an abstractionist counter-layer of imagery. It anticipates the "chaos art" of Dunleavy. . . .* It went on about the painting as if it had no connection to anything but art theory. But all Thorn cared about was the first sentence. GM 862—the year of the Gmintan Holocide.

Jemma was staring at her gravely, as if there were some implied expectation on her mind. Thorn went back to the shelves, this time for a history of the Holocide. It seemed like there were hundreds of them. At last she picked one almost at random and typed in "Diwali." There were uninformative references to the name scattered throughout the book. From the first two, she gathered that the Diwalis had been a Vind family associated with the government on Gmintagad. There were no mentions of Jemma.

She had left the door ajar and now heard the sounds of Hunter returning downstairs. Quickly she re-cased the books and erased her trail from the reader. She did not want him to find out just yet. This was her mystery to solve.

There wasn't another chance to sneak into Hunter's office before she returned to Magister Pregaldin's apartment on Weezer Alley. She found that he had cleared a table for them to work at, directly underneath the stuffed head of a creature with curling copper-colored horns. As he checked over the work she had done the note before, her eyes were drawn irresistibly to the portrait of Jemma across the room.

At last he caught her staring at it, and their eyes met. She blurted out, "Did you know that painting comes from Gmintagad?"

A shadow of frost crossed his face. But it passed quickly, and his voice was low and even when he said, "Yes."

"It was looted," Thorn said. "Everyone thought it was lost."

"Yes, I know," he said.

Accusatory thoughts were bombarding her. He must have seen them, for he said calmly, "I collect art from the Holocide."

"That's macabre," she said.

"A great deal of significant art was looted in the Holocide. In the years after, it was scattered, and entered the black markets of a dozen planets. Much of it was lost. I am reassembling a small portion of it, whatever I can rescue. It is very slow work."

This explanation altered the picture Thorn had been creating in her head. Before, she had seen him as a scavenger feeding on the remains of a tragedy. Now he seemed more like a memorialist acting in tribute to the dead. Regretting what she had been thinking, she said, "Where do you find it?"

"In curio shops, import stores, estate sales. Most people don't recognize it. There are dealers who specialize in it, but I don't talk to them."

"Don't you think it should go back to the families that owned it?"

He hesitated a fraction of a second, then said, "Yes, I do." He glanced over his shoulder at Jemma's portrait. "If one of them existed, I would give it back."

"You mean they're *all* dead? Every one of them?"

"So far as I can find out."

That gave the artwork a new quality. To its delicacy, its frozen-flower beauty, was added an iron frame of absolute mortality. An entire family, vanished. Thorn got up to go look at it, unable to stay away.

"The butterflies are all gone, too," she said.

Magister Pregaldin came up behind her, looking at the painting as well. "Yes," he said. "The butterflies, the girl, the family, the world, all gone. It can never be replicated."

There was something exquisitely poignant about the painting now. The only surviving thing to prove that they had all existed. She looked up at Magister Pregaldin. "Were you there?"

He shook his head slowly. "No. It was before my time. I have always been interested in it, that's all."

"Her name was Jemma," Thorn said. "Jemma Diwali."

"How did you find that out?" he asked.

"It was in a book. A stupid book. It was all about abstractionist counter-layers and things. Nothing that really explained the painting."

"I'll show you what it was talking about," the magister said. "Stand right there." He positioned her about four feet from the painting, then took the lamp and moved it to one side. As the light moved, the image of Jemma

Diwali disappeared, and in its place was an abstract design of interlocking spirals, spinning pinwheels of purple and blue.

Thorn gave an exclamation of astonishment. "How did that happen?"

"It is in the microscopic structure of the butterfly wings," Magister Pregaldin explained. "Later, I will show you one under magnification. From most angles they reflect certain wavelengths of light, but from this one, they reflect another. The skill in the painting was assembling them so they would show both images. Most people think it was just a feat of technical virtuosity, without any meaning."

She looked at him. "But that's not what you think."

"No," he said. "You have to understand, Vind art is all about hidden messages, layers of meaning, riddles to be solved. Since I have had the painting here, I have been studying it, and I have identified this pattern. It was not chosen randomly." He went to his terminal and called up a file. A simple algebraic equation flashed onto the screen. "You solve this equation using any random number for X, then take the solution and use it as X to solve the equation again, then take *that* number and use it to solve the equation again, and so forth. Then you graph all the solutions on an X and Y axis, and this is what you get." He hit a key and an empty graph appeared on the screen. As the machine started to solve the equation, little dots of blue began appearing in random locations on the screen. There appeared to be no pattern at all, and Thorn frowned in perplexity.

"I'll speed it up now," Magister Pregaldin said. The dots started appearing rapidly, like sleet against a window or sand scattered on the floor. "It is like graphing the result of a thousand dice throws, sometimes lucky, sometimes outside the limits of reality, just like the choices of a life. You spend the first years buffeted by randomness, pulled this way by parents, that way by friends, all the variables squabbling and nudging, quarreling till you can't hear your own mind. And then, patterns start to appear."

On the screen, the dots had started to show a tendency to cluster. Thorn could see the hazy outlines of spiral swirls. As more and more dots appeared in seemingly random locations, the pattern became clearer and clearer.

Magister Pregaldin said, "As the pattern fills in, you begin to see that the individual dots were actually the pointillist elements of something beautiful: a snowflake, or a spiral, or concentric ripples. There is a pattern to our lives; we just experience it out of order, and don't have enough data at first to see the design. Our path forward is determined by this invisible artwork, the creation of a lifetime of events."

"You mean, like fate?" Thorn said.

"That is the question." Her tutor nodded gravely, staring at the screen. The light made his face look planar and secretive. "Does the pattern exist before us? Is our underlying equation predetermined, or is it generated by the results of our first random choice for the value of X? I can't answer that."

The pattern on the screen was clear now; it was the same one hidden under the portrait. Thorn glanced from one to the other. "What does this have to do with Jemma?"

"Another good question," Magister Pregaldin said thoughtfully. "I don't know. Perhaps it was a message to her from the artist, or a prediction—one that never had a chance to come true, because she died before she could find her pattern."

Thorn was silent a moment, thinking of that other girl. "Did she die in the Holocide?"

"Yes."

"Did you know her?"

"I told you, I wasn't there."

She didn't believe him for a second. He *had* been there, she was sure of it now. Not only had he been there, he was still there, and would always be there.

*   *   *

Several days later Thorn stepped out of the front door on her way to classes, and instantly sensed something wrong. There was a hush; tension or expectation had stretched the air tight. Too few people were on the street, and they were casting glances up at the city. She looked up toward where the Corkscrew rose, a black sheet-iron spiral that looked poised to drill a hole through the sky. There was a low, rhythmic sound coming from around it.

"Bick!" she cried out when she saw the Waster heading home laden down with groceries, as if for a siege. "What's going on?"

"You haven't heard?" Bick said.

"No."

In a low voice, Bick said, "The Protector was assassinated last note."

"Oh. Is that good or bad?"

Bick shrugged. "It depends on who they blame."

As Bick hurried on her way, Thorn stood, balanced between going home and going on to warn Magister Pregaldin. The sound from above grew more distinct, as of slow drumming. Deciding abruptly, Thorn dashed on.

The denizens of Weezer Alley had become accustomed to the sight of Thorn passing through to her lessons. Few of them were abroad this forenote, but she nearly collided with one coming out of the tobacco shop. It was a renegade priest from Glory to God who had adopted the Waster lifestyle as if it were his own. Everyone called him Father Sin.

"Ah, girl!" he exclaimed. "So eager for knowledge you knock down old men?"

"Father Sin, what's that sound?" she asked.

"They are beating the doorways of their houses in grief," he said. "It is tragic, what has happened."

She dashed on. The sound had become a ringing by the time she reached Magister Pregaldin's doorway, like an unnatural Note. She had to wait several seconds after knocking before the door opened.

"Ah, Thorn! I am glad you are here," Magister Pregaldin said when he saw her. "I have something I need to. . . ." He stopped, seeing her expression. "What is wrong?"

"Haven't you heard the news, Magister?"

"What news?"

"The Protector is dead. Assassinated. That's what the ringing is about."

He listened as if noticing it for the first time, then quickly went to his terminal to look up the news. There was a stark announcement from the Protectorate, blaming "Enemies of God," but of course no news. He shut it off and stood thinking. Then he seemed to come to a decision.

"This should not alter my plans," he said. "In fact, it may help." He turned to Thorn, calm and austere as usual. "I need to make a short journey. I will be away for two days, three at most. But if it takes me any longer, I will need you to check on my apartment, and make sure everything is in order. Will you do that?"

"Of course," Thorn said. "Where are you going?"

"I'm taking the wayport to one of the other city-states." He began then to show her two plants that would need watering, and a bucket under a leaky pipe that would need to be emptied. He paused at the entrance to his bedroom, then finally gestured her in. It was just as cluttered as the other rooms. He took a rug off a box, and she saw that it was actually a small refrigerator unit with a temperature gauge on the front showing that the interior was well below freezing.

"This needs to remain cold," he said. "If the electricity should go out, it will be fine for up to three days. But if I am delayed getting back, and the inside temperature starts rising, you will need to go out and get some dry ice to cool it again. Here is the lock. Do you remember the recursive equation I showed you?"

"You mean Jemma's equation?"

He hesitated in surprise, then said, "Yes. If you take twenty-seven for the first value of X, then solve it five times, that will give you the combination. That should be child's play for you."

"What's in it?" Thorn asked.

At first he seemed reluctant to answer, but then realized he had just given her the combination, so he knelt and pecked it out on the keypad. A light changed to green. He undid several latches and opened the top, then removed an ice pack and stood back for her to see. Thorn peered in and saw nested in ice a ball of white feathers.

"It's a bird," she said in puzzlement.

"You have seen birds, have you?"

"Yes. They don't have them here. Why are you keeping a dead bird?"

"It's not dead," he said. "It's sleeping. It is from a species they call ice owls, the only birds known to hibernate. They are native to a planet called

Ping, where the winters last a century or more. The owls burrow into the ice to wait out the winter. Their bodies actually freeze solid. Then when spring comes, they revive and rise up to mate and produce the next generation."

The temperature gauge had gone yellow, so he fitted the ice pack back in place and latched the top. The refrigerator hummed, restoring the chest to its previous temperature.

"There was a . . I suppose you would call it a fad, once, for keeping ice owls. When another person came along with a suitable owl, the owners would allow them both to thaw so they could come back to life and mate. It was a long time ago, though. I don't know whether there are still any freezer owls alive but this one."

Another thing that might be the last of its kind. This apartment was full of reminders of extinction, as if Magister Pregaldin could not free his mind of the thought.

But this one struck Thorn differently, because the final tragedy had not taken place. There was still a hope of life. "I'll keep it safe," she promised gravely.

He smiled at her. It made him look strangely sad. "You are a little like an owl yourself," he said kindly. "Older than the years you have lived."

She thought, but did not say, that he was also like an owl—frozen for 141 years.

They left the apartment together, she heading for home and he with a backpack over his shoulder, bound for the waystation.

*   *   *

Thorn did not wait two days to revisit the apartment alone to do some true detective work.

It was the day of the Protector's funeral, and Glory to God was holding its breath in pious suspension. All businesses were closed, even in the Waste, while the mourning rituals went on. Whatever repercussions would come from the assassination, they would not occur this day. Still, Thorn wore the veil when she went out, because it gave her a feeling of invisibility.

The magister's apartment was very quiet and motionless when she let herself in. She checked on the plants and emptied the pail in order to give her presence the appearance of legitimacy. She then went into the magister's bedroom, ostensibly to check the freezer, but really to look around, for she had only been in there the one time. She studied the art-encrusted walls, the shaving mirror supported by mythical beasts, the armoire full of clothes that had once been fine but now were shabby and outmoded. As she was about to leave she spotted a large box—a hexagonal column about three feet tall—on a table in a corner. It was clearly an offworld artifact because it was made of wood. Many sorts of wood, actually: the surface was an inlaid honeycomb design. But there were no drawers, no cabinets, no way inside at all. Thorn immediately realized that it must be a puzzle box—and she wanted to get inside.

She felt all around it for sliding panels, levers, or springs, but could not find any, so she brought over a lamp to study it. The surface was a parquet of hexagons, but the colors were not arranged in a regular pattern. Most tiles were made from a blond-colored wood and a reddish wood, interrupted at irregular intervals by hexagons of chocolate, caramel, and black. It gave her the strong impression of a code or diagram, but she could not imagine what sort.

It occurred to her that perhaps she was making this more complex than necessary, and the top might come off. So she tried to lift it—and indeed it shifted up, but only about an inch, enough to disengage the top row of hexagons from the ones below. In that position she found she could turn the lower rows. Apparently, it was like a cylinder padlock. Each row of hexagons was a tumbler that needed to be turned and aligned correctly for the box to open. She did not have the combination, but knowing the way Magister Pregaldin's Vind mind worked, she felt sure that there would be some hint, some way to figure it out.

Once more she studied the honeycomb inlay. There were six rows. The top one was most regular—six blond hexagons followed by six red hexagons, repeating around the circumference of the box. The patterns became more colorful in the lower rows, but always included the repeating line of six blond hexagons. For a while she experimented with spinning the rows to see if she could hit on something randomly, but soon gave up. Instead, she fetched her slate from her backpack and photographed the box, shifting it on the table to get the back. When she was done, she found that the top would no longer lock down in its original position. The instant Magister Pregaldin saw it, he would know that she had raised it. It was evidently meant as a tamper detector, and she had set it off. Now she needed to solve the puzzle, or explain to him why she had been prowling his apartment looking for evidence.

She walked home preoccupied. The puzzle was clearly about sixes—six sides, six rows, six hexagons in a row. She needed to think of formulas that involved sixes. When she reached home she went to her room and started transferring the box's pattern from the photos to a diagram so she could see it better. All that afternote she worked on it, trying to find algorithms that would produce the patterns she saw. Nothing seemed to work. The thought that she would fail, and have to confess to Magister Pregaldin, made her feeling of urgency grow. The anticipation of his disappointment and lost trust kept her up long after she should have pulled the curtains against the per-petual sun and gone to bed.

At about six hours forenote a strange dream came to her. She was standing before a tree whose trunk was a hexagonal pillar, and around it was twined a snake with Magister Pregaldin's eyes. It looked at her mockingly, then took its tail in its mouth.

She woke with the dream vivid in her mind. Lying there thinking, she remembered a story he had told her, about some Capellan magister named Kekule, who had deduced the ringlike structure of benzene after dreaming of a snake. She smiled with the thought that she had just had Kekule's dream.

Then she bounded out of bed and out her door, pounding down the spiral steps to the kitchen. Hunter and Maya were eating breakfast together when she erupted into the room.

"Hunter! Do you have any books on chemistry?" she said.

He regarded her as if she were demented. "Why?"

"I need to know about benzene!"

The two adults looked at each other, mystified. "I have an encyclopedia," he said.

"Can I go borrow it?"

"No. I'll find it for you. Now try to curb your enthusiasm for aromatic hydrocarbons till I've had my coffee."

He sat there tormenting her for ten minutes till he was ready to go up to his office and find the book for her. She took the disk saying, "Thanks, you're the best!" and flew upstairs with it. As soon as she found the entry on benzene her hunch was confirmed: it was a hexagonal ring of carbon atoms with hydrogens attached at the corners. By replacing hydrogens with different molecules you could create a bewildering variety of compounds.

So perhaps the formula she should have been looking for was not a mathematical one, but a chemical one. When she saw the diagrams for toluene, xylene, and mesitylene she began to see how it might work. Each compound was constructed from a benzene ring with methyl groups attached in different positions. Perhaps, then, each ring on the box represented a different compound and the objective was to somehow align the corners as they were shown in the diagrams. But which compounds?

Then the code of the inlaid woods came clear to her. The blond-colored hexagons were carbons, the red ones were hydrogens. The other colors probably stood for elements like nitrogen or oxygen. The chemical formulae were written right on the box for all to see.

After an hour of scribbling and looking up formulae, she was racing down the steps again with her solutions in her backpack. She grabbed a pastry from the kitchen and ate it on her way, praying that Magister Pregaldin would not have returned.

He had not. The apartment still seemed to be dozing in its emptiness. She went straight to the box. As she dialed each row to line up the corners properly, her excitement grew. When the last ring slid into place, a vertical crack appeared along one edge. The sides swung open on hinges to reveal compartments inside.

There were no gold or rubies, just papers. She took one from its slot and unfolded it. It was an intricate diagram composed of spidery lines connecting geometric shapes with numbers inside, as if to show relationships or pathways. There was no key, nor even a word written on it. The next one she looked at was all words, closely written to the very edges of the paper in a tiny, obsessive hand. In some places they seemed to be telling a surreal story about angels, magic papayas, and polar magnetism; in others they disintegrated into garbled nonsense. The next document was a map of sorts, with coastlines and roads inked in, and landmarks given allegorical names like Perfidy, Imbroglio, and Redemption Denied. The next was a complex chart of concentric circles divided into sections and labeled in an alphabet she had never seen before.

Either Magister Pregaldin was a madman or he was trying to keep track of something so secret that it had to be hidden under multiple layers of code. Thorn spread out each paper on the floor and took a picture of it, then returned it to its pigeonhole so she could puzzle over them at leisure. When she was done she closed the box and spun the rings to randomize them again. Now she could push the top back down and lock it in place.

She walked home a little disappointed, but feeling as if she had learned something about her tutor. There was an obsessive and paranoid quality about the papers that ill fitted the controlled and rational magister. Clearly, there were more layers to him than she had guessed.

When she got home, she trudged up the stairs to return the encyclopedia to Hunter. As she was raising her hand to knock on his office door, she heard a profane exclamation from within. Then Hunter came rocketing out. Without a glance at Thorn he shot down the stairs to the kitchen.

Thorn followed. He was brewing coffee and pacing. She sat on the steps and said, "What's the matter?"

He glanced up, shook his head, then it boiled out: "One of the suspects I have been following was murdered last night."

"Really?" So he *did* know of Gmintas in hiding. Or had known. Thinking it over, she said, "I guess it was a good time for a murder, in the middle of the mourning."

"It didn't happen here," he said irritably. "It was in Flaming Sword of Righteousness. Damn! We were days away from moving in on him. We had all the evidence to put him on trial before the Court of a Thousand Peoples. Now all that work has gone to waste."

She watched him pour coffee, then said, "What would have happened if the Court found him guilty?"

"He would have been executed," Hunter said. "There is not the slightest doubt. He was one of the worst. We've wanted him for decades. Now we'll never have justice; all we've got is revenge."

Thorn sat quiet then, thinking about justice and revenge, and why one was so right and the other so wrong, when they brought about the same result. "Who did it?" she asked at last.

"If I knew I'd track him down," Hunter said darkly.

He started back up the stairs with his coffee, and she had to move aside for him. "Hunter, why do you care so much about such an old crime?" she asked. "There are so many bad things going on today that need fixing."

He looked at her with a tight, unyielding expression. "To forget is to condone," he said. "Evil must know it will pay. No matter how long it takes."

* * *

"He's such a phony," she said to Magister Pregaldin the next day.

She had returned to his apartment that morning to find everything as usual, except for a half-unpacked crate of new artworks in the middle of the living room. They had sat down to resume lessons as if nothing had changed, but neither of them could concentrate on differential equations. So Thorn told him about her conversation with Hunter.

"What really made him mad was that someone beat him," Thorn said. "It's not really about justice, it's about competition. He wants the glory of having bagged a notorious Gminta. That's why it has to be public. I guess that's the difference between justice and revenge: when it's justice somebody gets the credit."

Magister Pregaldin had been listening thoughtfully; now he said, "You are far too cynical for someone your age."

"Well, people are disappointing!" Thorn said.

"Yes, but they are also complicated. I would wager there is something about him you do not know. It is the only thing we can ever say about people with absolute certainty: that we don't know the whole story."

It struck Thorn that what he said was truer of him than of Hunter.

He rose from the table and said, "I want to give you a gift, Thorn. We'll call it our lesson for the day."

Intrigued, she followed him into his bedroom. He took the rug off the freezer and checked the temperature, then unplugged it. He then took a small two-wheeled dolly from a corner and tipped the freezer onto it.

"You're giving me the ice owl?" Thorn said in astonishment.

"Yes. It is better for you to have it; you are more likely than I to meet someone else with another one. All you have to do is keep it cold. Can you do that?"

"Yes!" Thorn said eagerly. She had never owned something precious, something unique. She had never even had a pet. She was awed by the fact that Magister Pregaldin would give her something he obviously prized so much. "No one has ever trusted me like this," she said.

"Well, you have trusted me," he murmured without looking. "I need to return some of the burden."

He helped her get it down the steps. Once onto the street, she was able to wheel it by herself. But before leaving, she threw her arms giddily around her tutor and said, "Thank you, Magister! You're the best teacher I've ever had."

Wheeling the freezer through the alley, she attracted the attention of some young Wasters lounging in front of a betel parlor, who called out loudly to ask if she had a private stash of beer in there, and if they could have some. When she scowled and didn't answer they laughed and called her a lush. By the time she got home, her exaltation had been jostled aside by disgust and fury at the place where she lived. She managed to wrestle the freezer up the stoop and over the threshold into the kitchen, but when she faced the narrow spiral stair, she knew this was as far as she could get without help. The kitchen was already crowded, and the only place she could fit the freezer in was under the table. As she was shoving it against the wall, Maya came down the stairs and said, "What are you doing?"

"I have to keep this freezer here," Thorn said.

"You can't put it there. It's not convenient."

"Will you help me carry it up to my room?"

"You're kidding."

"I didn't think so. Then it's got to stay here."

Maya rolled her eyes at the irrational acts of teenagers. Now Thorn was angry at her, too. "It has to stay plugged in," Thorn said strictly. "Do you think you can remember that?"

"What's in it?"

Thorn would have enjoyed telling her if she hadn't been angry. "A science experiment," she said curtly.

"Oh, I see. None of my business, right?"

"Right."

"Okay. It's a secret," Maya said in a playful tone, as if she were talking to a child. She reached out to tousle Thorn's hair, but Thorn knocked her hand away and left, taking the stairs two at a time.

In her room, Thorn gave way to rage at her unsatisfactory life. She didn't want to be a Waster anymore. She wanted to live in a house where she could have things of her own, not squat in a boyfriend's place, always one quarrel away from eviction. She wanted a life she could control. Most of all, she wanted to leave the Waste. She went to the window and looked down at the rusty ghetto below. Cynicism hung miasmatic over it, defiling everything noble and pure. The decadent sophistication left nothing unstained.

During dinner, Maya and Hunter were cross and sarcastic with each other, and Hunter ended up storming off into his office. Thorn went to her room and studied Magister Pregaldin's secret charts till the house was silent below. Then she crept down to the kitchen to check on the freezer. The temperature gauge was reassuringly low. She sat on the brick floor with her back to it, its gentle hum soothing against her spine, feeling a kinship with the owl inside. She envied it for its isolation from the dirty world. Packed away safe in ice, it was the one thing that would never grow up, never lose its innocence. One day it would come alive and erupt in glorious joy—but only if she could protect it. Even if she couldn't protect herself, there was still something she could keep safe.

As she sat there, The Note came, filling the air full and ringing through her body like a benediction. It seemed to be answering her unfocused yearning, as if the believers were right, and there really were a force looking over her, as she looked over the owl.

*   *   *

When she next came to Magister Pregaldin's apartment, he was busy filling the crate up again with treasures. Thorn helped him wrap artworks in packing material as he told her which planet each one came from. "Where are you sending them?" she asked.

"Offworld," he answered vaguely.

Together they lifted the lid onto the crate, and only then did Thorn see the shipping label that had brought it here. It was stamped with a burning red sword—the customs mark of the city-state Flaming Sword of Righteousness. "Is that where you were?" she said.

"Yes."

She was about to blurt out that Hunter's Gminta had been murdered there when a terrible thought seized her: What if he already knew? What if it were no coincidence?

They sat down to lessons under the head of the copper-horned beast, but Thorn was distracted. She kept looking at her tutor's large hands, so gentle when he handled his art, and wondering if they could be the hands of an assassin.

That night Hunter went out and Maya barricaded herself in her room, leaving Thorn the run of the house. She instantly let herself into Hunter's office to search for a list of Gmintas killed and brought to justice over the years. When she tried to access his files, she found they were heavily protected by password and encryption—and if she knew his personality, he probably had intrusion detectors set. So she turned again to his library of books on the Holocide. The information was scattered and fragmentary, but after a few hours she had pieced together a list of seven mysterious murders on five planets that seemed to be revenge slayings.

Up in her room again, she took out her replica of one of Magister Pregaldin's charts, the one that looked most like a tracking chart. She started by assuming that the geometric shapes meant planets and the symbols represented individual Gmintas he had been following. After an hour she gave it up—not because she couldn't make it match, but because she could never prove it. A chart for tracking Gmintas would look identical to a chart for tracking artworks. It was the perfect cover story.

She was still awake when Hunter returned. As she listened to his footsteps she thought of going downstairs and telling him of her suspicions. But uncertainty kept her in bed, restless and wondering what was the right thing to do.

*   *   *

There were riots in the city the next day. In the streets far above the Waste, angry mobs flowed, a turbulent tide crashing against the Protectorate troops wherever they met. The Wasters kept close to home, looking up watchfully toward the palace, listening to the rumors that ran ratlike between the buildings. Thorn spent much of the day on the roof, a self-appointed lookout. About five hours afternote, she heard a roar from above, as of many voices raised at once. There was something elemental about the sound, as if a force of nature had broken into the domed city—a human eruption, shaking the iron framework on which all their lives depended.

She went down to the front door to see if she could catch any news. Her survival instincts were alert now, and when she spotted a little group down the street, standing on a doorstep exchanging news, she sprinted toward them to hear what they knew.

"The Incorruptibles have taken the Palace," a man told her in a low voice. "The mobs are looting it now."

"Are we safe?" she asked.

He only shrugged. "For now." They all glanced down the street toward the spike-topped gates of the Waste. The barrier had never looked flimsier.

When Thorn returned home, Maya was sitting in the kitchen looking miserable. She didn't react much to the news. Thorn sat down at the table with her, bumping her knees on the freezer underneath.

"Shouldn't we start planning to leave?" Thorn said.

"I don't want to leave," Maya said, tears coming to her already-red eyes.

"I don't either," Thorn said. "But we shouldn't wait till we don't have a choice."

"Hunter will protect us," Maya said. "He knows who to pay."

Frustrated, Thorn said, "But if the Incorruptibles take over, there won't *be* anyone to pay. That's why they call themselves incorruptible."

"It won't come to that," Maya said stubbornly. "We'll be all right. You'll see."

Thorn had heard it all before. Maya always denied that anything was wrong until everything fell apart. She acted as if planning for the worst would make it happen.

The next day the city was tense but quiet. The rumors said that the Incorruptibles were still hunting down Protectorate loyalists and throwing them in jail. The nearby streets were empty except for Wasters, so Thorn judged it safe enough to go to Weezer Alley. When she entered Magister Pregaldin's place, she was stunned at the change. The apartment had been stripped of its artworks. The carpets were rolled up, the empty walls looked dented and peeling. Only Jemma's portrait still remained. Two metal crates stood in the middle of the living room, and as Thorn was taking it all in, a pair of movers arrived to carry them off to the waystation.

"You're leaving," she said to Magister Pregaldin when he came back in from supervising the movers. She was not prepared for the disappointment she felt. All this time she had been trustworthy and kept his secrets—and he had abandoned her anyway.

"I'm sorry, Thorn," he said, reading her face. "It is becoming too dangerous here. You and your mother ought to think of leaving, as well."

"Where are you going?"

He paused. "It would be better if I didn't tell you that."

"I'm not going to tell anyone."

"Forgive me. It's a habit." He studied her for a few moments, then put his hand gently on her shoulder. "Your friendship has meant more to me than you can know," he said. "I had forgotten what it was like, to inspire such pure trust."

He didn't even know she saw through him. "You're lying to me," she said. "You've been lying all along. You're not leaving because of the Incorruptibles. You're leaving because you've finished what you came here to do."

He stood motionless, his hand still on her shoulder. "What do you mean?"

"You came here to settle an old score," she said. "That's what your life is about, isn't it? Revenge for something everyone else has forgotten and you can't let go."

He withdrew his hand. "You have made some strange mistake."

"You and Hunter—I don't understand either of you. Why can't you just stop digging up the past and move on?"

For several moments he stared at her, but his eyes were shifting as if tracking things she couldn't see. When he finally spoke, his voice was very low. "I don't *choose* to remember the past. I am compelled to—it is my punishment. Or perhaps it is a disease, or an addiction. I don't know."

Taken aback at his earnestness, Thorn said, "Punishment? For what?"

"Here, sit down," he said. "I will tell you a story before we part."

They both sat at the table where he had given her so many lessons, but before he started to speak he stood up again and paced away, his hands clenching. She waited silently, and he came back to face her, and started to speak.

*   *   *

This is a story about a young man who lived long ago. I will call him Till. He wanted badly to live up to his family's distinguished tradition. It was a prominent family, you see; for generations they had been involved in finance, banking, and insurance. The planet where they lived was relatively primitive and poor, but Till's family felt they were helping it by attracting outside investment and extending credit. Of course, they did very well by doing good.

The government of their country had been controlled by the Alloes for years. Even though the Alloes were an ethnic minority, they were a diligent people and had prospered by collaborating with Vind businessmen like Till's family. The Alloes ruled over the majority, the Gmintas, who had less of everything—less education, less money, less power. It was an unjust situation, and when there was a mutiny in the military and the Gmintas took control, the Vinds accepted the change. Especially to younger people like Till, it seemed like a righting of many historical wrongs.

Once the Gminta army officers were in power, they started borrowing heavily to build hospitals, roads, and schools for Gminta communities, and the Vind banks were happy to make the loans. It seemed like a good way to dispell many suspicions and prejudices that throve in the ignorance of the Gminta villages. Till was on the board of his family bank, and he argued for extending credit even after the other bankers became concerned about the government's reckless fiscal policies.

One day, Till was called into the offices of the government banking regulators. Alone in a small room, they accused him of money laundering and corruption. It was completely untrue, but they had forged documents that seemed to prove it. Till realized that he faced a life in prison. He would bring shame to his entire family, unless he could strike a deal. They offered him an alternative: he could come to work for the government, as their representative to the Vind community. He readily accepted the job, and resigned from the bank.

They gave him an office and a small staff. He had an Alloe counterpart responsible for outreach to that community; and though they never spoke about it, he suspected his colleague had been recruited with similar methods. They started out distributing informational leaflets and giving tips on broadcast shows, all quite bland. But it changed when the government decided to institute a new draft policy for military service. Every young person was to give five years' mandatory service starting at eighteen. The Vinds would not be exempt.

Now, as you may know, the Vinds are pacifists and mystics, and have never served in the military of any planet. This demand by the Gminta government was unprecedented, and caused great alarm. The Vinds gathered in the halls of their Ethical Congresses to discuss what to do. Till worked tirelessly, meeting with them and explaining the perspective of the government, reminding them of the Vind principle of obeying the local law wherever they found themselves. At the same time, he managed to get the generals to promise that no Vind would be required to serve in combat, which was utterly in violation of their beliefs. With this assurance, the Vinds reluctantly agreed. And so mothers packed bags for their children and sent them off to training, urging them to call often.

Soon after, a new land policy was announced. Estates that had always belonged to the Alloes were to be redistributed among landless Gmintas. This created quite a lot of resistance; Till and his colleague kept busy giving interviews and explaining how the policy restored fairness to the land system. They became familiar to all as government spokespeople.

Then the decision was made to relocate whole neighborhoods of Alloes and Vinds so Gmintas could have better housing in the cities. Till could no longer argue about justice; now he could only tell people it was necessary to move in order to quiet the fears of the Gmintas and preserve peace.

People started to emigrate off-planet, but then the government closed down the waystations. This nearly caused a panic, and Till had to tell everyone it was merely to prevent people from taking their goods and assets offworld, thus draining the national wealth. He promised that individuals would be allowed to leave again soon, as long as they took no cash or valuables with them.

He no longer believed it himself.

It had been months since the young people had gone off to the army, and their families had heard nothing from them. Till had been telling everyone it was a period of temporary isolation, while the trainees lived in camps on the frontier to build solidarity and camaraderie. Every time he went out, he would be surrounded by anxious parents asking when they could expect to hear from their children.

Fleets of buses showed up to evacuate the Alloe and Vind families from their homes, and take them to relocation camps. Till watched his own neighborhood become a ghost town, and the certainty grew in him that the people were never coming back. One day he entered his supervisor's office unexpectedly and overheard someone saying, ". . . to the mortifactories." They stopped talking when they saw him.

You are probably thinking, "Why didn't he speak out? Why didn't he denounce them?" Try to imagine, in many respects life still seemed quite normal, and what he suspected was so unthinkable it seemed insane. And even if he could overcome that, there was no one to speak out to. He was alone, and he was not a very courageous person. His only chance was to stay useful to the government.

Other Vinds and Alloes who had been working alongside him started to vanish. Still the Gmintas wanted him to go on reassuring people; he did it so well. He had to hide what he suspected, to fool them into thinking that he was fooled himself. Every day he lived in fear of hearing the knock on his door that would mean it was his time.

It was his Alloe colleague who finally broke. They rarely let the man go on air anymore; his nerves were too shattered. But one day he substituted for Till, and in the midst of a broadcast shouted out a warning: "They are killing you! It is mass murder!" That was all he got out before they cut him off.

That night, well-armed and well-organized mobs broke into the remaining Alloe enclaves in the capital city. The government deplored the violence the next day, but suggested that the Alloes had incited it.

At that point they no longer had any need for Till. Once again, they gave him a choice: relocation or deportation. He could join his family and share their fate; or he could leave the planet. Death or life. I think I have mentioned he was not very courageous. He chose to live.

They sent him to Capella Two, a twenty-five-year journey. By the time he arrived, the entire story had traveled ahead of him by pepci, and everything was known. His own role was infamous. He was the vile collaborator who had put a benign face on the crime. He had soothed people's fears and deceived them into walking docilely to their deaths. In hindsight, it was inconceivable that he had not known what he was doing. All across the Twenty Planets, the name of Till Diwali was reviled.

*   *   *

He fell silent at last. Thorn sat staring at the tabletop, because she could not sort out what to think. It was all wheeling about in her mind: right and wrong, horror and sympathy, criminal and victim—all were jumbled together. Finally she said, "Was Jemma your sister?"

"I told you, I was not there," he said in a distant voice. "The man who did those things was not me."

He was sitting at the table across from her again, his hands clasped before him. Now he spoke to her directly. "Thorn, you are unitary and authentic now as you will never be again. As you pass through life, you will accumulate other selves. Always you will be a person looking back on, and separate from, the person you are now. Whenever you walk down a street, or sit on a park bench, your past selves will be sitting beside you, impossible to touch or interrogate. In the end there is a whole crowd of you wherever you go, and you feel like you will perish from the loneliness."

Thorn's whirling feelings were beginning to come to rest in a pattern, and in it horror and blame predominated. She looked up at Jemma's face and said, "She *died*. How could you do that, and walk away? It's inhuman."

He didn't react, either to admit guilt or defend his innocence. She wanted an explanation from him, and he didn't give it. "You're a monster," she said.

Still he said nothing. She got up, blind to everything but the intensity of her thoughts, and went to the door. She glanced back before leaving, and he was looking at her with an expression that was nothing like what he ought to feel—not shame, not rage, not self-loathing. Thorn slammed the door behind her and fled.

She walked around the streets of the Waste for a long time, viciously throwing stones at heaps of trash to make the rats come out. Above the buildings, the sky seemed even redder than usual, and the shadows blacker. She was furious at the magister for not being admirable. She blamed him for hiding it from her and for telling her—since, by giving her the knowledge, he had also given her a responsibility of choosing what to do.

*   *   *

When she got home the kitchen was empty, but she heard voices from the living room above. She was mounting the stairs when the voices rose in anger, and she froze. It was Hunter and Maya, and they were yelling at each other.

"Good God, what were you thinking?" Hunter demanded.

"She needed help. I couldn't say no."

"You knew it would bring the authorities down on us!"

"I had a responsibility—"

"What about your responsibility to me? You just didn't think. You never think; everything is impulse with you. You are the most immature and manipulative person I've ever met."

Maya's voice went wheedling. "Hunter, come on. It'll be okay."

"And what if it's not okay? What are you going to do then? Just pick up and leave the wreckage behind you? That's what you've been doing all your life—dragging that kid of yours from planet to planet, never thinking what it's doing to her. You never think what you're doing to anyone, do you? It's all just yourself. I never should have let you in here."

There were angry footsteps, and then Hunter was mounting the stairs.

"Hunter!" Maya cried after him.

Thorn waited a minute, then crept up into the living room. Maya was sitting there, looking tragic and beautiful.

"What did you do?" Thorn said.

"It doesn't matter," Maya said. "He'll get over it."

"I don't care about Hunter."

Mistaking what she meant, Maya smiled through her tears. "You know what? I don't care either." She came over and hugged Thorn tight. "I'm not really a bad mother, am I, Thorn?"

Cautiously, Thorn said, "No. . . ."

"People just don't understand us. We're a team, right?"

Maya held out her hand for their secret finger-hook. Once it would have made Thorn smile, but she no longer felt the old solidarity against the world. She hooked fingers anyway, because she was afraid Maya would start to cry again if she didn't. Maya said, "They just don't know you. Damaged child, poppycock—you're tough as old boots. It makes me awestruck, what a survivor you are."

"I think we ought to get ready to leave," Thorn said.

Maya's face lost its false cheer. "I can't leave," she whispered.

"Why not?"

"Because I love him."

There was no sensible answer to that. So Thorn turned away to go up to her room. As she passed the closed door of Hunter's office, she paused, wondering if she should knock. Wondering if she should turn in the most notorious Gminta collaborator still alive. All those millions of dead Alloes and Vinds would get their justice, and Hunter would be famous. Then her feet continued on, even before she consciously made the decision. It was not loyalty to Magister Pregaldin, and it was not resentment of Hunter. It was because she might need that information to buy her own safety.

*   *   *

The sound of breaking glass woke her. She lay tense, listening to footsteps and raised voices below in the street. Then another window broke, and she got up to pull back the curtain. The sun was orange, as always, and she squinted in the glare, then raised her window and climbed out on the roof.

Below in the street, a mob of white-clad Incorruptibles was breaking windows as they passed; but their true target obviously lay deeper in the Waste. She watched till they were gone, then waited to see what would happen.

From somewhere beyond the tower fans of the park she could hear shouts and clanging, and once an avalanche-like roar, after which a cloud of dust rose from the direction of Weezer Alley. After that there was silence for a while. At last she heard chanting. Fleeing footsteps passed below. Then the wall of Incorruptibles appeared again. They were driving someone before them with improvised whips made from their belts. Thorn peered over the eaves to see more clearly and recognized their victim—Ginko, the heshe from the Garden of Delights, completely naked, both breasts and genitals exposed, with a rope around hisher neck. The whips had cut into the delicate paisley of Ginko's skin, exposing slashes of red underneath.

At a spot beneath Thorn's perch, Ginko stumbled and fell. A mass of Incorruptibles gathered round. Two of them pulled Ginko's legs apart, and a third made a jerking motion with a knife. A womanlike scream made Thorn grip the edge of her rooftop, wanting to look away. They tossed the rope over a signpost and hoisted Ginko up by the neck, choking and clawing at the noose. The body still quivered as the army marched past. When they were gone, the silence was so complete Thorn could hear the patter of blood into a pool on the pavement under the body.

On hands and knees she backed away from the edge of the roof and climbed into her bedroom. It was already stripped; everything she valued or needed was in her backpack, ready to go. She threw on some clothes and went down the stairs.

Maya, dressed in a robe, stopped her halfway. She looked scattered and panicky. "Thorn, we've got to leave," she said.

"Right now?"

"Yes. He doesn't want us here anymore. He's acting as if we're some sort of danger to him."

"Where are we going?"

"I don't know. Some other planet. Some place without men." She started to cry.

"Go get dressed," Thorn told her. "I'll bring some food." Over her shoulder she added, "Pack some clothes and money."

With her backpack in hand, Thorn raced down to the kitchen.

She was just getting out the dolly for the ice owl's refrigerator when Maya came down.

"You're not taking that, are you?" Maya said.

"Yes, I am." Thorn knelt to shift the refrigerator out from under the table, and only then noticed it wasn't running. Quickly, she checked the temperature gauge. It was in the red zone, far too high. With an anguished exclamation, she punched in the lock code and opened the top. Not a breath of cool air escaped. The ice pack on top was gurgling and liquid. She lifted it to see what was underneath.

The owl was no longer nested snugly in ice. It had shifted, tried to open its wings. There were scratches on the insulation where it had tried to peck and claw its way out. Now it lay limp, its head thrown back. Thorn sank to her knees, griefstruck before the evidence of its terrifying last minutes— revived to life only to find itself trapped in a locked chest. Even in that stifling dark, it had longed for life so much it had fought to free itself. Thorn's breath came hard and her heart labored, as if she were reliving the ice owl's death.

"Hurry up, Thorn," Maya said. "We've got to go."

Then she saw what had happened. The refrigerator cord lay on the floor, no longer attached to the wall outlet. She held it up as if it were a murder weapon. "It's unplugged," she said.

"Oh, that's right," Maya said, distracted. "I had to plug in the curling iron. I must have forgotten."

Rage rose inside Thorn like a huge bubble of compressed air. "You *forgot*?"

"I'm sorry, Thorn. I didn't know it was important."

"I *told* you it was important. This was the last ice owl anywhere. You haven't just killed this one, you've killed the entire species."

"I said I was sorry. What do you want me to do?"

Maya would never change. She would always be like this, careless and irresponsible, unable to face consequences. Tears of fury came to Thorn's eyes. She dashed them away with her hand. "You're useless," she said, climbing to her feet and picking up her pack. "You can't be trusted to take care of anything. I'm done with you. Don't bother to follow me."

Out in the street, she turned in the direction she never went, to avoid having to pass what was hanging in the street. Down a narrow alley she sprinted, past piles of stinking refuse alive with roaches, till she came to a narrow side street that doglegged into the park. On the edge of the open space she paused under a portico to scan for danger; seeing none, she dashed across, past the old men's chess tables, past the bench where she had met Magister Pregaldin, to the entrance of Weezer Alley.

Signs of the Incorruptibles' passage were everywhere. Broken glass crunched underfoot and the contents of the shops were trampled under red dirt shoeprints. When Thorn reached the Garden of Delights, the entire street looked different, for the building had been demolished. Only a monstrous pile of rubble remained, with iron girders and ribs sticking up like broken bones. A few people climbed over the ruin, looking for survivors.

The other side of the street was still standing, but Magister Pregaldin's door had been ripped from its hinges and tossed aside. Thorn dashed up the familiar stairs. The apartment looked as if it had been looted—stripped bare, not a thing of value left. She walked through the empty rooms, dreading what she might find, and finding nothing. Out on the street again, she saw a man who had often winked at her when she passed by to her lessons. "Do you know what happened to Magister Pregaldin?" she asked. "Did he get away?"

"Who?" the man said.

"Magister Pregaldin. The man who lived here."

"Oh, the old Vind. No, I don't know where he is."

So he had abandoned her as well. In all the world, there was no one trust-worthy. For a moment she had a dark wish that she had exposed his secret. Then she realized she was just thinking of revenge.

Hoisting her pack to her shoulder, she set out for the waystation. She was alone now, only herself to trust.

There was a crowd in the street outside the waystation. Everyone seemed to have decided to leave the planet at once, some of them with huge piles of baggage and children. Thorn pushed her way in toward the ticket station to find out what was going on. They were still selling tickets, she saw with relief; the crowd was people waiting for their turn in the translation chamber. Checking to make sure she had her copy of Maya's credit stick, she joined the ticket line. She was back among her own kind, the rootless, migrant elite.

Where was she going? She scanned the list of destinations. She had been born on Capella Two, but had heard it was a harshly competitive place, so she decided against it. Ben was just an ice-ball world, Gammadis was too far away. It was both thrilling and frightening to have control over where she went and what she did. She was still torn by indecision when she heard someone calling, "Thorn!"

Clarity was pushing through the crowd toward her. "I'm so glad we found you," she said when she drew close. "Maya was here a little while ago, looking for you."

"Where is she now?" Thorn asked, scanning the crowd.

"She left again."

"Good," Thorn said.

"Thorn, she was frantic. She was afraid you'd get separated."

"We *are* separated," Thorn said implacably. "She can do what she wants. I'm on my own now. Where are you going, Clarity?"

Bick had come up, carrying their ticket cards. Thorn caught her hand to look at the tickets. "Alananovis," she read aloud, then looked up to find it on the directory. It was only eighteen light-years distant. "Can I come with you?"

"Not without Maya," Clarity said.

"Okay, then I'll go somewhere else."

Clarity put a hand on her arm. "Thorn, you can't just go off without Maya."

"Yes, I can. I'm old enough to be on my own. I'm sick of her, and I'm sick of her boyfriends. I want control of my life." Besides, Maya had killed the ice owl; Maya ought to suffer. It was only justice.

She had reached the head of the line. Her eye caught a name on the list, and she made a snap decision. When the ticket seller said "Where to?" she answered, "Gmintagad." She would go to see where Jemma Diwali had lived—and died.

*   *   *

The translation chamber on Gmintagad was like all the others she had seen over the years: sterile and anonymous. A technician led her into a waiting room till her luggage came through by the low-resolution beam. She sat feeling cross and tired, as she always did after having her molecules reassembled out of new atoms. When at last her backpack was delivered and she went on into the customs and immigration facility, she noticed a change in the air. For the first time in years she was breathing organically manufactured oxygen. She could smell the complex and decay-laden odor of an actual ecosystem. Soon she would see sky without any dome. The thought gave her an agoraphobic thrill.

She put her identity card into the reader, and after a pause it directed her to a glass-fronted booth where an immigration official in a sand-colored uniform sat behind a desk. Unlike the air, the man looked manufactured—a face with no wrinkles, defects, or stand-out features, as if they had chosen him to match a mathematical formula for facial symmetry. His hair was neatly clipped, and so, she noticed, were his nails. When she sat opposite him, she found that her chair creaked at the slightest movement. She tried to hold perfectly still.

He regarded her information on his screen, then said, "Who is your father?"

She had been prepared to say why her mother was not with her, but her father? "I don't know," she said. "Why?"

"Your records do not state his race."

His *race*? It was an antique concept she barely understood. "He was Capellan," she said.

"Capellan is not an origin. No one evolved on Capella."

"I did," Thorn stated.

He studied her without any expression at all. She tried to meet his eyes, but it began to seem confrontational, so she looked down. Her chair creaked.

"There are certain types of people we do not allow on Gmintagad," he said.

She tried to imagine what he meant. Criminals? Disease carriers? Agitators? He could see she wasn't any of those. "Wasters, you mean?" she finally ventured.

"I mean Vinds," he said.

Relieved, she said, "Oh, well that's all right, then. I'm not Vind." Creak.

"Unless you can tell me who your father was, I cannot be sure of that," he said.

She was speechless. How could a father she had never known have any bearing on who she was?

The thought that they might not let her in made her stomach knot. Her chair sent out a barrage of telegraphic signals. "I just spent thirty-two years as a lightbeam to get here," she said. "You've got to let me stay."

"We are a sovereign principality," he said calmly. "We don't *have* to let anyone stay." He paused, his eyes still on her. "You have a Vind look. Are you willing to submit to a genetic test?"

Minutes ago, her mind had seemed like syrup. Now it bubbled with alarm. In fact, she didn't *know* her father wasn't Vind. It had never mattered, so she had never cared. But here, all the things that defined her—her interests, her aptitudes, her internal doubts—none of it counted, only her racial status. She was in a place where identity was assigned, not chosen or created.

"What happens if I fail the test?" she asked.

"You will be sent back."

"And what happens if I don't take it?"

"You will be sent back."

"Then why did you even ask?"

He gave a regulation smile. If she had measured it with a ruler, it would have been perfect. She stood up, and the chair sounded like it was laughing. "All right. Where do I go?"

They took her blood and sent her into a waiting room with two doors, neither of which had a handle. As she sat there idle, the true rashness of what she had done crept up on her. It wasn't like running away on-planet. Maya didn't know where she had gone. By now, they would be different ages. Maya could be dying, or Thorn could be older than she was, before they ever found each other. It was a permanent separation. And permanent punishment for Maya.

Thorn tried to summon up the righteous anger that had propelled her only an hour and thirty-two years before. But even that slipped from her grasp. It was replaced with a clutching feeling of her own guilt. She had known Maya's shortcomings when she took the ice owl, and never bothered to safeguard against them. She had known all the accidents the world was capable of, and still she had failed to protect a creature that could not protect itself.

Now, remorse made her bleed inside. The owl had been too innocent to meet such a terrible end. Its life should have been a joyous ascent into air, and instead it had been a hellish struggle, alone and forgotten, killed by neglect. Thorn had betrayed everyone by letting the ice owl die. Magister Pregaldin, who had trusted her with his precious possession. Even, somehow, Jemma and the other victims of Till Diwali's crime—for what had she done but reenact his failure, as if to show that human beings had learned nothing? She felt as if caught in an iron-bound cycle of history, doomed to repeat what had gone before, as long as she was no better than her predecessors had been.

She covered her face with her hands, wanting to cry, but too demoralized even for that. It seemed like a self-indulgence she didn't deserve.

The door clicked and she started up at sight of a stern, rectangular woman in a uniform skirt, whose face held the hint of a sneer. Thorn braced for the news that she would have to waste another thirty-two years on a pointless journey back to Glory to God. But instead, the woman said, "There is someone here to see you."

Behind her was a familiar face that made Thorn exclaim in joy, "Clarity!"

Clarity came into the room, and Thorn embraced her in relief. "I thought you were going to Alananovis."

"We were," Clarity said, "but we decided we couldn't just stand by and let a disaster happen. I followed you, and Bick stayed behind to tell Maya where we were going."

"Oh, thank you, thank you!" Thorn cried. Now the tears that had refused to come before were running down her face. "But you gave up thirty-two years for a stupid reason."

"It wasn't stupid for us," Clarity said. "You were the stupid one."

"I know," Thorn said miserably.

Clarity was looking at her with an expression of understanding. "Thorn, most people your age are allowed some mistakes. But you're performing life without a net. You have to consider Maya. Somehow, you've gotten older than she is even though you've been traveling together. You're the steady one, the rock she leans on. These boyfriends, they're just entertainment for her. They drop her and she bounces back. But if you dropped her, her whole world would dissolve."

Thorn said, "That's not true."

"It *is* true," Clarity said.

Thorn pressed her lips together, feeling impossibly burdened. Why did *she* have to be the reliable one, the one who was never vulnerable or wounded? Why did Maya get to be the dependent one?

On the other hand, it was a comfort that she hadn't abandoned Maya as she had done to the ice owl. Maya was not a perfect mother, but neither was Thorn a perfect daughter. They were both just doing their best.

"I hate this," she said, but without conviction. "Why do I have to be responsible for her?"

"That's what love is all about," Clarity said.

"You're a busybody, Clarity," Thorn said.

Clarity squeezed her hand. "Yes. Aren't you lucky?"

The door clicked open again. Beyond the female guard's square shoulder, Thorn glimpsed a flash of honey-gold hair. "Maya!" she said.

When she saw Thorn, Maya's whole being seemed to blaze like the sun. Dodging in, she threw her arms around Thorn.

"Oh Thorn, thank heaven I found you! I was worried sick. I thought you were lost."

"It's okay, it's okay," Thorn kept saying as Maya wept and hugged her again. "But Maya, you have to tell me something."

"Anything. What?"

"Did you seduce a *Vind*?"

For a moment Maya didn't understand. Then a secretive smile grew on her face, making her look very pretty and pleased with herself. She touched Thorn's hair. "I've been meaning to tell you about that."

"Later," Bick said. "Right now, we all have tickets for Alananovis."

"That's wonderful," Maya said. "Where's Alananovis?"

"Only seven years away from here."

"Fine. It doesn't matter. Nothing matters as long as we're together."

She held out her finger for the secret finger-lock. Thorn did it with a little inward sigh. For a moment she felt as if her whole world were composed of vulnerable beings frozen in time, as if she were the only one who aged and changed.

"We're a team, right?" Maya said anxiously.

"Yeah," Thorn answered. "We're a team."

ADO

Connie Willis

The Monday before spring break I told my English lit class we were going to do Shakespeare. The weather in Colorado is usually wretched this time of year. We get all the snow the ski resorts needed in December, use up our scheduled snow days, and end up going an extra week in June. The forecast on the *Today* show hadn't predicted any snow till Saturday, but with luck it would arrive sooner.

My announcement generated a lot of excitement. Paula dived for her corder and rewound it to make sure she'd gotten my every word, Edwin Sumner looked smug, and Delilah snatched up her books and stomped out, slamming the door so hard it woke Rick up. I passed out the release/refusal slips and told them they had to have them back in by Wednesday. I gave one to Sharon to give Delilah. "Shakespeare is considered one of our greatest writers, possibly *the* greatest," I said for the benefit of Paula's corder. "On Wednesday I will be talking about Shakespeare's life, and on Thursday and Friday we will be reading his work."

Wendy raised her hand. "Are we going to read all the plays?"

I sometimes wonder where Wendy has been the last few years—certainly not in this school, possibly not in this universe. "What we're studying hasn't been decided yet," I said. "The principal and I are meeting tomorrow."

"It had better be one of the tragedies," Edwin said darkly.

*   *   *

By lunch the news was all over the school. "Good luck," Greg Jefferson the biology teacher said in the teacher's lounge. "I just got done doing evolution."

"Is it really that time of year again?" Karen Miller said. She teaches American lit across the hall. "I'm not even up to the Civil War yet."

"It's that time of year again," I said. "Can you take my class during your free period tomorrow? I've got to meet with Harrows."

"I can take them all morning. Just have your kids come into my room tomorrow. We're doing 'Thanatopsis.' Another thirty kids won't matter."

"'Thanatopsis?'" I said, impressed. "The whole thing?"

"All but lines ten and sixty-eight. It's a terrible poem, you know. I don't think anybody understands it well enough to protest. And I'm not telling anybody what the title means."

"Cheer up," Greg said. "Maybe we'll have a blizzard."

*   *   *

Tuesday was clear, with a forecast of temps in the sixties. Delilah was outside the school when I got there, wearing a red Seniors Against Devil Worship in the Schools T-shirt and shorts. She was carrying a picket sign that said, "Shakespeare is Satan's Spokesman." Shakespeare and Satan were both misspelled.

"We're not starting Shakespeare till tomorrow," I told her. "There's no reason for you not to be in class. Ms. Miller is teaching 'Thanatopsis.'"

"Not lines ten and sixty-eight, she's not. Besides, Bryant was a Theist, which is the same thing as a Satanist." She handed me her refusal slip and a fat manila envelope. "Our protests are in there." She lowered her voice. "What does the word 'thanatopsis' really mean?"

"It's an Indian word. It means, 'One who uses her religion to ditch class and get a tan.'"

I went inside, got Shakespeare out of the vault in the library and went into the office. Ms. Harrows already had the Shakespeare file and her box of kleenex out. "Do you have to do this?" she said, blowing her nose.

"As long as Edwin Sumner's in my class, I do. His mother's head of the President's Task Force on Lack of Familiarity with the Classics." I added Delilah's list of protests to the stack and sat down at the computer.

"Well, it may be easier than we think," she said. "There have been a lot of suits since last year, which takes care of *Macbeth*, *The Tempest*, *A Midsummer Night's Dream*, *The Winter's Tale*, and *Richard III*."

"Delilah's been a busy girl," I said. I fed in the unexpurgated disk and the excise and reformat programs. "I don't remember there being any witchcraft in *Richard III.*"

She sneezed and grabbed for another kleenex. "There's not. That was a slander suit. Filed by his great-great-grand-something. He claims there's no conclusive proof that Richard III killed the little princes. It doesn't matter anyway. The Royal Society for the Restoration of Divine Right of Kings has an injunction against all the history plays. What's the weather supposed to be like?"

"Terrible," I said. "Warm and sunny." I called up the catalog and deleted *Henry IV, Parts I and II*, and the rest of her list. "*Taming of the Shrew?*"

"Angry Women's Alliance. Also *Merry Wives of Windsor*, *Romeo and Juliet*, and *Love's Labour Lost.*"

"*Othello?* Never mind. I know that one. *Merchant of Venice?* The Anti-Defamation League?"

"No. The American Bar Association. And Morticians International. They object to the use of the word "casket" in Act III." She blew her nose.

* * *

It took us first and second period to deal with the plays and most of third to finish the sonnets. "I've got a class fourth period and then lunch duty," I said. "We'll have to finish up the rest of them this afternoon."

"Is there anything left for this afternoon?" Ms. Harrows asked.

"*As You Like It* and *Hamlet*," I said. "Good heavens, how did they miss *Hamlet?*"

"Are you sure about *As You Like It?*" Ms. Harrows said, leafing through her stack. "I thought somebody'd filed a restraining order against it."

"Probably the Mothers Against Transvestites," I said. "Rosalind dresses up like a man in Act II."

"No, here it is. The Sierra Club. 'Destructive attitudes toward the environment.'" She looked up. "What destructive attitudes?"

"Orlando carves Rosalind's name on a tree." I leaned back in my chair so

I could see out the window. The sun was still shining maliciously down. "I guess we go with *Hamlet*. This should make Edwin and his mother happy."

"We've still got the line-by-lines to go," Ms. Harrows said. "I think my throat is getting sore."

*   *   *

I got Karen to take my afternoon classes. It was sophomore lit, and we'd been doing Beatrix Potter—all she had to do was pass out a worksheet on *Squirrel Nutkin.* I had outside lunch duty. It was so hot I had to take my jacket off. The College Students for Christ were marching around the school carrying

picket signs that said, "Shakespeare was a Secular Humanist."

Delilah was lying on the front steps, reeking of suntan oil. She waved her "Shakespeare is Satan's Spokesman" sign languidly at me. "'Ye have sinned a great sin,'" she quoted. "'Blot me, I pray thee, out of thy book which thou has written.' Exodus Chapter 32, Verse 30."

"First Corinthians 13:3," I said. "'Though I give my body to be burned and have not charity, it profiteth me nothing.'"

*   *   *

"I called the doctor," Ms. Harrows said. She was standing by the window looking out at the blazing sun. "He thinks I might have pneumonia."

I sat down at the computer and fed in *Hamlet.* "Look on the bright side. At least we've got the E-and-R programs. We don't have to do it by hand the way we used to."

She sat down behind the stack. "How shall we do this? By group or by line?"

"We might as well take it from the top."

"Line one. 'Who's there?' The National Coalition Against Contractions."

"Let's do it by group," I said.

"All right. We'll get the big ones out of the way first. The Commission on Poison Prevention feels the 'graphic depiction of poisoning in the murder of Hamlet's father may lead to copycat crimes.' They cite a case in New Jersey where a sixteen-year-old poured Drano in his father's ear after reading the play. Just a minute. Let me get a kleenex. The Literature Liberation Front objects to the phrases, 'Frailty, thy name is woman,' and 'O, most pernicious woman,' the 'What a piece of work is man' speech, and the queen."

"The whole queen?"

She checked her notes. "Yes. All lines, references, and allusions." She felt under her jaw, first one side, then the other. "I think my glands are swollen. Would that go along with pneumonia?"

Greg Jefferson came in, carrying a grocery sack. "I thought you could use some combat rations. How's it going?"

"We lost the queen," I said. "Next?"

"The National Cutlery Council objects to the depiction of swords as deadly weapons. 'Swords don't kill people. People kill people.' The Copenhagen Chamber of Commerce objects to the line, 'Something is rotten in the state of Denmark.' Students Against Suicide, the International Federation of Florists, and the Red Cross object to Ophelia's drowning."

Greg was setting out the bottles of cough syrup and cold tablets on the desk. He handed me a bottle of valium. "The International Federation of Florists?" he said.

"She fell in picking flowers, " I said. "What was the weather like out there?"

"Just like summer," he said. "Delilah's using an aluminum sun reflector."

"Ass," Ms. Harrows said.

"Beg pardon?" Greg said.

"ASS, the Association of Summer Sunbathers objects to the line, 'I am too much i' the sun,'" Ms. Harrows said, and took a swig from the bottle of cough syrup.

*   *   *

We were only half-finished by the time school let out. The Nuns' Network objected to the line, "Get thee too a nunnery," Fat and Proud of It wanted the passage beginning, "Oh, that this too too solid flesh should melt," removed, and we didn't even get to Delilah's list, which was eight pages long.

"What play are we going to do?" Wendy asked me on my way out.

"*Hamlet,*" I said.

"*Hamlet?*" she said. "Is that the one about the guy whose uncle murders the king and then the queen marries the uncle?"

"Not any more," I said.

Delilah was waiting for me outside. "'Many of them brought their books together and burned them,'" she quoted. "Acts 19:19."

"'Look not upon me, because I am black, because the sun hath looked upon me,'" I said.

*   *   *

It was overcast Wednesday but still warm. The Veterans for a Clean America and the Subliminal Seduction Sentinels were picnicking on the lawn. Delilah had on a halter top. "That thing you said yesterday about the sun turning people black, what was that from?"

"The *Bible,*" I said. "Song of Solomon. Chapter one, verse six."

"Oh," she said, relieved. "That's not in the *Bible* anymore. We threw that out."

Ms. Harrows had left a note for me. She was at the doctor's. I was supposed to meet with her third period.

"Do we get to start today?" Wendy asked.

"If everybody remembered to bring in their slips. I'm going to lecture on Shakespeare's life," I said. "You don't know what the forecast for today is, do you?"

"Yeah, it's supposed to be great."

I had her collect the refusal slips while I went over my notes. Last year Delilah's sister Jezebel had filed a grievance halfway through the lecture for "trying to preach promiscuity, birth control, and abortion by saying Anne Hathaway got pregnant before she got married." Promiscuity, abortion, pregnant, and before had all been misspelled.

Everybody had remembered their slips. I sent the refusals to the library and started to lecture.

"Shakespeare—" I said. Paula's corder clicked on. "William Shakespeare was born on April 23, 1564, in Stratford-on-Avon."

Rick, who hadn't raised his hand all year or even given any indication that he was sentient, raised his hand. "Do you intend to give equal time to the Baconian theory?" he said. "Bacon was not born on April 23, 1564. He was born on January 22, 1561."

*   *   *

Ms. Harrows wasn't back from the doctor's by third period, so I started on Delilah's list. She objected to forty-three references to spirits, ghosts, and related matters, twenty-one obscene words (obscene misspelled), and seventy-eight others that she thought might be, such as pajock and cockles.

Ms. Harrows came in as I was finishing the list and threw her briefcase down. "Stress-induced!" she said. "I have pneumonia, and he says my symptoms are stress-induced!"

"Is it still cloudy out?"

"It is seventy-two degrees out. Where are we?"

"Morticians International," I said. "Again. 'Death presented as universal and inevitable.'" I peered at the paper. "That doesn't sound right."

Ms. Harrows took the paper away from me. "That's their 'Thanatopsis' protest. They had their national convention last week. They filed a whole set at once, and I haven't had a chance to sort through them." She rummaged around in her stack. "Here's the one on *Hamlet*. 'Negative portrayal of interment preparation personnel—'"

"The gravedigger."

"'—And innacurate representation of burial regulations. Neither a hermetically-sealed coffin nor a vault appear in the scene.'"

We worked until five o'clock. The Society for the Advancement of Philosophy considered the line, "There are more things in heaven and earth, Horatio, than are dreamt of in your philosophy," a slur on their profession. The Actor's Guild challenged Hamlet's hiring of non-union employees, and the Drapery Defense League objected to Polonius being stabbed while hiding behind a curtain. "The clear implication of the scene is that the arras is dangerous," they had written in their brief. "Draperies don't kill people. People kill people."

Ms. Harrows put the paper down on top of the stack and took a swig of cough syrup. "And that's it. Anything left?"

"I think so," I said, punching *reformat* and scanning the screen. "Yes, a couple of things. How about, 'There is a willow grows aslant a brook/That shows his hoar leaves in the glassy stream.'"

"You'll never get away with 'hoar,'" Ms. Harrows said.

*　　*　　*

Thursday I got to school at seven-thirty to print out thirty copies of *Hamlet* for my class. It had turned colder and even cloudier in the night. Delilah was wearing a parka and mittens. Her face was a deep scarlet, and her nose had begun to peel.

"'Hath the Lord as great delight in burnt offerings as in obeying the voice of the Lord?'" I asked. "First Samuel 15:22." I patted her on the shoulder.

"Yeow," she said.

*　　*　　*

I passed out *Hamlet* and assigned Wendy and Rick to read the parts of Hamlet and Horatio.

"'The air bites shrewdly; it is very cold,'" Wendy read.

"Where are we?" Rick said. I pointed out the place to him. "Oh. 'It is a nipping and an eager air.'"

"'What hour now?'" Wendy read.

"'I think it lacks of twelve.'"

Wendy turned her paper over and looked at the back. "That's it?" she said. "That's all there is to *Hamlet?* I thought his uncle killed his father and then the ghost told him his mother was in on it and he said 'To be or not to be' and Ophelia killed herself and stuff." She turned the paper back over. "This can't be the whole play."

"It better not be the whole play," Delilah said. She came in, carrying her picket sign. "There'd better not be any ghosts in it. Or cockles."

"Did you need some Solarcaine, Delilah?" I asked her.

"I *need* a Magic Marker," she said with dignity.

I got her one out of the desk. She left, walking a little stiffly, as if it hurt to move.

"You can't just take parts of the play out because somebody doesn't like them," Wendy said. "If you do, the play doesn't make any sense. I bet if Shakespeare were here, he wouldn't let you just take things out—"

"Assuming Shakespeare wrote it," Rick said. "If you take every other letter in line two except the first three and the last six, they spell 'pig,' which is obviously a code word for Bacon."

"Snow day!" Ms. Harrows said over the intercom. Everybody raced to the windows. "We will have early dismissal today at 9:30."

I looked at the clock. It was 9:28.

"The Over-Protective Parents Organization has filed the following protest: 'It is now snowing, and as the forecast predicts more snow, and as snow can result in slippery streets, poor visibility, bus accidents, frostbite, and avalanches, we demand that school be closed today and tomorrow so as not to endanger our children.' Buses will leave at 9:35. Have a nice spring break!"

"The snow isn't even sticking on the ground," Wendy said. "Now we'll never get to do Shakespeare."

*　　*　　*

Delilah was out in the hall, on her knees next to her picket sign, crossing out the word "man" in "Spokesman."

"The Feminists for a Fair Language are here," she said disgustedly. "They've got a court order." She wrote "person" above the crossed-out "man." "A court order! Can you believe that? I mean, what's happening to our right to freedom of speech?"

"You misspelled 'person,'" I said.

THE MIGRATORY PATTERN OF DANCERS

Katherine Sparrow

The inexorable pull to move south grows. The sun hums to me all day long that it's time to go, go, go. The night sky is even more persistent—every constellation in the big Montana sky makes arrows pointing south. My appetite increases and I develop a layer of fat on my belly. My senses grow more intricate—smells carry layers of meaning, gnats and mosquitoes become visible everywhere I look, and the normal sounds of human civilization hurt my ears with all their chaos.

And now my eyes have changed. The cornea and pupil widen so that the white is barely visible. A mercy that the genetic modifications left me normal eyes for summer and winter, but when it changes, it is unsettling for everyone. My vision increases three-fold. It is the last sign that it is time.

"Your eyes look funny," Marion says. My wife drops her fork onto her plate and starts to cry.

This is another sign, as real and inevitable as all the others.

"Josiah, don't go this time. Stay here. Stay safe. We'll manage, somehow." She cries harder. Marion is beautiful when she cries. She breaks my heart every time. "Why won't they ever leave you alone?"

We've been avoiding this for the last month as though time was not passing—as though summer was not heading toward fall. I don't know what to say to her. I never know what to say.

"I'll be leaving tomorrow morning." I reach out for her hand, but she pulls away from me. She doesn't want to touch me, to be any more vulnerable than I have already made her. Later there will be an intensity burning in her as she takes me into our room and undresses me, touches every part of my body as though there will be a test later and she must memorize it all. This too is another one of the signs.

*   *   *

Marion drives our old griesel out to a lonely stretch of road in Glacier National Park. She doesn't say goodbye to me, but holds me tight and then lets me go. Despite her words, she and I both know what I will do, if I have to. There are three other men waiting on the road.

"Good summer?" Scotty asks.

"Yep," I say. "Hot enough for you?"

"Yep."

There's Keith who's twenty-eight, the youngest and darkest skinned of us—he's mixed; Scotty, gay, thirty-seven, and a beast of a rider; and Hector, forty-four, Mexican but from the US. He doesn't speak Spanish but his wife and kids do. We're a strange migrating flock, not much in common, nothing like the huge numbers of wild birds who used to travel across the US and wore a monotony of feathers on their bodies. But once you see us dance, then you know we belong together.

"How you been, Josiah?" Hector asks. I feel his eyes looking me over, wondering about me now that I'm the oldest: now that Siv's dead.

"Ready to ride." Christ, I'm only fifty-six.

"Any one seen the new guy yet?" Keith asks.

Silence. It had been a good seven years without any casualties. Fourteen migrations without any big accidents: a stretch so long I think we all forgot what could happen. No one noticed Siv getting older. He didn't show any weakness, not up until the very end. And now we had a new guy coming on.

Our Sponsor arrives in a long black four door car spewing enough exhaust to make my eyes water. He steps out wearing sunglasses and skin stretched so tight over his face that he looks like he might pop. All the immortals look like that. Even though they have enough money to buy life, they have that look to them like it's been a long time since they've lived at all. We smile at him, each of us thinking, I reckon, about the last time we saw him.

He was yelling and calling us murderers as we all stood around the broken body of Siv. He threatened us with life in prison, even though we all knew he couldn't do a damn thing about it.

Now he's showing off his white as paint teeth and looking at us like we are racing horses: profitable flesh. He frowns as he looks at me. Other doors on his car open and men that look like him, but with cheaper clothing, get out. You can't get them to talk to you, I've tried.

The new rider comes out of the car and blinks like he's just waking up. It takes a while to get used to the eyes. He's too skinny—someone should have told him to fatten up—but otherwise he looks tough enough. He has thick black hair, olive skin, and a five o'clock shadow even though it's only noon. He looks us over. He smiles at Keith, who must be the leader, I can see him thinking, because he's the youngest and strongest. Keith smiles back enigmatically.

"This is Theo Anders, boys, and he's going to make me proud!" The Sponsor tries to act like one of the good old boys, but there's a billion dollars and ownership issues between us.

A trailer pulls up with our bicycles, and Scotty runs over to them. He's our resident gearhound. Our Sponsor chats him up about all the new components on his bike.

"No way! Awesome!" he says.

The new guy stands near us nervously. For him it's the most important day of his life so far. The first day of the migration. For the rest of us, it's not so special.

"Hey Theo, I'm Josiah," I say. "Welcome to the migration." I introduce him to Keith and Hector. "A man's first migration is the most dangerous," I say. "Just like with real birds. You won't know the route, the dances, or how to pace yourself. All kinds of changes will be coming on inside of you all the while you're expected to keep pedaling. Just don't do anything stupid."

"I had the operation three months ago. I've adjusted to the changes. The Sponsor told me everything I need to know," he says.

"That's what he'll have told you," I point my thumb at our owner, "but it's not true. It takes awhile for it all to settle in. They never know when they'll need a new rider, so there's never enough time to change."

"He said—"

Hector steps toward the fledgling and says quiet enough that only we can hear, "He only cares about getting you migrating as soon as possible. He doesn't care about you." Hector shakes his head and gives Keith and I a look like *can you believe this kid?* Nevermind that he was just as ignorant when he came on.

Theo's face turns a dirty pink. "You saying something bad about our Sponsor? That's against contract clause twelve B." His voice is too loud.

"Calm down," I tell him. "We're all friends here." But his words make me uneasy. Our owner has tried to get a man on the inside for years. Someone who will tell the truth of what actually happens on our migration. Maybe he's finally found one.

Theo eyes me again, and I can see he thinks I'm worthless. America never had any use for the old. I could tell him I'm going to be more useful to him than he can know, but I don't. Let him learn.

We grab our bikes with fat panniers loaded up with MRE's, protein bars, and watergel. The first day of our ride we're not riding hard: we're just getting onto our bikes, checking out the upgrades, and learning to ride again. It's a relief to get on the road and get moving. Tonight will be the first time in a week any of us will be able to sleep. When the change comes there's nothing for it but to start moving. That's what birds always did, and with how they modified us, we're no different. The bikes are custom made for each of us, and we get a new bike every migration.

Hector takes the lead and we ride slipstream on both sides of him on the two lane road. We look like a flock of geese flying in V formation. People say part of our augmentation is to copy the geese, but that's crap. We ride like them for the same reason they do: it's the best way to cut the wind. And with two thousand miles and twenty-two performances to hit in the next month, we'll need it. No matter how slick our bikes are, when it comes down to it they are still one-hundred-percent powered by our legs and nothing else. So we'll do anything we can to make it easier. We're lazy like that.

The Going-to-the-Sun-Road is smooth and lined with trees turning pretty colors in front of deep blue mountains that look like the ocean in rock form.

Keith races ahead then slams on his regenerative brakes. He races forward again, brakes, then pops the hover gear and his bike floats up three inches off the ground for about five feet. Bless the mechanics who figured that one out twenty-one migrations ago. It makes our ride almost manageable through the lower states. We won't need to hover in Montana where roads are still alright—cowboys will never give up the dream of driving, even if no one can afford the gas.

Scotty pops wheelies and bounces up and down on his bike. He's got all kinds of boing-boing with twice the shocks and gearing of any of us. He carries the extra weight and drag of them. He likes the challenge.

I bike elbows to the grooves of my handlebars, laying my forearms against the warm metal. The curve of my back likes being here with my neck craned toward the horizon. My helmet feels like something I've been missing, a part of my head returned. It feels easy, like I could sit here all day and pedal, which is good, because that's what I'll be doing. I straighten up and warm my hands under my armpits, reminding myself of all the ways to ride, all the muscle sets I can use.

Something big skitters across the upper edge of my vision and I turn my head, excited. But it must have been a bug, because there's nothing there. There aren't many wild birds left, but sometimes, out in the middle of nowhere, a little miracle will fly through the sky. I like to imagine them living out here and surviving, despite everything.

We reach our first campsite—an old RV campground with a sign up to welcome us. Hector twists around to confer with me, then takes us another ten miles so we can stretch our legs a little bit more.

"Aren't we supposed to stop there?" Theo asks.

I turn my head around and see he looks peeved.

None of the others answer him, so I say, "It's good to not be predictable. You never know when the Sponsor might try to show up with his cameras and get into our business."

"What do you have against him? That's his right. It's part of the contract," Theo says. "And what's our route? The Sponsor says we could add in a couple more dances if we rode faster."

Theo can't help talking stupid. He's like a baby eagle who's half pin feathers, half fluff. Even so, the other guys glare at him.

"Missoula to Stevensville, then Darby, then over to Wisdom," I say. "As soon as you've ridden it once, it'll imprint into you. Easy as riding a bike."

"What happens if our bikes break and we're not at the right spot?"

"Never happens."

"Never?" he asks.

"All the components are internalized. The wheels are braided tungsten-rubber. The frames are torture tested carbon-fiber. We'll break before these bikes do."

That gives him a moment's pause, then he asks, "You like being a migrator? You ever get tired of it and think of retiring?" There's something sly and mean to his words.

I don't answer him. There's no way to express the combination of love, rage, fear, hate, joy, and sorrow I feel about migrating. Most humans never have to know about that feeling.

"Back when I started," I say, and then grin at my grandpa words, "there used to be trackers on our bikes. They were real useful to our owner for planning our performances and getting the crowds ready. Except they always fell off or got broken somehow. That's what happens when he tries to spy on our migration: things get broken." I give him a knowing look.

He pauses for a moment, but then he starts in on me again. "He's made you all rich. You talk like it wasn't your choice, like he made you migrate."

The young are always under the illusion that they are free. "He owns enough of us as is. Two migrations every year. When a bird migrates his flock follow the same route every year, but where they stop and rest—every year is a little different."

"You study birds?" Theo asks.

"I've read some books, thought I should, since I am part bird."

Theo nods his head. "What else do you know about them?"

"They're quiet when they fly."

The sun is a cold sliver on the horizon by the time we stop. We set up camp—five orange tents staked down in one corner of a fallow field. Scotty lets into the fledgling about uniforms.

"The more flow to our costumes the better, but you have to be careful about tripping. What do you think, Theo?"

The fledgling doesn't know what to think, but Scotty doesn't mind. All he needs is a sounding post. We all have our tricks for getting through the migration—Scotty's is uniforms and gadgets. Hector's is his tattoos, one for every migration. Maybe mine is thinking about birds. Theo stays up late talking with him, getting in a couple of 'uh-huhs' and 'I guess sos' in between Scotty's monologue.

I zip into my tent and open up the sky window. It's a big sky in Montana, everyone knows that, but the way it makes me feel lonely is all my own. I miss Marion and our two girls, all grown up now. In a day or so I won't think much about them—everything will get focused down to the tunnel vision of migrating. I'm a man who lives dual lives with little overlap. But for the moment, I like to think about my family. I'd do just about anything for my wife and girls, like turn myself part way into a bird and migrate across the continent.

*   *   *

Three hundred and fifty miles later, give or take a dozen miles on my sore ass, we reach Yellowstone.

A huge banner stretches over the park's north entrance reading, "See the Dance of the Sandhill Crane!" We sit back on our bikes as we coast into the park. Keith has been singing an old camp song to himself, over and over.

"I like bananas, coconuts, and grapes—that's why they call me Tarzan of the apes! I like bananas . . ."

No one would blame me if I strangled him. Too bad I like Keith.

Theo is full of all kinds of talk again, playing the role of the good little stooge. He's riding behind Hector, who treats him like a mosquito just out of slapping range.

"What can we do to make the dance more exciting and draw in more people? It's great how the Sponsor is meeting us with more provisions, isn't it? He really takes care of us."

I bike steadily and let my leg muscles do the work. My left Achilles aches, but the rest of me feels strong. Yellowstone has crap roads that twist and turn on themselves like they were drunk when they laid the concrete. I pop and coast into hover a couple of times. Until the day I'm dead, I'll always love hovering.

There are whiffs of sulfur and foul minerals on the air. Yellowstone is nature's fartlands, but it's the most popular American park. Go figure. Cars pull over and line the roads, waving and honking at us as we pass.

Hector increases our pace and we turn down a long stretch of road that's less crowded. Even though it's not the first stop in the park, we go to Old Faithful first. It puts an extra fifty miles on our ride, but that's what the contract orders. We bike along the Madison River then down to the Upper Geyser Basin. The road loops back and around to where we start our performance, so we won't be seen ahead of time. We dismount just out of sight of the Anemone, Beehive, and Plume geysers.

Our Sponsor is there with the costumes and body paint that Scotty radioed to him after talking us all to death about what we should wear. It's not so different from last time. There's cloth sewn along the arms and attached to our shoulder blades with a long skeletal frame to approximate the sandhill crane wingspan. The rest is sleek gray material so tight it shows off every line and muscle of our bodies, save for the modesty crotch-cups. This is a family event, after all.

"And now, what you've all been waiting for. . . ." A tinny sounding drum roll pounds through the park. "Once thought to be extinct, the sandhill cranes have been resurrected for one day only! The oldest birds known to man! Closest in kin to dinosaurs! The sandhill cranes' mysterious movements might be how the dinosaurs danced! Please welcome the Western Migrators!"

The applause of five thousand people is a little unnerving. Theo takes a step backwards. We've painted our skin gray, except for our eyes, which are blackened, and our foreheads, which are a shocking red like the actual birds. Scotty leads the way forward, and we follow him, picking our legs along the ground carefully, straining our necks upward and moving them from side to side. Three of us move in unison for a couple steps then fall out of it, as though any uniformity were random. My legs are sore and my neck's stiff, but never mind that, a crane doesn't know about that. A thousand cameras click and follow our motions. As many people as they can fit into the bleachers lean forward and stare at us. A screen twenty feet above us projects our dance to everyone else. A kid starts crying.

We walk toward them slowly, until we are centered just right in front of the bleachers. Theo walks behind us, mimicking, not yet on the inside of what we are doing, not yet trusting the instincts within him. A force builds in my throat, and I raise my head to let out a loud, ugly "Augaroo-a-a-a, au!" The other birds . . . men sway away from me. Keith raises his arms and with it the long stretch of wings unfold behind him. He hops once, twice, up into the air. I cry out again.

Scotty echoes my cry, and Hector hops up into the air and moves his neck from side to side. He lands. A vent of steam hisses up from the ground, and we crouch down and spread our wings, except for Theo who's a beat off. He crouches down as quick as he can.

Don't think, be. Let it come, I'd tell him, but the bird within me takes hold. Grafted DNA and bird memory pulses through my muscles and limbs. My neck moves from side to side, tasting the air, feeling the wind against my cheek and the warm air blowing at us from beehive geyser. Anemone geyser starts gurgling and filling up with water, building pressure at the same time pressure builds in me. Everything is syncopated and my wings move with the rotation of the planet and sun.

Two birds start hopping up and down with their wings beating. Jumping toward each other, then popping back, testing their strength and virility. I crouch lower to the ground and sweep forward with my wings outstretched. Two hop over my wings. Another screams "Augaroo-a-a-a, garoo-a-a-a, au—a challenge and a promise. The cry passes to me, and I rise up tall and proud. I crouch down and jump up, my wings spread high above me as I twist upwards and fall back to the earth in a spiral. Beating my wings aggressively, I turn and face Theo—stare him in the eyes and lunge toward him twice, my body hinging at the waist. Still uncertain, he mimics my motions. I back away, feeling the heat of his movement, even if he can't feel it yet.

"Garoo-a-a-a!" he yells at me, moving closer to the bird inside of him. I step away and bend toward him. Keith joins our circle and spreads his wings, his gray and red face blank as a bird's. In unison, we run toward Plume geyser and, one by one, we jump across. The pit in the earth gurgles with boiling water below us. A dare, a challenge to the mother, and she lets us pass by, unburned. We turn and dance mirroring each other, facing the crowd of ragged Americans chewing on soya-dogs and deep-fried kelp bars.

Keith jumps up and does a somersault in the air. Theo does the same and I bend toward them, challenging, receding, moving. With a gurgle and suck, Plume geyser spews up and we run around it, our dance becoming more urgent as the hot mist hits us and stings.

People scream and clap their hands. Keith uses Theo's shoulders to launch himself up higher. Theo watches him, then does the same with me, his weight pushing off me as he twists into the air. We are birds and we are magnificent. We get lost in the movement that goes on and on, ebbs and flows, reinvents itself and repeats. Garoo-a-a-a. We end by sweeping our wings along the ground.

People clap and kids jump up and down on the flimsy metal seating. I smile up at them. There's few enough things the people of this country look forward to anymore, and I'm glad to be one of them. Young women with a hungry look to them check us out, as do a few men. Not that it will do them any good—none of us can be sexual on the migration. Just like birds, we have other fixations. Still, no one minds the appreciative stares.

We turn and walk away from them, back to the fake log cabins they put us up at.

Theo walks beside me, deciding, I guess, that I'm not so useless. You learn things about a man when you dance with him.

"That was . . . tell me about those birds."

"Sandhill cranes danced for courtship, hierarchy, territories, and maybe, sometimes just because they wanted to. At least that's what I think. They went extinct in May of 2012. Word went out that there was one surviving flock, and everyone shot at them, wanting to be the one to cause the extinction. We've got some of them in us. We've got every bird that we dance in us. They tell you that?"

Theo nods. "I didn't all the way believe it. But then, the dance . . . it was magical."

"Yep."

"What's your favorite bird dance?"

"California Condor. Huge, ugly, awkward vultures. We dance it in the Narrows of Zion. There's something about that bird. Some say it's the little sister to the Thunderbird."

"What's that?"

"A big old vengeful bird that stirred up storms with the beat of his wings. A birds that carries lightning bolts in his beak, at least that's what the Lakotan Indians say." I pat Theo on the back. He's okay. Sometimes you dance with a man, and you know you don't like him, plain and simple. But Theo's all right.

Yellowstone has fixed us up a huge dinner set up at one of their picnic table, and we eat like starving men. Like birds a long time between meals. There are platters of fat burgers with all the condiments; three kinds of slaws—red, white and green; potato salad with plenty of hard boiled eggs; and my favorite, this kind of chocolate cake that is gooey in the middle like they put the frosting on the inside.

We eat and eat and there is a light that shines out from each of us. They've genmodded us into gods, and here at American Valhalla, they feed us well.

Our Sponsor pops up out of nowhere, and his men follow behind him like a long dark shadow. He yanks everything good out of the day as he looks us over proudly. He plunks down different products on the table—sparkle ketchup, muscle-grow lotion, and bird-men model kits. One of his men sets up lights over the table and starts taking pictures. I look over at Theo in the washed out light and it hurts. I see all his pride turning into shame. For the first time he's realizing how the bird parts embedded into him exists to make money. Tie-ins, tell-alls, television, action figures, and that's not to mention all the tax write-offs our owner gets for having us dance at national parks. I lose my appetite as the Sponsor sits down at our table.

"How's the ride, boys? Any problems?" His men check our bikes and start resupplying them with provisions. "I brought you a surprise." The way he says it, I just know it's gonna be nasty.

One of his men brings old Ray to the table. Cruel. Being here and seein us remind Ray of all the things he's lost. It's been ten years since he last rode with us, and the years have not been kind. His red face is weather burned and even though he wears a big smile, I can see it's all uneasy sleep and hardship underneath. All ache inside to migrate, even though his body can't make it anymore.

"Hi boys." His southern drawl reminds me of all the good rides and dances we had. It makes me uneasy. I liked Ray. Hell, we all did.

"Hi Ray, have a seat. Have some food. Plenty of it," I say.

He sits down next to me. I glare at the Sponsor until he leaves our table. He stays within earshot, of course.

"How you been?" I ask.

Bleak eyes with a migrator's wide pupils meet mine, then dart away. Behind us I hear one of the geysers—probably Old Faithful—explode upwards as people clap and yell.

Ray takes a burger and studies it like maybe the answer is written on it. He sighs and says, "Couldn't be better. Best thing I ever did was quit the ride."

"Yeah, you look happy. You heard about Siv? That's why you're here, right?" I ask.

"Shame, that. Should have stopped while he could."

Everyone's looking at me and stuffing food into their mouths so they won't have to talk. Thanks, boys.

"He died well," I say, easy as I can. "I visited Jenny and his three kids. They're doing just fine, set up in Texas on an old sheep ranch."

" It's not worth it to die for the pension," Ray says loudly. Behind him the Sponsor looks smug. "A man should get to live after all that providing. He shouldn't have to die just to get his family taken care of. Hell, they give me plenty of money to live on."

"You call what you're doing living, Ray?" I say real quiet, just between him and me.

"The operation worked fine. They were able to reverse all the changes. I live like a normal man, Josiah. You should try it."

As clear as the bird eyes on his face, I know he's lying. I forgive him, because it's probably one of the things the Sponsor wants him to say.

"You want to give it all away? You want to die just so your wife can have nice things?" Ray asks.

It's a good thing he's old and ragged. I remember that he never got on so well with his wife. The woman was always angry at him for migrating, and could never forgive him for it during the months in between.

"That's why you're being paid to talk to us, Ray, because you don't need money? Where're you living?"

He looks down at his old man hands with dirt in the creases. "Here and there."

"You've got to do what you've got to do, Ray, but don't come around here questioning any migrator's decision, and don't ever talk bad about Siv again. He was a great rider."

"He was a fool."

"Leave. Now."

The Sponsor follows Ray, then calls back to us, "See you in Utah, boys."

That night, sitting around a good smelling cedar campfire, we talk about Siv. Theo sits next to me and does a good job of listening, for once. Maybe too good, like he's trying to memorize it to tell the Sponsor.

"Remember when Siv talked us into a detour up into the Rockies where he heard some raptors were nesting?" Scotty asks.

Chuckles all around.

"Four migrations back. We lost four days chasing those imagined birds," Hector explains for Theo's sake. "Everyday uphill on crap roads, too. Siv was crazy for nature."

"One time he talked us all into doing peyote so we could really know what it felt like to fly," I say. "Three of us almost jumped off a cliff."

"Josiah got so paranoid he tried to set our bikes on fire. And we all saw these huge birds, big as cars, circling over us in the sky, black as midnight, spookiest thing I've ever seen," Hector adds.

"Two days of headaches and diarrhea after that, and Siv wanted us to trip again, this time with mushrooms." Scotty laughs.

"He was a good man to have on the ride," I say.

"The best."

We get all quiet, maybe remembering the last time we were with him and what we had to do.

"What was Ray like?" Theo asks.

"Good enough." Damn fine, truth be told, but hell if any of us were going to reminisce about him.

"He doesn't look good," Scotty says. "I bet he regrets his decision."

"What decision?" Theo asks.

Silence all around.

It falls on me to talk to him, although he probably knows damn well what we are hinting at. Hector and Scotty make a fire and everyone is real quiet as I talk.

"Why'd you join us, Theo?"

"I've always wanted to dance. No money for dance anywhere else."

"No, not the reason you told the Sponsor. The real reason. You've got a big family, lots of siblings, probably, and maybe a girlfriend who wants to get married and have kids soon. That about right?"

He nods.

"All of us do, and the contract states that we'll get our fat paychecks so long as we migrate. Hell, in this economy, it's impossible to turn it down. But when we quit, our pension is set at five percent, nothing more. Maybe one man can live on that, but not well."

He nods again vaguely. He's young and will stay that way forever right?

"So long as we ride everyone is happy and you get to be the man that brings them security. You quit and your bird parts are telling you to go, only your body's crap and you're too poor to own a decent bike. What do they give you? Five percent of your wage, for the rest of your life. But under Federal law, if you are genetically modified and die on the job, they have to pay a lump sum of ten year's wages. Simple as that."

"Are you saying Siv killed himself and made it look like an accident?" Theo asks softly.

"I'm saying there are four men on this migration who will swear to every police investigator that it was an accident. I'm also saying that the Sponsor would pay a man, let's say a new migrator, good money to prove dancers don't die on accident. Then he wouldn't have to pay out one red cent when we died. Wouldn't you agree, Theo?"

The fledgling had the decency to blush.

* * *

We make a loop in Yellowstone and double back to Mammoth, then Tower Falls, and Yellowstone lake. We dance as Tundra Swans, American Kestrels, and Black Terns before we leave the park and cut through Wyoming into Idaho and the City of Rocks. The crowd there is small and some elderly hippie chicks try to join in our dance. Scotty comes close to breaking a leg. We haul ass the rest of the way through Idaho. Pretty country full of bright yellows and pink rock-face sticking out underneath rolling green hills. I'm feeling my body more than I would like, more than I have in the past.

Just before we hit the Utah border, black clouds hover all morning on the edge of the sky and grow as we bike toward them. We feel the electricity in that storm—migrating birds have metal in their heads to follow the magnetic poles, and so do we. It makes me feel buzzed. The temperature drops ten degrees and a mean wind kicks up. Bless the makers of our smart cloth that knows when to keep us warm.

We ride down a busted up highway that smells like grass and petrochemicals. There's no sign of anything human in sight. There's less and less on this stretch of highway every year. They bulldoze the old barns and farmhouses because the dirt is contaminated and they don't want anyone coming here to squat and then suing later for cancer.

Something big and dark flits across the sky. I look up, but there is nothing. A wall of rain rushes toward. When we hit it, there's so much rain it's three inches deep on the road.

Hector lets out a ululating cry and raises both of his hands in the air as he raises his head toward the sky. We all do the same. As I stare up at the whirling flecks of rain coming down, everything stops and is made eternal. Then we hunch over our bikes and peddle on.

My belly starts to feel shaky and two protein bars don't do anything to help it. It grows darker and colder. My arms feel rubbery and numb. Scotty sets a good pace to keep us warm, but not so fast that we keel over. He looks back at me, worried. I grin at him. Mind yourself, Scotty, I'll keep up. There have been other migrations where we've ridden all night just to stay warm, and we'll do that, if we have to.

Then a sway-backed barn as beautiful as a mansion comes into view, and Hector lets out another loud bird cry.

It's not that dry inside, and the moldy hay makes my nose itch, but it'll do. We climb up into the loft where it's drier and settle in to sleep, except for Theo. He sits in a corner near an open window and stares outside. I'm exhausted and need sleep more than the rest of them, but I go sit next to him anyway.

"Big storm," I say.

He nods.

"What're you thinking?"

A lightning strike illuminates his face. He looks worried. "I'm changing . . . more than I thought I would. More than he said I would," he says, not looking up from the hay his hands play with.

I wait for him to explain.

He holds out his arm. "Touch it."

I do. It feels smooth one way, prickly the other.

"Feathers," he says. "Real small ones."

I try not to, but it's been a long day. I laugh.

"It's not funny," he says.

"Yes it is. We all have weird side effects. Hell, that one might even be intentional. They don't exactly know what they are doing with our augmentations." I hold up one of my hands. The tan polish on one of my nails had chipped off to show the black. "I've got talons on my fingers and toes. Have to keep them trimmed real close or else they cut my wife. Keith, though he hates to admit it, loves to eat worms. Ask him about it. And don't ask Hector and Scotty about where their tale feathers."

Theo laughs.

"You're doing fine, Theo. You're riding well and dancing well. That's what this life's about."

"It's just . . . I can't go back, can I?"

"Nope."

"There's something . . . he offered me five years pay for every migrator I ratted on," Theo whispers.

"That's a mighty fine offer." And half of what the bastard would pay out otherwise, I think. "A man could get rich real quick, but there's a price for all that money."

There's an awkwardness between us. "Do you want to die, Josiah? Don't you want to keep living?"

"Did the Sponsor tell you migrators don't live as long as normal people, even without accidents?"

Silence.

"Course he didn't. It's true though. It's a heavy strain on the body."

"But don't you want to live?"

"Of course. No one wants to die, but we all do, don't we? You set your mind on getting through this migration. Leave the macabre thoughts to old men like me." I put my hand on his shoulder and let it rest there.

Lightning pulses outside, and I see what looks like a huge bird flying up in the middle of the storm.

When the morning sun wakes us up the world has been washed clean and pretty. We ride on and pop into hover over huge gashes in the road. We discover a diner that serves up pieces of peanut-butter chocolate pie that we eat as townspeople gawk at us.

*   *   *

In Colorado we run into some angry types. They catch up to us on a gut-busting climb out of Steamboat Springs up to Rabbit Ears Pass. They chug passed us spewing griesel fumes that smell like burnt french fries. The environmentalists have joined up with the local dance troupe and picked up some anti-genmod types by the looks of their bumper stickers. They stop their van about a quarter mile away from us. Ten of them all pile out to make a human line across the road. There's forest on both sides of us that we could run into, but we'd have to leave the bikes. We could ride back down the hill, but hell if we're going to.

"What should we do, Josiah?" Hector asks quietly.

One reason birds have died out, beyond all the toxins, is that they just couldn't find hospitable places to live.

"Let's just talk to them," I say.

We grind on up the hill and stop ten feet away. I'm bonked enough by the ride to be glad for the unscheduled stop, come what may, and squeeze some watergel into my mouth. I keep an eye on them and on my migrators. Usually protesters show up at performances and try to mess us up, but there's nothing but us and them out here.

"Morning," I call out.

Hatred thick as cream on each of their faces.

"Hacks," one of them says. She's a dancer, by the thin, ropy look to her. "You're not dancers. You're monkeys!"

"Freaks," a man says.

A bird streaks across the air above me, but when I look up, nothing's there.

Keith takes a step forward. I put a hand on his shoulder and he stays put. Ten to five ratio is not good odds, and we've got a dance to make by nightfall.

"Your owner destroys all the wildlife, and then gets tax breaks for sending you out to the parks and make people forget all the animals are gone," a hungry looking man says.

Anger grows among us. A tensing of bodies. A shifting of feet and stances. Like a dance. I feel my hands curl into fists and the desire to hit something grows in me. "We're just getting by, same as everyone," I say, calmly as I can. "Your beef's with our Sponsor. Go harass him." But they won't. He's too heavily guarded. "We're just men doing our jobs."

A woman spits on the ground, and I can see the time to talk is over. When they run at us, we do the same and start beating at each other in the middle of the road. Only it's not a fair fight. They pull out the kind of cheap sticky-tasers you can buy at any 7-11. They aim and fire and we wriggle on the ground and gasp for breath as they put collars around our necks and spray paint the panniers of our bike. They drive off.

"Fuck!" Scotty yells. He's the first one to get his legs back and stand up. He's wearing an inch thick collar that says "Bird Killer."

We sit up and look at each other. Keith is "Genefreak," Hector is "Corporate Slave," Theo is "Dance Whore, and mine says, "Earth Raper."

"Well, boys," I say, "looks like we got ourselves some new nicknames." We bike all the way to Echo Park with our new logos, too proud, I guess, to call our Sponsor for help. We bike through small one road towns and get laughed at by shiny clean Mormon kids lining the street to watch us. The collars rub our necks raw until we meet up with the Sponsor who hires a welder to cut them off.

From Echo Park we change out our tires for heavier threads and bike into the middle of Utah down old cattle roads along the Green river. We swim in the hot water every day and try to avoid the dead fish floating around. The only people out here are long-bearded men living in little blow away shacks. They glare at us even though they see us twice a year, every year. We stay up late and watch bats catch mosquitoes. We tell stories. I tell more than anyone else, which is unusual for me, but somehow I want to tell all of them about me and make sure they remember. When I talk it feels to me like the other riders no longer with us are listening in too.

When a goose dies on a migration, the other geese leave a spot for him in their slipstream, an empty space of air where he used to be. I wish we had something like that.

The migration drags on through Arches, Canyonlands, Rainbow Bridge, and Bryce Canyon. Everyone is still riding well and dancing well. I'm the only one who's feeling it, but I hide my aches and pains. Every night I'm so exhausted I don't ever want to move again. Every day brings us closer to the end: I remind myself of that daily.

"Josiah, we can ride slower," Keith says.

I glare at him. "You tired, Genefreak?"

I see birds all morning on the ride. They keep playing around the edge of my vision, then disappearing. They got a fancy word for that—heat-induced-hallucinations—but I could just swear they were real.

I bike alongside Theo. He keeps getting stuck in the sand drifts that cover the road into Zion. I show him how to peddle into them with just enough momentum to coast through. I lean over to point to Theo where he needs to stop pedaling, which is why I don't see the hole in the road that sends me end-o off my bike.

End-over-end-over-end, and then I hit the hard-rock ground with my legs, and something in my left leg snaps. Like a painful rubber band ricocheting up my calf and thigh, then biting into my ass. The pain's like getting a tooth pulled out, awful for a moment, then a kind of relief. Until I try to stand up, that is. I scream so loud tears pop out of my eyes.

"Don't move, Josiah," Scotty says.

I try to get up again, then I curl up on the ground and yell some more.

A torn Achilles takes six months to heal, and it's never very strong after that. Every migrators knows about leg injuries, and which ones are recoverable. This one isn't.

It gets real quiet between us all. There's a question that they don't want to ask, and I don't want to answer. I'd made my decision years ago, but it's different being here, having finally arrived where I always knew I'd end up. Finally, I say, "This'll be my last dance. As long as that's okay with you, Theo?"

We all look at him, but he won't look back at any of us. I can see the struggle going on inside of him, deciding what kind of man he is going to be. Finally, he nods his head and says, "I'm a migrator, aren't I?"

I ride tied up behind Theo and he uses up all his hover on me, riding gentle over all the rough spots. Scotty rides with my bike strapped onto his back. We take a trail through desert back-country so no one will catch sight of us. We're only thirty miles out from Zion, but it's the longest ride of my life. Funny how time stretches out at the least convenient times.

"Hey Theo," I say, just as the ridge of the Narrows comes into sight.

He looks sick. I remember the first time I was part of something like this on a migration. I tell him the same thing I was told. "This is nothing. Don't let it worry you. Okay?"

Theo hits a bump, and I hold back a groan. As soon as we get to the top of the canyon where the ropes are all set out, Hector radios in that we are starting the dance in four minutes. I hear the Sponsor start to complain and ask why, real anxious like, but Hector cuts him off.

They make a circle around me, and dress and harness me as gently and quickly as they can. The Sponsor will be on his way up the old canyon road. If he makes it here. . . .

Hector radios in again and says they better cue the music because we're starting right now. Scotty and Keith cut both the ropes that will hold me up. Not all the way through, but enough so they will snap. Later on the police will examine the ropes and suspect foul play, but there'll be four men swearing nothing happened. We walk to the edge of the canyon. Theo and Hector hold me up, and, as one, we all jump out into the Narrows Canyon, arcing and spinning around in the air, holding up our arms that are the wings of the California Condor.

The ropes are tethered to both sides of the canyon, and one rope pulls taut as I hit one side of the canyon, then kick out from it with my good leg. The harness pushes on the bulge of my snapped muscles. I hiss and grunt with the effort: the California condor has no vocal cords. Around me others hiss and flap. I spread my midnight wings out to their full length and look down at the canyon, at all the people looking up at me. I flow towards Keith, who grabs my hands, midair, and spins me around. I hit the other side of the canyon and swoop out from it. The other dancers fly around me. Their wings and hands touch me, saying goodbye. I see them with a clarity I don't think I've ever had before. I see the birds in them, and the men. I wish I could tell them this— that it is something more, not less—but there are only hisses and pain.

One of my ropes snaps and I fall hard, hitting one side of the canyon. Hard rock smashes across my head, back, and legs. People scream, though of course this is one of the reasons so many come to see us perform. The other rope holds me above the Narrows, above the silvery Virgin river that wants me to come home, and I kick out into the canyon. A sixth bird joins us, and I know that I don't want to die, am not ready to die yet. It is huge with twice the wingspan of any of us, and I feel the uplift from its wings as it flies beneath me. I recognize it is the bird I've been seeing the whole ride. I reach out to touch it. Its feathers are hot as fire. A Thunderbird. It fills my vision and there is nothing else. My body slams against the side of the canyon again, and the other rope snaps. My body falls, and it is all feathers and flight.

PEACH~CREAMED HONEY

Amal El~Mohtar

2011 RHYSLING WINNER, SHORT POEM CATEGORY

They say
she likes to suck peaches. Not eat them, suck them,
tilt her head back and let the juice drip
sticky down her chin, before licking, sucking,
swallowing the sunshine of it down. They say
she likes to tease her fruit, bite ripe summer flesh
just to get that drip going
down, down,
sweets her elbow with the slip of it,
wears it like perfume.

I say
she's got a ways to go yet, that girl,
just a blossom yet herself, still bashful 'round the bees. I say
no way a girl can tease like that
who's been bit into once or twice.

So I come 'round with just a little bit of honey,
just a little, little lick, just enough to catch her eye,
creamed peach honey, just the thing to bring her by.

And I know she'll let me tell her how the peaches lost their way
how they fell out of a wagon on a sweaty summer's day,

how the buzz got all around that there was sugar to be had,
and the bees came singing, and the bees came glad.
They sucked—she'll blush—I'll tell her, they sucked that fruit right dry,
'till it all got tangled up in the heady humming hive.
they made it into honey and they fed it to their queen,
and she shivered with the sweet, and she licked the platter clean,
and she dreamed of sunny meadows and she dreamed of soft ice cream—

I'll see her lick her lips, and I'll see her bite a frown,
and I'll see how she'll hesitate, look from me up to the town
and back, and she'll swallow, and she'll say "can I try?"
and I'll offer like a gentleman, won't even hold her eye.

Because she'll have to close them, see. She'll have to moan a bit.
and it's when she isn't looking
when she's sighing fit to cry,
that I'll lick the loving from her,
that I'll taste the peaches on her
that I'll drink the honey from her
suck the sweet of her surprise.

THE AXIOM OF CHOICE

David W. Goldman

The incident in the story's penultimate scene comes from something I stumbled upon several years ago—a message from a defunct e-mail discussion list that had been copied to a website (by now, also defunct).

In his 1996 message, Mike Beauchamp described a concert he'd just attended at the Brantford (Ontario) Folk Club. During one song introduction, musician Michael Doyle related an anecdote about reassuring an earlier listener that travelers always come back. Someone a few rows behind Beauchamp commented, "Sometimes they don't come back." Sitting in that section was Ariel Rogers, widow of legendary Canadian singer/songwriter Stan Rogers—victim of a 1983 airplane disaster.

"I think," Beauchamp wrote, "there is a song in there somewhere to be written."

301

The guy mentions a town that means nothing to you, but the remark topples Paul into laughter. Into his big, rumbling belly laugh, the one so deep and generous that during a gig it never fails to convince the audience that they're all in on the joke with you and him.

The three of you have lingered outside the darkened club an hour beyond the show's end. Your palms rest atop your guitar case, which stands vertical before you on the cracked sidewalk. Standing not quite as vertical, Paul steadies himself by pressing a hand against the club's brick wall, just below a photocopied poster bearing an image of his face looking very serious. (Dynamic singer-songwriter Paul Muroni! says the poster. Your name appears lower down, in smaller type.) One corner of the poster has come loose. It flips back and forth in the unseasonably warm gusts that blow down the narrow street.

"But really," says the guy, some old friend of Paul's whose name you've already forgotten, "why should you two spend tomorrow driving way up the coast for one damn gig, and then all the way back the next day? I'll fly you there tonight in my Cessna—tomorrow you can sleep in as long as you like." His arms sweep broad arcs when he speaks, the streetlamp across the road glinting off the near-empty bottle in his grip.

Paul rubs the back of his hand against his forehead, the way he always does when he's tired. You're both tired, three weeks into a tour of what seem like the smallest clubs in the most out-of-the-way towns along the twistiest roads in New England.

Paul looks at you, his eyes a bit blurry. "What do you think?" There's a blur to his voice, too. "I'm in no condition for decisions."

You're not sure that your qualifications for decision making are any better than his, given not only your sleep deprivation, but also the beers during the gig and the fifth of Scotch that the three of you have been passing around since.

If you ask Paul's friend to let you both spend the night here in town on the floor of his apartment, go to section 304.

If the thought of sleeping in until noon is too tempting to pass up, go to section 307.

304

This would be a different story.
Go to section 307.

307

The third time the little plane plummets and steadies, its propeller's buzz nearly lost beyond the pounding of rain on the cold aluminum hull, you turn to Paul.

"You know, maybe this wasn't the best decision."

But Paul's snores continue uninterrupted.

Usually you're the one who can sleep anywhere, anytime. Tonight, though, Paul has achieved a blend of exhaustion and inebriation that's vaulted him into a league beyond even your abilities.

"Hey," shouts Paul's friend, twisting around from the pilot seat, his head a silhouette in the dim glow of the control panel. "You ever used a parachute?"

For an instant you're aware of nothing but your own heartbeat.

Then the friend cackles. "Just kidding! Flown through worse than this, dozens of times. You two just sit back and enjoy the scenery."

You peer out the dark porthole. The only scenery is the shivering wing above, illuminated ghost-like in the fan of the plane's lights.

The plane bounces again. You picture aerial potholes.

If you unstrap yourself to check on your guitar in the back of the cabin, go to section 310.

If you pound on the pilot's seat and demand that he turn the plane around, go to section 312.

310

Go to section 324.

312

Go to section 324.

324

Ice-cold water splashes your face.

If you keep your eyes shut tight and try to ignore the water, go to section 325.

If you're confused about where you are and how you got here, go to section 326.

325

Ice-cold water splashes your face. You're terribly cold, except for your arms. You can't feel your arms.

If you wonder why you're so cold, go to section 327.

If you wonder what's wrong with your arms, go to section 328.

326

This is not the choice you make.

So this section doesn't really need to be here. If it were omitted, its absence wouldn't affect your story.

Go to section 325.

328

Ice-cold water splashes your face. You open your eyes to blackness.

You're floating in freezing, heaving water. You spit out a mouthful of brine as you realize that your numb arms are wrapped around something. Whatever it is, it's the only thing keeping you afloat.

You remember the plane, and the storm. It's still raining now, the drops plinking against your scalp even as ocean sloshes into your mouth.

The last thing you can remember is aerial potholes.

You realize that something is tangled really tightly around your arms.

If you try to work your arms free, go to section 335.

If your consciousness fades, go

338

"Now *that* is a guitar case!"

You open your eyes. A few inches away, blue medical scrubs wrap some-body's legs.

"The lining's not even damp." It's a woman's voice. The scrubs turn and she says, "Well, good morning, Sunshine! Joining us at last, are you?"

You blink and roll your head to look up toward her face. On the way you see the metal bed railing. Hospital, you think. The woman—in her early thir-ties probably, tall but pudgy, her brunette hair pulled into a ponytail, a stetho-scope slung around her neck—is grinning at you. Nurse, you think.

She points to a bedside table on which your guitar case lies open. Your head is too low to see inside.

"Coast Guard brought it over this morning," she says. "Figured you'd like to keep it close, the way it saved your life and all."

You see the case's shoulder strap—tooled leather, custom-made, presented to you by a lover three, no, four years ago to replace the case's broken handle—dangling in two jaggedly truncated scraps from each of their rivets.

Maybe the nurse notices the direction of your gaze. "They had to cut you free when they got you out of the water. That strap was so tight that your hands—"

She stops, as if she's caught herself saying more than she intended.

You look at your hands, resting atop the bed covers. They're wrapped in so much gauze that they look like two cantaloupe mummies. Both arms are also thickly wrapped, nearly to the shoulder. You try to bend one, and then the other. They don't move. Your arms don't move. What the hell—

"Calm down!" says the nurse. "Just relax. Those splints have to stay on for a week. They spent a whole night working on you in the OR. You don't want to put all that effort to waste now, do you?"

You let your head settle back into the pillow.

Your tongue sticks to the roof of your mouth for a second when you try to talk. "Working on me?"

"Well." She reaches down to adjust the covers over your chest. "Your hands got really banged up in the crash, and you were hypothermic, of course. And then that strap got tangled around your arms, choking off the circulation."

"So they had to, what, restore the circulation?"

For a second she doesn't answer. She reaches up and pulls her ponytail over her shoulder, and then slowly runs her fingers through its end.

"Yes," she says. "That's right." A brunette curl wraps around her finger. "Also—"

She straightens and takes a step away. "I should tell the doctors that you're awake. They'll give you a full report."

If you insist that she stop and tell you everything right now, go to section 341.

If you wait to hear what the doctors have to say, go to section 344.

341

"Well," she says, "your right hand is going to be fine. Except that they had to amputate the end of your pinkie finger. Just the last joint."

It takes you a moment to understand that word. Amputate.

But okay. Just the pinkie. You don't need that one to hold a pick. Not even finger picks. So that's okay. You'll still be able to play, no problem.

If that makes you think of Paul, and you ask how he's doing, go to section 350.

If you realize that the nurse hasn't said anything about Paul, nor the other guy, and you guess what her omissions must imply, and you recall that it was you who decided that flying would be the right choice, go to section 356.

356

"Okay," you say. Your voice is louder than it needs to be, and you speak quickly, as if you're drowning out some other voice. "And my left hand?"

Her finger tightens in her ponytail. "You're right-handed, aren't you?"

You nod. You're busy trying to not think, so you don't wonder why she asks that.

"There was more damage to your left hand. I'm afraid that they couldn't save all the fingers."

She has freckles across both cheeks. You hadn't noticed that before. Her eyes are green, like the eyes of the cat you had as a kid.

"You still have your thumb, though. And your middle finger should be fine. So you'll—"

If you think about Django Reinhardt, the Gypsy guitarist renowned for his prowess despite half his left hand being crippled by a fire, go to section 362.

If the only thing you can think about is how, just the other night, your biggest priority had been sleeping in until noon, go to section 373.

373

You stay in the hospital for three weeks. There's a lot of pain, and two more surgeries. You don't have insurance, of course, but the hospital's social worker says that they'll work out a payment plan for you. You meet her eyes when she says that; after a second she looks away.

This afternoon a therapist is making you squeeze a rubber ball with your left hand, but you keep dropping it. Each time he picks up the ball, without speaking, and puts it back into your hand. The two of you repeat this cycle for five minutes, glaring at each other.

Somebody punches you in the shoulder.

"Ow!" you say.

It's your nurse, the one with the freckles. You didn't notice her entrance.

"Get out," she says to the therapist. Her eyes, though, are locked on your face.

"Look at your hand," she tells you.

"What?"

"It's why you can't hold the ball. You never look at what you're doing."

"Fuck you," you say. And you turn away.

So you aren't watching when she reaches out and grabs your left wrist.

"Hey!"

She's stronger than you, despite your panic. She yanks up the hand and holds it before your face. "Look at it." Her other hand clamps onto your head so you can't twist away.

So you do it. You look at the hand. At the intact but twisted middle finger. At the half forefinger, wriggling like a decapitated worm. At the puckered stumps at the hand's outer edge.

"All right!" you shout at her. "I'm looking! Now let go!"

"No," she replies. "You're looking at this messed-up thing I'm holding. Now—" and suddenly you realize that her voice, this whole time, has been surprisingly gentle, almost a whisper, "—look at *your* hand."

It's not some immediate, magical thing. But after a few seconds you notice the thumb. And, yes, it's your thumb, exactly the same as it's always been. And that's your palm, with all its familiar lines and creases, including the scar from when you fell onto a rock as a kid. And the fingers—the parts that are still there—those are yours, too.

You lift your other hand, and she releases her hold as you press your two palms together. You turn them back and forth, back and forth, studying what's there. What's not.

If, for the first time since the crash, you start crying, go to section 378.

If she's brought back a memory from your college philosophy class, go to section 125.

125

The professor is roaming the aisles between desks, as he always does, speaking about determinism and free will. You try to pay attention, but you were up all night at a party, jamming some blues with a hot piano player and a lukewarm fiddler while everybody else drifted home or fell asleep in the corners. Now the only things keeping you awake are the cup of dorm coffee you swallowed on the way to class, and the good-looking redhead two rows down, across the aisle.

Somebody punches you in the shoulder.

"Ow!" you say.

The professor stands beside you, massaging his fist. "What's wrong?" he asks.

"You punched me! Why did you do that?"

He looks confused. "What do you mean? Oh—my fist?" He studies it. "Well, my fist has free will. It hit you for no reason."

"What?" You know that you've fallen into one of his Philosophical Dialogues, but you're pissed. "Your fist doesn't have its own will. It does what *you* decide."

"Yes, I suppose that's true." He draws out the moment, as if you've just given him something novel to consider. "Well, *I* have free will. *I* punched you for no reason."

You notice the redhead watching you.

You say, "People don't do things for no reason."

"You endorse determinism, then? The claim that everything that happens is predetermined by what's happened before? So I punched you because, say, I wanted to get your attention. And I wanted to get your attention because you were nodding off. And you were nodding off because—well, I suppose that's none of my business, is it?"

Your classmates snicker. Except the redhead, who smiles and raises an eyebrow.

"But," continues the professor, "don't I have free will? Can't I make unpredictable decisions, regardless of what's come before?"

You're about to speak when you have a sudden insight.

If you think you see how free will and determinism can coexist, how their apparent conflict is merely superficial, go to section 132.

If it strikes you that philosophy is bullshit, and after lunch you drop this course, and then pretty soon you decide to drop the whole university and become a professional musician, go to section 390.

390

You spend two more weeks in the hospital. The nurses explain about changing the bandages. The therapist gives you exercises to do, and a rubber ball.

When you're discharged you try to leave your guitar behind. But the nurse with the freckles makes you take it.

You drive—of course you can drive, you're right-handed—to Paul's memorial service. Lisa, Paul's wife, widow, hugs you tightly, careful to avoid your bandaged hands. You hug her back, but when you step apart there's a piece of the way she looks at you that you can't manage to interpret as sympathetic. Or friendly.

You sit in the rearmost row of folding chairs. The room fills with people all sitting still, watching and listening. Like a concert audience. Your forearms always tighten up right before a gig, and they do that now. But this time your legs tighten, too, and then they start shaking.

Somebody picks up a guitar to sing one of Paul's songs. Your heart hammers at twice the song's tempo as you push back your chair and sneak away.

You reach your apartment as the sun is setting. You lean the guitar case against its usual bookshelf. You're relieved to finally collapse into your own couch, surrounded by your comfortably familiar clutter. Then, after a few minutes, you take a closer look at your familiar clutter. CDs, sheet music, *Guitar Player* and *Dirty Linen* magazines, scattered picks, broken strings. The apartment doesn't feel so comfortable now.

You stare awhile at the telephone. But all your friends are musicians. You don't want to watch them as they try to say the right thing. As they try to not look at your hands.

If, despite all that, you do phone one of them, one of your oldest friends, go to section 402.

If you go out for a drive and after an hour come back with three fifths of Scotch, go to section 429.

429

Your savings—at least, the dollars you don't spend on the increasingly cheap whiskey that keeps you from hearing your own thoughts—let you hold onto the apartment for three months. The guitars and the mandolin buy you two more. It's nearly another two before the police show up for the eviction.

It's late spring by now, so your timing could have been worse. Your hand hurts a lot, though, and the prescriptions keep running out early—and your new pharmacy, who meets you each Wednesday in the alley behind the porn shop, isn't interested in your Medicaid card.

The guitar case—you've still got that. The way it saved your life and all. Also, with a rope tied to the strap-stumps you can sling it over your shoulder with all your stuff inside. The case whacks against your hip when you walk, but that's not so bad, and when the bottles in there clink against each other—on the happy occasions when there's more than one—you tell people that you're making music.

If you meet a guy at the shelter who convinces you to get into treatment, go to section 440.

If you tell that guy to go fuck himself, go to section 472.

472

You should, somehow, have gotten yourself down South someplace before winter arrived. Last night some asshole stole your shopping cart while you slept, so now your only possession that you're not wearing is the crappy cardboard sign asking people to help a vet. (It's pretty obvious that not everybody buys that when they first glance at you. But you always hold the sign with your left hand showing good and plain, and then nobody asks anything.)

This afternoon you kind of lost track of the time, and when you finally got to the shelter it was full. So now you're heading toward the bridge by the river, where at least you'll be out of the wind.

You must have turned the wrong way, though, because you're walking along right next to the frozen river. You look up, and then around, and finally you find the bridge, way the hell behind you.

As you turn, your foot slides onto the ice. Which isn't as thick as it looked. You yank it out quick, though, and it doesn't feel wet. Of course, both of your feet were already kind of numb.

If you think you can still make it to the bridge, go to section 476.

If the idea of just lying down right here and sleeping in until noon is too tempting to pass up, go to section 491.

491

You wake to noise and light. Your chest hurts. You squint against the glare and lift your head just enough to see that some asshole has stolen both your goddamn coats and all your shirts and left you lying here, covered in just a sheet like a corpse. You try to grab the railings and sit up, but your wrists are tangled in some straps and your arms don't move.

"Hey!" you yell. "Hey! Hey!"

Somebody grabs your shoulder. Red hospital scrubs. Nurse, you think.

Both of your shoulders get shoved down against the mattress. Your nurse says, "Take it easy."

"My case," you demand. "Where's my case?"

You twist around to see her freckles, but she's up behind your head too far.

"We've got your case, don't worry."

Of course you're not worried. "The Coast Guard," you explain to her.

"Sure," she says. "Take it easy."

Damn, she's not even listening to you! "The Coast Guard!" you repeat. "They're supposed to bring my case!"

If you keep trying to get through to her, until a warmth slides up inside your arm and then you feel sleepy, go to section 501.

If you shut up for a minute and look around and realize that you're not where you thought you were, and then you quietly ask the nurse if maybe you can stay here a few days and get some help, go to section 525.

501

You're sitting in a plastic chair, in a circle of people sitting in plastic chairs, in a bright hospital room with pale blue walls. There's a TV mounted high on one of the walls, but it's off right now.

"All right," says the guy in one of the chairs. He's the only one who's wearing shoes. Not these little socks with rough patches on their soles, at least if you put them on right.

The guy says, "The past couple days here in group we've been talking about what? Choices, right? Choices. Now I've got something I want you to try. I'm going to shut up for the next ten minutes, and for that ten minutes I invite each of you to think about the thing I'm about to explain. And each of you, you need to shut up, too, or else it's not fair to the others. Okay?"

He waits until everybody, including you, says okay, or at least nods.

"All right, so here's the thing. We've all had moments in our lives where we were faced with a choice. And we made our decision, and that choice sent our life down a certain path. And one thing led to another, and finally, well, here we all are." He looks around the circle, his gaze pausing on each person. When he looks at you, you stare right back at him and he gives you this little smile he does sometimes. Then he finishes looking around the circle, and then he shakes his head and says, "Here we all fucking are."

Everybody chuckles. This guy is all right. He's told you that his drug of choice, back when he wasn't the one wearing shoes to group, was meth. Normally you can't stand tweakers. But he's all right.

"So," he says, "here's what we're going to do for the next ten minutes. Each of us is going to think back to some choice we once made, some decision that at the time made sense, but that ever since, we've wished we could do over. All right? Now, I invite you to sit here and take yourself, in your head, back to that moment. But this time, this time you get to do it over. This time you make a different choice. And for the next ten minutes—maybe close your eyes, if you like—for the next ten minutes you get to watch how your life goes, step by step by step, after this different choice. Just follow it out slow and easy, okay? All right? Give it its fair chance. All right, here we go. I'm shutting up now for ten minutes."

You look around the circle. Most of the others are doing the same. A few have closed their eyes.

What the hell. You close your eyes.

If you ask Paul's friend to let you both spend the night on the floor of his apartment, go to section 304.

If that strikes you as too obvious—too predictable—and instead you're curious about how free will and determinism can coexist, go to section 132.

132

You pick an empty table and set down your tray, still thinking about your dialogue with the professor. As you're taking the second bite from your burger, the redhead from class sits down opposite you.

"Hi," says the redhead. "I'm Kerry."

You never finish the burger.

The two of you talk about how free will differs from unpredictability. How predetermination doesn't equate to constraint. How fists can't have free will because they don't have brains, but how brains are overrated.

Kerry is a year ahead of you—a junior—and a math major. (Kerry's the one who introduced the term *equate* into your conversation.)

You try not to be obvious about letting your gaze wander over what you can see of Kerry's body. You'd like to see more.

Then Kerry makes a stupid claim about the contrast Boethius drew between fatalism and divine omniscience.

If you steer the conversation back to the part about how brains are overrated, go to section 138.

If you get frustrated as you keep trying to explain why Kerry's claim is stupid, go to section 155.

138

You and Kerry have been spending all your evenings together at the library, and afterward at the Rathskeller or just wandering campus talking. But so far things haven't gotten past holding hands and kissing. Pretty intense kissing, true, but come on.

Apparently math majors are shy.

Tonight, though, the two of you are rolling around on your bed, and many items of clothing have been removed. A few minutes ago you almost blurted out something about hoping that Boethius's God was looking someplace else, but you suppressed the impulse.

As you yank off a sock, Kerry suddenly pulls away and says, "Do you have any . . . I mean, because I don't, not with me. . . ."

You don't either, but right at this instant you're not really up for a Philosophical Dialogue. "I'll get some tomorrow," you say, and you reach for Kerry's shoulder.

"Wait." Kerry eyes you reappraisingly.

If you say, "Just this one time," go to section 160.

If you offer an apologetic smile and sigh, and then, deliberately but gently, you put the sock back onto its foot, go to section 144.

144

You listen to the morning's birdsongs. Kerry's dorm is on the edge of campus, by the arboretum, so mornings are louder here than in your room. There's one bird who keeps hitting this little arpeggio with a syncopation on the last note that you're trying to memorize, so you can try it out later on guitar.

You're also trying to memorize how Kerry looks asleep. Just because you think that will make a good memory.

Eventually the alarm buzzes, and you two have to get out of bed.

A little later, you face each other over breakfast trays. (The first time you shared breakfast, you discovered that you both like oatmeal—with raisins, and definitely no brown sugar—and that neither of you can stand breakfast sausage.)

Kerry asks, "Figure it out yet?"

You've been teaching Kerry some basic music theory, and in return you're learning about set theory. Last night Kerry gave you a challenge: Suppose you're given some arbitrary sets. It doesn't matter how many or what's in them. Maybe one contains all the even numbers, while another contains red fire trucks, and a third includes the contents of your pants pockets on the morning of your fourteenth birthday. Whatever. Now prove that, without having to know exactly what's in each set, there is some other set that has at least one element in common with each of the given sets—but which isn't simply the union of all of them, as if you'd dumped all of the original sets into one big bag.

You did, in fact, figure this out, last night while you were brushing your teeth. But then the two of you got distracted by other, more entertaining, challenges.

"All right," you say. "I pick one element from each of the sets you give me. My new set is defined as the set containing precisely those elements. Ta-dah."

Orange juice in hand, Kerry nods. "Very good."

You grin, but Kerry's not finished.

"So who gave you permission to *pick* an element from each of those sets? There's nothing in the basic rules of set theory—the axioms—that says you can do that."

You frown. "Of course you can. It's obvious."

Kerry raises an eyebrow.

"Fine," you say. "I choose the smallest element in each set—that's well-defined, right?"

"What if one of the sets consists of all fractions bigger than zero? What's the smallest fraction?" Kerry reaches for your toast, which you've been neglecting.

Annoyed, you start to offer a counterproposal. But you catch yourself as you see its flaw. Which suggests a different solution—but no, that doesn't work, either. . . .

Finally Kerry says, "It does seem natural that you should be able to pick elements out of sets. But it turns out that there's no way to prove that you can do that, in general, based on the axioms of set theory. Most mathematicians agree with you that it should be allowed, though, so they add a new rule that specifically says you can do it. The Axiom of Choice."

Now you're annoyed again. "Then why didn't you tell me that up front? If this Axiom of Choice is simply one of the rules, why are we even discussing it?"

Kerry leans forward, one elbow skidding almost into a puddle of spilled coffee. "It's *not* one of the rules. Not one of the most basic, defining ones, anyway. You can build up a complete, self-consistent system of mathematics that doesn't include the Axiom of Choice. If you add it in, you end up with a slightly different system. One that includes a lot of new, interesting results, most of which *feel* right. So most mathematicians are fine with proofs that depend on the Axiom of Choice."

You glance at your watch. You'll both be late for class if you don't pick up your trays and get going. But a corner of Kerry's argument looks loose to you.

"So," you say, "you can do math either with this axiom or without it?"

"Right." Kerry stands up.

You remain in your seat. "Then, each mathematician has to *choose* whether or not to use the Axiom of Choice."

Kerry pauses and stares at you.

And then, slowly, Kerry nods, and slides the two trays in your direction. As if presenting you an award.

"I guess," says Kerry, "that says something about the rules of the *higher* system. The one in which we live."

If you stack both trays and carry them away, go to section 147.

If you push back Kerry's tray and grumble about hypocritical mathematicians, go to section 170.

147

That night, after you get under the covers, Kerry approaches the bed, naked.

"Tonight," says Kerry, "I want you to lie completely still. Got it? Now pay attention. Here's my hand. And here's my mouth. And here—" Kerry takes a step back, so you can get a really good look, "—is the rest of me."

Kerry draws out the moment.

"Choose."

If

502

"Okay, that's ten minutes."

You open your eyes to a circle of people sitting in plastic chairs, in a bright room with pale blue walls.

"So," says the guy with shoes. "Who wants to share something from their experience?"

If after a few seconds you raise your hand, go to section 511.

If it strikes you that group is bullshit, go to section 550.

550

One of the counselors is standing in your room, looking Very Serious.

"We can't do this without you," she says. She's in her forties, you guess, her dark hair braided and wrapped up on top of her head. You've decided that the lilt in her voice comes from Jamaica.

You lie completely still.

She sighs. "You only get to keep your bed if you're an active participant in ward activities. Do you understand me? If you're going to stay here, then you have to get yourself up and out of this room, and interact with the others."

She waits for you to respond. As if it matters what you might say.

Again she sighs. "At least come to the common room for lunch."

If the idea of lunch finally gives you a reason to get out of bed, go to section 557.

If you're finally recognizing that you're not the one making the decisions in your life, go to section 601.

601

Somebody has started a fire with some old campaign signs from a dumpster, and you join the others huddling around it. The bridge's supports block most of the wind, and after a while, for the first time today, you stop shivering.

"Nice hat," says a big guy, meaningfully.

Somebody at the hospital gave it to you when they kicked you out. It's the warmest thing you're wearing, stuffed with fleece, and with furry earflaps.

If you kick the guy in the nuts and run, go to section 615.

If you stand there waiting to see what the higher system is going to make you do next, go to section 620.

620

You're standing in line at the mission, leaning against the counter to take some weight off your feet. A lady asks whether you'd like brown sugar on your oatmeal.

If you shake your head and keep shuffling down the line, go to section 634.

If you stand there, waiting, until finally somebody drops a clump of brown sugar onto your oatmeal and shoves you ahead, go to section 652.

652

Your sign isn't working at all today. You glance down to your lap and notice that you're holding the sign with your good hand. Dumb.

A brown leather wallet drops onto the cracked sidewalk, right in front of you. The guy who must have dropped it is sauntering away, oblivious, eating one of those big pretzels.

Even without leaning closer, you can see a lot of bills in there. Probably cards, too—you could maybe sell those cards.

If you pick up the wallet and stick it inside your coat, go to section 664.

If you just sit there, and eventually somebody else notices the wallet and grabs it, go to section 701.

701

The sky is full of fluffy clouds today. You've got a good view, except for some tree branches. You must have slept on a park bench last night, since that's where you find yourself now. You can't recall the details, though.

If you're just going to lie there all day, go to section 701.

If eventually you get so bored that you sit up, go to section 702.

702

At first it's really early in the morning and you've got this part of the park to yourself. But soon a thickening parade of office workers marches past your bench. Some of them glance your way for a second, and then lift their coffee or their phone to block the view.

If you ask one of them what they think they're staring at, go to section 708.

If all you do is wait to see what's going to happen next, go to section 721.

721

There aren't as many office workers now, but between the kids and the joggers and the drunks there's still a sort of parade.

If you lie back down on the bench, go to section 724.

If your fist punches somebody in the shoulder for no reason, go to section 801.

801

"Ow!" says the woman who had just sat herself beside you on the bench. "What was that for?"

You're staring at your fist.

"No reason," you say.

"Yeah?" She squints at you for a few seconds.

Then she punches your arm. Pretty hard, actually.

"Hey!"

"So," she says, "if we're done with that, I have a proposition for you."

You give her a closer look. Mid-thirties. Dressed like a lot of women you used to know, in a long crinkly black skirt and a brightly striped top from Peru or Mexico or someplace like that. Hair falling in waves to the base of her neck.

Redhead.

She continues, "Community House—maybe you've heard of us? One of our residents got himself kicked out last night, so this is your lucky day. You get a bedroom to yourself, and three meals. Only two rules: You don't do anything illegal in the house, and you don't piss off everybody else."

You narrow your eyes. "So why are you choosing me?"

She nods toward your still-clenched fist.

"No reason," she says. "Now come on." She stands and begins walking away.

If you're fine with her making the decisions, go to section 808.

If you lie back down on the bench, go to section 815.

808

Your third afternoon at Community House, Irene—the redhead—invites you to come along with everybody to a movie.

In your mind you see a dark room full of people all sitting still, watching and listening. Your arms tighten up, and then you start shaking all over.

After a minute Irene says that maybe you should just stay here today.

If you insist on joining the outing, go to section 815.

If you're fine with Irene making the decisions, go to section 822.

822

A couple evenings later you and a few others are in the living room watching TV. When the show ends, Irene gets up and turns off the set. Nobody objects.

"I'm going to read awhile," she says. She crosses the room toward an armchair, pausing at the stereo to start up a CD.

The drums kick things off, and then comes the bass. A bottleneck guitar eases into some Delta blues.

You get shaky, and stand to leave.

"Wait a minute," she tells you, looking concerned. She turns off the CD. She glances around the room at the others. "I think I need some tea. Come on."

You follow her to the unoccupied kitchen. She runs water into the kettle. Not looking at you, she says, "Music. It's a problem?"

You don't feel entirely steady, so you slide into one of the wooden chairs at the kitchen table.

She lights a burner and sets down the kettle. "Especially guitar."

You let out the breath you've apparently been holding. "I used to play."

She pulls out the adjacent chair and sits. "And then your hands got messed up."

You nod. Though you don't know whether she's watching, because you're staring at your lap, where your hands are holding each other. As well as they can.

You've had this conversation enough times, back when you were in the hospital, to know that next she'll ask how that makes you feel. And then you'll be having a Therapeutic Dialogue.

You wait, but for several seconds she doesn't speak.

"That," she finally says, "truly sucks."

A minute later the kettle starts whistling, and she stands. You hear her open a cabinet.

"Damn. We're out of green. Chamomile okay?"

If you wait silently for your tea and then carefully pick it up with your right hand, go to section 831.

If you look up and say, "Sure. Thanks," go to section 845.

845

A week later there's a trip to an art gallery.

You go along.

If, when you're standing in a crowded room where everybody is attentively staring at the same big painting, your heart starts hammering and you have to leave, go to section 859.

If you don't leave, go to section 870.

870

You've been at Community House for three months now. Sometimes you help Irene or the other staff with grocery shopping. Often with cooking. Lately you've been able to sit still while CDs play, and a few nights ago you realized that your right hand was fingerpicking along with an old Ry Cooder track. (Though at that realization you did have to leave the room, and for a couple of hours it felt like all the fingers you don't have anymore were spasming in boiling water.)

But what surprises you the most, what truly astounds you, is that some of the other residents lately have been asking if they can talk with you. Have been asking your opinions about their stuff. As if it matters what you say.

This afternoon you're sitting at the kitchen table with Irene, stuffing fundraising envelopes. The sun is warm on the back of your neck. Through a screen, birds arpeggiate.

"I'm going to a concert next week," she says. "Some Canadian folksinger." She positions a stamp at an envelope's corner, presses it down with her thumb. "Come with me?"

"Sure," you say. "Thanks."

If you lift a fundraising letter from the pile and fold it precisely into thirds, giving the task absolutely all your attention and thinking hard about nothing else at all, go to section 884.

If there's no way you're going to let her drag you to that concert, go to section 896.

896

Could be worse, you think, sitting in the darkened room. The guy's guitar playing is rudimentary, but his lyrics actually make sense. And he's got an interesting, gravelly voice that he keeps sending out on surprising trajectories. It twists and soars until, sooner or later, it always ends up crashing back home.

Irene is working her usual nonchalance. But you've noticed her glancing your way every minute or two. You consider telling her that she can relax, that you're doing fine. Then you feel the singer's diminished chord echoed on your left hand's own phantom fretboard, and you think maybe you'd better wait a bit and see what develops.

Now he's introducing his next song, explaining that it's about a man sailing away on a long expedition, leaving the woman he loves to await his return. "Couple months ago," he says, "a guy came backstage after a show, looking really sad. And he told me how his girlfriend was about to leave for Europe for a year, and so he had to ask me about the traveler in my song: 'Did he come back?' And I told him, 'Of course he came back! This isn't a blues song!' He seemed reassured."

Everybody chuckles. Then, just as he leans forward and is about to start playing, you hear a soft voice.

"Sometimes they don't come back."

Two rows behind you sits a woman whose face you can't quite make out in the darkness. You can't be sure the comment came from her. But you think it's Lisa Muroni. Paul's wife, widow.

If you sink down into your seat and hope that Lisa doesn't recognize you, go to section 898.

If you sit up and try to pay attention to the singer, figuring that somehow you owe that to Paul, go to section 901.

901

You're sitting on the curb outside the club, watching cars and pedestrians. Two songs after the break you told Irene that you needed some air, but that she should stay for the final few tunes. After considering you for a few seconds, she nodded.

You're thinking about people who go away. About the ones who never come back.

And about the ones who do. Even if it takes them a long, long time.

The show lets out. Irene lowers herself to the curb by your side, and helps you watch traffic. She passes you her open can of ginger ale. You take a sip and pass it back.

After a while there are no more pedestrians and not many cars. Irene stands.

"Let's go back to the House," she says.

You look up at her.

And ask, "What if I don't?"

For a few seconds she squints at you.

And then, slowly, she nods. She hands you the empty soda can, as if presenting you an award.

"I guess that would be for you to find out."

You reach out your left hand and take the can between your thumb and middle finger. The can wobbles in your uncertain grip, catching a glint from a nearby streetlamp. And in that glint, for just a second, your life takes a step back so you can get a really good look.

If you return with her to the House, and over the following days realize that helping other people is something you could learn to be good at—

If tonight's show has left you wondering whether you could learn to play guitar left-handed or maybe pick up some different instrument, or take voice lessons, because you're realizing that during these past couple years a lot of new songs have been growing in you—

If you think that maybe you should get back together with some of your oldest friends, maybe even look up that lover of four, no, six years ago—

If you think that it's time, finally, to forget your old life and hitchhike out to Minneapolis, say, or Seattle, and find a job, maybe take some classes (starting, you think, with philosophy)—

You lower the soda can to the ground.

And you choose.

CLUB STORY

John Clute

from *The Encyclopedia of Science Fiction: Third Edition* (2011–),
sf-encyclopedia.com

It was way more than simply gratifying to stand beside Octavia Butler, in one of the goodly as-if worlds we make, and to receive a Solstice Award this year; and I'm very happy consequently to supply a sample of my stuff at Catherine Asaro's invitation. However. The problem with most of the nonfiction I've done is that most of it is in the form of reviews, which get republished elsewhere and which are in any case not entirely right for this context. The problem with most of my nonreview nonfiction pieces is that they are either too narrowly focused, or too long, to belong here—in any case most of the general pieces I'd want to preserve have already been packed into a collection Beccon Publications put out last year, Pardon This Intrusion: Fantastika in the World Storm. *And the problem with taking something from* The Encyclopedia of Science Fiction, *versions of which have taken much of my time for the last 35 years, was that most of what I write there is entries: not quite the thing. But I thought a bit, and realized there were a few, extended entries like* Edisonade *or* Hitler Wins, *that might fit. In the end I selected* Club Story, *an entry (and a tool for describing genre) that has seemed to get bigger (and with more to describe) almost daily.*

So before it gets too long, here it is, modestly tampered with for readability outside its initiating context. What I've done is mainly remove hyperlink indications from the text. You can assume that any author without birth/death data immediately appended has a linked-to entry in the SFE, and that capitalized words or terms, like Time Opera, link to entries. I've also drastically simplified the ascription practice for citing titles and their dates. The piece is divided into two parts. Part Two is where I get punch-drunk. Thanks for your patience.

CLUB STORY

1. Assemblages of tales told within an enabling frame-story to a group of companions in a sheltered venue were not always known as club stories, a term of nineteenth-century provenance that does not, perhaps, very adequately encompass the implications of the *Decameron* (*circa* 1372) by Giovanni Boccaccio (1313–1375), or the *Canterbury Tales* (written before 1400) by Geoffrey Chaucer (*circa* 1343–1400). Only in hindsight, moreover, does the term do much to expand upon our knowledge of the colloquium format used by Sir Thomas More to disengage the presentation of *Utopia* (1516) from any fixed register of seriousness or advocacy. It may, however, be applied very cautiously to the actual proceedings of the Scriblerus Club (founded 1712, disbanded 1745), of which Jonathan Swift (almost all of whose work was distanced through the use of satirical masks) was a founding member; and to suggest the nature of occasional publications as by Martin Scriblerus, mostly written by John Arbuthnot (1667–1735). But Club Story is still a term of only tangential utility until recent centuries—even though there is clearly a thin line of connection between the Platonic colloquium and imaginary nineteenth-century gatherings—when it surfaces through, for instance, the specific homage paid by Robert Louis Stevenon in the title of his *New Arabian Nights* (1882), and its successor, *More New Arabian Nights: The Dynamiter* (1885) with Fanny Van de Grift Stevenson (1840–1914), perhaps the first collection in English fully to express the ambience of the nineteenth-century form. The familiar club story—such as Charles Dickens adumbrated in *Master Humphrey's Clock* (1840–1841), and Edgar Allan Poe, though with only one auditor, clearly exploited in "A Descent into the Maelström" (May 1841 *Graham's Lady's and Gentleman's Magazine*), and which Stevenson and those he influenced brought to maturity—is a far cry from the great assemblages of European medieval material from which culture-founding creators like Boccaccio and Chaucer took their inspiration. Nor does the modern club story normally refract complex Eastern models—from the fifth-century *Pañchatantra* to the multi-sourced *Arabian Nights* themselves—in which a frame-story figure like Scheherazade recounts a series of tales under orders;

European examples of this category do not seem very common, though *The Pentamerone* (1634–1636) by Giambattista Basile (*circa* 1575–1632) roughly fits the model. Any focus on these culture-creating world-encompassing story assemblages makes it clear that the range of implications held within the term club story cannot be addressed by taking the nineteenth-century model as a template. To describe the form as a tall tale told by one man to other men in a sanctum restricted to those of similar class and outlook, who agree to believe in the story for their mutual comfort, and who themselves may (or may not) tell a tale in turn, is to submit to a particularly narrow understanding of a very broad and deep tradition. But the term itself remains useful.

Club story collections featuring a solo raconteur who is *not under coercion*— they only occur within the last century or so—are not in fact very common, though the most famous modern club story sequences—the Mulliner collections by P G Wodehouse, beginning with *Meet Mr Mulliner* (coll 1927) and continuing for several years, and the five Jorkens collections by Lord Dunsany, beginning with *The Travel Tales of Mr Joseph Jorkens* (coll 1931) and continuing for two decades—do focus on one storyteller who tells a number of tales, some featuring the storyteller himself, some recounting urban fantasies and other implausibilities. But both Mulliner and Jorkens are volunteers. As narrators, they are inherently unreliable, though the club story format, if it does not support the truth of their tales, does at least sanction the safely enclosed telling of them.

For club stories as narrowly defined, whether or not narrated by a single figure, safe telling is vital. Certainly it was no coincidence that the form should have become popular in the UK towards the end of the nineteenth century, for by this point the *texture* of Western World had begun to show marks of strain throughout, an effect that had been gradually intensifying for more than a century. Through the *fin de siècle* period climaxing finally in the death of Queen Victoria, and through the years leading up to World War One, the great progressive march of Western history had begun to seem more and more problematical, and the swollen empires of Europe were increasingly being characterized in fiction—especially in the literatures of the fantastic—as entities fatally vulnerable to infection. For socially dominant white UK males, whose sense of reality was beginning to fray under the assault of women, and Darwin, and dark strains of Marx, and Freud, and Flaubert, and Zola, the club story created a kind of psychic Polder against the epistemological insecurities of the dawning new world. By foregrounding that sense of sanctuary, authors and readers could sideline the question of the believability of the tall tale; and the tale could therefore be accepted by the males to whom it was addressed not for its intrinsic plausibility but—defiantly—as part of a shared conspiracy to maintain an inward-looking, mutually supportive consensus that the world outside could continue to be gossiped about, and manipulated, in safety. Most club stories are set literally in safe havens, most are told by men to men, and most are conservative in both style and content, though they are conveyed in a tone of moderate self-mockery, an example of this being Jerome K Jerome's *After Supper Ghost Stories* (coll 1891) which, though set not in a club but around the table after Christmas Eve dinner, softly parodies the club-story format and the tales told therein. Most club story collections incline more to fantasy than sf, though most incorporate some sf material. Some of the exploits recounted in Andrew Lang's *The Disentanglers* (1902) are of sf interest, however, though more frequently—as in G K Chesterton's *The Club of Queer Trades* (1905)— examples of the form read more like lubricated Satire than fantasy.

Further examples from before World War Two include John Kendrick Bang's *Roger Camerden: A Strange Story* (1887); Stanley W's *The Cassowary: What Chanced in the Cleft Mountains* (1906); Alfred Noyes's *Tales of the Mermaid Tavern* (1914), a set of narrative poems told in Shakespeare's pub; *Zeppelin Nights: A London Entertainment* (1916) by Ford Madox Ford and Violet Hunt (1866–1942), and *Foe-Farrell* (1918) by Sir Arthur Quiller-Couch (1863– 1944): these two later examples both being tales which come close to repre- senting World War One as something not amenable to solace (see below); H Rider Haggard's *Hew-Heu; Or, the Monster* (1924); Cameron Blake's *Only Men on Board* (1933); *The Salzburg Tales* (1934) by Christina Stead (1902–1983), which evoke Boccaccio, as does a slightly earlier Anthology series, *The New Decameron* (1919–1929); and Wyndham Lewis's *Count Your Dead—They Are Alive!; Or, a New War in the Making* (1937), whose puppet-like disputants augur World War Two. Of more established genre interest are Saki's *The*

Chronicles of Clovis (1907), though much less uniformly cast in the club story format than his nonfantastic *Reginald* (1904); John Buchan's *The Runagates Club* (1928); and T H White's *Gone to Ground* (1935), which—as these tales are told by survivors of a final Holocaust—resembles the Ford/Hunt and Quiller-Couch volumes cited above by stretching to its limit the capacity of the form to comfort (again, see below).

In "Sites for Sore Souls: Some Science-Fictional Saloons" (Fall 1991 *Extrapolation*), Fred Erisman loosens the argument made above that the club story can be understood in terms of denial; he suggests that sf club stories—or in his terms saloon stories—respond more straightforwardly to a human need for venues in which an "informal public life" can be led. Although Erisman assumes that the paucity of such venues in America is reflected in the UK, and therefore significantly undervalues the unspoken but clearly felt ambience of the pub in Arthur C Clarke's cosily Recursive *Tales from the White Hart* (1957), his comments are clearly helpful in understanding the persistence of the club story in US sf. Beginning with L Sprague de Camp's and Fletcher Pratt's *Tales from Gavagan's Bar* (1953), it has been a feature of magazine sf for nearly half a century, partly perhaps because imaginary American saloons and venues like conventions—where the genuine affinity groups that generate and consume American sf tend to foregather—are similar kinds of informal public space. Further examples of the club story in the USA, not all of them set in "saloons," are assembled in Poul Anderson's *Tales of the Flying Mountains* (1970); Sterling Lanier's *The Peculiar Exploits of Brigadier Ffellowes* (1972) and *The Curious Quests of Brigadier Ffellowes* (1986); Isaac Asimov's several volumes of nonfantastic **Black Widowers** mysteries, starting with *Tales of the Black Widowers* (1974); Spider Robinson's **Callahan** books, starting with *Callahan's Crosstime Saloon* (1977); Larry Niven's **Draco Tavern** tales, which appear mostly in *Convergent Series* (1979) and *Limits* (1985); and *Tales from the Red Lion* (2007) by John Weagly (1968–). A further Poul Anderson example, the **Nicholas van Rijn** story "The Master Key" (July 1964 *Analog*), pastiches Rudyard Kipling's use of the club-story format. There are many others; some individual stories are assembled in Darrell Schweitzer's and George Scithers's *Tales from the Spaceport Bar* (1987) and *Another Round at the Spaceport Bar* (1989). Almost certainly the most important sf novel to have been organized around a club story frame is Dan Simmons's Time Opera, *Hyperion* (1989), which is very loosely based on Chaucer's *Canterbury Tales* [see above]; and Rana Dasgupta's *Tokyo Cancelled* (2005) very effectively applies the model to the contemporary world.

2. But there is more to the club story form than its capacity to fix tall tales into sanctums where it is safe to pretend to believe them. Fixing a tale into place can be a double-edged sword. Superficially, locking a story into the moment of its telling may seem to constitute a narratological insistence that the *meaning* of the story is itself locked down by the visibility of its telling; but for at least three reasons, it is in fact dangerous to make a story visible. One: each and every club story represents a bringing into the present tense of witness a story which, it is claimed, *has already happened*, which is to say the world of the auditors was in some sense false or incomplete *before the truth was told*. The Club Story brings together the past and the future. Two: it could be argued that the more visible a story is, the less reliable any paraphrastic abstraction of that story will be, for what is almost inevitably exposed by paraphrase is the essential elusiveness of Story, what might be called the polysemy of the visible when narrated. Three: it seems clear that to make a story visible within a club story frame is primarily to enforce not meaning but *witness*, for the story has now been *told* to auditors whose very attentiveness affirms the storyable world: it is, in a clear sense, impossible to deny the existence of a story once told in this fashion, in this context. The club story is a vessel explicitly shaped for the mandatory reception of raw story. There are few genuinely great club stories, but all of them are threatening.

It may be more than a rhetorical gesture to note that at least two paradigm creations in the nearly new-born realm of the fantastic, the Frankenstein Monster and the Vampire—both transgressive figures central to the evolution of sf, and fantasy, and horror—were created within the context of the club story. In the middle of a famous 1816 walking tour in Switzerland, Lord Byron, John Polidori, Mary Wollstonecraft Shelley and Percy Bysshe Shelley (1892–1822) were forced by rain to stay inside at the Villa Diodati on the shores of Lake Geneva. After an evening recital of readings taken from an assembly of *Schauerroman* tales told in a club story frame—*Das Gespensterbuch* ["The Ghost Book"] (1811–1815) by Johann August Apel (1771–1816) and Friedrich August Schulze (1770–1849) writing together as Friedrich Laun— Byron suggested that each member of the party make up a similar tale to be told on a subsequent night. Though there is no clear evidence as to what was actually recounted aloud, both Polidori's and Mary Shelley's eventually published narratives—*The Vampyre: A Tale* (1819) and *Frankenstein; Or, the Modern Prometheus* (1818)—came out of that club-story moment, and both stories exhale the intrusiveness—the first words spoken by Frankenstein's "monster" are "Pardon this intrusion"—of tales that enforce witness. (It might be noted that Chuck Palahniuk's *Haunted: A Novel of Stories* (2005)—which suggestively treats a writing workshop/retreat in club story terms—is set in a "theatre" referred to as the Villa Diodati.) In Germany at about the same time, transgressive authors like E T A Hoffmann—whose *Die Serapionsbruder* ["The Serapion Brothers"] (1818–1821) is a club story assembly—and Ludwig Tieck (1773– 1853)—whose *Phantasus* (1812–1816) is also presented in club story form— were publishing work of oneiric power that hit, as it were, below the belt.

Though James de Mille's *A Strange Manuscript Found in a Copper Cylinder* (1888) is a powerful precursor, and works as a corrosive dismantling of Imperialism's exploitative gaze upon worlds that comment upon its pretences, the great period for the club story, for the club story that threatens rather than consoles, comes rather later: during the 1890s, exactly when reactive club story writers (see above) were beginning to construct Polders against a sense that the Western imperium had become fragile. The four greatest novellas of that decade are probably Arthur Machen's "The Great God Pan" (1894), H G Wells's *The Time Machine: An Invention* (1895), *The Turn of the Screw* (1898) by Henry James (1843–1916) and Joseph Conrad's *Heart of Darkness* (in *Youth: A Narrative; and Two Other Stories*, 1902). Each of them is a club story. Each of them constitutes a witness against any stable understanding of a darkening world. The case of *The Time Machine* is central to the history of sf: the Time Traveller recounts his Scientific Romance–inflected epic of long inevitable decline to a group of auditors who are forced to recognize his tale by virtue of the fact that he returns like some inverted Hero of the Thousand Faces to irrefutably *tell* it. In *Heart of Darkness*—whose setting and tone reflect the contemplative witnessing of the Gustave Doré New Zealander, who gazes upon the same darkening Thames that Marlow and his auditors have sailed into—a tale almost totally resistant to paraphrastic analysis is recounted, at times somewhat bewilderedly, by Marlow, whose pilgrimage into the heart of darkness at the head of the Congo leaves him whited like a sepulchre: Kurtz's cry of "The horror! The horror!" is in fact—after decades of critical analysis—beyond all understanding: though we *suspect* he sees what the future will hold. In conveying his witness to this overwhelming cry, and by enforcing his auditors' witness to that prophetic experience, *Heart of Darkness* perfectly exemplifies the deep power available within the club story format. A club story that has been told cannot be untold.

WHAT WE FOUND

Geoff Ryman

Can't sleep. Still dark. Waiting for light in the East.

My rooster crows. Knows it's my wedding day. I hear the pig rooting around outside. Pig, the traditional gift for the family of my new wife. I can't sleep because alone in the darkness there is nothing between me and the realization that I do not want to get married. Well, Patrick, you don't have long to decide.

The night bakes black around me. Three-thirty a.m. In three hours, the church at the top of the road will start with the singing. Two hours after that, everyone in both families will come crowding into my yard.

My rooster crows again, all his wives in the small space behind the house. It is still piled with broken bottles from when my father lined the top of that wall with glass shards.

That was one of his good times, when he wore trousers and a hat and gave orders. I mixed the concrete, and passed it up in buckets to my eldest brother, Matthew. He sat on the wall like riding a horse, slopping on concrete and pushing in the glass. Raphael was reading in the shade of the porch. "I'm not wasting my time doing all that," he said. "How is broken glass going to stop a criminal who wants to get in?" He always made me laugh, I don't know why. Nobody else was smiling.

When we were young my father would keep us sitting on the hot, hairy sofa in the dark, no lights, no TV because he was driven mad by the sound of the generator. Eyes wide, he would quiver like a wire, listening for it to start up again. My mother tried to speak and he said, "Sssh. Sssh! There it goes again."

"Jacob, the machine cannot turn itself on."

"Sssh! Sssh!" He would not let us move. I was about seven, and terrified. If the generator was wicked enough to scare my big strong father, what would it do to little me? I keep asking my mother what does the generator do?

"Nothing, your father is just being very careful."

"Terhemba is a coward," my brother Matthew said, using my Tiv name. My mother shushed him, but Matthew's merry eyes glimmered at me: *I will make you miserable later.* Raphael prized himself loose from my mother's grip and stomped across the sitting room floor.

*   *   *

People think Makurdi is a backwater, but now we have all you need for a civilized life. Beautiful banks with security doors, retina ID, and air conditioning; new roads, solar panels on all the streetlights, and our phones are stuffed full of e-books. On one of the river islands they built the new hospital; and my university has a medical school, all pink and state-funded with laboratories that are as good as most. Good enough for controlled experiments with mice.

My research assistant Jide is Yoruba and his people believe that the grandson first born after his grandfather's death will continue that man's life. Jide says that we have found how that is true. This is a problem for Christian Nigerians, for it means that evil continues.

What we found in mice is this. If you deprive a mouse of a mother's love, if you make him stressed through infancy, his brain becomes methylated. The high levels of methyl deactivate a gene that produces a neurotropin important for memory and emotional balance in both mice and humans. Schizophrenics have abnormally low levels of it.

It is a miracle of God that with new generation, our genes are knocked clean. There is a new beginning. Science thought this meant that the effects of one life could not be inherited by another.

What we found is that high levels of methyl affect the sperm cells. Methylation is passed on with them, and thus the deactivation. A grandfather's stress is passed on through the male line, yea unto the third generation.

Jide says that what we have found is how the life of the father is continued by his sons. And that is why I don't want to wed.

My father would wander all night. His three older sons slept in one room. Our door would click open and he would stand and glare at me, me particularly, with a boggled and distracted eye as if I had done something outrageous. He would be naked; his towering height and broad shoulders humbled me, made me feel puny and endangered. I have an odd-shaped head with an indented V going down my forehead. People said it was the forceps tugging me out: I was a difficult birth. That was supposed to be why I was slow to speak, slow to learn. My father believed them.

My mother would try to shush him back into their bedroom. Sometimes he would be tame and allow himself to be guided; he might chuckle as if it were a game and hug her. Or he might blow up, shouting and flinging his hands about, calling her woman, witch, or demon. Once she whispered, "It's you who have the demon; the demon has taken hold of you, Jacob."

Sometimes he shuffled past our door and out into the Government street, sleeping-walking to his and our shame.

In those days, it was the wife's job to keep family business safe within the house. Our mother locked all the internal doors even by day to keep him inside, away from visitors from the church or relatives who dropped in on their way to Abuja. If he was being crazy in the sitting room, she would shove us back into our bedroom or whisk us with the broom out into the yard. She would give him whisky if he asked for it, to get him to sleep. Our mother could never speak of these things to anybody, not even her own mother, let alone to us.

We could hear him making noises at night, groaning as if in pain, or slapping someone. The baby slept in my parents' room and he would start to wail. I would stare into the darkness: was Baba hurting my new brother? In the morning his own face would be puffed out. It was Raphael who dared to say something. The very first time I heard that diva voice was when he asked her, sharp and demanding, "Why does that man hit himself?"

My mother got angry and pushed Raphael's face; slap would be the wrong word; she was horrified that the problem she lived with was clear to a five-year-old. "You do not call your father 'that man'! Who are you to ask questions? I can see it's time we put you to work like children used to be when I was young. You don't know what good luck you had to be born into this household!"

Raphael looked back at her, lips pursed. "That does not answer my question."

My mother got very angry at him, shouted more things. Afterward he looked so small and sad that I pulled him closer to me on the sofa. He crawled up onto my lap and just sat there. "I wish we were closer to the river," he said, "so we could go and play."

"Mamamimi says the river is dangerous." My mother's name was Mimi, which means truth, so Mama Truth was a kind of title.

"Everything's dangerous," he said, his lower lip thrust out. A five-year-old should not have such a bleak face.

By the time I was nine, Baba would try to push us into the walls, wanting us hidden or wanting us gone. His vast hands would cover the back of our heads or shoulders and grind us against the plaster. Raphael would look like a crushed berry, but he shouted in a rage, "No! No! No!"

Yet my father wore a suit and drove himself to work. Jacob Terhemba Shawo worked as a tax inspector and electoral official.

Did other government employees act the same way? Did they put on a shell of calm at work? He would be called to important meetings in Abuja and stay for several days. Once Mamamimi sat at the table, her white bread uneaten, not caring what her children heard. "What you go to Abuja for? Who you sleep with there, Wildman? What diseases do you bring back into my house?"

We stared down at our toast and tea, amazed to hear such things. "You tricked me into marriage with you. I bewail the day I accepted you. Nobody told me you were crazy!"

My father was not a man to be dominated in his own house. Clothed in his functionary suit, he stood up. "If you don't like it, go. See who will have you since you left your husband. See who will want you without all the clothes and jewelry I buy you. Maybe you no longer want this comfortable home. Maybe you no longer want your car. I can send you back to your village, and no one would blame me."

My mother spun away into the kitchen and began to slam pots. She did not weep. She was not one to be dominated either, but knew she could not change how things had to be. My father climbed into his SUV for Abuja in his special glowering suit that kept all questions at bay, with his polished head and square-cornered briefcase. The car purred away down the tree-lined Government street with no one to wave him good-bye.

*   *   *

Jide's full name is Babajide. In Yoruba it means Father Wakes Up. His son is called Babatunde, Father Returns. It is something many people believe in the muddle of populations that is Nigeria.

My work on mice was published in *Nature* and widely cited. People wanted to believe that character could be inherited; that stressed fathers passed incapacities on to their grandchildren. It seemed to open a door to inherited characteristics, perhaps a modified theory of evolution. Our experiments had been conclusive: not only were there the non-genetically inherited emotional tendencies, but we could objectively measure the levels of methyl.

My father was born in 1965, the year before the Tiv rioted against what they thought were Muslim incursions. It was a time of coup and counter-coup. The violence meant my grandfather left Jos, and moved the family to Makurdi. They walked, pushing some of their possessions and my infant father in a wheelbarrow. The civil war came with its trains full of headless Igbo rattling eastward, and air force attacks on our own towns. People my age say, oh those old wars. What can Biafra possibly have to do with us, now?

What we found is that 1966 can reach into your head and into your balls and stain your children red. You pass war on. The cranky old men in the villages, the lack of live music in clubs, the distrust of each other, soldiers everywhere, the crimes of colonialism embedded in the pattern of our roads. We live our grandfathers' lives.

Outside, the stars spangle. It will be a beautiful clear day. My traditional clothes hang unaccepted in the closet and I fear for any son that I might have. What will I pass on? Who would want their son to repeat the life of my father, the life of my brother? Ought I to get married at all? Outside in the courtyard, wet with dew, the white plastic chairs are lined up for the guests.

*   *   *

My Grandmother Iveren would visit without warning. Her name meant "Blessing," which was a bitter thing for us. Grandmother Iveren visited all her children in turn no matter how far they moved to get away from her: Kano, Jalingo, or Makurdi.

A taxi would pull up and we would hear a hammering on our gate. One of us boys would run to open it and there she would be, standing like a princess. "Go tell my son to come and pay for the taxi. Bring my bags, please."

She herded us around our living room with the burning tip of her cigarette, inspecting us as if everything was found wanting. The Intermittent Freezer that only kept things cool, the gas cooker, the rack of vegetables, the many tins of powdered milk, the rumpled throw rug, the blanket still on the sofa, the TV that was left tuned all day to Africa Magic. She would switch it off with a sigh as she passed. "Education," she would say, shaking her head. She had studied literature at the University of Madison, Wisconsin, and she used that like she used her cigarette. Iveren was tiny, thin, very pretty, and elegant in glistening blue or purple dresses with matching headpieces.

My mother's mother might also be staying, rattling out garments on her sewing machine. Mamagrand, we called her. The two women would feign civility, even smiling. My father lumbered in with suitcases; the two grandmothers would pretend that it made no difference to them where they slept, but Iveren would get the back bedroom and Mamagrand the sofa. My father then sat down to gaze at his knees, his jaws clamped shut like a turtle's. His sons assumed that that was what all children did, and that mothers always kept order in this way.

Having finished pursuing us around our own house, she would sigh, sit on the sofa, and wait expectantly for my mother to bring her food. Mamamimi dutifully did so—family being family—and then sat down, her face going solid and her arms folded.

"You should know what the family is saying about you," Grandmother might begin, smiling so sweetly. "They are saying that you have infected my son, that you are unclean from an abortion." She would say that my aunt

Judith would no longer allow Mamamimi into her house and had paid a woman to cast a spell on my mother to keep her away.

"Such a terrible thing to do. The spell can only be cured by cutting it with razor blades." Grandmother Iveren looked as though she might enjoy helping.

"Thank heavens such a thing cannot happen in a Christian household," my mother's mother would say.

"Could I have something to drink?"

From the moment Grandmother arrived, all the alcohol in the house would start to disappear: little airline sample bottles, whisky from my father's boss, even the brandy Baba had brought from London. And not just alcohol. Grandmother would offer to help Mamamimi clean a bedroom; and small things would be gone from it forever, jewelry or scarves or little bronzes. She sold the things she pilfered, to keep herself in dresses and perfume.

It wasn't as if her children neglected their duty. She would be fed and housed for as long as any of us could stand it. Even so, she would steal and hide all the food in the house. My mother went grim-faced, and would lift up mattresses to display the tins and bottles hidden under it. The top shelf of the bedroom closet would contain the missing stewpot with that evening's meal. "It's raw!" my mother would swelter at her. "It's not even cooked! Do you want it to go rotten in this heat?"

"I never get fed anything in this house. I am watched like a hawk!" Iveren complained, her face turned toward her giant son.

Mamamimi had strategies. She might take to her room ill, and pack meat in a cool chest and keep it under her bed. Against all tradition, especially if Father was away, she would sometimes refuse to cook any food at all. For herself, for Grandmother, or even us. "I'm on strike!" she announced once. "Here, here is money. Go buy food! Go cook it!" She pressed folded money into our hands. Raphael and I made a chicken stew, giggling. We had been warned about Iveren's cooking. "Good boys, to take the place of the mother," she said, winding our hair in her fingers.

Such bad behavior on all sides made Raphael laugh. He loved it when Iveren came to stay, with her swishing skirts and dramatic manner and drunken stumbles; loved it when Mamamimi behaved badly and the house swelled with their silent battle of wills.

Grandmother would say things to my mother like: "We knew that you were not on our level, but we thought you were a simple girl from the country and that your innocence would be good for him." Chuckle. "If only we had known."

"If only I had," my mother replied.

My father's brothers had told us stories about Granny. When they were young, she would bake cakes with salt instead of sugar and laugh when they bit into them. She would make stews out of only bones, having thrown the goat away. She would cook with no seasoning so that it was like eating water, or cook with so many chillies that it was like eating fire.

When my uncle Eamon tried to sell his car, she stole the starter motor. She was right in there with a monkey wrench and spirited it away. It would cough and grind when potential buyers turned the key. When he was away, she put the motor back in and sold the car herself. She told Eamon that it had been stolen. When Eamon saw someone driving it, he had the poor man arrested, and the story came out.

My other uncle, Emmanuel, was an officer in the Air Force, a fine-looking man in his uniform. When he first went away to do his training, Grandmother told all the neighbors that he was a worthless ingrate who neglected his mother, never calling her or giving her gifts. She got everyone so riled against him that when he came home to the village, the elders raised sticks against him and shouted, "How dare you show your face here after the way you have treated your mother!" For who would think a mother would say such things about a son without reason?

It was Grandmother who reported gleefully to Emmanuel that his wife had tested HIV positive. "You should have yourself tested. A shame you are not man enough to satisfy your wife and hold her to you. All that smoking has made you impotent."

She must be a witch, Uncle Emmanuel said, how else would she have known when he himself did not?

Raphael would laugh at her antics. He loved it when Granny started asking us all for gifts—even the orphan girl who lived with us. Iveren asked if she couldn't take the cushion covers home with her, or just one belt. Raphael yelped with laughter and clapped his hands. Granny blinked at him. What did he find so funny? Did my brother like her?

She knew what to make of me: quiet, well behaved. I was someone to torment.

I soon learned how to behave around her. I would stand, not sit, in silence in my white shirt, tie, and blue shorts.

"Those dents in his skull," she said to my mother once, during their competitive couch-sitting. "Is that why he's so slow and stupid?"

"That's just the shape of his head. He's not slow."

"Tuh. Your monstrous first-born didn't want a brother and bewitched him in the womb." Her eyes glittered all over me, her smile askew. "The boy cannot talk properly. He sounds ignorant."

My mother said that I sounded fine to her and that I was a good boy and got good grades in school.

My father was sitting in shamed silence. What did it mean that my father said nothing in my favor? Was I stupid?

"Look to your own children," my mother told her. "Your son is not doing well at work, and they delay paying him. So we have very little money. I'm afraid we can't offer you anything except water from the well. I have a bad back. Would you be so kind to fetch water yourself, since your son offers you nothing?"

Grandmother chuckled airily, as if my mother was a fool and would see soon enough. "So badly brought up. My poor son. No wonder your children are such frights."

That very day my mother took me round to the back of the house, where she grew her herbs. She bowed down to look into my eyes and held my shoulders and told me, "Patrick, you are a fine boy. You do everything right. There is nothing wrong with you. You do well in your lessons, and look how you washed the car this morning without even being asked."

It was Raphael who finally told Granny off. She had stayed for three months. Father's hair was corkscrewing off in all directions and his eyes had a trapped light in them. Everyone had taken to cooking their own food at night, and every spoon and knife in the house had disappeared.

"Get out of this house, you thieving witch. If you were nice to your family, they would let you stay and give you anything you want. But you can't stop stealing things." He was giggling. "Why do you tell lies and make such trouble? You should be nice to your children and show them loving care."

"And you should learn how to be polite." Granny sounded weak with surprise.

"Ha-ha! And so should you! You say terrible things about us. None of your children believes a thing you say. You only come here when no one else can stand you and you only leave when you know you've poisoned the well so much even you can't drink from it. It's not very intelligent of you, when you depend on us to eat."

He drove her from the house, keeping it up until no other outcome were possible. "Blessing, our Blessing, the taxi is here!" pursuing her to the gate with mockery. Even Matthew started to laugh. Mother had to hide her mouth. He held the car door open for her. "You'd best read your Bible and give up selling all your worthless potions."

Father took hold of Raphael's wrists gently. "That's enough," he said. "Grandmother went through many bad things." He didn't say it in anger. He didn't say it like a wild man. Something somber in his voice made Raphael calm.

"You come straight out of the bush," Grandmother said, almost unperturbed. "No wonder my poor son is losing his mind." She looked directly at Raphael. "The old ways did work." Strangely, he was the only one she dealt with straightforwardly. "They wore out."

*   *   *

Something happened to my research.

At first the replication studies showed a less marked effect, less inherited stress, lower methyl levels. But soon we ceased to be able to replicate our results at all.

The new studies dragged me down, made me suicidal. I felt I had achieved something with my paper, made up for all my shortcomings, done something that would have made my family proud of me if they were alive.

Methylation had made me a full Professor. Benue State's home page found room to feature me as an example of the university's research excellence. I sought design flaws in the replication studies; that was the only thing I published. All my life I had fought to prove I wasn't slow, or at least hide it through hard work. And here before the whole world, I was being made to look like a fraud.

Then I read the work of Jonathan Schooler. The same thing had happened to him. His research had proved that if you described a memory clearly you ceased to remember it as well. The act of describing faces reduced his subjects' ability to recognize them later. The effects he measured were so huge and so unambiguous, and people were so intrigued by the implications of what he called verbal overshadowing, that his paper was cited 400 times.

Gradually, it had become impossible to replicate his results. Every time he did the experiment, the effect shrank by thirty percent.

I got in touch with Schooler, and we began to check the record. We found that all the way back in the 1930s, results of E.S.P. experiments by Joseph Banks Rhine declined. In replication, his startling findings evaporated to something only slightly different from chance. It was as if scientific truths wore out, as if the act of observing them reduced their effect.

Jide laughed and shook his head. "We think the same thing!" he said. "We always say that a truth can wear out with the telling."

That is why I am sitting here writing, dreading the sound of the first car arriving, the first knock on my gate.

I am writing to wear out both memory and truth.

*   *   *

Whenever my father was away, or sometimes to escape Iveren, Mamamimi would take all us boys back to our family village. It is called Kawuye, on the road toward Taraba State. Her friend Sheba would drive us to the bus station in the market, and we would wait under the shelter, where the women cooked rice and chicken and sold sweating tins of Coca-Cola. Then we would stuff ourselves into the van next to some fat businessman who had hoped for a row of seats to himself.

Matthew was the firstborn, and tried to boss everyone, even Mamamimi. He had teamed up with little Andrew from the moment he'd been born. Andrew was too young to be a threat to him. The four brothers fell into two teams and Mamamimi had to referee, coach, organize, and punish.

If Matthew and I were crammed in next to each other, we would fight. I could stand his needling and bossiness only so long and then wordlessly clout him. That made me the one to be punished. Mamamimi would swipe me over the head and Matthew's eyes would tell me that he'd done it deliberately.

It was hot and crowded on the buses, with three packed rows of sweating ladies, skinny men balancing deliveries of posters on their laps, or mothers dandling heat-drugged infants. It was not supportable to have four boys elbowing, kneeing, and scratching.

Mamamimi started to drive us herself in her old green car. She put Matthew in the front so that he felt in charge. Raphael and I sat in the back reading, while next to us Andrew cawed for Matthew's attention.

Driving by herself was an act of courage. The broken-edged roads would have logs pulled across them, checkpoints they were called, with soldiers. They would wave through the stuffed vans but they would stop a woman driving four children and stare into the car. Did we look like criminals or terrorists? They would ask her questions and rummage through our bags and mutter things that we could not quite hear. I am not sure they were always proper. Raphael would noisily flick through the pages of his book. "Nothing we can do about it," he would murmur. After slipping them some money, Mama would drive on.

As if by surprise, up and over a hill, we would roller-coaster down through maize fields into Kawuye. I loved it there. The houses were the best houses for Nigeria and typical of the Tiv people, round and thick-walled with high pointed roofs and tiny windows. The heat could not get in and the walls sweated like a person to keep cool. There were no wild men waiting to leap out, no poison grandmothers. My great-uncle Jacob—it is a common name in my family—repaired cars with the patience of a cricket, opening, snipping, melting, and reforming. He once repaired a vehicle by replacing the fan belt with the elastic from my mother's underwear.

Raphael and I would buy firewood, trading some of it for eggs, ginger, and yams. We also helped my aunty with her pig-roasting business. To burn off the bristles, we'd lower it onto a fire and watch grassfire lines of red creep up each strand. It made a smell like burning hair and Raphael and I would pretend we were pirates cooking people. Then we turned the pig on a spit until it crackled. At nights we were men, serving beer and taking money.

We both got fat because our pay was some of the pig, and if no one was looking, the beer as well. I ate because I needed to get as big as Matthew. In the evenings the generators coughed to life and the village smelled of petrol and I played football barefoot under lights. There were jurisdictions and disagreements, but laughing uncles to adjudicate with the wisdom of a Solomon. So even the four of us liked each other more in Kawuye.

Then after whole weeks of sanity, my mother's phone would sing out with the voice of Mariah Carey or an American prophetess. As the screen illuminated, Mamamimi's face would scowl. We knew the call meant that our father was back in the house, demanding our return.

Uncle Jacob would change the oil and check the tires and we would drive back through the fields and rock across potholes onto the main road. At intersections, children swarmed around the car, pushing their hands through open windows, selling plastic bags of water or dappled plantains. Their eyes peered in at us. I would feel ashamed somehow. Raphael wound up the window and hollered at them. "Go away and stop your staring. There's nothing here for you to see!"

Baba would be waiting for us reading *ThisDay* stiffly, like he had broomsticks for bones, saying nothing.

After that long drive, Mama would silently go and cook. Raphael told him off. "It's not very fair of you, Popsie, to make her work. She has just driven us back all that way just to be nice to us and show us a good time in the country."

Father's eyes rested on him like drills on DIY.

That amused Raphael. "Since you choose to be away all the time, she has to do all the work here. And you're just sitting there." My father rattled the paper and said nothing. Raphael was twelve years old.

*　　*　　*

I was good at football, so I survived school well enough. But my brother was legendary.

They were reading *The Old Man and The Sea* in English class, and Raphael blew up at the teacher. She said that lions were a symbol of Hemingway being lionized when young. She said the old fisherman carrying a mast made him some sort of Jesus with his cross. He told her she had a head full of nonsense. I can see him doing it. He would bark with sudden laughter and bounce up and down in his chair and declare, delighted, "That's blasphemy! It's just a story about an old man. If Hemingway had wanted to write a story about Jesus, he was a clever enough person to have written one!" The headmaster gave him a clip about the ear. Raphael wobbled his head at him as if shaking a finger. "Your hitting me doesn't make me wrong." None of the other students ever bothered us. Raphael still got straight As.

Our sleepy little bookshops, dark, wooden, and crammed into corners of markets, knew that if they got a book on chemistry or genetics they could sell it to Raphael. He set up a business to buy textbooks that he knew Benue State was going to recommend. At sixteen he would sit on benches at the university, sipping cold drinks and selling books, previous essays, and condoms. Everybody assumed that he was already being educated there. Tall, beautiful students would call him "sah." One pretty girl called him "Prof." She had honey-colored, extended hair, and a spangled top that hung off one shoulder.

"I'm his brother," I told her proudly.

"So you are the handsome one," she said, being kind to what she took to be the younger brother. For many weeks I carried her in my heart.

The roof of our Government bungalow was flat and Raphael and I took to living on it. We slept there; we even climbed the ladder with our plates of food. We read by torchlight, rigged mosquito nets, and plugged the mobile phone into our netbook. The world flooded into it; the websites of our wonderful Nigerian newspapers, the BBC, Al Jazeera, *Nature*, *New Scientist*. We pirated Nollywood movies. We got slashdotcom; we hacked into the scientific journals, getting all those ten-dollar PDFs for free.

We elevated ourselves above the murk of our household. Raphael would read aloud in many different voices, most of them mocking. He would giggle at news articles. "Oh, story! Now they are saying Fashola is corrupt. Hee hee hee. It's the corrupt people saying that to get their own back."

"Oh this is interesting," he would say and read about what some Indian at Caltech had found out about gravitational lenses.

My naked father would pad out like an old lion gone mangy and stare up at us, looking bewildered as if he wanted to join us but couldn't work out how. "You shouldn't be standing out there with no clothes on," Raphael told him. "What would happen if someone came to visit?" My father looked as mournful as an abandoned dog.

*　*　*

Jacob Terhemba Shawo was forced to retire. He was only forty-two. We had to leave the Government Reserved Area. Our family name means "high on the hill," and that's where we had lived. I remember that our well was so deep that once I dropped the bucket and nothing could reach it. A boy had to climb down the stones in the well wall to fetch it.

We moved into the house I live in now, a respectable bungalow across town, surrounded with high walls. It had a sloping roof, so Raphael and I were no longer elevated.

The driveway left no room for Mamamimi's herb garden, so we bought a neighboring patch of land but couldn't afford the sand and cement to wall it off. Schoolchildren would wander up the slope into our maize, picking it or sometimes doing their business.

The school had been built by public subscription and the only land cheap enough was in the slough. For much of the year the new two-story building rose vertically out of a lake like a castle. It looked like the Scottish islands in my father's calendars. Girls boated to the front door and climbed up a ramp. A little beyond was a marsh, with ponds and birds and water lilies: beautiful but it smelled of drains and rotting reeds.

We continued to go to the main cathedral for services. White draperies hung the length of its ceiling, and the stained-glass doors would accordion open to let in air. Local dignitaries would be in attendance and nod approval as our family lined up to take communion and make our gifts to the church, showing obeisance to the gods of middle-class respectability.

But the church at the top of our unpaved road was bare concrete, always open at the sides. People would pad past my bedroom window and the singing of hymns would swell with the dawn. Some of the local houses would be village dwellings amid the aging urban villas.

Chickens still clucked in our new narrow back court. If you dropped a bucket down this well, all you had to do was reach in for it. The problem was to stop water flooding into the house. The concrete of an inner courtyard was broken and the hot little square was never used, except for the weights that Raphael had made for himself out of iron bars and sacks of concrete. Tiny and rotund, he had dreams of being a muscleman. His computer desktop was full of a Nigerian champion in briefs. I winced with embarrassment whenever his screen sang open in public. What would people think of him, with that naked man on his netbook?

My father started to swat flies all the time. He got long sticky strips of paper and hung them everywhere—across doorways, from ceilings, in windows. They would snag in our hair as we carried out food from the kitchen. All we saw was flies on strips of paper. We would wake up in the night to hear him slapping the walls with books, muttering, "Flies flies flies."

The house had a tin roof and inside we baked like bread. Raphael resented it personally. He was plump and felt the heat. My parents had installed the house's only AC in their bedroom. He would just as regularly march in with a spanner and screwdriver and steal it. He would stomp out, the cable dragging behind him, with my mother wringing her hands and weeping. "That boy! That crazy boy! Jacob! Come see to your son."

Raphael shouted, "Buy another one! You can afford it!"

"We can't, Raphael! You know that! We can't."

And Raphael said, "I'm not letting you drag me down to your level."

Matthew by then was nearly nineteen and had given up going to university. His voice was newly rich and sad. "Raphael. The whole family is in trouble. We would all like the AC, but if Baba doesn't get it, he wanders, and that is a problem, too."

I didn't like it that Raphael took it from our parents without permission. Shamefaced with betrayal of him, I helped Matthew fix the AC back in our parents' window.

Raphael stomped up to me and poked me with his finger. "You should be helping me, not turning tail and running!" He turned his back and said, "I'm not talking to you."

I must have looked very sad because later I heard his flip-flops shuffling behind me. "You are my brother and of course I will always talk to you. I'm covered in shame that I said such a thing to you." Raphael had a genius for apologies, too.

* * *

When Andrew was twelve, our father drove him to Abuja and left him with people, some great-aunt we didn't know. She was childless, and Andrew had come back happy from his first visit sporting new track shoes. She had bought him an ice cream from Grand Square. He went back.

One night Raphael heard Mother and Father talking. He came outside onto the porch, his fat face gleaming. "I've got some gossip," he told me. "Mamamimi and Father have sold Andrew!"

"Sold" was an exaggeration. They had put him to work and were harvesting his wages. In return he got to live in an air-conditioned house. Raphael giggled. "It's so naughty of them!" He took hold of my hand and pulled me with him right into their bedroom.

Both of them were decent, lying on the bed with their books. Raphael announced, very pleased with himself. "You're not selling my brother like an indentured servant. Just because he was a mistake and you didn't want him born so late and want to be shot of him now."

Mamamimi leapt at him. He ran, laughter pealing, and his hands swaying from side to side. I saw only then that he had the keys for the SUV in his hand. He pulled me with him out into the yard, and then swung me forward. "Get the gate!" He popped himself into the driver's seat and roared the engine. Mamamimi waddled after him. The car rumbled forward, the big metal gate groaned open, dogs started to bark. Raphael bounced the SUV out of the yard, and pushed its door open for me. Mamamimi was right behind, and I didn't want to be the one punished again, so I jumped in. "Good-bye-yeee!" Raphael called in a singsong voice, smiling right into her face.

We somehow got to Abuja alive. Raphael couldn't drive, and trucks kept swinging out onto our side of the road, accelerating and beeping. We swerved in and out, missing death, passing the corpses of dead transports lined up along the roadside. Even I roared with laughter as lorries wailed past us by inches.

Using the GPS, Raphael foxed his way to the woman's house. Andrew let us in; he worked as her boy, beautifully dressed in a white shirt and jeans, with tan sandals of interwoven strips. In we strode and Raphael said, very pleasantly at first, "Hello! *M'sugh!* How are you? I am Jacob's son, Andrew's brother."

I saw at once this was a very nice lady. She was huge like a balloon, with a child-counseling smile, and she welcomed us and hugged Andrew to her.

"Have you paid my parents anything in advance for Andrew's work? Because they want him back, they miss him so much."

She didn't seem to mind. "Oh, they changed their minds. Well of course they did, Andrew is such a fine young man. Well, Andrew, it seems your brothers want you back!"

"I changed their minds for them." Raphael always cut his words out of the air like a tailor making a bespoke garment. Andrew looked confused and kept his eyes on the embroidery on his jeans.

Andrew must have known what had happened because he didn't ask why it was us two who had come to fetch him. Raphael had saved him, not first-born Matthew—if he had wanted to be saved from decent clothes and shopping in Abuja.

When we got back home, no mention was made of anything by anyone. Except by Raphael, to me, later. "It is so interesting, isn't it, that they haven't said a thing. They know what they were doing was wrong. How would they like to be a child and know their parents had sent them to work?" Matthew said nothing either. We had been rich; now we were poor.

*　　*　　*

Jide and I measured replication decline.

We carried out our old experiment over and over and measured methyl as levels declined for no apparent reason. Then we increased the levels of stress. Those poor mice! In the name of science, we deprived them of a mother and then cuddly surrogates. We subjected them to regimes of irregular feeding and random light and darkness and finally electric shocks.

There was no doubt. No matter how much stress we subjected them to, after the first spectacular results, the methyl levels dropped off with each successive experiment. Not only that, but the association between methyl and neurotropin suppression reduced as well—objectively measured, the amount of methyl and its effect on neurotropin production were smaller with each study. We had proved the decline effect. Truth wore out. Or at least, scientific truth wore out.

We published. People loved the idea and we were widely cited. Jide became a Lecturer and a valued colleague. People began to speak of something called Cosmic Habituation. The old ways were no longer working. And I was thirty-seven.

*　　*　　*

With visitors, Raphael loved being civil, a different person. Sweetly and sociably, he would say, "*M'sugh*," our mix of hello, good-bye, and pardon me. He loved bringing them trays of cold water from the Intermittent Freezer. He remembered everybody's name and birthday. He hated dancing, but loved dressing up for parties. Musa the tailor made him wonderful robes with long shirts, matching trousers, shawls.

My father liked company, too, even more so after his Decline. He would suddenly stand up straight and smile eagerly. I swear, his shirt would suddenly look ironed, his shoes polished. I was envious of the company, usually men from his old work. They could get my father laughing. He would look young then, and merry, and slap the back of his hand on his palm, jumping up to pass around the beer. I wanted him to laugh with me.

Very suddenly Matthew announced he was getting married. We knew it was his way of escaping. After the wedding he and his bride would move in with her sister's husband. He would help with their fish farm and plantation of nym trees. We did well by him: no band, but a fine display of food. My father boasted about how strong Matthew was, always captain. From age twelve he had read the business news like some boys read adventure stories. Matthew, he said, was going to be a leader.

My father saw me looking quiet and suddenly lifted up his arms. "Then there is my Patrick who is so quiet. I have two clever sons to go alongside the strong one." His hand felt warm on my back.

By midnight it was cool and everybody was outside dancing, even Raphael, who grinned, making circular motions with his elbows and planting his feet as firmly as freeway supports.

My father wavered up to me like a vision out of the desert, holding a tin of High Life. He stood next to me watching the dancing and the stars. "You know," he said, "your elder brother was sent to you by Jesus." My heart sank: *Yes, I know, to lead the family, to be an example.*

"He was so unhappy when you were born. He saw you in your mother's arms and howled. He is threatened by you. Jesus sent you Matthew so that you would know what it is to fight to distinguish yourself. And you learned that. You are becoming distinguished."

I can find myself being kind in that way; suddenly, in private with no one else to hear or challenge the kindness, as if kindness were a thing to shame us.

I went back onto the porch and there was Raphael looking hunched and large, a middle-aged patriarch. He'd heard what my father said. "So who taught Matthew to be stupid? Why didn't he ever tell him to leave you alone?"

* * *

My father's skin faded. It had always been very dark, so black that he would use skin lightener as a moisturizer without the least bleaching effect. Now very suddenly, he went honey-colored; his hair became a knotted muddy brown. A dried clot of white spit always threatened to glue his lips together, and his eyes went bad, huge and round and ringed with swollen flesh like a frog's. He sprouted thick spectacles, and had to lean his head back to see, blinking continually. He could no longer remember how to find the toilet from the living room. He took to crouching down behind the bungalow with the hens, then as things grew worse, off the porch in front of the house. Mamamimi said, "It makes me think there may be witchcraft after all." Her face swelled and went hard until it looked like a stone.

On the Tuesday night before he died, he briefly came back to us. Tall, in trousers, so skinny now that he looked young again. He ate his dinner with good manners, the fou-fou cradling the soup so that none got onto his fingers. Outside on the porch he started to talk, listing the names of all his brothers.

Then he told us that Grandmother was not his actual mother. Another woman had borne him, made pregnant while dying of cancer. Grandfather knew pregnancy would kill her, but he made her come to term. She was bearing his first son.

Two weeks after my father was born, his real mother had died, and my grandfather married the woman called Blessing.

Salt instead of sugar. Iveren loved looking as though she had given the family its first son. It looked good as they lined up in church. But she had no milk for him. Jacob Terhemba Shawo spent his first five years loveless in a war.

My father died three days before Matthew's first child was born. Matthew and his wife brought her to our house to give our mother something joyful to think about.

The baby's Christian name was Isobel. Her baby suit had three padded Disney princesses on it and her hair was a red down.

Matthew chuckled. "Don't worry, Mamamimi, this can't be Grandpa, it's a girl."

Raphael smiled. "Maybe she's Grandpa born in woman's body."

Matthew's wife clucked her tongue. She didn't like us and she certainly didn't like what she'd heard about Raphael. She drew herself up tall and said, "Her name is Iveren."

Matthew stared at his hands; Mamamimi froze; Raphael began to dance with laughter.

"It was my mother's name," the wife said.

"Ah!" cried Raphael. "Two of them, Matthew. Two Iverens! Oh, that is such good luck for you!"

I saw from my mother's unmoving face, and from a flick of the fingers, a jettisoning, that she had consigned the child to its mother's family and Matthew to that other family, too. She never took a proper interest in little Iveren.

But Grandmother must have thought that they had named the child after her. Later, she went to live with them, which was exactly the blessing I would wish for Matthew.

*   *   *

Raphael became quieter, preoccupied, as if invisible flies buzzed around his head. I told myself we were working too hard. Both of us had been applying for oil company scholarships. I wanted both of us to go together to the best universities: Lagos or Ibadan. I thought of all those strangers, in states that were mainly Igbo or Yoruba or maybe even Muslim. I was sure we were a team.

In the hall bookcase a notice appeared. DO NOT TOUCH MY BOOKS. I DON'T INTERFERE WITH YOUR JOB. LEAVE ALL BOOKS IN ORDER.

They weren't his alone. "Can I look at them, at least?"

He looked at me balefully. "If you ask first."

I checked his downloads and they were all porn. I saw the terrible titles of the files, which by themselves were racial and sexual abuse. A good Christian boy, I was shocked and dismayed. I said something to him and he puffed up, looking determined. "I don't live by other people's rules."

He put a new password onto our machine so that I could not get into it. My protests were feeble.

"I need to study, Raphael."

"Study is beyond you," he said. "Study cannot help you."

At the worst possible time for him, his schoolteachers went on strike because they weren't being paid. Raphael spent all day clicking away at his keyboard, not bothering to dress. His voice became milder, faint and sweet, but he talked only in monosyllables. "Yes. No. I don't know." Not angry, a bit as though he was utterly weary.

That Advent, Mamamimi, Andrew, Matthew and family went to the cathedral, but my mother asked me to stay behind to look after Raphael.

"You calm him," Mamamimi said, and for some reason that made my eyes sting. They went to church, and I was left alone in the main room. I was sitting on the old sofa watching some TV trash about country bumpkins going to Lagos.

Suddenly Raphael trotted out of our bedroom in little Japanese steps wearing one of my mother's dresses. He had folded a matching cloth around his head into an enormous flower shape, his face ghostly with makeup. My face must have been horrified: it made him chatter with laughter. "What the well-dressed diva is wearing this season."

All I thought then was, *Raphael, don't leave me.* I stood up and I pushed him back toward the room; like my mother, I was afraid of visitors. "Get it off, get it off, what are you doing?"

"You don't like it?" He batted his eyelashes.

"No I do not! What's got into you?"

"Raphael is not a nurse! Raphael does not have to be nice!"

I begged him to get out of the dress. I kept looking at my telephone for the time, worried when they would be back. Above all else I didn't want Mama to know he had taken her things.

He stepped out of the dress, and let the folded headdress trail behind him, falling onto the floor. I scooped them up, checked them for dirt or makeup, and folded them up as neatly as I could.

I came back to the bedroom and he was sitting in his boxer shorts and flip-flops, staring at his screen and with complete unconcern was doing something to himself.

I asked the stupidest question. "What are you doing?"

"What does it look like? It's fun. You should join in." Then he laughed. He turned the screen toward me. In the video, a man was servicing a woman's behind. I had no idea people did such things. I howled and covered my mouth, laughing in shock. I ran out of the room and left him to finish.

Without Raphael I had no one to go to and I could not be seen to cry. I went outside and realized that I was alone. What could I say to my mother? Our Raphael is going mad? For her he had always been mad. Only I had really liked Raphael and now he was becoming someone else, and I was so slow I would only ever be me.

He got a strange disease that made his skin glisten but a fever did not register. It was what my father had done: get illnesses that were not quite physical. He ceased to do anything with his hair. It twisted off his head in knots and made him look like a beggar.

He was hardly ever fully dressed. He hung around the house in underwear and flip-flops. I became his personal Mamamimi, trying to stop the rest of the family finding out, trying to keep him inside the room. In the middle of the night, he would get up. I would sit up, see he wasn't there, and slip out of the house trying to find him, walking around our unlit streets. This is not wise in our locality. The neighborhood boys patrol for thieves or outsiders, and they can be rough if they do not recognize your face. "I'm Patrick, I moved into the house above the school. I'm trying to find my brother Raphael."

"So how did you lose him?"

"He's not well, he's had a fever, he wanders."

"The crazy family," one of them said.

Their flashlights dazzled my eyes, but I could see them glance at each other. "He means that dirty boy." They said that of Raphael?

"He's my brother. He's not well."

I would stay out until they brought him back to me, swinging their AK-47s. He could so easily have been shot. He was wearing almost nothing, dazed like a sleepwalker, and his hair in such a mess. Raphael had always been vain. His skin Vaselined with the scent of roses, the fine shirt with no tails designed to hang outside the trousers and hide his tummy, his nails manicured. Now he looked like a laborer who needed a bath.

Finally one night, the moon was too bright and the boys brought him too close to our house. My mother ran out of the groaning gate. "Patrick, Patrick, what is it?"

"These boys have been helping us find Raphael," was all I said. I felt ashamed and frustrated because I had failed to calm him, to find him myself, to keep the secret locked away, especially from Mamamimi.

When my mother saw him she whispered, "Wild man!" and it was like a chill wind going through me. She had said what I knew but did not let myself acknowledge. Again, it was happening again, first to the father, then to the son.

I got him to bed, holding both his arms and steering him. Our room was cool as if we were on a mountain. I came back out into the heat and Mamamimi was waiting, looking old. "Does he smoke gbana?" she asked.

I said I didn't think so. "But I no longer know him."

In my mind I was saying, *Raphael, come back*. Sometimes my mother would beseech me with her eyes to do something. Such a thing should not befall a family twice.

*   *   *

Makurdi lives only because of its river. The Benue flows into the great Niger, gray-green with fine beaches that are being dug up for concrete and currents so treacherous they look like molded jellies welling up from below. No one swims there, except at dusk, in the shallows, workmen go to wash, wading out in their underwear.

Raphael would disappear at sunset and go down the slopes to hymn the men. It was the only time he dressed up: yellow shirt, tan slacks, good shoes. He walked out respectfully onto the sand and sang about the men, teased them, and chortled. He would try to take photographs of them. The men eyed him in fear, or ignored him like gnarled trees, or sometimes threw pebbles at him to make him go away. The things he said were irresponsible. Matthew and I would be sent to fetch him back. Matthew hated it. He would show up in his bank suit, with his car that would get sand in it. "Let him stay there! He only brings shame on himself!"

But we could not leave our brother to have stones thrown at him. He would be on the beach laughing at his own wild self, singing paeans of praise for the beauty of the bathers, asking their names, asking where they lived. Matthew and I would be numb from shame. "Come home, come home," we said to him, and to the laborers, "Please excuse us, we are good Christians, he is not well." We could not bring ourselves to call him our brother. He would laugh and run away. When we caught him, he would sit down on the ground and make us lift him up and carry him back to Matthew's car. He was made of something other than flesh; his bones were lead, his blood mercury.

"I can't take more of this," said Matthew.

It ended so swiftly that we were left blinking. He disappeared from the house as usual; Mamamimi scolded Andrew to keep out of it and rang Matthew. He pulled up outside our gates, so back we went past the university, and the zoo where Baba had taken us as kids, then down beyond the old bridge.

This time was the worst, beyond anything. He was wearing one of Mamamimi's dresses, sashaying among construction workers with a sun umbrella, roaring with laughter as he sang.

He saw us and called waving. "*M'sugh*! My brothers! My dear brothers! I am going swimming."

He ran away from us like a child, into the river. He fought his way into those strong green currents, squealing like a child, perhaps with delight, as the currents cooled him. The great dress blossomed out then sank. He stumbled on pebbles underfoot, dipped under the water, and was not seen again.

"Go get him!" said Matthew.

I said nothing, did nothing.

"Go on, you're the only one who likes him." He had to push me.

I nibbled at the edge of the currents. I called his name in a weak voice as if I really didn't want him back. I was angry with him as if he was now playing a particularly annoying game. Finally I pushed my way in partly so that Matthew would tell our mother that I'd struggled to find him. I began to call his name loudly, not so much in the hope of finding him as banishing this new reality. *Raphael. Raphael,* I shouted, meaning this terrible thing cannot be, not so simply, not so quickly. Finally I dove under the water. I felt the current pull and drag me away by my heels. I fought my way back to the shore but I knew I had not done enough, swiftly enough. I knew that he had already been swept far away.

On the bank, Matthew said, "Maybe it is best that he is gone." Since then, I have not been able to address more than five consecutive words to him.

That's what the family said, if not in words. Best he was gone. The bookcase was there with its notice. I knew we were cursed. I knew we would all be swept away.

Oh story, Raphael seemed to say to me. *You just want to be miserable so you have an excuse to fail.*

We need a body to bury, I said to his memory.

It doesn't make any difference; nobody in this family will mourn. They have too many worries of their own. You'll have to take care of yourself now. You don't have your younger brother to watch out for you.

The sun set, everyone else inside the house. I wanted to climb up onto a roof, or sit astride the wall. I plugged the mobile phone into the laptop, but in the depths of our slough I could not get a signal. I went into our hot, unlit hall and pulled out the books, but they were unreadable without Raphael. Who would laugh for me as I did not laugh? Who would speak my mind for me as I could never find my mind in time? Who would know how to be pleasant with guests, civil in this uncivil world? I picked up our book on genetics and walked to the top of the hill, and sat in the open unlit shed of a church and tried to read it in the last of the orange light. I said, Patrick, you are not civil and can't make other people laugh, but you can do this. This is the one part of Raphael you can carry on.

I read it aloud, like a child sounding out words, to make them go in as facts. I realized later I was trying to read in the dark, in a church. I had been chanting nonsense GATTACA aloud, unable to see, my eyes full of tears. But I had told myself one slow truth and stuck to it. I studied for many years.

Whenever I felt weak or low or lonely, Raphael spoke inside my indented head. I kept his books in order for him. The chemistry book, the human genetics book. I went out into the broken courtyard and started to lift the iron bars with balls of concrete that he had made. Now I look like the muscular champion on his netbook. Everything I am, I am because of my brother.

I did not speak much to anyone else. I didn't want to. Somewhere what is left of Raphael's lead and mercury is entwined with reeds or glistens in sand.

*   *   *

To pay for your application for a scholarship in those days you had to buy a scratch card from a bank. I had bought so many. I did not even remember applying to the Benue State Scholarship Board. They gave me a small stipend, enough if I stayed at home and did construction work. I became one of the workmen in the shallows.

Ex-colleagues of my father had found Matthew a job as a clerk in a bank in Jos. Matthew went to live with Uncle Emmanuel. Andrew's jaw set, demanding to be allowed to go with him. He knew where things were going. So did Mamamimi, who saw the sense and nodded quietly, yes. Matthew became Andrew's father.

We all lined up in the courtyard in the buzzing heat to let Matthew take the SUV, his inheritance. We waved good-bye as if half the family were just going for a short trip back to the home village or to the Chinese bakery to buy rolls. Our car pulled up the red hill past the church and they were gone. Mamamimi and I were alone with the sizzling sound of insects and heat and we all walked back into the house in the same way, shuffling flat-footed. We stayed wordless all that day. Even the TV was not turned on. In the kitchen, in the dark, Mamamimi said to me, "Why didn't you go with them? Study at a proper university?" and I said, "Because someone needs to help you."

"Don't worry about me," she said. Not long afterward she took her rusty green car and drove it back to Kawuye for the last time. She lived with Uncle Jacob and the elders. I was left alone in this whispering house.

*   *   *

We had in our neglected, unpaid, strike-ridden campus a mathematician, a dusty and disordered man who reminded me of Raphael. He was an Idoma man called Thomas Aba. He came to Jide and me with his notebook and then unfolded a page of equations.

These equations described, he said, how the act of observing events at a quantum level changed them. He turned the page. Now, he said, here is how those same equations describe how observing alters effects on the macro level.

He had shown mathematically how the mere act of repeated observation changed the real world.

We published in *Nature*. People wanted to believe that someone working things out for themselves could revolutionize cosmology with a single set of equations. Of all of us, Doubting Thomas was the genius. Tsinghua University in Beijing offered him a Professorship and he left us. Citations for our article avalanched; Google could not keep up. People needed to know why everything was shifting, needing to explain both the climate-change debacle and the end of miracles.

Simply put, science found the truth and by finding it, changed it. Science undid itself, in an endless cycle.

Some day the theory of evolution will be untrue and the law of conservation of energy will no longer work. Who knows, maybe we will get faster-than-light travel after all?

Thomas still writes to me about his work, though it is the intellectual property of Tsinghua. He is now able to calculate how long it takes for observation to change things. The rotation of the Earth around the Sun is so rooted in the universe that it will take four thousand years to wear it out. What kind of paradigm will replace it? The Earth and the Sun and all the stars secretly overlap? Outside the four dimensions they all occupy the same single mathematical point?

So many things exist only as metaphors and numbers. Atoms will take only fifty more years to disappear, taking with them quarks and muons and all the other particles. What the Large Hadron Collider will most accelerate is their demise.

Thomas has calculated how long it will take for observation to wear out even his observation. Then, he says, the universe will once again be stable. History melts down and is restored.

My fiancée is a simple country girl who wants a Prof for a husband. I know where that leads. To Mamamimi. Perhaps no bad thing. I hardly know the girl. She wears long dresses instead of jeans and has a pretty smile. My mother's family knows her.

The singing at the church has started, growing with the heat and sunlight. My beautiful suit wax-printed in blue and gold arches reflects the sunlight. Its cotton will be cool, cooler than all that lumpy knitwear from Indonesia.

We have two weddings; one new, one old. So I go through it all twice: next week, the church and the big white dress. I will have to mime love and happiness; the photographs will be used for those framed tributes: "Patrick and Leticia: True Love Is Forever." Matthew and Andrew will be here with their families for the first time in years and I find it hurts to have brothers who care nothing for me.

I hear my father saying that my country wife had best be grateful for all that I give her. I hear him telling her to leave if she is not happy. This time, though, he speaks with my own voice.

Will I slap the walls all night or just my own face? Will I go mad and dance for workmen in a woman's dress? Will I make stews so fiery that only I can eat them? I look down at my body, visible through the white linen, the body I have made perfect to compensate for my imperfect brain.

Shall I have a little baby with a creased forehead? Will he wear my father's dusty cap? Will he sleepwalk, weep at night, or laugh for no reason? If I call him a family name, will he live his grandfather's life again? What poison will I pass on?

I try to imagine all my wedding guests and how their faces would fall if I simply walked away, or strode out like Raphael to crow with delight, "No wedding! I'm not getting married, no way José!" I smile; I can hear him say it; I can see how he would strut.

I can also hear him say, *What else is someone like you going to do except get married? You are too quiet and homely. A publication in* Nature *is not going to cook your food for you. It's not going to get you laid.*

I think of my future son. His Christian name will be Raphael but his personal name will be Ese, which means Wiped Out. It means that God will wipe out the past with all its expectations.

If witchcraft once worked and science is wearing out, then it seems to me that God loves our freedom more than stable truth. If I have a son who is free from the past, then I know God loves me too.

So I can envisage Ese, my firstborn. He's wearing shorts and running with a kite behind him, happy, clean, and free, and we the Shawos live on the hill once more.

I think of Mamamimi kneeling down to look into my face and saying, "Patrick, you are a fine young boy. You do everything right. There is nothing wrong with you." I remember my father, sane for a while, resting a hand on the small of my back and saying, "You are becoming distinguished." He was proud of me.

Most of all I think of Raphael speaking his mind to Matthew, to Grandma, even to Father, but never to me. He is passing on his books to me in twilight, and I give him tea, and he says, as if surprised, *That's nice. Thank you.* His shiny face glows with love.

I have to trust that I can pass on love as well.

EXCERPT FROM *AMONG OTHERS*

Jo Walton

MAY 1st, 1975

The Phurnacite factory in Abercwmboi killed all the trees for two miles around. We'd measured it on the mileometer. It looked like something from the depths of hell, black and looming with chimneys of flame, reflected in a dark pool that killed any bird or animal that drank from it. The smell was beyond description. We always wound up the car windows as tight as tight when we had to pass it, and tried to hold our breath, but Grampar said nobody could hold their breath that long, and he was right. There was sulphur in that smell, which was a hell chemical as everyone knew, and other, worse things, hot unnamable metals and rotten eggs.

My sister and I called it Mordor, and we'd never been there on our own before. We were ten years old. Even so, big as we were, as soon as we got off the bus and started looking at it we started holding hands.

It was dusk, and as we approached the factory loomed blacker and more terrible than ever. Six of the chimneys were alight, four belched out noxious smokes.

"Surely it is a device of the Enemy," I murmured.

Mor didn't want to play. "Do you really think this will work?"

"The fairies were sure of it," I said, as reassuringly as possible.

"I know, but sometimes I don't know how much they understand about the real world."

"Their world is real," I protested. "Just in a different way. At a different angle."

"Yes." She was still staring at the Phurnacite, which was getting bigger and scarier as we approached. "But I don't know how much they understand about the angle of the every day world. And this is definitely in that world. The trees are dead. There isn't a fairy for miles."

"That's why we're here," I said.

We came to the wire, three straggly strands, only the top one barbed. A sign on it read "No Unauthorised Admittance. Beware Guard Dogs." The gate was far around the other side, out of sight.

"Are there dogs?" she asked. Mor was afraid of dogs, and dogs knew it. Perfectly nice dogs who would play with me would rouse their hackles at her. My mother said it was a method people could use to tell us apart. It would have worked, too, but typically of her, it was both terrifyingly evil and just a little crazily impractical.

"No," I said.

"How do you know?"

"It would ruin everything if we go back now, after having gone to all this trouble and come this far. Besides, it's a quest, and you can't give up on a quest because you're afraid of dogs. I don't know what the fairies would say. Think of all the things people on quests have to put up with." I knew this wasn't working. I squinted forward into the deepening dusk as I spoke. Her grip on my hand had tightened. "Besides, dogs are animals. Even trained guard dogs would try to drink the water, and then they'd die. If there really were dogs, there would be at least a few dog bodies at the side of the pool, and I don't see any. They're bluffing."

We crept below the wire, taking turns holding it up. The still pool was like old unpolished pewter, reflecting the chimney flames as unfaithful wavering streaks. There were lights below them, lights the evening shift worked by.

There was no vegetation here, not even dead trees. Cinders crunched underfoot, and clinker and slag threatened to turn our ankles. There seemed to be nothing alive but us. The star-points of windows on the hill opposite seemed ridiculously out of reach. We had a school friend who lived there, we had been to a party once, and noticed the smell, even inside the house. Her father worked at the plant. I wondered if he was inside now.

At the edge of the pool we stopped. It was completely still, without even the faintest movement of natural water. I dug in my pocket for the magic flower. "Have you got yours?"

"It's a bit crushed," she said, fishing it out. I looked at them. Mine was a bit crushed too. Never had what we were doing seemed more childish and stupid than standing in the centre of that desolation by that dead pool holding a pair of crushed pimpernels the fairies had told us would kill the factory.

I couldn't think of anything appropriate to say. "Well, un, dai, tri!" I said, and on "Three" as always we cast the flowers forward into the leaden pool, where they vanished without even a ripple. Nothing whatsoever happened. Then a dog barked far away, and Mor turned and ran and I turned and pelted after her.

"Nothing happened," she said, when we were back on the road, having covered the distance back in less than a quarter of the time it had taken us as distance out.

"What did you expect?" I asked.

"The Phurnacite to fall and become a hallowed place," she said, in the most matter-of-fact tone imaginable. "Well, either that or huorns."

I hadn't thought of huorns, and I regretted them extremely. "I thought the flowers would dissolve and ripples would spread out and then it would crumble to ruin and the trees and ivy come swarming over it while we watched and the pool would become real water and a bird would come and drink from it and then the fairies would be there and thank us and take it for a palace."

"But nothing at all happened," she said, and sighed. "We'll have to tell them it didn't work tomorrow. Come on, are we going to walk home or wait for a bus?"

It had worked, though. The next day, the headline in the Aberdare *Leader* was "Phurnacite Plant Closing: Thousands of Jobs Lost."

*   *   *

I'm telling that part first because it's compact and concise and it makes sense, and a lot of the rest of this isn't that simple.

Think of this as a memoir. Think of it as one of those memoirs that's later discredited to everyone's horror because the writer lied and is revealed to be a different colour, gender, class and creed from the way they'd made everybody think. I have the opposite problem. I have to keep fighting to stop making myself sound more normal. Fiction's nice. Fiction lets you select and simplify. This isn't a nice story, and this isn't an easy story. But it is a story about fairies, so feel free to think of it as a fairy story. It's not like you'd believe it anyway.

Mori Phelps 1979 Very Private. This is NOT a vocab book!

"Et haec, olim, meminisse iuvabit!" Virgil, The Aeneid

WEDNESDAY, SEPTEMBER 5TH, 1979

"And how nice it'll be for you," they said, "to be in the countryside. After coming from, well, such an industrialised place. The school's right out in the country, there'll be cows and grass and healthy air." They want to get rid of me. Sending me off to boarding school would do nicely, that way they can keep on pretending I didn't exist at all. They never looked right at me. They looked past me, or they sort of squinted at me. I wasn't the sort of relative they'd have put in for if they'd had any choice. *He* might have been looking, I don't know. I can't look straight at him. I kept darting little sideways glances at him, taking him in, his beard, the colour of his hair. Did he look like me? I couldn't tell.

There were three of them, his older sisters. I'd seen a photograph of them, much younger but their faces exactly the same, all dressed as bridesmaids and my Auntie Teg next to them looking as brown as a berry. My mother had been in the picture too, in her horrid pink wedding dress—pink because it was December and we were born the June after and she did have some shame— but *he* hadn't been. She'd torn him off. She'd ripped or cut or burned him out of all the wedding pictures after he'd run off. I'd never seen a picture of him, not one. In L.M. Montgomery's *Jane* of *Lantern Hill*, a girl whose parents were divorced recognised a picture of her father in the paper without knowing it. After reading that we'd looked at some pictures, but they never did anything for us. To be honest, most of the time we hadn't thought about him much.

Even standing in his house I was almost surprised to find him real, him and his three bossy half-sisters who asked me to call them Aunt. "Not aunty," they said. "Aunty's common." So I called them Aunt. Their names are Anthea and Dorothy and Frederica, I know, as I know a lot of things, though some of them are lies. I can't trust anything my mother told me, not unless it's checked. Some things books can't check, though. It's no use my knowing their names anyway, because I can't tell them apart, so I don't call them aunt anything, just aunt. They call me "Morwenna," very formally.

"Arlinghurst is one of the best girls schools in the country," one of them said.

"We all went there," another chimed in.

"We had the jolliest time," the third finished. Spreading what they're saying out like that seems to be one of their habits.

I just stood there in front of the cold fireplace looking up under my fringe and leaning on my cane. That was something else they didn't want to see. I saw pity in one of their faces when I first got out of the car. I hate that. I'd have liked to sit down, but I wasn't going to say so. I can stand up much better now. I will get better, whatever the doctors said. I want to run so much sometimes my body aches with longing more than the pain from my leg.

I turned around to distract myself and looked at the fireplace. It was marble, very elaborate, and there were branches of copper birch leaves arranged in it. Everything was very clean, but not very comfortable. "So we'll get your uniforms right away, today in Shrewsbury, and take you down there tomorrow," they said. Tomorrow. They really can't wait to get rid of me with my ugly Welsh accent and my limp and worst of all my inconvenient existence. I don't want to be here either. The problem is that I don't have anywhere else to be. They won't let you live alone until you're sixteen, I found that out in the Home. And he is my father even if I'd never seen him before. There is a sense in which these women really are my aunts. That makes me feel lonelier and further away from home than I ever had. I miss my real family, who have let me down.

The rest of the day was shopping, with all three aunts, but without him. I didn't know if I was glad or sorry about that. The Arlinghurst uniform had to come from special shops, just like my grammar school uniform did. We'd been so proud when we passed the eleven plus. The cream of the Valleys, they said we were. Now that's all gone, and instead they're forcing on me this posh boarding school with its strange requirements. One of the aunts had a list, and we bought everything on it. They're certainly not hesitating about spending money. I've never had this much spent on me. Pity it's all so horrible. Lots of it is special games kits. I didn't say I won't be using them any time soon, or maybe ever. I keep turning away from that thought. All my childhood we had run. We'd won races. Most of the school races we'd been racing each other, leaving the rest of the field far behind. Grampar had talked about the Olympics, just dreaming, but he had mentioned it. There had never been twins at the Olympics, he said.

When it came to shoes, there was a problem. I let them buy hockey shoes and running shoes and daps, for gym, because either I can use them or not. But when it comes to the uniform shoes, for every day, I had to stop them. "I have a special shoe," I said, not looking at them. "It has a special sole. They have to be made, at the orthopaedic. I can't just buy them."

The shop assistant confirmed that we can't just buy them in the school pattern. She held up a school shoe. It was ugly, and not very different from the clumpy shoes I have. "Couldn't you walk in these?" one of the aunts asked.

I took the school shoe in my hands and looked at it. "No," I said, turning it over. "There's a heel, look." It was inarguable, though the school probably thinks the heel is the minimum any self respecting teenage girl will wear.

They didn't mean to totally humiliate me as they clucked over the shoes and me and my built up sole. I had to remind myself of that as I stood there like a rock, a little painful half-smile on my face. They wanted to ask what's wrong with my leg, but I outfaced them and they didn't quite dare. This, and seeing it, cheered me up a little. They gave in on the shoes, and say the school will just have to understand. "It's not as if my shoes were red and glamorous," I said.

That was a mistake, because then they all stared at my shoes. They are cripple shoes. I had a choice of one pattern of ladies' cripple shoes, black or brown, and they are black. My cane's wooden. It used to belong to Grampar, who is still alive, who is in hospital, who is trying to get better. If he gets better, I might be able to go home. It's not likely, considering everything, but it's all the hope I have. I have my wooden keyring dangling from the zip of my cardigan. It's a slice of tree, with bark, it came from Pembrokeshire. I've had it since before. I touched it, to touch wood, and I saw them looking. I saw what they saw, a funny little spiky crippled teenager with a piece of tatty wood. But what they ought to see is two glowing confident children. I know what happened, but they don't, and they'd never understand it.

"You're very English," I said.

They smiled. Where I come from, "Saes" is an insult, a terrible fighting word, the worst thing you can possibly call someone. It means "English." But I am in England now.

We ate dinner around a table that would have been small for sixteen, but with a fifth place laid awkwardly for me. Everything matched, the tablemats, the napkins, the plates. It couldn't be more different from home. The food was, as I'd expected, terrible, leathery meat and watery potatoes and some kind of green spear-shaped vegetable that tastes of grass. People have told me all my life than English food is awful, and it's reassuring that they were right. They talked about boarding schools, which they all went to. I know all about them. Not for nothing have I read Greyfriars and Mallory Towers and the complete works of Angela Brazil.

After dinner, *he* asked me into his study. The aunts didn't look happy about it, but they didn't say anything. The study was a complete surprise, because it's full of books. From the rest of the house, I'd have expected neat old leatherbound editions of Dickens and Trollope and Hardy (Gramma loved Hardy) but instead the shelves are chock-a-block with paperbacks, and masses of them are SF. I actually relaxed for the first time in this house, for the first time in his presence, because if there are books perhaps it won't be all that bad. There were other things in the room, chairs, a fireplace, a drinks tray, a record player, but I ignored or avoided them and walked as fast as I clumsily could to the SF shelf.

There was a whole load of Poul Anderson I haven't read. Stuffed on the top of the As there was Anne McCaffrey's *Dragonquest*, which looks as if it's the sequel to "Weyrsearch" which I read in an anthology. On the shelf below there was a John Brunner I haven't read. Better than that, two John Brunners, no, three John Brunners I haven't read. I felt my eyes start to swim.

I spent the summer practically bookless, with only what I took with me when I ran away from my mother—the three volume paperback *Lord of the Rings*, of course, Ursula Le Guin's *The Wind's Twelve Quarters, Volume 2*, which I will defend against all comers as the best single author short story collection of all time, ever, and John Boyd's *The Last Starship From Earth*, which I'd been in the middle of at the time and which hadn't stood up to re-reading as much as one might hope. I have read, though I didn't bring it with me, Judith Kerr's *When Hitler Stole Pink Rabbit* and the comparison between the child in that bringing a new toy instead of the loved Pink Rabbit when they left the Third Reich have been uncomfortably with me whenever I've looked at the Boyd recently.

"Can I—" I started to ask.

"You can borrow any books you want, just take care of them and bring them back," he said. I snatched the Anderson, the McCaffrey, the Brunners. "What have you got?" he asked. I turned and showed him. We both looked at the books, not at each other.

"Have you read the first of these?" he asked, tapping the McCaffrey.

"Out of the library," I said. I have read the entire science fiction and fantasy collection of Aberdare library, from Anderson's *Ensign Flandry* to Roger Zelazny's *Creatures of Light and Darkness*, an odd thing to end on, and one I'm still not certain about.

"Have you read any Delany?" he asked. He poured himself a whisky and sipped it. It smelled weird, horrible.

I shook my head. He handed me an Ace double, one half of it "Empire Star" by Samuel R. Delany Jr. I turned it over to look at the other half, but he tutted impatiently, and I actually looked at him for a moment.

"The other half's just rubbish," he says, dismissively, stubbing out a cigarette with unnecessary force. "How about Vonnegut?"

I have read the complete works of Kurt Vonnegut, Jr, up to date. Some of it I have read standing up in Lears bookshop in Cardiff. *God Bless You Mr. Rosewater* is very strange, but *Cat's Cradle* is one of the best things I've ever read. "Oh yes," I said.

"What Vonnegut?"

"All of it," I said, confidently.

"*Cat's Cradle?*"

"*Breakfast of Champions, Welcome to the Monkey House . . .*" I reeled off the titles. He was smiling. He looked pleased. My reading has been solace and addiction but nobody has been pleased with me for it before.

"How about *The Sirens of Titan?*" he asked, as I wound down.

I shook my head. "I've never heard of it!"

He set down his drink, bent down and got the book, hardly looking at the shelves, and added it to my pile. "How about Zenna Henderson?"

"*Pilgrimage,*" I breathed. It is a book that speaks to me. I love it. Nobody else I've met has ever read it. I didn't read it from the library. My mother had it, an American edition with a hole punched in the cover. I don't even think there is a British edition. Henderson wasn't in the library catalogue. For the first time, I realised that if he is my father, which in some sense he is, then long ago he *knew* her. He married her. He had the sequel to *Pilgrimage* and two collections. I took them, very uncertain of him. I could hardly hold my book pile one handed. I put them all in my bag, which was on my shoulder, where it always is.

"I think I'll go to bed and read now," I said.

He smiled. He has a nice smile, nothing like our smiles. I've been told all my life that we looked like him, but I can't see it. If he's Lazarus Long to our Laz and Lor, I'd expect to have some sense of recognition. We never looked anything like anyone in our family, but apart from the eye and hair colour I don't see anything. It doesn't matter. I have books, new books, and I can bear anything as long as there are books.

THURSDAY, SEPTEMBER 6TH, 1979

My father drove me to school. In the back seat was a neat suitcase I never saw before, in which one of the aunts assured me is all the uniform, neatly laid out. There was also a leather satchel, which she said is school supplies. Neither of them were scuffed at all, and I think they must be new. They must have cost the earth. My own bag held what it had held since I ran away, plus the books I have borrowed. I clutched it tightly and resisted their attempts to take it from me and put it with the luggage. I nodded at them, my tongue frozen in my mouth. It's funny how impossible it would be to cry, or show any strong emotion, with these people. They are not my people. They are not like my people. That sounded like the first lines of a poem, and I itched to write them down in my notebook. I got into the car, awkwardly. It was painful. At least there was room to straighten my leg once I was in. Front seats are better than back seats, I've noticed that before.

I managed to say thank you as well as goodbye. The Aunts each kissed me on the cheek.

My father didn't look at me as he drove, which meant I could look at him, sideways. He was smoking, lighting each cigarette with the butt of the last, just like her. I wound down my window to have some air. I still don't think he looks the least bit like us. It isn't just the beard. I wondered what Mor would have made of him, and pushed the thought away hard. After a little while he said, puffing, "I've put you down as Markova."

It's his name. Daniel Markova. I've always known that. It's the name on my birth certificate. He was married to my mother. It's her name. But I've never used it. My family name is Phelps, and that's how I've gone to school. Phelps means something, at least in Aberdare, it means my grandparents, my family. Mrs. Markova means that madwoman my mother. Still, it will mean nothing to Arlinghurst.

"Morwenna Markova is a bit of a mouthful," I said, after rather too long.

He laughed. "I said that when you were born. Morwenna and Morganna."

"She said you chose the names," I said, not very loudly, staring out of the open window at the moving patchwork of flat fields full of growing things. Some of them are stubble and some of them have been ploughed.

"I suppose I did," he said. "She had all those lists and she made me choose. They were all very long, and very Welsh. I said it would be a mouthful, but she said people would soon shorten it. Did they?"

"Yes," I said, still staring out. "Mo, or Mor. Or Mori." Mori Phelps is the name I will use when I am a famous poet. It's what I write inside my books now. Ex libris Mori Phelps. And what has Mori Phelps to do with Morwenna Markova and what's likely to happen to her in a new school? I will laugh about this one day, I told myself. I will laugh about it with people so clever and sophisticated I can't imagine them properly now.

"And did they call your sister Mog?" he asked.

He hadn't asked me about her before. I shook my head, then realised he was driving and not looking at me. "No," I said. "Mo, or Mor, both of us."

"But how could they tell you apart?" He wasn't looking at all, he was lighting another cigarette.

"They couldn't." I smiled to myself.

"You won't mind being Markova at school?"

"I don't care. And anyway, you're paying for it," I said.

He turned his head and looked at me for a second, then back to the road. "My sisters are paying for it," he said. "I don't have any money except what they allow me. Do you know my family situation?"

What is there to know? I knew nothing about him apart from the fact that he was English, which has caused me no end of playground fights, that he married my mother when he was nineteen and then ran off two years later when she was in hospital having another baby, a baby that died because of the shock. "No," I said.

"My mother was married to a man named Charles Bartleby. He was quite wealthy. They had three daughters. Then the war came. He went off to fight in France in 1940 and was captured there and put in a prisoner of war camp. My mother left my three little sisters with their grandmother Bartleby, in the Old Hall, the house we've just left. She went to work in an RAF canteen, to do what she could for the war effort. There she met and fell in love with a Polish flying officer called Samuel Markova. He was a Jew. I was born in March 1944. In September 1944 Bartleby was liberated from the camp and came home to England, where he and my mother obtained a divorce. She married my father, who had just learned that his entire family in Poland had been killed."

Had he had a wife and children too? I felt sure he had. A Polish Jew! I am part Polish. Part Jewish? All that I know about Judaism comes from *A Canticle for Leibovitz* and *Dying Inside*. Well, and the bible, I suppose.

"My mother had some money of her own, but not very much. My father left the RAF after the war and worked in a factory in Ironbridge. Bartleby left his money, and his house, to my sisters. When I was thirteen my mother died in an accident. My sisters, who were grown up by then, came to her funeral. Anthea offered to pay to send me to school, and my father accepted. They've been subsidising me ever since. As you know, I married part way through university."

"What happened to Bartleby?" I asked. He couldn't have been much older than my grandfather.

"He shot himself when the girls turned twenty-one," he said, in a tone of voice that closed off further questions.

"What do you . . . do?" I asked.

"They hold the purse-strings, but I manage the estate," he said. He dropped the butt of a cigarette into the ash tray, which was overflowing. "They pay me a salary, and I live at the house. Very Victorian really."

"Have you lived there ever since you ran off?" I asked.

"Yes."

"But they said they didn't know where you were. My grandfather went there and talked to them, all this way." I was indignant.

"They lied." He wasn't looking at me at all. "Did it bother you so much that I ran away?"

"I've run away from her too," I said, which didn't answer his question but which seemed to be enough.

"I knew your grandparents would look after you," he said.

"They did," I said. "You needn't have worried about that."

"Ah," he said.

So then I realised guiltily how my very presence in his car was actually a huge reproach. For one thing, there is only one of me, when he abandoned twins. For another, I am crippled. Thirdly, I am there at all; I ran away. I had to ask for his help—and worse, I had to use the social services to ask for his help. Clearly the arrangements he made for us were far from adequate. In fact, my existence there at that moment demonstrated to him that he is a rotten parent. And, truth be told, he is. My mother notwithstanding, running out on babies isn't an acceptable thing to do—and in fact, as an abstraction, abandoning babies with her is particularly and unusually irresponsible. But I have run away from her too.

"I wouldn't have grown up any other way," I said. My grandparents. The Valleys. Home. "Truly. There was so much about it to love. I couldn't have had a better childhood."

"I'll take you to meet my father soon, perhaps at half term," he said. He was signalling to turn, and we turned between two elms, both dying, and onto a gravel drive that crunched under the car wheels. It was Arlinghurst. We had arrived.

The first thing that happened in school was the fight about chemistry. It's a big gracious house in it's own grounds, looking stately and Victorian. But the place smells like a school, chalk, boiled cabbage, disinfectant, sweat. The headmistress was well-mannered and distant. She didn't give my father permission to smoke, which wrong footed him. Her chairs are too low, I had trouble getting out of mine. But none of that would matter if it wasn't for the timetable she handed me. First, there are three hours of games every day. Second, art and religious education are compulsory. Third, I can have either chemistry or French, and either Latin or biology. The other choices were very simple, like physics or economics, and history or music.

Robert Heinlein says, in *Have Space Suit, Will Travel* that the only things worth studying are history, languages, and science. Actually, he adds maths, but honestly they left out the mathematical part of my brain. Mor got all the maths. Having said that, it was the same for both of us, we either understood it instantly or you might as well have used a drill to get it into our heads. "How can you understand Boolean algebra when you still have problems with the concept of long division?" my maths teacher had asked in despair. But Venn diagrams are easy, while long division remains challenging. Hardest of all were those problems about people doing incomprehensible things with no motivation. I was inclined to drift away from the sum to wonder why people would care what time two trains passed each other (spies) be so picky about seating arrangements (recently divorced people) or, which to this day remains incomprehensible, run the bath with no plug in.

History, languages and science pose me no such problems. When you need to use maths in science, it always makes sense, and besides, they let you use a calculator.

"I need to do both Latin and biology, and both French and chemistry," I said, looking up from the timetable. "But I don't need to do art or religious education, so it'll be easy to rearrange."

The headmistress went through the roof at this, because clearly time-tables are sacred, or something. I didn't listen all that much. "There are over five hundred girls in this school, do you propose I inconvenience them all to accommodate you?"

My father, who has no doubt also read Heinlein, backed me up. I'll take Heinlein over a headmistress any day. Eventually we ended up with a compromise in which I'll surrender biology if I get to take all three of the others, which can be arranged with a little shuffling between classes. I'll take chemistry with a different class, but I don't care about that. It felt like enough of a victory for now, and I consented to be shown my dorm and meet my house-mistress and "new friends."

My father kissed my cheek when he said goodbye. I watched him out of the front door and saw him lighting a cigarette the second he was in the open air.

FRIDAY, SEPTEMBER 7TH, 1979

It turns out to be a joke about the countryside.

Well, it is true in a way. Arlinghurst stands alone in its playing fields, surrounded by farmland. There isn't an inch of land within twenty miles that someone isn't using. There are cows, stupid ugly things, black and white like toy cows, not brown like the real cows we'd seen on holiday. (How now, brown cow? Nobody could talk to these.) They mill about in the fields until it is time for milking then they walk in a line into the farmyard. I figured it out this afternoon, when they let me take a walk around the grounds, that these cows are stupid. Bovine. I knew the word, but I hadn't quite appreciated how literal it could be.

I come from the Welsh Valleys. There's a reason they're called "The Valleys." They're steep narrow glaciated valleys without much flat land at the bottom. There are valleys just like them all over Wales. Most of them have a church and a few farms, maybe a thousand people in the whole valley. That's what they can naturally support. Our valley, the Cynon Valley, like its neighbours, has a population of more than a hundred thousand, all living in Victorian terraced houses, terraced up the hillsides like grapes, stuck together in rows with barely room between to hang out washing. The houses and the people are jammed together, like in a city, worse than a city, except that it isn't a city. But away from those rows, it was wild. And even in them, you could always lift up your eyes.

You could lift up your eyes to the hills from whence cometh your help—a psalm that always seemed self evident to me. The hills were beautiful, were green and had trees and sheep, and they were always there. They were wild, in the sense that anyone could go there at any time. They didn't belong to anyone, unlike the flat farmed fenced-in countryside around the school. The hills were common land. And even down in the valleys there were rivers and woods and ruins, as the ironworks ceased to be used, as the industrial places were abandoned. The ruins sprouted plants, returned to the wild, then the fairies moved in. What we thought would happen with the Phurnacite really did happen. It just took a little longer than we'd imagined.

We spent our childhood playing in the ruins, sometimes alone and sometimes with other children or with the fairies. We didn't realise what the ruins were, not for a long time. There was an old ironworks near Auntie Florrie's house where we used to play all the time. There were other children there, and we'd play with them sometimes, wonderful games of hide and seek, chasing through. I didn't know what an ironworks was. If pressed, I'd have worked out the etymology that someone must have once worked iron there, but nobody ever pressed me. It was a place, a thing. It was all over rosebay willow-herb in the autumn. It was unusual that we knew what it was.

Most of the ruins where we played, in the woods, didn't have names and could have been anything. We called them witch's cottage, giant's castle, fairy palace, and we played that they were Hitler's last redoubt or the walls of

Angband, but they were really old crumbling relics of industry. The fairies hadn't built them. They'd moved in with the green things after people had abandoned them. The fairies couldn't make anything, not anything real. They couldn't do anything. That's why they needed us. We didn't know that. There were a lot of things we didn't know, that we didn't think to ask. Before the people came I suppose the fairies would have lived in the trees and not had houses. The farmers would have put out milk for them, perhaps. There wouldn't have been so many of them either.

The people had come to the Valleys, or rather their ancestors had, at the beginning of the Industrial Revolution. Under the hills there were iron and coal, and the Valleys were the boom towns of their day, filling up with people. If you've ever wondered why there wasn't a Welsh immigration to the New World on the scale of the Irish or Scottish ones it isn't because the people didn't need to leave their farms in the same way. It's because they had somewhere of their own to go. Or at least, they thought it was their own. English people came too. The Welsh language lost out. Welsh was my grandmother's first language, my mother's second language and I can only fumble along in it. My grandmother's family had come from west Wales, from Carmarthenshire. We still had relatives there, Mary-from-the-country and her people.

My ancestors came like everyone else, after iron was discovered, and coal. People started building smelters on the spot, railroads to take it out, houses for workers, more smelters, more mines, more houses until the valleys were solid strips of habitation up and down. The hills were always there between, and the fairies must have huddled in the hills. Then the iron ran out, or was cheaper to produce somewhere else, and while there was still coal mining it was a pitiful remnant of the boom of a hundred years before. Iron works were abandoned. Pits closed down. Some of the people left, but most stayed. It was home by then. By the time we were born, chronic unemployment was a fact of life and the fairies had crept back down into the valleys and taken over the ruins that nobody wanted.

We grew up playing freely in the ruins and had no real sense of this history. It was a wonderful place for children. It was abandoned and grown over and ignored, and once you slipped away from the houses it was wild.

You could always go up the mountain into real countryside, which had rocks and trees and sheep, grey-coated from coal dust and unappealing. (I can't understand how people are sentimental about sheep. We used to shout "Mint sauce!" at them to get them to run away. Auntie Teg always winced at that and told us not to, but we kept on doing it. They'd come down into the valley and knock over dustbins and destroy gardens. They were the reason you had to keep gates shut.) But even down in the valley, running through everything were the seams of trees and ruins running everywhere, through and under and parallel to the town. It wasn't the only landscape we knew. We went to Pembrokeshire on holiday, and up to the real mountains, the Brecon Beacons, and to Cardiff, which is a city, with city shops. The Valleys were home, they were the landscape of normality, and we never questioned it.

The fairies never said they built the ruins. I doubt we asked, but if we had they'd just have laughed, as they did at most of our questions. They were just inexplicably there or, some days inexplicably not there. Sometimes they would talk to us, and other times flee from us. Like the other children we knew, we could play with them or without them. All we really needed was each other and our imagination.

The places of my childhood were linked by magical pathways, ones almost no adults used. They had roads, we had these, they were for walking, they were different and extra, wider than a path but not big enough for cars, sometimes parallel to the real roads and sometimes cutting from nowhere to nowhere, from an elven ruin to the labyrinth of Minos. We gave them names but we knew unquestioningly that the real name for them was "dramroads." I never turned that word over in my mouth and saw it for what it was: Tram road. Welsh mutates initial consonants. Actually all languages do, but most of them take centuries, while Welsh does it while your mouth is still open. Tram to dram, of course. Once there had been trams running on rails up those dramroads, trams full of iron ore or coal. So empty and leaf-strewn, used by nobody but children and fairies, once they'd been little railroads.

It wasn't that we didn't know history. Even if you only count the real world, we knew more history than most people. We'd been taught about cavemen and Normans and Tudors. We knew about Greeks and Romans. We knew masses of personal stories about World War II. We even knew quite a lot of family history. It just didn't connect to the landscape. And it was the landscape that formed us, that made us who we were as we grew in it, that affected everything. We thought we were living in a fantasy landscape when in actually we were living in a science fictional one. In ignorance, we played our way through what the elves and giants had left us, taking the fairies' possession for ownership. I named the dramroads after places in *The Lord of the Rings* when I should have recognised that they were from *The Chrysalids*.

It's amazing how large the things are that it's possible to overlook.

MOVEMENT

Nancy Fulda

It is sunset. The sky is splendid through the panes of my bedroom window; billowing layers of cumulous blazing with refracted oranges and reds. I think if only it weren't for the glass, I could reach out and touch the cloudscape, perhaps leave my own trail of turbulence in the swirling patterns that will soon deepen to indigo.

But the window is there, and I feel trapped.

Behind me my parents and a specialist from the neurological research institute are sitting on folding chairs they've brought in from the kitchen, quietly discussing my future. They do not know I am listening. They think that, because I do not choose to respond, I do not notice they are there.

"Would there be side effects?" My father asks. In the oppressive heat of the evening, I hear the quiet *Zzzap* of his shoulder laser as it targets mosquitoes. The device is not as effective as it was two years ago: the mosquitoes are getting faster.

My father is a believer in technology, and that is why he contacted the research institute. He wants to fix me. He is certain there is a way.

"There would be no side effects in the traditional sense," the specialist says. I like him even though his presence makes me uncomfortable. He chooses his words very precisely. "We're talking about direct synaptic grafting, not drugs. The process is akin to bending a sapling to influence the shape of the grown tree. We boost the strength of key dendritic connections and allow brain development to continue naturally. Young neurons are very malleable."

"And you've done this before?" I do not have to look to know my mother is frowning.

My mother does not trust technology. She has spent the last ten years trying to coax me into social behavior by gentler means. She loves me, but she does not understand me. She thinks I cannot be happy unless I am smiling and laughing and running along the beach with other teenagers.

"The procedure is still new, but our first subject was a young woman about the same age as your daughter. Afterwards, she integrated wonderfully. She was never an exceptional student, but she began speaking more and had an easier time following classroom procedure."

"What about Hannah's . . . talents?" my mother asks. I know she is thinking about my dancing; also the way I remember facts and numbers without trying. "Would she lose those?"

The specialist's voice is very firm, and I like the way he delivers the facts without trying to cushion them. "It's a matter of trade-offs, Mrs. Didier. The brain cannot be optimized for everything at once. Without treatment, some children like Hannah develop into extraordinary individuals. They become famous, change the world, learn to integrate their abilities into the structures of society. But only a very few are that lucky. The others never learn to make friends, hold a job, or live outside of institutions."

"And . . . *with* treatment?"

"I cannot promise anything, but the chances are very good that Hannah will lead a normal life."

I have pressed my hand to the window. The glass feels cold and smooth beneath my palm. It appears motionless although I know at the molecular level it is flowing. Its atoms slide past each other slowly, so slowly; a transformation no less inevitable for its tempo. I like glass—also stone—because it does not change very quickly. I will be dead, and so will all of my relatives and their descendants, before the deformations will be visible without a microscope.

I feel my mother's hands on my shoulders. She has come up behind me and now she turns me so that I must either look in her eyes or pull away. I look in her eyes because I love her and because I am calm enough right now to handle it. She speaks softly and slowly.

"Would you like that, Hannah? Would you like to be more like other teenagers?"

Neither yes nor no seems appropriate, so I do not say anything. Words are such fleeting, indefinite things. They slip through the spaces between my thoughts and are lost.

She keeps looking at me, and I consider giving her an answer I've been saving. Two weeks ago she asked me whether I would like a new pair of dancing shoes and if so, what color. I have collected the proper words in my mind, smooth and firm like pebbles, but I decide it is not worth speaking them. Usually by the time I answer a question, people have forgotten that they asked it.

The word they have made for my condition is temporal autism. I do not like it, both because it is a word and because I am not certain I have anything in common with autists beyond a disinclination for speech.

They are right about the temporal part, though.

My mother waits twelve-point-five seconds before releasing my shoulders and returning to sit on the folding chair. I can tell she is unhappy with me, so I climb down from the window ledge and reach for the paper sack I keep tucked under my bed. The handles are made of twine, rough and real against my fingers. I press the sack to my chest and slip past the people conversing in my bedroom.

Downstairs I open the front door and stare into the breathtaking sky. I know I am not supposed to leave the house on my own, but I do not want to stay inside, either. Above me the heavens are moving. The clouds swirl like leaves in a hurricane: billowing, vanishing, tumbling apart and restructuring themselves; a lethargic yet incontrovertible chaos.

I can almost feel the earth spinning beneath my feet. I am hurtling through space, a speck too small to resist the immensity of the forces that surround me. I tighten my fingers around the twine handles of the sack to keep myself from spinning away into the stratosphere. I wonder what it's like to be cheerfully oblivious of the way time shapes our existence. I wonder what it's like to be like everyone else.

*   *   *

I am under the brilliant sky now, the thick paper of the sack crackling as it swings against my legs. I am holding the handles so tightly that the twine bites into my fingers.

At my feet the flytraps are opening, their spiny blossoms stretching upwards from chips and cracks in the pavement. They are a domestic variety gone wild, and they are thriving in the nurturing environment provided by this part of town. Our street hosts a flurry of sidewalk cafes, and the fist-sized blossoms open every evening to snare crumbs of baguettes or sausage fragments carried by the wind from nearby tables.

The flytraps make me nervous, although I doubt I could communicate to anyone why this is so. They feel very much like the clouds that stream overhead in glowing shades of orange and amber: always changing, always taking on new forms.

The plants have even outgrown their own name. They seldom feed on flies anymore. The game of out-evolving prey has become unrewarding, and so they have learned to survive by seeming pleasant to humanity. The speckled patterns along the blossoms grow more intricate each year. The spines snap closed so dramatically when a bit of protein or carbohydrate falls within their grasp that children giggle and hasten to fetch more.

One flytrap, in particular, catches my attention. It has a magnificent blossom, larger and more colorful than any I have seen before, but the ordinary stem is too spindly to support this innovation. The blossom lies crushed against the sidewalk, overshadowed by the smaller, sturdier plants that crowd above it.

It is a critical juncture in the evolutionary chain, and I want to watch and see whether the plant will live to pass on its genes. Although the flytraps as a whole disquiet me, this single plant is comforting. It is like the space between one section of music and another; something is about to happen, but no one knows exactly what. The plant may quietly extinguish, or it may live to spawn the next generation of flytraps; a generation more uniquely suited to survival than any that has come before.

I want the flytrap to survive, but I can tell from the sickly color of its leaves that this is unlikely. I wonder, if the plant had been offered the certainty of mediocrity rather than the chance of greatness, would it have accepted?

I start walking again because I am afraid I will start crying.

I am too young. It is not fair to ask me to make such a decision. It is also not fair if someone else makes it for me.

I do not know what I should want.

* * *

The old cathedral, when it appears at the end of the avenue, soothes me. It is like a stone in the midst of a swirling river, worn smooth at the edges but mostly immune to time's capricious currents. Looking at it makes me think of Daniel Tammet. Tammet was an autistic savant in the twenty-first century who recognized every prime from 2 to 9,973 by the pebble-like quality they elicited in his mind. Historical architecture feels to me the way I think Tammet's primes must have felt to him.

The priest inside the building greets me kindly, but does not expect a response. He is used to me, and I am comfortable with him. He does not demand that I waste my effort on fleeting things—pointless things—like specks of conversation that are swept away by the great rush of time without leaving any lasting impact. I slip past him into the empty room where the colored windows cast shadows of light on the walls.

My footsteps echo as I pass through the doorway, and I feel suddenly alone.

I know that there are other people like me, most of them from the same ethnic background, which implies we are the result of a recent mutation. I have never asked to meet them. It has not seemed important. Now, as I sit against the dusty walls and remove my street shoes, I think maybe that has been a mistake.

The paper sack rustles as I pull from it a pair of dancing slippers. They are *pointe* shoes, reinforced for a type of dancing that human anatomy cannot achieve on its own. I slide my feet into position along the shank, my toes nestling into the familiar shape of the toe box. I wrap the ribbons carefully, making sure my foot is properly supported.

Other people do not see the shoes the same way I do. They see only the faded satin, battered so much that it has grown threadbare, and the rough wood of the toe box where it juts through the gaps. They do not see how the worn leather has matched itself to the shape of my foot. They do not know what it is like to dance in shoes that feel like a part of your body.

I begin to warm my muscles, keenly aware of the paths the shadows trace along the walls as sunset fades into darkness. When I have finished the last of my *pliés* and *jetés,* stars glimmer through the colored glass of the windows, dizzying me with their progress. I am hurtling through space, part of a solar system flung towards the outer rim of its galaxy. It is difficult to breathe.

Often, when the flow of time becomes too strong, I crawl into the dark space beneath my bed and run my fingers along the rough stones and jagged glass fragments that I have collected there. But today the *pointe* shoes are connecting me to the ground. I move to the center of the room, rise to full point . . .

And wait.

Time stretches and spins like molasses, pulling me in all directions at once. I am like the silence between one movement of music and the next, like a water droplet trapped halfway down a waterfall that stands frozen in time. Forces press against me, churning, swirling, roaring with the sound of reality changing. I hear my heart beating in the empty chamber. I wonder if this is how Daniel Tammet felt when he contemplated infinity.

Finally I find it; the pattern in the chaos. It is not music, precisely, but it is very like it. It unlocks the terror that has tightened my muscles and I am no longer a mote in a hurricane. I am the hurricane itself. My feet stir up dust along the floor. My body moves in concordance with my will. There are no words here. There is only me and the motion, whirling in patterns as complex as they are inconstant.

Life is not the only thing that evolves. My dancing changes every day, sometimes every second, each sequence repeating or extinguishing based on how well it pleases me. At a higher level in the fractal, forms of dance also mutate and die. People call ballet a timeless art, but the dance performed in modern theatres is very different from the ballet that originally emerged in Italy and France.

Mine is an endangered species in the performance hierarchy; a neoclassical variant that no one remembers, no one pays to watch, and only a few small groups of dancers ever mimic. It is solitary, beautiful, and doomed to destruction. I love it because its fate is certain. Time has no more hold on it.

When my muscles lose their strength I will relinquish the illusion of control and return to being yet another particle in the rushing chaos of the universe, a spectator to my own existence. But for now I am aware of nothing except my own movement and the energy rushing through my blood vessels. Were it not for physical limitations, I would keep dancing forever.

*   *   *

My brother is the one who finds me. He has often brought me here and waits with electronics flickering at his temples while I dance. I like my brother. I feel comfortable with him because he does not expect me to be anything other than what I am.

By the time I have knelt to unlace my dance shoes my parents have arrived also. They are not calm and quiet like my brother. They are sweaty from the night air and speak in tense sentences that all jumble on top of each other. If they would bother to wait I might find words to soothe their frantic babble. But they do not know how to speak on my time scale. Their conversations are paced in seconds, sometimes in minutes. It is like the buzzing of mosquitoes in my ears. I need days, sometimes weeks to sort my thoughts and find the perfect answer.

My mother is close to my face and seems distressed. I try to calm her with the answer I've been saving.

"No new shoes," I say. "I couldn't dance the same in new shoes."

I can tell that these are not the words she was looking for, but she has stopped scolding me for leaving the house unaccompanied.

My father is also angry. Or perhaps he is afraid. His voice is too loud for me, and I tighten my fingers around the paper sack in my hands.

"Stars above, Hannah, do you have any idea how long we've been looking for you? Gina, we're going to have to do something soon. She might have wandered into the Red District, or been hit by a car, or—"

"I don't want to be rushed into this!" Mother's voice is angry. "Dr. Renoit is starting a new therapy group next month. We should—"

"I don't know why you're so stubborn about this. We're not talking about drugs or surgery. It's a simple, noninvasive procedure."

"One that hasn't been tested yet! We've been seeing progress with the ABA program. I'm not willing to tfhrow that away just because . . ."

I hear the *Zzzap* of father's shoulder laser. Because I have not heard the whine of a mosquito, I know that it has targeted a spec of dust. This does not surprise me. In the years since father bought the laser the mosquitoes have changed, but the dust is the same as it was millennia ago.

A moment later I hear mother swear and swat at her shirt. The mosquito whizzes past my ear as it escapes. I have been keeping track of the statistics over the years. Mother's traditional approach to mosquitoes is no more effective than Father's hi-tech solution.

*   *   *

My brother takes me home while my parents argue about the future. I sit in his room while he lies down and activates the implants at his temples. Pinpricks of light gleam across his forehead, flickering because he's connected to the Vastness. His mind is wide, now. Wide and broadening; horizons without end. Each pulse of his neurons flares across the thoughtnets to stimulate the neurons of others, just as theirs are stimulating his.

Forty minutes later my grandparents pause by the open doorway. My grandparents do not understand the Vastness. They do not know that the drool pools at his cheek because it is hard to perceive the faint messages from the body when the mind is ablaze with stimuli. They see the slackness of his face, the glassy eyes staring upwards, and they know only that he is far away from us, gone somewhere they cannot follow, and that they think must be evil.

"It isn't right," they mutter, "letting the mind decay like that. His parents shouldn't let him spend so much time on that thing."

"Remember how it was when we were young? The way we'd all crowd around the same game console? Everyone in the same room. Everyone seeing the same screen. Now that was bonding. That was healthy entertainment."

They shake their heads. "It's a shame young people don't know how to connect with each other anymore."

I do not want to listen to them talk, so I stand up and close the door in their faces. I know they will consider the action unprovoked, but I do not care. They know the words for temporal autism, but they do not understand what it means. Deep inside, they still believe that I am just bad mannered.

Faintly, beyond the door, I hear them telling each other how different young people are from the way they used to be. Their frustration mystifies me. I do not understand why old people expect the younger generations to hold still, why they think, in a world so full of tumult, children should play the same games their grandparents did.

I watch the lights flare at my brother's temples, a stochastic pattern that reminds me of the birth and death of suns. Right now, he is using a higher percentage of his neural tissue than anyone born a hundred years ago could conceive of. He is communicating with more people than my father has met in his entire lifetime.

How was it, I wonder, when *Homo habilis* first uttered the noises that would lead to modern language? Were those odd-sounding infants considered defective, asocial, unsuitable to interact with their peers? How many genetic variations bordered on language before one found enough acceptance to perpetuate?

My grandparents say the Vastness is distorting my brother's mind, but I think it is really the opposite. His mind is built to seek out the Vastness, just like mine is attuned to the dizzying flow of seconds and centuries.

*   *   *

Night collides into morning, and somewhere along the way I fall asleep. When I wake the sky beyond my brother's window is bright with sunlight. If I bring my face close to the glass, I can just see the flytrap with the magnificent blossom and the crumpled stem. It is too early to tell whether it will survive the day.

Outside the neighbors greet each other; the elderly with polite nods or handshakes, the teenagers with shouts and gestured slang. I wonder which of the new greetings used this morning will entrench themselves into the vocabulary of tomorrow.

Social structures follow their own path of evolution—variations infinitely emerging, competing, and fading into the tumult. The cathedral at the end of our street will one day host humans speaking a different language, with entirely different customs than ours.

Everything changes. Everything is always changing. To me, the process is very much like waves hitting the tidal rocks: Churn, swirl, splash, churn . . . Chaos, inevitable in its consistency.

It should not be surprising that, on the way from what we are to what we are becoming, there should be friction and false starts along the way. Noise is intrinsic to change. Progression is inherently chaotic.

Mother calls me for breakfast, then attempts to make conversation while I eat my buttered toast. She thinks that I do not answer because I haven't heard her, or perhaps because I do not care. But it's not that. I'm like my brother when he's connected to the Vastness. How can I play the game of dredging up memorized answers to questions that have no meaning when the world is changing so rapidly? The heavens stream past outside the windows, the crustal plates are shifting beneath my feet. Everything around me is either growing or falling apart. Words feel flat and insignificant by comparison.

Mother and father have avoided discussing synaptic grafting with each other all morning, a clear indication that their communication strategies must once again evolve. Their conversations about me have always been strained. Disputed phrases have died out of our family vocabulary, and my parents must constantly invent new ones to fill the gaps.

I am evolving too, in my own small way. Connections within my brain are forming, surviving, and perishing, and with each choice I make I alter the genotype of my soul. This is the thing, I think, the my parents most fail to see. I am not static, no more than the large glass window that lights the breakfast table. Day by day I am learning to mold myself to a world that does not welcome me.

I press my hands to the window and feel its cool smoothness beneath my skin. If I close my eyes I can almost feel the molecules shifting. Let it continue long enough, and the pane will someday find its own shape, one constrained not by the hand of humans but by the laws of the universe, and by its own nature.

I find that I have decided something.

I do not want to live small. I do not want to be like everyone else, ignorant of the great rush of time, trapped in frantic racing sentences. I want something else, something that I cannot find a word for.

I pull on mother's arm and tap at the glass, to show her that I am fluid inside. As usual, she does not understand what I am trying to tell her. I would like to clarify, but I cannot find the way. I pull my ballet slippers from the rustling paper bag and place them on top of the information packet left by the neuroscientist.

"I do not want new shoes," I say. "I do not want new shoes."

SAUERKRAUT STATION

Ferrett Steinmetz

"The sauerkraut is what makes us special," Lizzie explained as she opened up the plastic door to show Themba the hydroponic units. She scooped a pale green head of cabbage from the moist sand and placed it gently into Themba's cupped hands.

She held her breath as Themba cradled it in his palm, hoping: *Please. Please don't tell me that stuff grows everywhere at home.*

Themba ran a dark brown finger along the cabbage's veins, then let loose a sigh of wonder. "That's *marvelous*," he said.

Lizzie puffed out her chest. Themba had passed her final test. At ten years old, Themba was two years younger, six inches shorter, and eight shades darker than Lizzie was, and she'd known him for a record three days and nine hours. That made him her best friend ever.

Themba leaned in through the access hatch to grab for another cabbage, but one of his escorts hauled him back out by the scruff of his red-and-gold kaftan. Lizzie was sure Themba would protest this time, but he ignored them as always. "You grow that stuff in here?" he asked her. "In *space?*"

"Yup," Lizzie said proudly, watching the escorts inspect the hydroponic basin for traps. "Momma says there are thousands of refill stations across the Western Spiral, but only *we* have genuine, home-made sauerkraut—one jar for ten indo-dollars, four for thirty. I know captains who chart an extra point on their jump-charts just to take some of our kim-chi home with 'em, yessiree."

"You gotta tell me how to make this stuff!" Themba stuck a thumb inside the jar of sauerkraut—the escorts had already tested it—and licked the juice off. "I mean, if it's not a trade secret or anything."

"It's pretty simple," Lizzie said—though secretly, she wondered if Momma *would* mind her sharing. "I can show you now, if the stoops don't get in my way."

"Aw, they're good eggs. Come on, fellas, give us some room. It's been three days, it's not like she's going to go all homi on me *now*."

The escorts squeezed reluctantly back out of the station kitchen, a convenience nook just large enough to allow two people to defrost prefabbed meals for the daily guests. Lizzie could see their muscles flex as they squatted on the aluminum cafeteria benches outside, glaring at Lizzie through the serving window.

Themba's escorts creeped Lizzie out; they had wrinkle-free faces that never smiled. They were utterly unlike Themba, whose broad, flat-nosed face was so expressive it flickered from mischievous grins to repentant sadness in the twinkle of an eye. Themba wore colorful, flowing robes, his cornrowed hair dotted with beads; his guards wore crisp, gunmetal-gray uniforms.

"I've never cooked!" said Themba, rubbing his hands together at the unexpected freedom. "All my food gets brought to me. So when I'm staying with the Gineer heads of state, I'll make sauerkraut for them. They'll all ask, 'Where did you learn this amazing recipe?' and I'll say, 'In *space*.'"

"That'll impress them?"

"You kidding? To hear that actual, grown food came from an outpost? In a system with no habitable planets? When I'm done, they'll all be begging to live in space stations."

"Themba, you are *awesome*," laughed Lizzie. "I hope your ship's busted forever."

Themba blushed. "I love it here, but I need to get to my reward."

"What's your reward?"

"I'm gonna be—"

One of the guards stood up, so fast he banged his knee against the cafeteria tables. Themba glanced over nervously.

"It's a secret," he whispered. "A *state* secret. But it's gonna be awesome."

If Themba said it was awesome, Lizzie believed him. Themba was the only visitor to Sauerkraut Station who'd ever understood just how awesome her home was.

It was one of Lizzie's duties to show their guests' children around for the handful of hours it took Gemma and Momma to resupply their ships. Space travel was both expensive and time-consuming, so the kids were spoiled and cranky. Most wrinkled their noses and told her it stank in here, which it most certainly did *not*—Lizzie had lived her all her life, and she was sure she would have noticed any funny smells.

Determined to prove how glorious life in space was, she always took them on the full tour, displaying all the miracles that kept her family alive in the void.

Lizzie took them for a walk all the way around the main hallway, explaining how the central, cigar-like axis rotated to give Sauerkraut Station its artificial gravity. She told them why the station looked like a big umbrella—Lizzie didn't know what an umbrella was, but the dirters always nodded—it was because the axis had a great, solar-paneled thermal hood on the end that shielded them from the sun. That hood simultaneously kept the heat off so they weren't boiled alive *and* generated electricity to keep their servers running—a clever design that her great-great-Gemma had pioneered.

To finish, she showed them the cabbages, which took a lot of time and precious energy to grow.

"We have cabbages at home," they yawned. "Can't we go for a spacewalk? Or watch the ships dock?"

Of course they couldn't go outside. Lizzie only got *her* first spacewalk after months of training—and considering Sauerkraut Station only entertained five ships a week during the busy season, they weren't likely to see any other ships.

So her guests inevitably went down to press their noses against the observation deck window—the only window on the station looking outside. That baffled her; why would anyone want to look at a boring old dust belt? They didn't even know the constellations.

Themba hadn't wrinkled his nose.

Momma had towed Themba's crippled ship down off the edge of the system's gravity well. He'd entered the station with a cautious wonder bordering on reverence. And when Lizzie had showed Themba the banks of magnets that kept the worst of the radiation off, he'd asked all sorts of questions.

When she'd offered to show him the EVAC suits, which Lizzie had never done before, Themba held up his hand to stop her.

"My Dad says tourist stuff's all the same," he'd said. "Ships are ships. What's important is the people who run it. What do *you* do for fun?"

So she'd taken him to the observation deck to point out her Daddy's body. She told him how he orbited by once every forty-seven days, and they always held up a candle for him.

Themba saluted Lizzie's father, real solemn and sad, like a soldier. He didn't tell her it was creepy; instead, he asked what Daddy had been like.

So Lizzie showed him Daddy's constellation. She traced the family shapes on the narrow, scratched porthole of the observation deck: Daddy's bear-constellation, Gemma's turbine-constellation, Momma's battleship. Themba started making up his own constellations until Lizzie explained that you only got to pick your own constellation when you turned thirteen.

He stopped. She'd liked that.

So Lizzie showed him how to make wishes off the microshields, where you said a question out loud three times and if a meteoroid got zapped before you could count to thirty, your wish would come true. And by the time Themba and Lizzie were done, Lizzie's last wish was that Themba would stay here forever.

Even though he was two years younger, he seemed older, because his Dad hauled him around the galaxy on diplomatic trips. He had lots of crazy stories. And though Lizzie wasn't too clear on how life actually *worked* on a planet, Themba never got tired of answering her questions.

Which was why Lizzie would show Themba how to make sauerkraut. Maybe Momma didn't want Themba to know; maybe it was a secret. But Themba was worth Momma's anger.

"Okay," Lizzie said. She put Themba's cabbage head down on the cutting surface and reached for a knife. "You—"

One of Themba's escorts grabbed her wrist. Lizzie cried out, dropping the knife. She looked at the cafeteria—how could they have gotten through the kitchen door that fast?

"Fellas, *fellas*!" Themba shouted, waving them off. "Come on, it's a kitchen, there's knives, what's the problem?"

The escort kicked the knife over to the other, who examined it closely.

"You okay, Lizzie?" Themba rubbed her hand. His fingers were pleasantly warm.

"It's fine," Lizzie said. And really, it was. If his escorts weren't so stupidly paranoid, they'd have let Gemma repair their ship in the mechbay instead of waiting for their own customized mechanics to arrive. And then Themba would have been gone in seven hours, not ninety-one.

"Come on," Themba begged them. "Give me the knife."

The escorts exchanged flat glances. Then they shoved her back into a corner, interposing themselves between Lizzie and Themba, then handed him the knife handle-first.

"I guess that's okay," Themba shrugged. "What do I do with this?"

"Take the cabbage," Lizzie said, craning her head to look out from underneath the escort's armpit. "Cut it in thirds . . ."

Lizzie had never taught anyone before, but even so she thought Themba was a little clumsy. He would have cut himself twice—but his escorts reached out, quick as a meteoroid, to grab the blade before it cut him.

"You're doing well," Lizzie said. Themba smiled. Even with the escorts in between them, it felt—well, special. It was simple work, chopping and canning, but making sauerkraut was like the metal beams that framed the station, fundamental and strong; she'd never shared that part of herself before.

"This is fun," Themba said. "Now I put in, what? Carrots?"

Themba dumped the last of the ingredients into a plastic tub, then proudly hoisted his special sauerkraut.

"What now?"

"Well," she said. "It's gotta ferment."

Themba bit his lip. "How long's that take?" And when Lizzie hesitated, knowing that it was longer than they had, Themba grabbed her arm.

"Promise me you'll keep it," he said, looking absurdly serious. "Keep it here until I come back. Please?"

"I'll have to hide it," Lizzie said. "Otherwise, Momma will sell it."

"Show me where."

They squeezed past the escorts and darted into the tiny airlock to the fermenting chambers, which were kept on a separate circulation vent. As it was, the damp, yogurty-vinegar sour smell almost made Themba topple over.

The chambers were small and cool, stacked with giant plastic tubs that bubbled over with foam-flecked sauerkraut. Lizzie hunted for the perfect space to store Themba's batch. His escorts bumped heads, fighting to peer through the tiny porthole.

"Come with me when I leave, Lizzie," Themba whispered. "They don't want you along, but I bet if I begged they'd bring you."

Lizzie froze; it had never occurred to her that she could go anywhere else. She was going to grow up and die on Sauerkraut Station, just like five generations of Denahues before her.

"Where—where are you going?"

"I'm gonna be a *hostage*," Themba said, and from the dreamy way he said it Lizzie just knew it was the best thing in the whole 'verse. "They'll give me the softest beds and the nicest food and all the games I want while Daddy talks to the Gineer. He says I'll be treated like a king while he's gone, but it could be years. It'll be lonely. With you, we could cook, we could play VR hockey . . ."

Lizzie fumbled for a marker and scrawled a big "T" on the top of Themba's tub.

"You like me that much?"

"Everyone's all stiff where I live," Themba said. "Grab the wrong fork at dinner, they talk for months. But you, you're just . . . cool."

Lizzie blushed as she shoved Themba's tub underneath a pile of well-aged kraut containers. No one had ever called her cool. But now all she could think of was Momma and Gemma, and how they'd just gotten Lizzie up to speed to take her slot on this three-man station. Momma should have hired someone new to take Daddy's place when he'd died five years back. Gemma had harangued Momma enough to get someone new, but Momma was firm: the family would get by without outsiders.

Fortunately, that was when Themba's escorts forced their way through the airlock, running a med-scanner over Themba's body.

For the rest of the day, Themba acted like he hadn't said anything, but Lizzie felt like she'd eaten a sugar bar. By the time she went to bed, she was vibrating with the secret.

Momma combed Lizzie's hair, as she always did before bedtime.

"What's gotten into you, Elizabeth?" Momma asked. "You're all snarls and tangles, and not just in your hair."

Gemma had tried combing once, and even though Gemma was great with engines and cuddles, she was terrible with hair. But Momma was coolly methodical, softly tugging each snarl, and when she was done she left Lizzie with the cleanest, freest hair you could imagine. It was the most soothing feeling, being in Momma's hands.

But ever since Daddy had launched himself into orbit, Momma had gotten brittle. Daddy's death wasn't Momma's fault, Lizzie had understood that even when she was six—Daddy was just a cook, and should never have been out on the hull. But Momma had been dreadful ill thanks to a flu she'd caught from some inbound flight; Daddy had been dumb enough to try and do a woman's job repairing air leaks, and in his haste he'd forgotten to tether himself.

Back then, Momma had hugged; now, she gave orders. The only sign of the old, loving Momma was in that careful combing, and Lizzie was afraid that if she left—or even mentioned leaving—Momma might stop combing her hair.

"You lose someone dear to you, you start making distance," Gemma had told her. "She still loves you, but she's terrible afraid of losing you. You gotta approach her just right, or she'll shut down on you like a crashed server."

Lizzie tried to think of a nice way to put it, but nothing came to mind. So she blurted it out: "Themba wants me to be a hostage."

Momma's brush stopped in mid-stroke. "Does he."

Lizzie leaned back into her Momma, hoping to restart the brushing, but nothing came. So she turned around and said, "He says he wants the company." That didn't seem like enough reason to leave the station, so she added: "He's my best friend, Momma."

"I'm sure he is, Lizzie." Momma was looking at the dented metal of the bedroom wall, like she often did these days.

"I'll need you here," Momma concluded. Lizzie's heart sank—but the brush started moving through her hair again, comforting and careful. "I'll be ordering some hydroponic prefab farms tomorrow morning; you'll need to help install them. And it's time you learned how to pilot."

That was an expected bonus; she'd been bugging Mom to let her learn to fly for years, but Momma said that girls under fourteen shouldn't fly unassisted near a dust belt. It was about as close as the new Momma came to an apology.

"That's real nice of you, Momma," Lizzie said politely.

"Changes are coming," Momma replied, and kissed her on the cheek. Lizzie nearly forgotten what that felt like.

The next afternoon, Themba's special-ordered mechanics docked at the station in a big mil-spec ship that bristled with gun ports. Lizzie had hoped that maybe it would take the techs weeks to fix Themba's ship, but Gemma had already told her it was a simple repair; they just wouldn't let Gemma touch it without a Level IV Gineer security clearance.

Sure enough, six hours after the mechanics arrived, Themba came to say his goodbyes. She squeezed him tight, trying to store the memory away for future nights.

"So you gonna come?" he whispered.

"I can't. My family needs me."

He nodded. "I thought so," he said. "But it's good, I guess. I'm helping my Daddy forge friendships, you're helping your Momma stay in business. Our parents need us. That's good, isn't it?"

Lizzie tried to say yes, but she burst out in tears instead, and then Themba buried his face in her neck. "Come back when you're done?"

Themba put his hand on the bright breast of his kaftan and promised that he would. And then Lizzie watched her best friend of four whole days, eighteen hours, and twenty-three minutes leave.

She hoped she'd see him again, but she doubted it. Things had a way of disappearing in space.

*　　*　　*

The guests at Sauerkraut Station told Lizzie stories of a world without maintenance. It seemed incomprehensible to Lizzie. How could a garden just spring up when you weren't looking?

When she was younger, she'd asked the customers about these worlds, expecting that if she asked enough people then one would eventually relent and admit that yeah, it was all a lie, just like the Vacuum Vipers that Dad had told her nestled inside incautious little girls' spacesuits, waiting to bite anyone who didn't check their EVA suits carefully.

But no; somber businessmen and travelling artists alike assured her that yes, water dripped freely down from the air, and helper faerie-bees flew seeds into every crevice. Gemma had even taken Lizzie down to the rec room, where customers paid money to kick their feet up on one of eight overstuffed foot-rests and pull a rented screenmask down over their heads, to show Lizzie the videos she'd taken of her planetside adventures. It had taken some convincing before Lizzie had believed that it wasn't a special effects trick.

What would it be like to live in a world that could get by without you? Lizzie's world was held together by checklists of chores and maintenance. Lizzie's world *needed* her.

For the first time, though, her needful world didn't feel like enough.

In every room, she found something she'd forgotten to tell Themba. Her daily tasklist became a litany of things she should have said to Themba, a constant ache of wondering what he would have thought.

When she straightened the cramped sliding-cabinet beds of the twelve guest chambers, she would have told Themba of all the crazy things people left behind—ansibles, encrypted veindrives, even a needler-rifle once. When she re-tightened the U-bends of the shower stalls, which provided luke-warm dribbles of water to customers for a nominal fee, she thought about how Themba would have wanted to see the central heating system, would have squirmed into the central axis to look at the boiler. And her worst chore of all would have been a joy with Themba there; normally, Lizzie hated pushing all the spare part bins away from the walls of Gemma's repair bay so she could scan the walls for metal fatigue.

But with Themba, she would have tugged up the heavy metal plate in the floor to expose the hidden compartment full of emergency supplies. Then she would have whispered about the hidden *hidden* compartment below that they never dared open, lest they disturb the dust at the bottom.

Then, afterwards, she and Themba and Gemma would have all clambered into the punctured ship that was crammed edgewise into the beams of the dockbay's ceiling—that contentious collection of parts that Momma called a junker, and that Gemma insisted was a classic waiting to be restored. And Gemma would have hugged them both as she told Themba the story of Great-Gemma and the Pirates.

But that was stupid. Themba's father had brought him to hundreds of planets. Why would he be impressed by a secret compartment? Sauerkraut was a novelty to Themba the first time—but when his hands stung from chopping a hundred heads of cabbage, would he still smile? When his shoulders ached from serving defrosted sausages and Insta-Ryz buns to six-hour guests, would he still want to stay?

Of course he wouldn't. He had chefs now.

And when Momma's voice boomed down from the conning tower to alert her that a new collection of guests was on its way, Lizzie took her place by the station's airlock with new vision. Momma always told her that the guests were weary from nearly a month in the transit-ships—they wanted a happy smile, a home-cooked meal, a touch on the shoulder. Lizzie had seen them as just another chore.

Now, when the airlock hissed and let in that first blast of body-odor-and-ganja laced air, Lizzie sniffed deep. As the guests emerged, stretching their arms and looking around in blink-eyed wonder, Lizzie saw them not as chores, but as people. Where had they come from? Where they were headed *to*, and what would it be like to stand in those strange and beautiful places?

As she drifted off to sleep, Lizzie pressed her face against the air vent, imagining a breeze—a wind stirred by no fan, only the goodness of the world itself. And she longed, *burned*, to feel that wind on her skin, to feel sunshine unfiltered by glassteel faceplates.

She needed to talk to Gemma.

Gemma was busy reducing the leakage on the junker's engine. Still, she dropped down the knotted chain ladder to invite her up into the cramped cockpit—their private talking-to space. Gemma took off her protective face-mask, shook out her long gray hair, and patted the lap of her oily coveralls.

Lizzie curled up into Gemma's hug, resting her boots on the curve of the junker's dashboard. Momma was practical, giving Lizzie the biology-talk of why you never played doctor with the customers—but Gemma was the one who told her how Momma and Daddy had fallen in love and made Lizzie.

"Gemma," she asked, "What was it like, when you ran away?"

"Sounds like someone has a case of Station Fever," said Gemma. "You counted the walls yet, girl?"

"228," said Lizzie.

"Only 228 walls in Sauerkraut Station," Gemma nodded, clucking her tongue in sympathy. "All the walls you've ever seen. And each of those walls feels like it's squeezing you. There's gotta be someplace bigger out there, and you're gonna die if you don't step into it. That it?"

Lizzie nodded eagerly, feeling like Gemma had just opened an airlock inside her.

"Perfectly normal at your age," Gemma concluded. "Is it that kid you liked?"

"Themba."

Gemma waved her hand in the air, like she was trying to clear away smoke. "Themba, whatever. He's not important in the specific—for me, it was a merchant marine. Sea-green hair, storm-gray eyes, all adventure and spitfire. The important thing is that he made me think of *someplace else*. And then I had to go."

"Daddy said you made your Momma furious," Lizzie said.

"Oh, how I did!" Gemma's titanium-gray eyes twinkled. "Left her with just my brother—a two-man crew for a three-man station. It was years before they forgave me."

"I guess it would be mean to leave you with all that work," Lizzie said. But Gemma planted her finger right in the center of Lizzie's chest.

"My happiness shouldn't enter into it, Lizzie," she said firmly. "Only you know what's gonna make you happy. That's why you should go if you need to, Lizzie—you have to follow your own dreams."

Lizzie felt absurdly grateful.

"*But* planets are big and careless," Gemma continued. "I'll tell you what

I told your Momma: You get swallowed up there. There's so much room to spare that people just wander away. They don't need you like station folk do.

"And us spacers are fools down there, Lizzie; you've seen how they make us look in the VDRs. They laughed at me for recycling waste urine, for refusing to bathe more'n once a month, for jumping when the wind whistled. Eventually the loneliness ate me up inside, and I crept back home to take my licks. My family forgave me—that's what families do—but I never forgave myself."

Lizzie thought how easy Themba had made it seem. Gemma pursed her lips thoughtfully, then added:

"I hate to say it, Lizzie, but Themba's probably forgotten you by now."

"Themba would *never* forget me!"

Lizzie hadn't meant to yell. Gemma just nodded wearily.

"That's exactly what I thought about my merchant marine, 'Lizabeth."

Lizzie knew Gemma didn't really mean that. Whenever Gemma talked about the nameless merchant marine who was her Momma's pa, it was always with such a regretful fondness. It was a hurt, Lizzie could tell, but a useful hurt, like the way your muscles ached after a long day of wiping off solar panels.

But Momma must have noticed her loneliness, because within a few days the chores started racking up. Shipments of wiring and water tanks arrived, and Lizzie spent whole days in her EVA-suit tethering vacuum-safe cargo packs to the surface storage hooks.

Then one day she saw a gigantic construct-tug blotting out the stars, a ship big enough to hold whole stations inside its belly, and soon after that a ferry-trawler dragged two huge shiny new rooms towards them, gleaming in the sun. Momma explained that the new hydroponics modules were here, two new rooms and twelve new walls for Lizzie to check.

It was exciting and dangerous work, since adding any new chambers to the station's architecture could cause any number of dangers; hull breaches, orbit eccentricity, brownouts. The last time they'd added a room was well before Lizzie was born.

"Why do we need more hydroponics, Momma?"

"We're gonna need more independence," Momma said. "This'll give us extra oxygen and more food once the shortages start coming."

"What shortages?" But Momma refused to talk about it. Gemma nodded grimly in agreement.

Prepping for the addition was a lot of work: Lizzie and Momma had to go over the hull with electrostatic rags to clear it of grit, and then pushed a layer of fresh sealant over everything so the surface was smooth and ready. Then, all three of them maneuvered the bulky units to the hull carefully so the new units *almost* touched—one bump might cause it to fuse in the wrong place—then clamped and vacuum-welded the metal.

Then the real welding started, which Momma wouldn't let Lizzie do because the torches could burn through the sleeve of an EVAC suit.

Next, they filled the chambers with cheap test helium to see whether there was any leakage, which of course there was, leading to tedious sealant application. And then there was the big danger when they closed down the station for a day; they air-locked off the rest of the station, broke the vacuum-seal on the new rooms, then carefully opened up the old rooms one by one until they were sure the bond would hold and they wouldn't lose any expensive oxygen. Lizzie's ears popped until they pumped in enough fresh O2 to regain equilibrium.

Lizzie was exhausted, because it wasn't like her other chores had stopped. She still had to greet the incoming guests and fill the sauerkraut vats and serve meals. At one point Lizzie fell asleep on the counter, right in the middle of serving dinner. She woke to find Momma, smiling as if she hadn't just put in a twenty-hour day, handing plates of thawed bratwurst to grateful travelers . . . And Lizzie felt shamed for being so weak, even though Momma never mentioned it, that she worked triple-shifts.

When that was done, they had to prime the hydroponics—filling the circulation system with nutrient water, lining the trays with diahydro grit, planting the seedlets. They even installed locks, which was weird; the old chamber never had locks.

On the day of the new hydroponics opening, Lizzie was thrilled to find that Momma had splurged for a sugar-cake. Everyone wore the celebration hats from storage, and Momma gave Lizzie some wonderful news: Lizzie was in charge of all the hydroponics.

"You grew those cabbages better than I could," Momma said proudly. "You got your Daddy's native thumb." That made Lizzie beam with pride, and she stayed up after shutdown cycle tending to the tender shoots of soybeans and oxyvines.

When she harvested her first ear of corn, she went to the observation deck and duct-taped it to the window so Daddy would see it on his next orbit.

Yet every day, she wondered what Themba was doing. She asked Momma about sending him a text, but Momma said intra-planet textbursts were expensive. All their money was tied up in the new hydroponics, anyway.

That was when the Gineer arrived.

Lizzie went to greet the incoming customers, but when the airlocks cycled, it didn't smell of BO and pot; it stank of ozone and WD-40. She started to say, "Welcome to Sauerkraut Station, the homiest place in the stars," like always, but as she did there was a "HUP!" from the inside and ten soldiers came tramping out in a neat line.

It was almost like a dance, the way they came out; each soldier had the same bulging foreheads of Themba's escorts, a sure sign of vat-grown folks. And like Themba's escorts, they wore reflective jet-blue uniforms with plastic gold piping on the shoulders, though these uniforms had a dullness to them; some of them had tiny, ragged holes.

Unlike Themba's escorts, they clasped black needlers. They fanned out before the airlock in a triangle pattern, and when their eyes moved the tip of their rifles followed their gaze, ready to spray death at whatever they saw. Lizzie trembled as those rifle-barrels swept across her, but she locked her knees, determined not to show disrespect to a paying guest.

When they were done, they yelled "CLEAR!" The commander came striding out of the back, as calm as her troops were nervous. She was flat-foreheaded, tight-skinned as a drum, with a long rope of braided red hair tied neatly around her waist. Her suit was spotless, which could have meant she'd never seen combat, but to Lizzie that seemed unthinkable; she was thin, sharp, attendant.

The commander bowed deeply, palms touching.

"Hold no fear, little one," said the commander. "Your reinforcements have arrived, free of charge and ready to sacrifice health for safety. Would you escort me to your mother, Elizabeth, so I might formally inform her of the transfer?"

Lizzie matched the commander's stern politeness. But when Lizzie ushered the commander into the comm room, Momma stiffened. She stood up to her full height to greet the commander—though the top of her head barely reached the commander's neck.

"I thank you for your assistance, commander," Momma said. "But I also regret to tell you that we shan't need it."

"I think you'll find that you will have great need of our aid in the months to come. I have tales of the depredations the Intraconnected Web have inflicted upon defenseless locales. But could I share these cautionary warnings in private, without . . . ?" And the commander jerked her chin towards Lizzie.

"My daughter is my tertiary command structure, and is privy to all conversations," Momma snapped back, which surprised Lizzie. "And while I appreciate what you're trying to do, it'll only tear us apart."

"You know war's been declared, Mrs. Denahue," said the commander. "You chose your position well; you're one of three stations that stand between the Gineer empire and the Trifold Manifest. That's been beneficial for tourism, but when war comes—well, do you *really* think the Intraconnected Web will respect your home-grown capitalism?"

"Actually, it was my great-gramma chose the location," Momma said tightly. "And you know we support the Gineer. But if you surround us with gunships, then you make us not a waypoint, but a *target*. The Web might respect our neutrality, they might not, but they sure as hell will shoot if you contest us. You might win that battle, but we'll lose everything."

"We have a new line of ships specially designed to defend stations such as this," the commander said. "And if something happens, we'll reimburse you for any combat losses . . ."

Momma barked out a laugh. "And then we'll be known as a Gineer station, and be drawn into every war after that. No offense, commander, but you think short-term. My family's been here for five generations; I want it here for five more. I'm not getting drawn in."

The commander pursed her lips. "And if we decide to garrison this station?"

Lizzie didn't know what garrisoning meant, but the intent was clear enough Lizzie froze. But Momma simply looked sad, like she did when they caught customers trying to hack free time from the VDR machines.

"It's that desperate?" she asked. "This soon?"

"We're confident in our chances. But it would help to take this place."

Momma eased her hand down into her pocket, gripping something.

"My faith is in the Gineer," she said. "But my hand is always on the self-destruct switch."

The commander frowned, pulling new creases into pristine skin.

"Look," Momma added quickly, thumping her left breast. "I support you folks, my heart to God. As long as you don't go bandying it about, I'll give you folks six percent off of any refueling costs I have, to give you an edge on that Web menace."

"Twenty."

"Twenty's a lot in wartime. We could—Elizabeth, would you mind fetching the commander some sauerkraut?"

The negotiations took several hours. Momma called Gemma up to help set the terms, leaving Lizzie to serve hot dogs and kraut to the soldiers. But the soldiers didn't relax; they ate like they expected someone to snatch it away from them at any moment, then asked for seconds.

By the time they took off, everyone was exhausted. Momma still took the time to comb Lizzie's hair.

"I hate them," Lizzie said. "They're mean."

"Who?" Momma asked, surprised. "The Gineer?"

"They were mean to you, and mean to Themba. They tried to take our home."

"Actually, sweetie, I meant it when I said the Web are bad news. Themba's people are no better . . ."

"*Themba* wouldn't try to rule our station."

Momma shrugged. "We don't choose allies," she said. "That's how we weather storms. Some day you'll understand."

Still, Lizzie felt her hatred of the Gineer burning in her. They were cruel, cruel people, and suddenly she feared for Themba.

* * *

Over the next few weeks, traffic picked up and ships docked every day, carrying harried-looking people away from the upcoming war. Momma had to start rationing fuel.

Predictably, the Gineer started shouting when Momma said she could only spare enough fissionable material to get them to Swayback Station, a mere five systems over. And when they stopped shouting they started begging, thrusting handfuls of cash at Momma, certain that everything was for sale. But Momma couldn't afford to stock up too heavily on any one currency.

The Web folks were disappointed, but took the news with a grim resignation. They were used to shortages.

Web or Gineer, though, every guest was desperate for food—especially when Lizzie explained that sauerkraut didn't go bad. They bought huge jars, so Lizzie had to stay up late at night chopping more cabbage.

But the Web folks seemed disheartened at having to spend money for food; they'd sigh, their pockmarked faces faded to a pale, overmilked coffee color thanks to weeks locked inside darkened ships.

"The Intraconnected used to provide for its citizens," they said, gesturing to their families huddled miserably behind them. "I'm a stamp-press mechanic, not a soldier! They tried to make me switch tasks. They said my children would be provided for in the unlikely event of my sacrifice—but I couldn't. I couldn't risk it . . ."

They were so polite, so peaceful, so like Themba, that Lizzie gave them extra dollops of sauerkraut.

The Gineer were pushier. Their smooth faces were plastered with makeup, men and women alike, pancaking their cheeks to hide the blemishes that had cropped up once they couldn't get their weekly gene-treatments. Lizzie didn't see anything wrong with a pimple, but tell that to the Gineer. They held up suitcases packed with useless stuff—gameboxes and electric hair-curlers—and lamented that *this* was all they could carry.

Yet in their suitcases they carried photos of their families. They were eager to tell Lizzie stories about the beautiful house they'd saved for, the beloved husband they'd negotiated so cleverly for to get their marriage authorization. They stroked the pictures with their fingers when they talked about the past, as if they were rubbing a genie's lamp for a wish—and then told Lizzie how the house had been bombed to splinters, the husband crunched under rubble.

Lizzie tried to tell herself that the Gineer had it coming. But then she imagined losing *her* home, seeing *her* Momma dead, and her anger dissolved into pity.

"You can't listen to their stories, Lizzie," said Momma. "It takes too much time. We need to get them out of the station as soon as possible."

Then there were the soldiers. Whether they were Web or Gineer, they were all lean-limbed, clean-cut, eager; they each told Lizzie how the other side had started it, and they pumped their fists at the idea of dispensing proper justice.

Lizzie bit her lip when the Gineer soldiers trash-talked the Web. Smart-mouthing was bad for business.

After a few months, a sour-looking Gineer with a bushy white mustache limped out of the airlock. His patched white suit hung in unflattering rags off his stick-thin frame. He chomped at a ganja cigar with malice, his wrinkled cheeks pulling in and out like a pump.

He sniffed the air and scowled.

"Smells like ass in here," he said.

"I've lived here all my life," Lizzie shot back, forgetting to be polite. "And if there was a smell, I would have noticed."

The man chuckled, bemused; it set Lizzie's hackles on edge. "You vacuum rats are so superbly *cute*," he said, ruffling her hair. "I'm Doc Ventrager. You must be my apprentice, Elizabeth. Inform your Momma of my presence, and update her that I shan't physic anyone in this sauerkraut fart of a place until I get a fresh deodorizer in my quarters."

Momma was slumped over her comm unit, half asleep. "That's right," she said, gulping a cup of tea. "I forgot he was arriving. It's time you learned medicine, Lizzie; in these times, it's good to have a sawbones handy. From now on, your spare time will be spent with Doc Ventrager."

Lizzie nearly suffocated from the unfairness of it all. "But I was supposed to learn how to *fly*!"

"Circumstances have changed, and so must you, Elizabeth. Instead of paying us rent, the doc is earning his keep teaching you to set bones—and you'll both do good business here, sadly enough. Now show him to the medbay."

Though Lizzie had dutifully run their syscheck routines once a month, she had no idea what all of the headsets and plastic wands in the medbay actually did—but judging from the harrumphing noises Doc Ventrager made as he picked them up and slapped them back down, he wasn't impressed. Momma stood behind him anxiously, chewing her lip. The Doc had Lizzie unlock the doors to the medicine cabinet, then peered in at the neat rows of antibiotics, opiates, and sutures.

"Well, at least *that's* well-stocked," he said.

"My great-grandma installed all this herself, after the pirates came," Lizzie protested. "It all works."

He flicked ash on the floor. "Thank the stars that despite their predilection for genegineering, the Gineer haven't altered the core organs of the human body in the past century." He turned to Momma. "Install that deodorizer and give me a free hand over pricing, and I'll educate your offspring with these antiques."

"Sold," said Momma. Lizzie said nothing. She wasn't sure she wanted to be under Doc Ventrager's tutelage.

As it turned out, Doc Ventrager had brought his own equipment, and he expected Lizzie to carry it all for him. He pointed out where the leather satchels and tanks should go as Lizzie struggled under their weight. As she ferried them out from the ship, Doc Ventrager seemed to sum up everything that was wrong about Gineer folks—even if Ventrager's pockmarked face meant he wasn't exactly a normal Gineer.

The next morning, she checked the hydroponics and then went to the medlab. "Right," the Doc said. He pointed to a tank, where child-sized things with gray, wrinkled flesh floated in a stinking green fluid. "Let's see what you're made of. Fish one out, deposit it 'pon the table."

They were so small that at first Lizzie thought they *were* children—and then she realized their ears and noses were funny. Lizzie ran her palm across the stiffened flesh, feeling its hard, horned hands, its antenna-like ears, the little snippet of flesh on its butt that looked like a leftover from a bad vacuu-forming job.

"What are these?" she asked.

"Pigs," said the Doc. "A lot cheaper than anatomy clones, that's for damn sure."

She frowned. "I thought you were supposed to teach me about humans."

"Pig bones and organs are close enough to hum-spec for the rudiments of injury repair," the Doc said, absent-mindedly cleaning a sharp knife on his gown. "You know how to stitch a wound? To set a bone?"

"No."

He handed her the knife. "Time you learned. Now cut."

* * *

Doc Ventrager was a hard but efficient taskmaster; Lizzie learned that he'd spent years training girls and boys at stations all around the 'verse.

"You're damn lucky," he said, after a long day treating simulated decompression injuries. "Most kids have to learn this all in theory. They can't call me when someone's EVA suit rips; it'd take three weeks to get there. So their first major field operation is on their dying Momma—holding her down while she's thrashing, shrieking, soaked crimson in blood . . ."

Lizzie sensed the test buried in the Doc's words; he was trying to frighten her with thoughts of her Momma. She said nothing.

The Doc nodded and took a long drag off of his reefer cigarette, blowing the sweet smoke into the room to overwhelm the "gangrenous reek" he smelled.

"But you, missy," he said, tipping his cigar at her, "Will acquire a chance to watch the *real* show. By the time this conflict's ebbed its course, you shall be qualified to teach."

She found out what he meant when the first Gineer warship arrived, one engine nearly shot to splinters.

Gemma immediately started working up a repair estimate, but the sergeant was more interested in cornering Doc. "We received some specially withering fire in a rear-guard action," he explained. "We had to escape before resupplying, and so several soldiers have severe infections. What's the charge to cleanse gangrene?"

"Allow me a gander," the Doc said, looking satisfied for the first time since Lizzie had known him. Doc walked, preening, into the ship, but Lizzie almost threw up from the smell.

Twenty soldiers rested on pallets against the wall, most with broken limbs that had healed in horrid ways. They bit down on pieces of plastic, trying not to shriek; the last of the painkillers had been used up weeks ago.

"Oh, that's a *fine* mess," the Doc said, rubbing his hands together. "The quote is one-ninety per head."

"*One-ninety?*" the sergeant said. "That's three times normal rate."

"You possess superior alternatives?" the Doc said. "No. You do not. You can sew 'em up now and have 'em heal en route to the next battle . . . or you can keep your funds walleted and remove them from your roster. Either way's acceptable to me."

"One-ninety's blackmail."

"Excuse me," Lizzie said politely, ostensibly to Doc Ventrager but speaking loud enough that the sergeant could overhear her, "Don't forget that Momma said the Gineer get eight percent off at Sauerkraut Station."

"I never heard of that. Even if I had, it wouldn't apply to me."

"You're on the station, aren't you?"

"Goddammit," he said. "I will speak with your Momma." But didn't; instead, he went down to one-seventy. Lizzie felt a malicious price at seeing the Doc's greed quashed.

And she felt pride when she cleaned her first batch of wounds. Though she'd drained pus on the dead pigs, Lizzie hadn't been sure how she'd take to it once she was working on live men. Judging from the sergeant's pleased reactions, she did a fine job.

The Doc grumbled at having to work for such low rates, snarling at everyone like their injuries were their own damn fault. "You went to war," he snapped. Lizzie, on the other hand, tried to be nicer, even if they were stupid, Themba-hating soldiers.

More ships came in, Web and Gineer alike, each carrying loads of injured people, so fast that Lizzie almost forgot to tend to the hydroponics. She diagnosed complications arising from welding burns, set broken legs from failed rig-drops, irrigated chemical lung-burns, treated vacuum explosions. When she rinsed off the cabbages, flecks of blood washed off her hands.

She wanted to take pleasure in the Gineer soldiers' agony, telling herself that it was just punishment for picking on the Web. But all soldiers screamed when they were hurt, and when they were dying they all wanted to talk to their Momma or their brother or their husband. They all wanted to see their families one last time.

Lizzie cried so much, she felt like her whole body was drying up. But never in front of the soldiers.

Momma combed her hair, told Lizzie how proud she was. "But you have to get the Doc to work faster, Lizzie," she said. "They have to be out the next day."

Lizzie hated letting down Momma, but if she rushed Doc Ventrager then people died. When she was alone, she squeezed her fists tightly enough to leave half-moon cuts in the palms of her hands.

After a few months of surgical assistance, the Doc handed off the minor operations to Lizzie. The Doc made it clear that even though she was doing doctor duties now, any profits from her surgeries went to him. That was better; surgery was like any other repair work. You took care, and measured twice before cutting once. The fact that she'd spent four hours a day in surgery for the past five months helped—and now she could go at her own speed.

Still, the soldiers always panicked when the twelve-year-old girl hooked them up to the anesthetizer. She reassured them that this was nothing, just removing a slug buried next to a lung, she'd done it twenty times before. And if they struggled against the straps, their fellow soldiers laughed and said, *hey, man, haven't you heard about the Angel of Sauerkraut Station? Settle down, man, she makes miracles.*

But no matter how busy things got, every night Momma brushed Lizzie's hair.

"Those ships are deathtraps, Momma," she complained, anguished. "There's no supplies; they get cooped up in there, stew in their own disease. Why don't they just build one big ship with a medlab?"

"One atomic bomb would take it out," she said. "Or heck, one kamikaze run. Spaceships are fragile, interconnected—like bodies, really. The more chambers you add, the more possibility that one hit ripples across all of them."

"But . . ."

Momma pursed her lips in disapproval. "Little ships are easy to churn out, Lizzie. They let you land soldiers across a wider area. They're built cheap and disposable, to carry cheap and disposable cargo."

A thought occurred to Lizzie. "We've had ships full of Web soldiers," she said. "And ships full of Gineer."

Momma smiled in approval. "You noticed."

"But never at the same time."

"Interstellar ships are very slow," she said. "The chances of two enemy fleets showing up on the same day are slim."

"But if they did?"

Momma kissed Lizzie on the head. "Why do you think I've been riding you so hard to get everyone out of the station?"

That thought kept Lizzie up at nights. But not for too long, because between the surgeries and the sauerkraut and the hydroponics, Lizzie was working eighteen-hour days. She slept deep.

She couldn't sleep long, though; the station was so packed with folks that their groans kept her awake. They slept fitfully in the hallways, with their heads on their backpacks, and when they woke it was always with a scream. And when she woke, startled, Lizzie smelt the fresh stench of infected wounds, body odor, and—yes, there it was—sauerkraut wafting through the vents. Its briny scent was stark against all the other recycled smells.

The Doc was right. Sauerkraut Station *did* smell. She hated him for revealing that. And she hated the way he kept raising his prices.

"I possess a mere two hands," he said after sending another Web soldier back to her doom. "As such, my time's at a premium."

"It'd take you one hand and three minutes," Lizzie shot back. "All that girl needed was a proper implantation of bowel sealant."

Lizzie was surprised at how blunt she was with Doc—but she was doing half the work these days, and most of the trickier stuff.

Doc just looked irritated. "Why shouldn't I make it worth my while?" he asked. "I'm an old man. War's the only time I can fill my coffers."

"I have to tend to the hydroponics," Lizzie said, snapping off her surgical gloves. She made her way down to the lounge where the wounded Web soldiers keened. Their sergeants fed them watered-down painkillers—which wouldn't stop their ruptured bowels from flooding their bodies with infection.

They were all bald, dark-skinned. It was like seeing a row of Thembas, sweating in agony.

"Hush," she said, kneeling down, taking the stolen hypodermic of sealant out from under her shirt. "I'll fix you."

The look in their eyes was so pathetically grateful that it would be worth Momma's anger.

*　　*　　*

The Doc had dragged Lizzie to the comm tower by her ear.

"The girl's *undercutting* me!" he cried to Momma. "She's working for free! The Web soldiers are waiting for *her* to treat them!"

Lizzie stood tall, ready for the slap. Momma had only hit her twice in her life, both times for being careless around vacuum—but she'd never disobeyed anyone so flagrantly before.

Instead, a curl of a smile edged around Momma's mouth.

"It's free work," she said. "She's an apprentice, no?"

Doc's face flushed. "Yeah—but . . ."

"She's getting extra medical practice in. That's why I brought you on board, you remember—to teach her?"

"Not at *my expense*! I didn't come here to get into competition, goddammit—I arrived with the intent of a monopoly!"

"I never promised you'd be the only doctor here," Momma said coolly. "I promised you free room and board as long as you served as *a* doctor. Check your contract."

"That's letter of the law," the Doc snapped. "That's *planetary* talk. I deserve better than—"

"I've been quite happy with your service here, Mister Ventrager," Momma said, cutting him off. "But if you're not satisfied, there's no time frame to your contract."

Doc Ventrager's hands twitched, as though he was thinking of taking a swing at Momma. Momma's hand dropped to her taser.

"Fine," he said, biting down so hard on his cigar that it snapped in half. "I hereby proffer you my summary resignation."

"Best wishes, Mister Ventrager," Momma said pleasantly to the Doc as he stormed out of the comm room.

Lizzie stepped forward to wrap her arms around Momma, but Momma looked suddenly solemn. "Well, Lizzie," she said. "You're the ship's doctor, now. Are you ready?"

Lizzie wasn't sure. But she realized she hadn't left herself another choice.

*　　*　　*

The irony was that within weeks, Lizzie was charging prices as bad as Doc Ventrager's. But that wasn't her fault; there just wasn't the medicine.

The trade routes had dried up. The freighters told her that pirates and privateers were running rampant. Both Web and Gineer officials complained bitterly whenever the pirates struck—but everyone knew that the pirates were only allowed to operate if they gave a cut to their sponsoring government, and the privateers carried brands authorizing them to steal.

Thankfully, after what Great-Gemma had done to them long ago, the pirates wouldn't touch Sauerkraut Station. But Momma wondered how long *that* age-old story would keep the pirates at bay—especially now that things were getting desperate.

Meanwhile, Lizzie bargained hard on the rare occasions she found a merchant with a case of Baxitrin or Rosleep. She got it for what passed for a good price these days. Lizzie hated sending poverty-stricken soldiers off with untreated wounds, but Lizzie found it was easier to set a price and refuse anyone who couldn't pay. When Lizzie chose who to subsidize that week, it made her responsible for the dead.

Food was scarce, too. The Web soldiers told rumors of other refill stations staffed by skeletal families, reduced to trading away fissionable materials in exchange for a case of protein bars. Lizzie tended to the vegetables in the hydroponics chambers with extra-special care, grateful for Momma's planning.

Occasionally, Lizzie stun-tagged hungry soldiers who pried at the food chamber locks—mostly Gineer scoundrels, as she'd expected. She lectured the Web troopers, though, sending them back thoroughly ashamed.

Fortunately, there were fewer ships. The war seemed to be spreading out. But the soldiers were getting meaner.

In the beginning, they'd all been fresh-faced and kind, talking about home with a wistful attitude; these new soldiers' faces were hidden under grizzled beards and puckered scars. All they talked about was war.

The Gineer soldiers shouted at her because this God-damned dry waste of a station had no alcohol to buy. The Web yelled because where had the Angel of Sauerkraut Station been when Ghalyela took a bullet to the head?

Lizzie tried to be nice, but "nice" just seemed to slide right off of them. They'd lost something vital out there.

Both sides threatened her when Lizzie tried to explain that she they had to pay for the Baxitrin. The Web grumbled, but the veterans were quick to explain that this was the Angel of Sauerkraut Station; Lizzie had done work for free, back when she could. They pulled their friends away with an apology.

The Gineer soldiers, however, had only known her as Doc's assistant. And Doc Ventrager's cruelty had become legendary.

"I can give you a six percent discount," she always explained, looking as wide-eyed and kid-startled as she could. "But there's just not enough to go around. You understand, don't you?"

That worked until a soldier with a head wound took a swing at her.

Fortunately, Momma taught her how to use a stun gun back when she was six. Lizzie pressed her back against the wall as the other eight wounded soldiers looked dully at the twitching man on the ground, then looked at Lizzie as she frantically tried to reload her stunner—

Finally they laughed, a scornful mirthless cough of a thing.

"Punked by a *kid*," they chuckled, helping their friend up. "No wonder this asshole needs medical attention."

They joked about how maybe Freddie could get beaten up by a teddy bear for an encore. But not a one of them seemed to think there was anything wrong with trying to beat up Lizzie.

Shaken, Lizzie worked on that whole troop for free, handing out precious supplies like they were sauerkraut.

She'd apologized to Momma for using up so much medicine at a net loss. Momma just hugged her. Lizzie froze with the newness of it all; she couldn't remember the last time she'd smelled Momma's hair.

"It's getting bad," Momma agreed. "If I could, I'd install a deadman's switch to dump knockout gas into the chambers to keep you safe, but . . ."

"Nobody has any," Lizzie finished.

"It could be worse," Momma said, putting the best face on it. "Imagine what would have happened if Doc Ventrager had stayed."

Still, Lizzie alternately hated herself for being paranoid, then hated the station for requiring paranoia. Lizzie counted the people in the hallways now, moved quickly from room to room so she'd never be too outnumbered; she squeezed her taser's rubberized grip until the bare metal poked through. She sighed with relief every time they got the latest batch of ships out beyond the Oort cloud.

She was trying to catch up on sleep before the next patrol ship of soldiers arrived, when she woke to a sizzling *pop*. Her hair rippled; a soft current buzzed through her. The vent next to her bed puffed stale ozone and wheezed to a halt.

When she opened her eyes, there was nothing to see. *Did that current blind me?*

Then she heard the awful silence, a void so utterly complete it took a moment to put a name to it:

The motors had stopped.

There were no creaks from the gyros, no hiss of water through the pipes, no hum from the meteoroid shields. It was the sound of space, a horrid nothing, dead and empty in a place that should have a million parts moving to keep her alive.

"Momma?" She tried to yell, but her mouth had gone dry.

Lizzie fumbled at the latches of her emergency supply case to get a flashlight, banging her knees. *This is a mechanical failure*, she told herself; *we'll get this fixed, and everything will be fine.* Except there was no light reflected down the hallways. The walls were shiny metal, each room normally ablaze with control panels and LEDs; she saw not a glimmer.

She clicked the flashlight on. The LED stayed dark.

"*Momma!*" This time, it was a shriek.

"Circuit-friers!" came Gemma's voice, echoing from down the hall. "Gotta be pirates—goddammit, nobody's supposed to *use* those on civilian targets!"

"Our systems are toast, Lizzie," Momma yelled from the control tower. "Even the self-destruct's dead. I'm going for the box."

"What box?" Gemma asked, her voice sharp. "Oh—no, love, too soon. Don't show your hand before we hear what they have to say."

Lizzie swallowed back bile. She reached out and wandered forward, hoping to hug Gemma, but without light the echoes in the hallways went every which way.

There was the dull *clank* of hull bashing hull. Lizzie was flung into the opposite wall. That wasn't a gentle docking, when computers guided you in with micromovements; this was manual dock, a hard impact that crushed airlock collars and risked depressurization. The central gyros creaked in protest.

Lizzie tried to make her way to the conn tower, but everything was jumping around in the dark. She followed the walls as best she could, but the distances seemed infinitely large. All the while Gemma yelled *stay calm, we can talk . . .*

More clanking. A hiss. She wasn't by the conn tower, she'd blundered to the airlock. She turned and ran, but a set of white-hot flashlight beams skittered along the walls, targeting her. Something exploded against the wall, sending slivers of shrapnel into her legs—

"It's a kid!" someone yelled. "No fire! No fire!"

Someone grabbed her shoulders, wrenched her arms behind her back. Just before they pulled the hood over her head, she saw the camo-green uniform of a Web soldier.

*   *   *

The Web searched the halls with IR detectors, looking for other guests. Gemma, Momma, and Lizzie sat in the cafeteria with their hands crossed primly on their laps, pointedly not looking at the soldiers who aimed needle-jets at their hearts.

When the soldiers smashed the locks off the kitchen cabinets, it hurt Lizzie like a blow; she'd installed those locks. Momma winced, too. Lizzie wanted to protest as the gaunt soldiers reached in with skeletal hands and chomped the raw cabbages with glee, but she didn't dare. In the harsh glare of the portable spotlights, the soldiers assigned to guard them looked envious and angry; they couldn't keep their eyes off of the dancing shadows in the next room, where food was being wolfed down. And when they looked at Lizzie and Gemma and Momma, who were skinny but not emaciated like they were, their dark brows narrowed.

The commander, a leonine black woman with gray streaks in her hair, walked in. "Place is clear," she said to the guards. "Get in there and get your bellies full. I'll talk to our newest citizens."

The commander had the ketone-scented breath of a starving woman, yet she pulled up a chair as though she had all the time in the world.

"Muh—maybe you should eat first," Lizzie said.

The commander smiled and stroked Lizzie's hair. Her touch was light, delicate, comforting; a mother's touch.

"Bless you, child," she said. "I'm afraid that yes, we will be eating your food. That's a philosophy you're going to have to learn."

Momma scowled. "I take it the war's not going well."

"We're staging a tactical retreat. This way-station has been useful, but at this stage we can't afford it to benefit our enemy. If we just leave you here, you'll give our enemy fissionables, food—we can't have that."

Behind her, her soldiers looted the kitchen. The new arrivals dug into the tubs of sauerkraut with both hands, shoving their mouths full of shredded cabbage with a fierce and frightening satisfaction. The ones with full bellies had begun toting the remaining food supplies back to the airlock, moving quickly.

"We won't give them anything," Lizzie begged. "We've been rooting for you, we don't want to help those awful Gineer . . ."

The commander smiled wearily. "I know you mean that, child, but you can't enforce it. Refuse to sell it, and they'll take it. They're as desperate as we are. We can't afford to leave you here."

"So you're going to kill us?" Momma asked, putting her arm around Lizzie.

"Despite the Gineer propaganda, we're not barbarians," the commander snapped. "My troops will strip this outpost to bare metal—but we'll take you with us. We'll escort you to the nearest free Web holding where you'll be safe."

"In between combat missions? That could take years," Gemma said.

"The Web's more efficient than you give us credit for. The good news is that we'll consider your ship's materiel your entry fee to the Intraconnected Collective—you're citizens now. It'll be a better life, child; no more worrying about air, food, or clothing." She ruffled Lizzie's hair, as though to prove what a wonderful world it would be. "Just as you provided for us today, we will provide for you. I'll personally recommend you for a surgeon's career when you hit planetfall."

Lizzie felt like she'd been punched in the chest. She'd had dreams about leaving, yes—but that left Sauerkraut Station where she could come back to it. The commander was talking about forced relocation, putting her in a place full of strangers, and taking everything she'd loved as payment.

The soldiers smashed in the door to the fermentation chamber. Momma and Gemma blinked back tears. Lizzie knew why; Momma had installed that airlock when she was Lizzie's age, the first time Gemma had trusted her with the welder.

Everything in this station was her birthright, purchased by one Denahue and installed by another. The Web would take away this history to give her someone else's hand-me-downs. And everything that five generations of Denahues had built would be so much floating debris.

Choking back tears, Lizzie watched as the soldiers hauled the tubs of sauerkraut out—and then she saw it.

A small container with a scrawled "T."

"NOT THAT ONE!" Lizzie yelled, leaping off the bench before anyone could stop her.

She tackled the soldier, sending a stack of tubs clattering to the floor; she clutched Themba's sauerkraut and to her chest.

The commander bent her wrists back to make her let go; another soldier took it away. "THAT'S THEMBA'S!" she yelled. "YOU CAN'T HAVE THAT ONE! I HAVE TO SAVE IT FOR HIM FOR WHEN HE—HE COMES BACK—"

Lizzie was already sobbing as the commander carried her back to the table, dropping her into Momma's arms.

"I understand the challenges of parenting," the commander said stiffly to Momma. "And your daughter's proven herself an ally. But you *will* settle her down, or it's the cuffs." She unholstered a pair of handcuffs, swung them lightly off the end of one finger.

Momma stroked Lizzie's hair, hugging her tight. Lizzie cried until Themba's container was out of sight—and then a thought occurred to her.

"Could you at least relocate us to Themba's house?" she asked. "He's my best friend."

The commander hesitated. "A *Web* citizen was your best friend? Is that why . . . why you were the Angel?"

"Oh yes," Lizzie gushed. "We played together for four whole days. He asked me to come with him—he'll be glad to show me around his home, I just know it."

"It's—an unusual request . . ."

"*Please,*" she begged. She looked to Momma for support, but Momma and Gemma were studying the tops of their boots. "If I can be with Themba again, it's . . . okay."

"I can't promise. But . . . Themba's a common name. Can you give me more details?"

"He was a hostage."

The commander flinched. The handcuffs fell to the floor.

Gemma let loose a choked cry. Momma reached over, and both Momma and Gemma were crying now, and that scared Lizzie worse than anything.

"Sweetie . . ." The commander reached out to take Lizzie's hands. "We gave our innocent sons to the Gineer as a token of our good will. We thought showing them our beautiful children would help them deal in good faith.

"And . . . when the Gineer broke the treaties, they probably shot the hostages. That's how hostages work."

Betrayed, Lizzie looked to Gemma and Momma. "You *knew?*"

"She said 'probably,' love," Gemma said, sniffling. "We did news-scans, but never found his name . . ."

Lizzie felt the tears on her cheeks before she realized she was crying again, huge whoops of pain that seemed to erupt from her like air squirting into vacuum. She'd been holding everything in, all the anguish of the war, and now that everything was lost she was flying apart into nothing, nothing at all.

"We'll find someplace good for you," the commander promised. Lizzie slapped her.

"You killed *everything*!" she shrieked. "*You made everything dead*!"

The commander touched her fingers to her swelling cheek in disbelief. Behind her, her soldiers froze; they cradled the sauerkraut containers awkwardly, not sure whether to keep moving or go for their guns.

Momma, her arms protectively around Lizzie, glared them all down.

"You've taken everything from her, now," she said. "Every last illusion. Will you take her home from her, too? Is *that* who you are?"

"You'd *die*!" the commander shot back, exasperated. "Your circuits are blown. And the Gineer are hot on our heels—so we can't leave you with fissionables, or food, or medical supplies. We have to leave *now*, and all you'll have left is a metal tube with a puff of air. Would you rather die in space than live in the Intraconnected Commonwealth?"

Lizzie turned to Momma, wondering what she'd say—but was surprised to find Momma was waiting for *her* answer. And even though Momma's face was patient and kind, Lizzie could see it in Momma's eyes:

Momma would rather die here.

She had spent forty-three years in Sauerkraut Station. Here, she was a commander; in the collective, she'd be a quirky neighbor. Brought to dirt, Momma would become the stereotypical planetfaller that was the butt of every

VDR comedy's joke: terrified of the outdoors, obsessively closing every door behind her, frozen by the overwhelming choices at supermarkets. Laughed at by everyone.

Yet Momma's gaze told the truth: *I would endure all of that. For you.*

Lizzie thought about that, then gripped her mother's hand. Her Momma gripped Gemma's hand. Three generations of Denahues turned to face the commander.

"This is our home," said Lizzie.

*   *   *

The Web troops left, burying them in black. In the darkness, Momma and Gemma hugged her tight.

"You're a true Denahue," Momma said, wetting Lizzie's neck with tears.

"You did us proud, Lizzie," Gemma assured her, enfolding them both inside her strong, stringy arms.

"But I'm gonna *die* a Denahue," Lizzie said. "We're gonna suffocate inside a tin can . . ."

Momma sighed, a warm stream of breath that rustled Lizzie's hair. "We got hope, Lizzie. Not a lot, but some."

"What do you mean?"

Gemma took Lizzie by the hand and they fumbled their way carefully to the mech-bay. She placed Lizzie's palms at the back of the now-empty hidden storage crèche.

"Tell me, Lizzie," Gemma said, her voice wavering. "I know they found the hidden compartment. But did they find the double-blind?"

The *hidden* hidden compartment! Lizzie had forgotten. And as she ran her hands along it, she whooped in happiness as she realized it was unopened.

"I guess it's still there," Momma said. "Now we'll see if the shielding held."

"It's shielded," Gemma said firmly. "*My* Momma made sure of that."

"She couldn't test it, though," Momma replied. "How could she, without frying the station? And we haven't checked the integrity of the backup hardware—well, since Lizzie was born, at least."

Gemma was unconcerned. "Momma stored stuff to last."

Lizzie's sweaty hands unbolted the last of the secret latches. She tossed the panel aside with a clatter. *Come on*, she thought, running fingertips around the edge of what felt like an emergency supply box. She grabbed at what felt like a flashlight.

A blue flicker illuminated the mechbay.

"Goddammit, *yes*!" Lizzie cried, and Momma didn't even cluck her tongue at the swearing.

The light was thin, barely enough to pierce the gloom, but Lizzie aimed it into the cramped cabinet. Fit neatly like a puzzle was a set of oxygen tanks, two backup servers, a case of shielded fissionables, a set of power tools, a month's supply of food, and a full meteoroid shielding kit. Lizzie let out another whoop and turned to hug Momma.

Momma pushed her away, looking grim.

"Sweetie," she whispered. "We're still probably gonna die."

Lizzie shivered. It was the truth.

*   *   *

The worst part about Momma and Gemma leaving was that Lizzie couldn't even wave goodbye. She stood on the other side of the welded door, doing the math one last time. Math was all she'd been doing for the last ninety-four hours, and the end results were merciless.

As a rough guideline, Lizzie knew the average human exhausts the oxygen in about 500 cubic feet of air per day. There were three of them. The station had 99,360 cubic feet of air, not counting airlock losses. Since the oxyscrubbers were fried along with everything else, that gave them two months before they suffocated on CO_2.

They did not have two months' worth of food.

Lizzie had begged hard, and the commander had left them with two weeks' worth of rations. There had been a year's supply of protein bars stored in the double-blind, but mold had crept in and gnawed most of it into a dry, inedible fuzz. Their water supplies were even worse: a mere thirty gallons.

And even that didn't matter unless they could get the meteoroid shield back up and running. Without that, as Gemma so colorfully put it, this place would be a tin shack on a firing range. Their first order of business was to get that running—which took twenty sleepless hours. (Thankfully, as Gemma pointed out, great-great-Gemma was wise indeed, spending the extra money for a shield that could be completely swapped out without ever leaving the ship's confines.)

When they were done, Momma and Gemma collapsed into a four-hour nap that had to keep them awake for thirty, but Lizzie had an idea. She felt her way out in darkness, conserving the power on her flashlight.

As she stepped out of the bunk room, she bonked her head against the door frame.

The station's gravity was artificial, created by a near-frictionless rotating drum; judging from the new creaks the station had acquired and then lessening gravity, Lizzie judged the impact of the Web ship must have crushed something inside, creating drag. A few days, and there would be no gravity at all.

Yet another deadline.

Lizzie carefully bobbed like a balloon down to the hydroponics room, then dunked her hands in the growing chambers.

Her wrists were engulfed in cold, moist sand.

She sighed with relief. The Web had drained the water tanks, but they *hadn't*removed the water in the diatomaceous earth. Lizzie didn't know how much water was there precisely, but it was enough to feed the roots of seven hundred square feet of plants. All she had to do was filter the silt out with a bedsheet and a bucket before the gravity stopped.

The next day, they looked at Gemma's salvage ship, stuck so high in the rafters and looking so damaged that the Web had left it behind. Gemma ran a quick test; a lot of it was fried, but the junker's older circuits weren't as finicky as the newer installs.

"Say it," Gemma crowed.

Momma lowered her head. "It was a good idea to keep the junker, Momma."

The junker had been designed for short hops out to the edge of the solar system, but in a pinch Gemma could rig it for cross-system travel . . . Assuming that there were enough supplies in the double-blind. Assuming that a jury-rigged drive wouldn't conk out in mid-jump, leaving them drifting through empty space—Lizzie knew the junker was already a hot zone, leaking scandalous amounts of waste energy.

Then Lizzie thought about how crowded it was in there when it was just her and Gemma cuddled inside the spaceship. She pictured all three of them there crammed in there, plus the food and water to feed them, the oxyscrubbers straining under a triple load—

Even if, as Momma pointed out—*if*—they successfully made the jump to Swayback Station, there was no guarantee the Web hadn't stripped Swayback as well. Lizzie pointed out it was a leap hubward, away from Web territories—but Momma retorted that fissionable material had already been scarce. There was no guarantee the Swaybacks, rumored to be a particularly mercenary family, would lend them fissionables for the week-long jump to Mekrong planetfall.

And Mekrong? Did Mekrong have the supplies to refit Sauerkraut Station? If they did, could Momma afford to buy it?

A single missed link meant either death or bankruptcy. Out here, the two were pretty much one and the same.

"And even if we *could* all squeeze in there," Momma agonized, putting her face into her hands, "We couldn't. The Web were fleeing a pursuing force. That means the Gineer will probably be here soon—we already know they wanted our station. If we all stay here and wait for help, the Gineer aren't any more likely to help us out than the Web was. But if all three of us leave, the Gineer can jump our claim and refurbish our station for their needs."

"That's not a bad thing, staying behind," Gemma mused. "The station's not comfortable, but it's stable. We got a working distress beacon in the closet. They'll hear it."

"No guarantee they'll stop, though," Momma said. "Not in war. Not for a dead station."

"True," Lizzie said. "But I bet they'd stop for a little girl."

The silence was punctuated only by the groans of the ship's axis slowing. "Don't say that, Lizzie." Momma's voice was hoarse.

"I have to, Momma," Lizzie replied, feeling light-headed but oddly sure. "You can take two weeks' supplies on the ship with you—that gets you to Swayback. And two people *have* to go to Swayback—without our usual bank-feed to draw from, one of you might have to stay behind at the station as insurance. And someone has to stay here, or we might just as well have traded our station to the Web. The math says one person stays."

"That's me," she said, her voice only trembling a little bit. "I'm smaller than you. I eat less, I breathe less. Leave me with all the protein bars and the water in the sand, and I bet I could last for—for three, maybe four months. Someone's sure to come before then."

Lizzie tried to sound more certain than she was. Her plan assumed that nothing further went wrong with the station. That Lizzie didn't go crazy from being cooped up in a lightless ship. That the soldiers who answered her distress call weren't soldiers who thought it was okay to beat up a little girl. But Lizzie's future was a teetering stack of uncertainties; this plan was the best of a bad batch.

Momma argued fiercely for a time—so furiously that Lizzie realized that Momma had already considered this plan. She just hadn't wanted to acknowledge it. And when Momma was forced to admit there was no other way, Momma squeezed her tight and wept. It was only the second time Lizzie had seen Momma weep since Daddy had died, and both times in the same day, and that scared her to the core.

Momma took Lizzie in her lap and combed her hair one last time while Gemma finished soldering the junker into shape. "You know I love you, right?"

Lizzie did, but it was good to hear it now. She buried her face in her mother's chest, trying to inhale Momma's scent so deeply it would carry her through blackness and terror. All her life, Momma had always been just a couple of rooms away; now, Momma was going to be systems away, crossing the void in a half-dead ship, and Lizzie would have no way of knowing what happened.

"Maybe I should have gone to planetfall," Momma muttered, rubbing her hands on her pants. "Maybe I should have—"

That questioning was the most terrible thing of all. Momma *never* doubted.

"It's okay," Lizzie said. "Daddy's out there. He'll protect me."

Momma looked sad, and then desperate, and then she floated with Lizzie to the observation window—the only native source of light in the whole station now—and spread her fingers across the scratched window.

Momma said other things before she left, but that was what Lizzie remembered: the terrifying fear and love as Momma said a silent prayer to Daddy, the stars reflected her eyes.

Without electricity, the airlocks didn't work. So Lizzie said her goodbyes, and then pressed her ear to the wall as Momma and Gemma welded themselves behind a door, then started up the ship, then rammed through a weakened hatch and into space. The only confirmation she had of their leaving was the hollow metal *thoom* that resounded through the station walls.

She prayed they'd make it. But whether they were alive or dead, for the first time in her life, Lizzie was alone.

*   *   *

Back when they'd had guests, Lizzie had bragged how even if all the servers crashed irrevocably, Sauerkraut Station would still remain a livable environment until rescue could arrive. The thermal hood that covered the axis like a great, trembling umbrella was the brilliant part of Great-Great Gemma's design. It intercepted all the solar emanations that might otherwise cook the axis, transmitting both heat and electricity back into the station. It was an elegant design that required little monitoring, and no complicated circuitry; the core of the station's axis served as a boiler room, keeping the station heated to human-habitable temperatures even in the deep cold of space.

But, Lizzie thought after the first day, it made for lousy viewing.

She pressed her nose against the observation deck window, looking for signs of Momma and Gemma. It was suffocatingly black; the thermal hood blocked all the sunlight, leaving Lizzie to strain her eyes to the faint illumination of reflected starlight. The only real light came from the sporadic purple bursts of the meteoroid shields zapping another microparticle.

Yet that was the only place that had any light. The rest of the ship, quite sanely, had no weak points to expose to the sucking vacuum outside. Every corridor was a lightless prison.

On the first day, Lizzie had to dare herself not to turn on her flashlight.

She hugged the hard plastic to her chest, shivering. For the first time in her life, nobody would answer if she called out for help. The emptiness of the station seemed to have its own personality—a mocking smirk, hidden in darkness.

By the time Lizzie half-skipped, half-floated up to the observation deck on the second day—at least she thought it was the second day, it was hard to tell without the usual lightcycles—the observation deck was tinged with a strange glow. It was her eyes adjusting, she knew that, but the deck felt like the ship's lights during a brownout.

Part of Lizzie wanted to stay at the observation deck all the time. A wiser part understood that if she stayed there in the light, eventually she'd be too terrified to venture back down into the chill void of Sauerkraut Station's hallways—and so she forced herself, trembling, back to where the water supplies and her bed and the repair kits were.

On the fifth maybe-day, Lizzie almost died.

The gravity had finally dropped to near-zero, and she'd let go of the doorway to push herself off the wall. But in the darkness, she'd misjudged her foot position, and instead of kicking off into space, she just stomped on empty air.

Lizzie tried to whirl around, to get ahold of something—but flailed and touched nothing but air. She knew she must be drifting, slowly, down the middle of the main corridor, towards the observation deck. But she could see nothing; this deep into the station, there was no difference between having her eyes open and her eyes shut.

From here, the observation deck was an eighth of a mile away.

How fast had she been going when she let go? It couldn't have been more than a couple of inches a minute. She was drifting, slowly, like a speck of dust, down the middle of a long and empty hallway.

Lizzie shrieked. Her voice echoed back, colder and shriller, as if the station itself was throwing her words back at her. She punched, she clapped, she frog-kicked, hoping to feel the pain of her hands smashing against metal. Her hands only slapped the globs of water hanging in the air.

There was nothing to push off of. There was no way to get free.

"MOMMA!" she shrieked. "GEMMA!"

Lizzie saw it all in her mind; she was drifting down the dead center of the hallway, slow as syrup. She'd eventually brush up against the gentle curve of the western wall—but that might take weeks.

She might starve before her body bumped metal.

She pictured her dead body ragdolling slackly against the wall and rebounding, just another dead thing floating in a dead ship. The doc had told her what happened to dead men when they rotted . . .

She was still screaming, but now she was shrieking at the stupid Web. "I ROOTED FOR YOU!" she said. "I TRUSTED YOU! AND NOW YOU LEFT ME TO DIE, YOU STUPID . . . STUPID IDIOTS! I HOPE YOU ALL DIE LIKE ME IN YOUR HORRIBLE WAR!"

Then she realized it was only five days maybe five days and Momma hadn't thought the Gineer would show for weeks and she was going to die and bounce around this ship.

Lizzie didn't know how long she hung there, yelling like a madwoman; it felt like hours. But after too long a time it finally occurred to her: *silly, just take off your clothes*. And once she flung her shoes away, that gave her enough motion to thump against a doorway a minute or two later.

It was a childish mistake, the kind of thing Daddy would have laughed at her for. But the panic of that moment never left her. From then on, she strapped herself to the bed when she slept, and she always carried a small canister of oxygen so she could jet herself to safety.

Without gravity, going to the bathroom was an abominable chore, a filthy thing that contaminated the very air. The air stank of human waste and rotting sauerkraut. That made eating a precursor to horror, so she ate only when she grew faint from hunger. She stopped going to the observation deck because floating through the hallway's splatters made her sick.

All she wanted to do was stay in bed. But what would happen to her muscles?

Things started to coalesce from the blackness.

At first it was little sparkles here and there, but the sparkles turned into constellations, and then firespark-white lines connected the dots to turn them into great silver airlocks. The airlocks hissed open. And as Lizzie pushed her way past the glowing doorways, she glided into a vast hydroponics chambers, the skies ribbed with water-pipes hissing down clean cool rain.

She looked down, and her fingertips brushed across waxy, familiar goodness; rows of cabbages floated below her. The cabbages danced joyfully, a strange and careful motion like two ships docking. Thousands of pale green heads bobbed beneath her fingers, like little men bowing.

She saw a flash of braided brown hair.

"*Themba!*" she cried.

"Play," said Themba, his voice just as full of joy and life as always, and as his cornrowed skull dipped under the dancing cabbages, she realized that Themba was playing hide and seek with her. She launched after him, laughing—and rammed into a cabinet.

As she shook off the sting of it, the blackness swallowed her up.

She tried to tether herself to the bed, but in the darkness she heard scuttling*things* coming for her. She felt fine hairs brushing against her skin, hoping to find an anchor on her flesh to drill deep.

She shrieked, and the walls of the station fell away, and she was walking on the panels of the outside hull.

Daddy walked with her.

His desiccated hand was all rattly inside his punctured spacesuit, but he held her wrist like they were going for a walk around the corridors back in the good old days. Lizzie didn't have a suit, but that didn't matter; it was a beautiful day. She closed her eyes, felt warmth of the sun on her face.

"You're dying, Lizzie," Dad said.

"I know," Lizzie shrugged.

"It's only been two weeks." His face was smashed in like a crushed cabbage—but still kind. "You gotta be strong. Trust me, Lizziebutt, I know what you're going through." He gestured up to point at himself, a dot far out in space.

"Aw, Daddy," Lizzie said, hugging him tight. Her squeeze sent a puff of dry, dead air shooting out through his cracked faceplate.

"It's no good hugging you any more, Daddy," she said.

He nodded. "Only the living can give comfort," he said. "That's why you gotta stay alive, Lizziebutt."

"But you came for me," she protested.

"That's cause I know how empty things are. You've been doing this for just fourteen days; I've been out here five years. But I wouldn't be out here drifting if I hadn't screwed up. I lost my footing, and drifted out, and wham—I was gone. You know how hard it is to get a glimpse of you only once every seven weeks?"

"I miss you, Daddy," she said, laying down on the panels and closing her eyes. "It's nice here."

"You gotta do stuff, Lizzie. Or you're gonna go crazier than you already have. So I'm gonna make things worse to give you something to do. It might kill you, too. But what wouldn't, these days?"

Daddy knelt down and swept her up in an embrace, then he leapt off like a ballet dancer to launch himself into space. He whirled around like a gyro and flung Lizzie back into the station.

She busted through the hull with a horrible *pong* noise, and there was a hiss as all the air came whooshing out, and Lizzie realized that she was struggling against her bedstraps.

There was new light in here. A sliver of stars, shimmering behind a fluttering stream of purple.

Something had broken through the hull.

A very real hissing came from a finger-sized hole on the wall. A meteoroid had punctured the alloyed metal like a bullet fired from space. If that meteor had gone three feet to the right, it would have punctured Lizzie's stomach.

She reached down for the emergency sealer-patch under her bed with the familiarity of practice of years of hull breach drills. She turned on the flashlight, and her head exploded; the light made her just as blind with white as she'd been blind with black.

As she slapped the sealer on, she peered out the gap; the plasma hummed. The shields were holding.

So why had a meteoroid made it through?

When she was done, she floated back to the observation deck. It was almost too bright to see now, a strobing purple.

How could she have ever thought it was dark? It was *radiant* in here.

But looking out the window, she saw meteoroids sizzling against the shields. There was maybe one a minute—*way* more than usual. She pressed her face to the window, trying to see what looked different.

Sure enough, Daddy's bear-constellation had slipped off the side of the window, and she could only make out the top three stars of Great-Gemma's turbine-constellation. If the stars were changing position, then the station was drifting off-course—through the fringe of the dust belt and into the nearby asteroid belt. The shields were designed to burn off small inbound particles . . . But large ones would still penetrate. Without thrusters to prevent her from drifting into the denser part of the belt, the shields would fail.

*　　*　　*

Lizzie tried to get the thrusters back on-line, but it was no use; even if she'd had enough fissionables to start a reaction, the reactor itself was laced with yards of blown-out circuitry. She'd thought about controlled hull breaches, maybe jetting her way to safety with air, but some calculations scrawled on a filthy whiteboard showed her that the displaced air wouldn't be enough to significantly affect the station's mass. And even if she could have moved the station, she didn't have a clear idea which way the ship was drifting. She might knock it deeper into the field.

All her life, Momma had taught her that everything came down to guts and brains, but this put the lie to it: she was dice rattling around in a cup, her life determined by sheer randomness. Nothing she had could prevent the larger meteoroids from breaking through. Every *punk!* meant that a rock had blown through the hull, and by sheer dumb luck it hadn't blown through her.

It was like trying to drift off to sleep with a gun pressed against your stomach.

Lizzie pulled herself around the station in an exhausted haze, her arms aching, trying to make herself a moving target. The station seemed to expand and contract at will, the sign of some malicious intelligence; at times it felt like a vast dock and she was a bat, fluttering madly around inside emptiness. Other times it was all walls, and the space outside compressed in. Sometimes she'd fall asleep in mid-pull and not even realize it until the next *ponk* woke her up.

Ponk. She'd survived. Again.

She had 99,000 cubic feet of lightless air to protect. Her universe was reduced to patching. Her universe had always been patching.

There was no time for sleep; everything was a coma-fugue. She had nightmares about patching horrible, howling holes, then realized she was awake. Once, she fell asleep mid-weld and woke up with her hair on fire.

The station hissed like a boiling kettle.

All the while Daddy and Momma and Themba and Gemma and all the Web and Gineer commanders floated behind her like balloons on a string, babbling in languages that made no sense. They told her the war was over, and everyone went home. They told her to give up, the station was dying and so was she. They told her that all her memories were dreams—there was just her in these stripped-out hallways, blind and numb, forever and ever.

Lizzie was dust. She was air. She was the taste of cabbages.

A flare of light came from the observation deck, so bright it filled the station. She floated over to see, her eyes tearing up; Dad was there, pressing his collapsed face against the window, telling her that it was okay, a meteor was coming to end her misery . . .

. . . And it was the catastrophic clang, the big one, a huge sound like a hammer smashing all the metal in the world. Lizzie was flung into the wall, bathed in light, enveloped in such pain and terror that she shrieked and shrieked and kept screaming until Daddy split in four and hauled her down to hell.

*   *   *

She opened her eyes. It took an effort.

She was blinded by the soft glare of fluorescent lights. A repetitive beep changed pitches, keeping time with her heart.

Turning her head to peer at the monitors raised a sweat underneath the stiff blue robe she was wearing. She tried to slide her hand up off the starched bedsheets, but only managed to make her heart monitor spike. Gravity held her tight to the bed.

At least her vitals looked good.

"It's *my ship*," Lizzie protested, using all her strength to lift her head off the pillow. "My *home*."

"We know that."

Lizzie jumped. A nurse was dressed in a close-fit Gineer uniform with a blood-red cross-and-sickle emblazoned on the front, his long hair slicked back under a nurse's cap. He had a friendly smile.

"'My ship, my ship,'" he said, placing a cool hand on her forehead. "That's all you'd said when we pulled you from the wreckage. And after everything you went through to secure that glorious lifestyle of yours, Elizabeth, our most profound generals decided that we couldn't remove it from you. You are a hero."

Hero? Lizzie thought. She hadn't done anything but survive.

But the nurse called in a couple of Web commanders, older women with sad eyes, and they told her that she'd been in an induced coma for almost two months while they restimulated bone growth and removed excess radiation from her body. In that time, her story had been transmitted to all corners of the galaxy—the discovery of a small girl working diligently to keep her home alive for her family. Elizabeth "Lizzie" Denahue, they said, was now known as an example of the tenacity that only family loyalty could generate.

"But I'm not Gineer," Lizzie protested.

"Doesn't matter," said the nurse. "It's a nice story. After all the consternation, people ache for a comforting tale."

She thought about the word "nice," and logically there was only one reason they could possibly think this was nice.

"So where's Momma?"

"Smart girl," one of the commanders said affectionately. "She's back on the station, refitting it with donated equipment. We almost snuffed you out in towing it back, you know; we thought no one could be alive inside that, it had drifted so badly out of orbit. We were just looking to refurbish it . . . But you were in there, Elizabeth. There was barely any air left, but you were there."

Lizzie nodded weakly. "Can I see Momma?"

"Of course, sweetie," said the nurse. "We just have to fly her in from the station."

Momma came about an hour later, looking haggard and scared and more beautiful than Lizzie could have imagined. They hugged, though Momma had to help lift Lizzie's arms around her waist.

"They told me what happened, Lizzie," Momma said. "We were on our way back, I swear—Gemma had to take a down-planet contract to pay for emergency supplies. But the folks at Swayback were *real* helpful once I explained what happened. We owe them a big one, Lizzie."

Lizzie flipped her wrist at the room around them. "So why are the Gineer . . . ?"

"The war's over, Lizzie. The Web was using some real unconventional weaponry, and the Gineer did something . . . Well, equally unconventional to end it. Something so big they've had to restructure the whole jumpweb around it. On the bright side, that means there's lots of contracting work building stations. What you're in right now is a rescue and refit ship designed to find stragglers like us."

"The war's over?"

Momma smiled and put a cool cloth on Lizzie's head. "Yep."

"Who won?"

Her Momma sighed. "Does it matter?"

Lizzie thought about it. It didn't. She squeezed Momma's hand, happy to have what counted.

* * *

There was a lot of cleanup to be done.

Lizzie was still weak from being weightless for almost two months, but the Gineer had muscle treatments—so as soon as Lizzie could walk within a day or two, Momma put her to work. Internal circuitry had to be replaced, the hull had to be reinforced, the hydroponics rebuilt, the air scrubbed. Thankfully, Momma and the charity mechanics had done the real work of getting the central gyros up and running; rebalancing a station was a job for ten people, not two.

It was hard. The starvation and weightlessness had marked her permanently; her eyes now had deep hollows underneath them, and her arms sometimes went numb, especially when she was using a wrench. Her legs swelled up fierce for no reason.

But now, when she went to bed, Momma combed her hair. That was the only luxury she needed.

Gemma was stuck back on Mekrong for the time being. Until the station was fully functional again, they needed cash. Gemma was doing her part for the family by taking contract work and sending the money back home. Lizzie wrote emails every day, and the charity ship tightbeamed them back for free.

But eventually the charity ship left and the ships started docking again. The folks travelling now were odd mixes that Lizzie had never seen before; gladhanding carpetbaggers looking for new opportunities, grieving families on their way back to homes they weren't sure still existed, scarred soldiers-turned-adrenaline junkies.

Gineer and Web folks mixed uneasily in the waiting rooms. Sometimes shouting matches broke out. And when voices were raised, Lizzie would limp in, and every person would go fall silent as the Angel of Sauerkraut Station glared at them.

"Your war's done enough to me," she said.

They stopped.

Some folks wanted to meet the little girl who'd survived in vacuum for nine weeks, and seemed disappointed when she wasn't more visibly scarred. Lizzie asked about that, and Momma got out the filthy gray coveralls they'd found Lizzie in.

"If you wear these," Momma said, her face unreadable, "People will hand you their money."

Lizzie looked at the rags. They stank of memories.

"Not for all the money in the world," she said.

Momma hugged her proudly. "Good girl." And she tossed the rags into the incinerator and pushed the "on" button.

But Lizzie did notice that Sauerkraut Station was now being called Survivor Station. Momma left up a few of the sturdier hull-patches Lizzie had made, and put plaques over them that noted where Elizabeth Denahue had made these patches to survive during her nine-week ordeal in the asteroid belt. She also put donation boxes below them "To help rebuild the station." They filled up nicely.

A few weeks later, the prisoner exchanges started up, and station was once again filled with soldiers—this time miserable-looking wretches who barely spoke. The handful of survivors had been kept in POW camps, and now they were being shipped back like embarrassing refuse.

They were suffering from scurvy, lice, malnutrition. Most were too weak to move. Lizzie wished she could have done more, but mostly what they needed was clean quarters and a steady supply of food. Neither looked likely in their futures, sadly enough.

She was in one of the prisoner ships, wearing a newly-bought HAZMAT suit and using a viral scanner to double-check the POWs for communicable diseases, when she saw Themba.

He was curled up underneath a pile of bigger kids. She was surprised to find him older—but where Lizzie had grown, Themba had shrunk. His neat cornrows were crusted with sores, his fine robes replaced by a gray prisoner's suit.

She pressed her hand against his forehead; she could feel his heat through the suit.

Themba was delirious, muttering something unintelligible over and over as though it was the only thing keeping him sane.

She hugged him, then turned angrily to the Web captain. "What's he doing here?" she demanded. "He was a hostage! You were supposed to take *care* of him!"

The captain shuffled uncomfortably. "Of that, I know nothing," he said, consulting the records. "This says he's an orphan. We're shipping him back to the collective. They'll find him a good home."

"They most certainly will *not*," Lizzie said, and thumbed open the airlock.

She took Themba in her arms, terrified by how easily she could lift him, and carried him off the ship. She brought him to the single cot that passed for a medbay these days, got a cold water rag for his forehead.

Momma stormed in. "Lizzie, what in blazes are you doing? After everything we've been through to stay neutral, we're *not* getting involved in politics *now*!"

"Momma," she said, "It's *Themba*."

"Think I didn't know that? We're not a charity ship, Lizzie. We're barely making enough to refit the station as it is. Another mouth might put us under."

"His dad's dead! Where's he gonna go?"

"Back to the Web. That's where he belongs."

"With strangers?"

"*Think*, Lizzie. The boy is—*was*—a diplomat's son. Outsiders are trouble on space stations. They're used to having endless space, used to having endless air. They have all *sorts* of problem with a life like ours. If they don't make— make some dumb mistake that gets their ass killed, then they spend the entire time feeling cooped up and desperate. I know you think you're doing him a favor, Elizabeth, but trust me. He'll hate it."

"He loved it here."

"For a day. A few months and he'll beg us to leave. And even if he doesn't, we'd have to train him from scratch to teach him to survive—and even then he'll never be as good as us . . ."

"He's not that way, Momma—he—"

They were shouting—but somehow Themba's high, whistling voice cut through the air, desperately repeating what he'd been muttering since he'd been put on the POW ship:

"*two heads sliced cabbage, fennel, salt water . . . two heads sliced cabbage, fennel, salt water. . . .*"

Momma stopped, and her face scrunched up with a strange mixture of sorrow and happiness. Then she turned to stare at the undecorated metal wall of the medbay—but Lizzie finally realized that Momma was staring *past* the walls, past the station, stroking her wedding band as she looked to the stars for an answer.

Momma swallowed, hard.

"I suppose this is the way of things," she said, her voice so soft Lizzie could barely hear her. "All right. He's crew."

Momma knelt down, kissed Themba on his forehead. Then she walked out of the room to bribe the captain, which would deplete their meager savings further—but Lizzie didn't care. She hugged her best friend, feeling the warmth of his skin on hers.

His eyes refocused, looked at her—and he laughed.

"Welcome home, Themba," Lizzie whispered, not letting go. "Welcome home."

THE CARTOGRAPHER WASPS
AND THE ANARCHIST BEES

E. Lily Yu

For longer than anyone could remember, the village of Yiwei had worn, in its orchards and under its eaves, clay-colored globes of paper that hissed and fizzed with wasps. The villagers maintained an uneasy peace with their neighbors for many years, exercising inimitable tact and circumspection. But it all ended the day a boy, digging in the riverbed, found a stone whose balance and weight pleased him. With this, he thought, he could hit a sparrow in flight. There were no sparrows to be seen, but a paper ball hung low and inviting nearby. He considered it for a moment, head cocked, then aimed and threw.

Much later, after he had been plastered and soothed, his mother scalded the fallen nest until the wasps seething in the paper were dead. In this way it was discovered that the wasp nests of Yiwei, dipped in hot water, unfurled into beautifully accurate maps of provinces near and far, inked in vegetable pigments and labeled in careful Mandarin that could be distinguished beneath a microscope.

The villagers' subsequent incursions with bee veils and kettles of boiling water soon diminished the prosperous population to a handful. Commanded by a single stubborn foundress, the survivors folded a new nest in the shape of a paper boat, provisioned it with fallen apricots and squash blossoms, and launched themselves onto the river. Browsing cows and children fled the riverbanks as they drifted downstream, piping sea chanteys.

At last, forty miles south from where they had begun, their craft snagged on an upthrust stick and sank. Only one drowned in the evacuation, weighed down with the remains of an apricot. They reconvened upon a stump and looked about themselves.

"It's a good place to land," the foundress said in her sweet soprano, examining the first rough maps that the scouts brought back. There were plenty of caterpillars, oaks for ink galls, fruiting brambles, and no signs of other wasps. A colony of bees had hived in a split oak two miles away. "Once we are established we will, of course, send a delegation to collect tribute.

"We will not make the same mistakes as before. Ours is a race of explorers and scientists, cartographers and philosophers, and to rest and grow slothful is to die. Once we are established here, we will expand."

It took two weeks to complete the nurseries with their paper mobiles, and then another month to reconstruct the Great Library and fill the pigeonholes with what the oldest cartographers could remember of their lost maps. Their comings and goings did not go unnoticed. An ambassador from the beehive arrived with an ultimatum and was promptly executed; her wings were made into stained-glass windows for the council chamber, and her stinger was returned to the hive in a paper envelope. The second ambassador came with altered attitude and a proposal to divide the bees' kingdom evenly between the two governments, retaining pollen and water rights for the bees—"as an acknowledgment of the preexisting claims of a free people to the natural resources of a common territory," she hummed.

The wasps of the council were gracious and only divested the envoy of her sting. She survived just long enough to deliver her account to the hive.

The third ambassador arrived with a ball of wax on the tip of her stinger and was better received.

"You understand, we are not refugees applying for recognition of a token territorial sovereignty," the foundress said, as attendants served them nectars in paper horns, "nor are we negotiating with you as equal states. Those were the assumptions of your late predecessors. They were mistaken."

"I trust I will do better," the diplomat said stiffly. She was older than the others, and the hairs of her thorax were sparse and faded.

"I do hope so."

"Unlike them, I have complete authority to speak for the hive. You have propositions for us; that is clear enough. We are prepared to listen."

"Oh, good." The foundress drained her horn and took another. "Yours is an old and highly cultured society, despite the indolence of your ruler, which we understand to be a racial rather than personal proclivity. You have laws, and traditional dances, and mathematicians, and principles, which of course we do respect."

"Your terms, please."

She smiled. "Since there is a local population of tussah moths, which we prefer for incubation, there is no need for anything so unrepublican as slavery. If you refrain from insurrection, you may keep your self-rule. But we will take a fifth of your stores in an ordinary year, and a tenth in drought years, and one of every hundred larvae."

"To eat?" Her antennae trembled with revulsion.

"Only if food is scarce. No, they will be raised among us and learn our ways and our arts, and then they will serve as officials and bureaucrats among you. It will be to your advantage, you see."

The diplomat paused for a moment, looking at nothing at all. Finally she said, "A tenth, in a good year—"

"Our terms," the foundress said, "are not negotiable."

The guards shifted among themselves, clinking the plates of their armor and shifting the gleaming points of their stings.

"I don't have a choice, do I?"

"The choice is enslavement or cooperation," the foundress said. "For your hive, I mean. You might choose something else, certainly, but they have tens of thousands to replace you with."

The diplomat bent her head. "I am old," she said. "I have served the hive all my life, in every fashion. My loyalty is to my hive and I will do what is best for it."

"I am so very glad."

"I ask you—I beg you—to wait three or four days to impose your terms. I will be dead by then, and will not see my sisters become a servile people."

The foundress clicked her claws together. "Is the delaying of business a custom of yours? We have no such practice. You will have the honor of watching us elevate your sisters to moral and technological heights you could never imagine."

The diplomat shivered.

"Go back to your queen, my dear. Tell them the good news."

*   *   *

It was a crisis for the constitutional monarchy. A riot broke out in District 6, destroying the royal waxworks and toppling the mouse-bone monuments before it was brutally suppressed. The queen had to be calmed with large doses of jelly after she burst into tears on her ministers' shoulders.

"Your Majesty," said one, "it's not a matter for your concern. Be at peace."

"These are my children," she said, sniffling. "You would feel for them too, were you a mother."

"Thankfully, I am not," the minister said briskly, "so to business."

"War is out of the question," another said.

"Their forces are vastly superior."

"We outnumber them three hundred to one!"

"They are experienced fighters. Sixty of us would die for each of theirs. We might drive them away, but it would cost us most of the hive and possibly our queen—"

The queen began weeping noisily again and had to be cleaned and comforted.

"Have we any alternatives?"

There was a small silence.

"Very well, then."

The terms of the relationship were copied out, at the wasps' direction, on small paper plaques embedded in propolis and wax around the hive. As paper and ink were new substances to the bees, they jostled and touched and tasted the bills until the paper fell to pieces. The wasps sent to oversee the installation did not take this kindly. Several civilians died before it was established that the bees could not read the Yiwei dialect.

Thereafter the hive's chemists were charged with compounding pheromones complex enough to encode the terms of the treaty. These were applied to the papers, so that both species could inspect them and comprehend the relationship between the two states.

Whereas the hive before the wasp infestation had been busy but content, the bees now lived in desperation. The natural terms of their lives were cut short by the need to gather enough honey for both the hive and the wasp nest. As they traveled farther and farther afield in search of nectar, they stopped singing. They danced their findings grimly, without joy. The queen herself grew gaunt and thin from breeding replacements, and certain ministers who understood such matters began feeding royal jelly to the strongest larvae.

Meanwhile, the wasps grew sleek and strong. Cadres of scholars, cartographers, botanists, and soldiers were dispatched on the river in small floating nests caulked with beeswax and loaded with rations of honeycomb to chart the unknown lands to the south. Those who returned bore beautiful maps with towns and farms and alien populations of wasps carefully noted in blue and purple ink, and these, once studied by the foundress and her generals, were carefully filed away in the depths of the Great Library for their southern advance in the new year.

The bees adopted by the wasps were first trained to clerical tasks, but once it was determined that they could be taught to read and write, they were assigned to some of the reconnaissance missions. The brightest students, gifted at trigonometry and angles, were educated beside the cartographers themselves and proved valuable assistants. They learned not to see the thick green caterpillars led on silver chains, or the dead bees fed to the wasp brood. It was easier that way.

When the old queen died, they did not mourn.

*   *   *

By the sheerest of accidents, one of the bees trained as a cartographer's assistant was an anarchist. It might have been the stresses on the hive, or it might have been luck; wherever it came from, the mutation was viable. She tucked a number of her own eggs in beeswax and wasp paper among the pigeonholes of the library and fed the larvae their milk and bread in secret. To her sons in their capped silk cradles—and they were all sons—she whispered the precepts she had developed while calculating flight paths and azimuths, that there should be no queen and no state, and that, as in the wasp nest, the males should labor and profit equally with the females. In their sleep and slow transformation they heard her teachings and instructions, and when they chewed their way out of their cells and out of the wasp nest, they made their way to the hive.

The damage to the nest was discovered, of course, but by then the anarchist was dead of old age. She had done impeccable work, her tutor sighed, looking over the filigree of her inscriptions, but the brilliant were subject to mental aberrations, were they not? He buried beneath grumblings and labors his fondness for her, which had become a grief to him and a political liability, and he never again took on any student from the hive who showed a glint of talent.

Though they had the bitter smell of the wasp nest in their hair, the anarchist's twenty sons were permitted to wander freely through the hive, as it was assumed that they were either spies or on official business. When the new queen emerged from her chamber, they joined unnoticed the other drones in the nuptial flight. Two succeeded in mating with her. Those who failed and survived spoke afterward in hushed tones of what had been done for the sake of the ideal. Before they died they took propolis and oak-apple ink and inscribed upon the lintels of the hive, in a shorthand they had developed, the story of the first anarchist and her twenty sons.

*   *   *

Anarchism being a heritable trait in bees, a number of the daughters of the new queen found themselves questioning the purpose of the monarchy. Two were taken by the wasps and taught to read and write. On one of their visits to the hive they spotted the history of their forefathers, and, being excellent scholars, soon figured out the translation.

They found their sisters in the hive who were unquiet in soul and whispered to them the strange knowledge they had learned among the wasps: astronomy, military strategy, the state of the world beyond the farthest flights of the bees. Hitherto educated as dancers and architects, nurses and foragers, the bees were full of a new wonder, stranger even than the first day they flew from the hive and felt the sun on their backs.

"Govern us," they said to the two wasp-taught anarchists, but they refused.

"A perfect society needs no rulers," they said. "Knowledge and authority ought to be held in common. In order to imagine a new existence, we must free ourselves from the structures of both our failed government and the unjustifiable hegemony of the wasp nests. Hear what you can hear and learn what you can learn while we remain among them. But be ready."

* * *

It was the first summer in Yiwei without the immemorial hum of the cartographer wasps. In the orchards, though their skins split with sweetness, fallen fruit lay unmolested, and children played barefoot with impunity. One of the villagers' daughters, in her third year at an agricultural college, came home in the back of a pickup truck at the end of July. She thumped her single suitcase against the gate before opening it, to scatter the chickens, then raised the latch and swung the iron aside, and was immediately wrapped in a flying hug.

Once she disentangled herself from brother and parents and liberally distributed kisses, she listened to the news she'd missed: how the cows were dying from drinking stonecutters' dust in the streams; how grain prices were falling everywhere, despite the drought; and how her brother, little fool that he was, had torn down a wasp nest and received a faceful of red and white lumps for it. One of the most detailed wasp's maps had reached the capital, she was told, and a bureaucrat had arrived in a sleek black car. But because the wasps were all dead, he could report little more than a prank, a freak, or a miracle. There were no further inquiries.

Her brother produced for her inspection the brittle, boiled bodies of several wasps in a glass jar, along with one of the smaller maps. She tickled him until he surrendered his trophies, promised him a basket of peaches in return, and let herself be fed to tautness. Then, to her family's dismay, she wrote an urgent letter to the Academy of Sciences and packed a satchel with clothes and cash. If she could find one more nest of wasps, she said, it would make their fortune and her name. But it had to be done quickly.

In the morning, before the cockerels woke and while the sky was still purple, she hopped onto her old bicycle and rode down the dusty path.

*   *   *

Bees do not fly at night or lie to each other, but the anarchists had learned both from the wasps. On a warm, clear evening they left the hive at last, flying west in a small tight cloud. Around them swelled the voices of summer insects, strange and disquieting. Several miles west of the old hive and the wasp nest, in a lightning-scarred elm, the anarchists had built up a small stock of stolen honey sealed in wax and paper. They rested there for the night, in cells of clean white wax, and in the morning they arose to the building of their city.

The first business of the new colony was the laying of eggs, which a number of workers set to, and provisions for winter. One egg from the old queen, brought from the hive in an anarchist's jaws, was hatched and raised as a new mother. Uncrowned and unconcerned, she too laid mortar and wax, chewed wood to make paper, and fanned the storerooms with her wings.

The anarchists labored secretly but rapidly, drones alongside workers, because the copper taste of autumn was in the air. None had seen a winter before, but the memory of the species is subtle and long, and in their hearts, despite the summer sun, they felt an imminent darkness.

The flowers were fading in the fields. Every day the anarchists added to their coffers of warm gold and built their white walls higher. Every day the air grew a little crisper, the grass a little drier. They sang as they worked, sometimes ballads from the old hive, sometimes anthems of their own devising, and for a time they were happy. Too soon, the leaves turned flame colors and blew from the trees, and then there were no more flowers. The anarchists pressed down the lid on the last vat of honey and wondered what was coming.

Four miles away, at the first touch of cold, the wasps licked shut their paper doors and slept in a tight knot around the foundress. In both beehives, the bees huddled together, awake and watchful, warming themselves with the thrumming of their wings. The anarchists murmured comfort to each other.

"There will be more, after us. It will breed out again."

"We are only the beginning."

"There will be more."

Snow fell silently outside.

*   *   *

The snow was ankle-deep and the river iced over when the girl from Yiwei reached up into the empty branches of an oak tree and plucked down the paper castle of a nest. The wasps within, drowsy with cold, murmured but did not stir. In their barracks the soldiers dreamed of the unexplored south and battles in strange cities, among strange peoples, and scouts dreamed of the corpses of starved and frozen deer. The cartographers dreamed of the changes that winter would work on the landscape, the diverted creeks and dead trees they would have to note down. They did not feel the burlap bag that settled around them, nor the crunch of tires on the frozen road.

She had spent weeks tramping through the countryside, questioning bee-keepers and villagers' children, peering up into trees and into hives, before she found the last wasps from Yiwei. Then she had had to wait for winter and the anesthetizing cold. But now, back in the warmth of her own room, she broke open the soft pages of the nest and pushed aside the heaps of glistening wasps until she found the foundress herself, stumbling on uncertain legs.

When it thawed, she would breed new foundresses among the village's apricot trees. The letters she received indicated a great demand for them in the capital, particularly from army generals and the captains of scientific explorations. In years to come, the village of Yiwei would be known for its delicately inscribed maps, the legends almost too small to see, and not for its barley and oats, its velvet apricots and glassy pears.

*   *   *

In the spring, the old beehive awoke to find the wasps gone, like a nightmare that evaporates by day. It was difficult to believe, but when not the slightest scrap of wasp paper could be found, the whole hive sang with delight. Even the queen, who had been coached from the pupa on the details of her client state and the conditions by which she ruled, and who had felt, perhaps, more sympathy for the wasps than she should have, cleared her throat and trilled once or twice. If she did not sing so loudly or so joyously as the rest, only a few noticed, and the winter had been a hard one, anyhow.

The maps had vanished with the wasps. No more would be made. Those who had studied among the wasps began to draft memoranda and the first independent decrees of queen and council. To defend against future invasions, it was decided that a detachment of bees would fly the borders of their land and carry home reports of what they found.

It was on one of these patrols that a small hive was discovered in the fork of an elm tree. Bees lay dead and brittle around it, no identifiable queen among them. Not a trace of honey remained in the storehouse; the dark wax of its walls had been gnawed to rags. Even the brood cells had been scraped clean. But in the last intact hexagons they found, curled and capped in wax, scrawled on page after page, words of revolution. They read in silence.

Then—

"Write," one said to the other, and she did.

RAY OF LIGHT

Brad R. Torgersen

My crew boss Jake was waiting for me at the sealock door. I'd been eight hours outside, checking for microfractures in the metal hull. Tedious work, that. I'd turned my helmet communicator off so as not to be distracted. The look on Jake's face spooked me.

"What's happened?" I asked him, seawater dripping from the hair of my beard.

"Jenna," was all I got in reply. Which was enough.

I closed my eyes and tried to remain calm, fists balled around the ends of a threadbare terrycloth towel wrapped around my neck.

For a brief instant the hum-and-clank activity of the sub garage went away, and there was only my mental picture of my daughter sitting in her mother's lap. Two, maybe three years old. A delightful nest of unruly ringlets sprouting at odd angles from her scalp. She'd been a mischief-maker from day one—hell on wheels in a confined space like Deepwater 12.

Jenna was much older now, but that particular memory was burned into my brain because it was the last time I remember seeing my wife smile.

"Tell me," I said to my boss.

Jake ran a hand over his own beard. All of us had given up shaving years ago, when the gel, cream, and disposable razors ran out.

"It seems she went for a joyride with another teenager."

"How the hell did they get a sub without someone saying something?"

"The Evans boy, Bart, he's old enough to drive. I've had him on rotation with the other men for a few weeks, to see if he'd take to it. We need all the help we can get."

"Yeah, yeah, skip it, where are they now?"

Jake coughed and momentarily wouldn't meet my gaze.

"We don't know," he said. "I tasked Bart with a trip to Deepwater 4, the usual swap-and-trade run. He's now—they're now—two hours overdue."

"The acoustic transponder on the sub?" I said.

"It's either broken, or they turned it off."

"Good hell, even idiots know not to do that."

Jake just looked at me.

I pivoted on a heel and headed back the way I'd come. With my wetsuit still on I didn't have to change. I'd grab the first sub I could muscle out of its cradle. Over my shoulder I said, "Whoever is on the next sortie, tell 'em I'm giving 'em the day off."

"Where are you going to look?" Jake said. "It's thousands of miles of dark water in every direction."

"I know a place," I said. "Jenna told me about it once."

* * *

My daughter was four when she first began asking the inevitable questions.

"How come we don't live where it's dry and sunny?"

All three of us were perched at the tiny family table in our little compartment. Lucille didn't even look up from her plate. As if she hadn't heard Jenna at all. Too much of that lately, for my taste. But I opted to not call my wife out on it. Lucille had become hot and cold—either she was screaming mad, or stone quiet. And I'd gotten tired of the screaming, so I settled for the quiet.

Folding my hands thoughtfully in front of me, I considered Jenna's inquiry.

"There isn't anywhere that's dry and sunny. Not anymore."

"But Chloe and Joey are always going to the park to play," Jenna said. "I want to go to the park too."

I grimaced. *Chloe and Joey* was a kids' show from before . . . from before everything. Lucille had been loathe to let Jenna watch it, but had caved when it became obvious that *Chloe and Joey* were the only two people—well, animated talking teddy bears actually—capable of getting our daughter to sit still and be silent for any length of time. We'd done what every parent swears they won't do, and the LCD had become our babysitter. Now it was biting us in the butt.

My wife stabbed at the dark green leaves on her plate, the tines on her fork making pronounced *tack!* noises on the scarred plastic.

"There used to be parks," I said. "But everything is covered in ice now. And it's dark, not sunny. You can't even see the sun anymore."

"But why?" Jenna said, her utensils abandoned on the table.

The room lost focus and I briefly remembered my NASA days. Those had been happy times. Washington was pumping money back into the program because the Chinese were threatening to land on the moon.

I'd been on the International Space Station when the aliens abruptly came. It was a gas. I got to pretend I was a celebrity, being interviewed remotely by the news, along with my crewmates.

The mammoth alien ship parked next to us in orbit, for three whole days—a smoothed sphere of nickel-iron, miles and miles in circumference. No obvious drive systems nor apertures for egress. No sign nor sound from them which might have indicated their intentions.

Then the big ship promptly broke orbit and headed inward, towards Venus.

Six months later, the sun began to dim . . .

"It's hard to explain," I said to Jenna, noting that my wife's fork hovered over her last bit of hydroponic cabbage. "Some people came from another place—another star far away. We thought they would be our friends, but they wouldn't talk to us. They made the sunshine go away, and everything started getting cold really fast."

"They turned off the sun?" Jenna said, incredulous.

"Nothing can turn off the sun," I said. "But they did put something in the way—it blocks the sun's light from reaching Earth, so the surface is too cold for us to live there anymore."

I remembered being ordered down in July. We landed in Florida. It was snowing heavily. NASA had already converted over—by Presidential order—to devising emergency alternatives. The sun had become a shadow of itself, even at high noon. We cobbled together a launch: NASA's final planetary probe, to follow the path of the gargantuan alien ship and find out what was going on.

The probe discovered a mammoth cloud orbiting just inside of Earth's orbit: countless little mirrors, each impossibly thin and impossibly rigid. No alien ship in sight, but the cloud of mirrors was enormous, and growing every day. By themselves, they were nothing. But together they were screening out most of the sun's light. A little bit more gone, every week.

"So now we have to live at the bottom of the ocean?" Jenna asked.

"Yes," I said. "It's the only place warm enough for anything to survive."

Which may or may not have been true. In Iceland they'd put their money on surface habitats constructed near their volcanoes. Chancy gamble. Irregular eruptions made it dangerous, which is why the United States had abandoned the Big Island plan in Hawaii. Besides, assuming enough light was blocked, cryogenic precipitation would be a problem. First the oxygen would rain out, and then, eventually, the nitrogen too. Which is why the United States had also abandoned the Yellowstone plan.

People were dying all over the world when NASA and the Navy began deploying the Deepwater stations. The Russians and Chinese, the Indians, all began doing the same. There was heat at the boundaries between tectonic plates. Life had learned to live without the sun near hydrothermal vents. Humans would have to learn to live there too.

And we did, after a fashion.

I explained this as best as I could to my daughter.

She grew very sad. A tiny, perplexed frown on her face.

"I don't want to watch Chloe and Joey anymore," she said softly.

Lucille's fork clattered onto the floor and she fled the compartment, sobbing.

* * *

Number 6's electronics, air circulator, and propulsion motor blended into a single, complaining whine as I pushed the old sub through the eternal darkness along the bottom of the Pacific Ocean. Occasionally I passed one of the black smokers—chimneys made of minerals deposited by the expulsion of superheated water from along the tectonic ridge. The water flowed like ink from the tops of the smokers. Tube worms, white crabs and other life shied away from my lights.

I was watching for the tell-tale smoker formation that Jenna had told me about. It was a gargantuan one, multiple chimneys sprouting into something the kids had dubbed the Gak's Antlers. Dan McDermott had joined the search and was 200 yards behind me, his own lights arrayed in a wide pattern, looking.

We both spotted our target at the same time.

I could see why the kids might have liked the spot. In addition to the bizarre beauty of the Antlers, there was a shallow series of depressions surrounding the base—each just big enough to settle a sub down into. Cozy. Private.

I saw the top of a single sub, just barely poking up over the rock and sand.

I asked Dan to hang back while I pinged them with the short-range sonar. When I got no answer I motored right up to the edge of the depression, turned my exterior lights on extra-bright and aimed them down through the half-sphere pilot's canopy.

I blushed and looked away.

Then I flashed my lights repeatedly until the two occupants inside got the hint and scrambled to get their clothes on. One of them—a girl, I think, though not Jenna—dropped into the driver's seat and flipped a few switches until my short-range radio scratched and coughed at me.

"Hate to ruin your make-out," I said.

"Who are you?" came the girl's tense voice. Too young, I thought.

"Not your father, if it makes any difference," I said.

"How did you get here?"

"Same as you."

A boy's head poked into view. He took the radio mic from the girl.

"Get out of here, this is our place," he said, his young voice cracking with annoyance. I was tempted to tell him to shove his blue balls up his ass, then remembered myself when I'd been that young, coughed quietly into my arm while I steadied my temper, and tried diplomacy.

"I swear," I said. "I won't tell a soul about this little noogie nook. I just want to get my daughter back alive. Jenna Leighton is her name. She's about your age."

"Jenna?" said the girl.

"You know her?"

"I know her name. She's part of the Glimmer Club."

The boy tried to shush her, and take the mic away. "That's a secret!"

"Who cares now?" the girl said. "We're busted anyway."

"What's the Glimmer Club?" I said.

The girl chewed her lip for a moment.

"Please," I said. "It could be life or death."

"It's probably easiest if I just show you," she said. "Give me a few minutes to warm up our blades. I'll tell you what I can once we're under way."

*　　*　　*

Jenna was six when Lucille went to live on Deepwater 8. At the time, it had seemed reasonable. A chance for my wife to get away from her routine at home, be around some people neither of us had seen in awhile, and get the wind back into her sails. It certainly wouldn't be any worse than it had been, with all the bickering and chronic insomnia. The doc had said it would do Lucille some good, so we packed her off and waved goodbye.

On Jenna's bunk wall there was an LCD picture frame that cycled through images, as a night light. I originally loaded it with cartoon characters, but once she swore off *Chloe and Joey* I let her choose her own photos from the station's substantial digital library.

I was surprised to see her assemble a collection of sunrises, sunsets, and other images of the sun—a thing she'd never seen. At night, I sometimes stood in the hatchway to the absurdly small family lavatory and watched Jenna lying in her blankets, eyes glazed and staring at the images as they gently shuffled past.

"What are you thinking about?" I once asked.

"How come it didn't burn you up?" she said.

"What?"

"Teacher told us the sun is a big giant ball of fire."

"That's true."

"Then why didn't it burn everyone up?"

"It's too far away for that."

"How far?"

"Millions of miles."

"Oh."

A few more images blended from one to the next, in silence.

"Daddy?"

"Yes?" I said, stroking Jenna's forehead.

"Am I ever going to get to see the sun? For real?"

I stopped stroking. It was a hell of a good question. One I wasn't sure I was qualified to know the answer to. Differences between the orbital speed of the mirror cloud and Earth's orbital velocity, combined with dispersion from the light pressure of the solar wind, would get Earth out from behind the death shadow eventually. How long this would take, or if it could happen before the last of us gave out—a few thousand remaining, from a population of over ten *billion*—was a matter of debate.

"Maybe," I said. "The surface is a giant glacier now. We can't even go up to look at the sky anymore because the ice has closed over the equator and it's too thick for our submarines to get through. If the sun comes back, things will melt. But it will probably take a long, long time."

Jenna turned in her bunk and stared at me, her eyes piercing as they always were when she was thinking.

"Why did the aliens do it?"

I sighed. That was the best question of all.

"Nobody knows," I said. "Some people think the aliens live a long, long time, and that they came to Earth and did this once or twice before."

"But why block out the sunshine? Especially since it killed people?"

"Maybe the aliens didn't know it would kill people. Last time the Earth froze over like it's frozen now, there were no people on the Earth, so the aliens might not have known better."

"But you tried to say hello," she said. "When you were on the space station.

283

You told them you were there. You tried to make friends. They must be really mean, to take the sun away after all you did. The aliens . . . are bullies."

I couldn't argue with that. I'd thought the same thing more than once.

"Maybe they are," I said. "But there's not much we could do about it when they came, and there's not much we can do about it now, other than what we are doing. We've figured out how to live on the sea floor where it's still warm, and where the aliens can't get to us. We'll keep on finding a way to live here—as long as it takes."

I was a bit surprised by the emotion I put into the last few words. Jenna watched me.

I leaned in and kissed her cheek.

"Come on, it's time to sleep. We both have to be up early tomorrow."

"Okay Daddy," she said, smiling slightly. "I wish Mama could give me a kiss goodnight too."

"You and me both," I said.

"Daddy?"

"Yes?"

"Is Mama going to be alright?"

I paused, letting my breath out slowly.

"I sure hope so," I said, settling into the lower bunk beneath my daughter's—a bunk originally built for two, which felt conspicuously empty.

*　　*　　*

The clubhouse was actually a restored segment of Deepwater 3, long abandoned since the early days of the freeze-up.

Each of the Deepwater stations were built as sectional rings—large titanium cylinders joined at their ends to form spoked hexagons and octagons. Deepwater 3 had been stripped and sat derelict since a decompression accident killed half her crew. We'd taken what could be taken, and left the hulk to the elements.

The kids had really busted their butts getting it livable again.

I admired their chutzpah as I motored alongside the revived segment, its portholes gleaming softly with light. They'd re-rigged a smaller, cobbled-together heat engine to take advantage of the exhaust from the nearby hydro-thermal vents, and I was able to mate the docking collar on my sub with the collar on the section as easy as you please.

The girl and boy from the other station didn't stick around to watch. They took me and Dan just far enough for us to see the distant light from the once-dead station, then fled. I didn't ask their names, but I didn't have to. I'd promised them anonymity in exchange for their help, and was eager to get onboard and find out what might have happened to my daughter. So far as I knew, I was the first adult to even hear about this place.

Only, nobody was home.

Dan hung around outside, giving Deepwater 3 a once-over with his lights and sonar, while I slowly went through the reactivated section.

It was a scene from a fantasy world.

They'd used cutting torches to rip out all the bulkheads, leaving only a few, thick support spars intact. The deck had been buried in soft, white, dry sand and the concave ceiling had been painted an almost surreal sky blue. Indirect lights made the ceiling glow, while a huge heat lamp had been welded into the ceiling at one end, glaring down across the "beach" with a mild humming sound. Makeshift beach chairs, beach blankets, and other fur-niture were positioned here and there, as the kids had seen fit.

Several stand-alone LCD screens had been wired into the walls, with horse-shoes of disturbed sand surrounding them. I carefully approached one of the LCDs—my moist suit picking up sand on my feet and legs. Cycling through the LCD's drive I discovered many dozens of movies and television programs. Informational relics from before the aliens came. Videos about flying, and surfing, hiking, camping, and lots and lots of nature shows.

I went to two more LCD screens, and found similar content.

I walked to the middle of the section—realizing that I hadn't stood in a space that unconfined and open since before we'd all gone below—and used my mobile radio to call for Dan.

He hooked up at the docking collar on the opposite end of the section, and came in under the "sun," stopping short and whistling softly.

"Can you believe this?" I said.

Like me, Dan was an oldster from the astronaut days. Though he'd never had any children, nor even a girlfriend, since his wife had died in the mad rush to get to sea when the mirror cloud made life impossible on the surface.

"They've been busy," Dan said. "Is there anyone else here?"

"Not a soul," I said. "Though it looks like they left in a hurry."

"How can you figure?"

"Lights were left on."

I looked around the room again, noting how many teenagers might fit into the space, and the countless prints in the sand, the somewhat disheveled nature of the blankets.

"Frankie and Annette, eat your hearts out," I said.

Dan grunted and smiled. "I was at party or two like that, back in flight school."

"Me too," I admitted. "But something tells me they didn't just come here to get laid. Look at what they've been watching."

"Porn?" Dan said.

"No . . . yes. But not the kind you think."

I flipped on the LCDs and started them up playing whatever video was queued in memory. Instantly, the space was filled with the sound of crashing waves, rock music, images of people sky-diving and hang-gliding, aerial sweeps of the Klondike, the Sahara, all shot on clear days. Very few clouds in the sky. It was non-stop *sunshine* from screen to screen to screen.

Dan wasn't smiling anymore. He stared at the heat lamp in the ceiling, and the false sky, and then back at the sand.

"You ever go to church when you were a kid?" Dan asked me.

"Not really. Dad was an atheist, and mom a lapsed Catholic."

"I went to church when I was a kid. Baptist, then Episcopal, then Lutheran. My dad was a spiritual shopper. Anyway, wherever we went, certain things were always the same. The pulpit, the huge bible open to a given scripture, the wooden pews. But more than that, they all *felt* a certain way. They had a vibe. You didn't have to get the doctrine to understand what the building was meant for."

"What does this have to do with anything, Dan?" I said, getting exasperated.

"Look around, man," Dan said, holding his arms wide. "This is a house of worship."

I stared at everything, not comprehending. Then, suddenly, it hit me.

"The club isn't a club."

"What?"

"The Glimmer Club. That's what she called it. She said many of the younger teens and a few of the older ones had started it up a couple of years ago. Not every kid was a member, but most of the other kids heard rumors. To be a member, you had to swear total secrecy."

My father had tended to consider all religions nuts, but he'd reserved special ire for the ones he called cults: the cracked up fringe groups with the truly dangerous beliefs. He'd pointed to Jonestown as a textbook example of what could go wrong when people let belief get out of hand.

I experienced a quick chill down my spine.

"They're not coming back," I said.

"Where would they go?" Dan asked.

But I was already running across the sand to the hatch for my sub.

*   *   *

Jenna was ten years old when her mother committed suicide.

Neither of us was there when it happened of course. Lucille had moved around from station to station for her last several months, until the separate crew bosses on each of the stations got fed up with her behavior. Ultimately she put herself into a sea lock without a suit on, and flooded the lock before anyone could stop her. By the time they got the lock dry and could bring her out, she was gone. And I was left trying to explain all of this to Jenna, who cried for 48 hours straight, then slept an additional day in complete physical and emotional exhaustion.

For me, it was painful—but in a detached kind of way. Lucille and I had been coming apart for years. The docs mutually agreed that sunlight deprivation may have been part of the problem. It had happened with several others, all of whom had had to seek light therapy to try to compensate for their depression. In Lucille's case, the light therapy hadn't worked. In fact, nothing had seemed to brake her long, gradual decline into despair. I'd kept hoping Jenna—a mother's instinctive selflessness for the sake of her child—would pull Lucille through. But in hindsight it was clear Jenna had actually made things worse.

These thoughts I kept strictly to myself in the weeks and months that followed Lucille's departure from the living world. I poured myself into my role as Daddy and held Jenna through many a sad night when the bad dreams and missing Mommy got her and there was nobody for Jenna to turn to but me. Eventually the nightmares stopped and Jenna started to get back to her old self—something I was so pleased about I had a difficult time expressing it in words.

For Jenna's 12th birthday I gave her a computer pad I'd squirreled away before committing to the deep. My daughter had been going nuts decorating half the station with chalk drawings—our supply of paper having long since been exhausted. The pad was an artist's model, with several different styli and programs for Jenna to use. It liberated her from the limited medium of diatoms-on-metal, and fairly soon all of the LCDs in our little family compartment were alive with her digital paintings.

It was impressive stuff. She threw herself into it unlike anything I'd ever seen before. Vistas and landscapes, stars and planets, and people. Lots of people. Lots of filtered representations of Lucille, usually sad. I dutifully recorded it all onto the family portable drive where I hoped, perhaps one day, if humanity made it out of this hole alive, Jenna's work might find a wider audience. She'd certainly won over many of the other people on Deepwater 12, and was even getting some nice feedback from some of the other stations as well.

In retrospect, I probably should have seen the obvious.

All of Jenna's art—with rare exception—had one thematic element in common.

It all featured the *sun*. In one form or another. Sometimes as the focus of the work, but more often as merely an element.

All kids do it, right? The ubiquitous yellow ball in the crayon sky, with yellow lines sprouting out of it? Only, Jenna's suns were warmer, more varied in hue and color. They became characters in their own right. When she discovered how to use the animation software on the pad, she went whole-hog building breathtaking sequences of the sun rising, the sun setting; people and families frolicking beneath our benevolent yellow dwarf star called Sol.

If ever the aliens who'd taken our star from us entered Jenna's mind, it didn't show up in her work. But then, few of us thought of the aliens in any real sense anymore. They'd come, and so far as we knew, they'd gone. Dealing with the repercussions of their single, apocalyptic action had become far, far more important to all of us than dealing with the aliens themselves.

I remembered this as Number 6 creaked and groaned around me, the pressure warning lights letting me know that I was coming up too quickly— risking structural damage if I didn't bleed off pressure differences between the inside and the outside of the sub.

Dan wasn't with me. I'd convinced him to go back and let the others know about the Glimmer Club, and what the kids had done with Deepwater 3 behind our backs. He'd also been tasked with explaining why I'd disobeyed direct orders from a crew boss, risking my life and the old sub to chase a wild hair through the vast, dark ocean.

I couldn't be sure I was right. All I had to go on was a short conversation I'd had with Jenna on her 15th birthday, just a few months earlier.

At that age she spent most of her time with the other teens on the station, as teenagers throughout history have always been prone to do. Old me had stopped being the focus of her attention right about the time she'd hit puberty.

Which was why that particular conversation stood out.

"Dad," she said, "Does anyone ever go check anymore?"

"On what?"

"On the surface. Up top."

"We used to send people all the time, but the thicker the ice got— especially when the equator closed over—the less point there seemed to be in it. So I don't think anyone has tried in several years."

"Why not? We can't just give up, can we? I mean, why are we doing any of this if people aren't going to ever go back to the surface?"

She had a good point. I am afraid I hemmed and hawed my way through that one, leaving her with a perplexed and somewhat unhappy expression on her face. If any of her friends had gotten better answers from their parents, I never found out. Though I now suspected that our big failure as adults had been our inability to imagine that our children wouldn't be satisfied to just scratch out a living on the ocean floor.

We who'd been through the freeze-out from the surface, we'd seen the destruction and the death brought by the forever night. We felt fortunate to be where we were. Alive.

But our kids? For them, the ice layer on the surface had become a thing of myth. An impenetrable but invisible bogey monster, forever warned about, but never seen nor experienced. For the Glimmer Club, I suspect, it got to the point where they wondered if all of the adults weren't crazy, or conspiring in a plot. How did anyone *really* know that the surface was frozen over? That aliens had blocked the sun?

To blindly accept a fundamental social truth upon which everyone agrees, is just part of what makes us human.

But in every era, however dark or desperate, there have also always been hopeful questioners.

*   *   *

I'd not slept for almost two days, and knew it when I caught myself slumped at the controls, chin in my chest; the sub's primitive autopilot beeping plaintively at me.

Sonar pings still didn't show me any subs.

But they hadn't shown me the underside of the ice sheet yet, either.

I used the sub's computer to run some calculations—based on the last known measurements to have been taken on the ice sheet's thickness. I used these to double check where I thought I was, versus what the instruments were telling me, and sat back to ponder.

Assuming the Glimmer Club had ascended as a group, without significant deviation—because the subs only have so much air and battery life to go around—I'd expected to spot them by now. Or at least hear them. Several quick pauses to capture and analyze ambient water noise had yielded depressing silence. Not even the cry of whales filled the sea anymore, because the whales and other sea mammals had all died out together.

If the aliens had had no regard for human sapience, what about the other intelligent creatures who had once called the Earth home?

If ever the oceans re-opened and humans reclaimed the planet, we'd find it an awfully empty place.

Exhausted, I kept going up.

*　　*　　*

Sonar pingbacks brought me awake the second time. There. A single object, roughly about the size of a sub. It was drifting ever so lazily back towards the bottom.

I spent a few minutes echo-locating, and when I did, my blood ran cold. There was a big crack in the pilot's canopy and the top hatch was hanging open. Dreading what I might find, I pointed my lights into the canopy and examined the interior of the little sub, down its entire length. If I'd expected to see bodies, I was relieved to see only emptiness. Trained from birth to salvage, they'd stripped the sub and continued on.

Wherever that happened to be.

Additional sonar pings sent back nothing. The ocean was silent in all directions, as black and lonely as space had ever been. On instinct alone, I resumed the long voyage to the ice.

*　　*　　*

The gentle rocking of the sub wasn't what woke me.

It was the occasional thumping against the hull.

I sat straight up, almost ripping my headset off in the process My neck and back hurt, and my hands were unsteady as I grasped the controls.

No telling how long I'd been out that time. I scanned the control board and the autopilot seemed satisfied. When I saw that the depth gauge read zero, I had to tap the screen a few times. Something had to be wrong. The knocking on the hull suggested I'd found the lower boundary of the ice sheet, where the sea water grudgingly turned to sludge. I'd never actually been up this high since the oceans closed over, so maybe the equipment was wonky this close to the frozen crust?

I hit my lights, but just a few of them because I didn't have all the battery life left in the world.

It took me at least a minute to figure out what I was seeing.

A lapping line of water sloshed halfway up the canopy.

Had I drifted into an air pocket on the underside of the ice?

Scanning upward with the lights revealed nothing but blackness.

But wait, not *black* blackness. There was a distinct hint of color in the void.

I slowly reached a hand down and flicked the lights off, letting the gentle rocking of the boat and the knocking of the hull fill my ears. The blackness was pinpricked with white dots, and there was a gloaming light in the very far distance. Only, gloaming wasn't the right word. The light slowly but perceptibly began to grow in strength, and the blackness overhead began to graduate from obsidian, to purple, and finally flared into dark blue at the far, far horizon.

No!

My hands were shaking badly. I almost couldn't hit the switch to extend the sub's single, disused radio aerial. A tiny motor whined somewhere behind me, and I waited until the motor stopped before I gently rested my headset back onto my scalp, a gentle hiss of static filling my ears.

I depressed the SEND button on the sub's control stick.

"This is Max Leighton speaking for Deepwater 12, the United States. If anyone can hear and understand this broadcast, please respond."

The static crackled lifelessly.

It was a vain hope. My signal couldn't go too far. But I had to try.

"I say again, this is Thomas Leighton speaking—"

"Daddy?"

My breath caught in my throat. It had been a single word, broken by crackling interference. But it was probably the most beautiful word I'd ever heard spoken in my entire life.

"Jenna," I said softly into my mic. "Please tell me that's you?"

"You're just in time," her voice said. If I was relieved beyond words, she sounded excited to the point of bursting. But not because of me.

"Just in time for what?" I said.

"The sun!" she said. "We got here just as it was going down and had to spend the night on the surface. We opened the top hatches and the air is breathable! Very cold, but breathable. Oh Daddy, we knew it. We all knew it. I'm so glad you're here with us."

"Where the hell is *here*, Jenna, I can't see another soul."

"Go out on top and take a look," was all she said.

It took me a minute to get the interior hatch to Number 6's stubby sail open, then I climbed up the short ladder, banging side to side in the tight tunnel as the sub kept rocking. At the top hatch I paused, hands on the locking wheel. Nobody had breathed fresh air in almost two decades. Had I merely imagined my daughter's voice? It certainly was true I'd been in better mental states. Sleep deprivation will do that to you.

But I'd certainly come too far to stop. So, what the hell?

The wheel complained, then spun, and there was a hiss as the last bit of pressure difference bled off from the inside of the sub to the outside. If I'd done it right when I came up, I'd not get the bends—no deadly nitrogen bubbles in the blood. If I'd done it wrong . . . too late now.

Jenna had been right. The air was brutally frigid, and moving fast. Almost a wind. But also so invigorating that I pulled myself up all the way out of the sail and rested my butt on the edge of the hatch. I looked out across the rolling sea of slushy ice—which appeared to extend for many, many miles in all directions.

I also saw the sails of the other subs. Four of them. The kids on those boats waved to me, and I waved back with both arms. If I'd been promising myself at the start of this trip that I'd skin Jenna alive when I found her, that anger had long since melted into a bewildering feeling of astonished wonderment.

Because Jenna was right. The sun certainly was coming up.

And not an apparitional, atrophied sun; as we'd all seen in the last days before going to sea.

This was the real deal.

It crested the horizon like a phoenix, a blast of yellow-orange rays shooting across the sky and into the belly of a bank of clouds to our west. The clouds lit up brilliantly, and there was a raucous cheer from the other subs—all the kids out on deck to see the miracle.

I suddenly found myself cheering too. No, *howling*. I was on my feet, dangerously close to toppling off the sail and into the slush below, but I couldn't make it stop. I yelled until my voice was hoarse.

I looked around and saw all the kids standing, hips and knees rocking in time to the rhythm of their bobbing craft, eyes closed and arms stretching out to the sky, waiting . . . waiting . . .

I suddenly knew what they were waiting for. I did the same.

When the rays hit my skin—old, dark, and wrinkled—my nerves exploded with warmth. Stupendous, almost orgasmic warmth. No electric heater was capable of creating such a feeling.

I came back to myself and thought I saw my daughter waving to me from the sails of one of the other subs.

I jumped into the icy sea, and swam in great strokes.

Pulling myself out onto the back of Jenna's sub, I ignored the smiling but reserved faces of the other teenagers and used handrails on the sail to pull myself up to Jenna's level.

I didn't ask if it was okay for a hug, as I'd been doing since she'd turned 13.

She had to politely tap my shoulders to get me to release her.

"Sorry," I said, noting that water from my beard had gotten her face wet.

"It's okay," she said, wiping it with her palms.

"I found the clubhouse," I said. "I was afraid that you—all of you—had gone off and done something really stupid."

Jenna looked down.

"Are you mad that I didn't tell you?"

"At first," I said. "But it doesn't matter now. This is . . . this is just . . . incredible."

The sun had gained in the sky. The old, dark neoprene of my wet suit was growing hot and uncomfortable. I unzipped and pulled my arms and head out of the top, letting it drape around my waste. Delicious rays of light bathed my exposed, gray-haired chest. An unreasoning, almost explosive feeling of giddiness had seized me, and I had to fight to maintain my bearing as the kids on the sub—all the kids on all the subs—began laughing and shoving each other into the water, paddling about and crooning like seals.

"Have you been in contact with anyone else?" I asked.

"We kept trying the radio," Jenna said, never moving away from my arm which had found its way protectively around her shoulders. "But you were the first person we heard."

"I wonder how many of the satellites still work," I said, looking up into the fantastically, outrageously blue sky. "We could rig a dish, one of the old VSAT units. I think we still have some down below . . ."

"We aren't going back," Jenna said suddenly, detaching herself.

I looked at my daughter.

"Where else can you possibly go?"

"We don't care, dad. We're just not going back *there*. We swore it amongst the group. All of us."

"And what if the ice had still been solid? What would you have done then?" I said, a burst of sea wind suddenly giving me goosebumps.

"We don't know."

"You're goddamned lucky there was a gap to get through. Air to breathe. I am not sure any of us have enough oxygen or battery power to get all the way back down. Jenna, for all I knew, you and the others were going to get yourselves killed."

Jenna didn't meet my gaze.

"Somebody had to do something," she said. "We had to know if there was a chance the sun had returned. We hoped. *We hoped so much*. You and Jake and the others—everybody from before the freeze-up—it was like you'd all given up. Everyone determined not to die, but also determined not to live, either."

I nodded my head, slowly.

"So what's the plan now?" I asked.

She looked up at me, smiling again.

"Baja."

"What?"

"The Baja Peninsula is supposed to be a couple hundred miles northeast of here. We'll sail until we hit the shore."

"And if you simply hit the pack ice?"

"We'll leave the subs, and keep going."

"Do you have any idea what you're saying? Where's your food, where's your water, what kind of clothes do any of you have? What—"

"We're not going back, daddy!"

She'd shouted it at me, her fists balled on my chest.

"Okay, okay," I said, thinking. "But consider this. You all stand a much better chance if you have help. Now that we know the ice is clearing and the air is breathable—and that the sun is back out again, by God—we can bring the others up. All of the Deepwater crews, and the stations too. It will take time, but if we do it in an organized, methodical fashion, we'll all stand a better chance of making land. Though I am not quite sure what we can expect to find when we get there."

Some of the other kids had pulled themselves out of the water to come listen to me talk. A few of them were nodding their heads in agreement.

"If you want," I said to them, looking around, "I'll be the one to go back down. But I'll need to get some air and electric power off these other subs first. I sure hope you all brought enough food to last a week or two. It's going to be at least that long, or longer, before anyone else comes up from below."

*　　*　　*

I went back down with what few reserves the kids could give me, about nine hundred digital pictures of the open water, the marvelously full sun, and the blue, blue sky—and a hell of a lot of hope in my heart.

It wouldn't be easy. Not all of the adults would want to believe me, at first. And raising the stations after so long at depth was liable to be even more dangerous than sinking them had been in the first place.

But I suspected Jenna was right. We couldn't go back. Not after what I'd just seen.

So I slowly dropped back down, gently, gently. Like a feather. The old sub wouldn't last a fast trip to the bottom, just as it wouldn't have lasted a fast trip to the top.

And though the darkness had resumed its hold, I felt light as a bird on the breeze.

Three days later, I stood in Deepwater 12's sub garage.

Dan had dutifully spread the word ahead of me, and he was in a crowd of adults as I slowly climbed down off Number 6's sail.

"You didn't find them," Jake said sternly. I could sense his extreme piss-off as I walked across the deck towards the group. Discipline was vital on the Deepwater crews, and I'd violated that discipline so extremely, I'd be lucky if Jake didn't bust my nose for me.

"Oh, I found 'em all right," I said.

"Dead?" Dan said, voice raised slightly.

"No," I said. "Take a look."

I tossed Dan the camera I'd used on the surface.

He looked at me questioningly, and I just looked back.

Dan turned the camera over, its little LCD screen exposed, and flipped the switch to slide show.

Adults crowded around Dan, including Jake.

They gasped in unison.

"It can't be," Dan said, voice caught in his throat.

"It is," I said. "And if you all don't mind, my daughter is waiting for us to join her up top. We've got a land expedition that needs support. I promised her I'd get her and the other kids the help they'd need to make it successful."

Dan cycled through the pictures and began playing one of the video files I'd also shot. The camera's little speaker blared loudly laughing, shouting teens and the sloshing of water against the hull of the sub I'd been standing on when I took the footage.

I noted tears falling down the faces of many of my compatriots. And for a tiny instant, I wished that Lucille had lived long enough to see this.

No matter. Lucille was a memory, but it was apparent I'd given the living something they'd desperately needed, without evening knowing it. Just as much as I'd desperately needed it when I first opened Number 6's top hatch and smelled the tangy, frigid salt air whipping through my hair.

Jake, the crew boss, was shouting orders—with a wide smile on his face—while the camera made its way reverently from hand to hand.

I looked up at the ceiling, my eyes glazing and my spirit going up through the black deep to the top where Jenna waited. Hang on, little one. Dad'll be back soon.

EXCERPT FROM *THE FREEDOM MAZE*

Delia Sherman

The Freedom Maze is a double historical time-travel novel, with chapters set in 1960 framing the main narrative, set in 1860. The narratives are linked by the central character of Sophie Martineau, who, in traditional children's-book fashion, is sent for the summer to the country. There she finds adventure in the shape of a sassy magical Creature, who grants her not-very-well-worded wish by transporting her into the past. This excerpt opens with Sophie's arrival in 1860, which she soon finds out is quite different from the Good Old Days her grandmother is always longing for.

—Delia Sherman

CHAPTER 6

"Where's here?" Sophie asked.

Her only answer was a fading giggle.

And wasn't it just her luck, she thought, to the get the kind of magic creature that would transport her somewhere and leave her without explanation? Just like the Natterjack in *The Time Garden*, come to think of it. And the Natterjack had always shown up when the children really needed it. Irritating as the Creature was, she was sure it would, too.

In the meantime, here she was, back in the Good Old Days, in a room that both was and was not hers.

Every piece of furniture seemed to come from somewhere else. The princessy bed with its high headboard, was from Mama's room, but what was that gauzy material hanging from the half-tester? The mirrored armoire and dresser belonged in Grandmama's room, and the last time Sophie had seen that desk, it was in the parlor. The familiar faded wallpaper was gone, and so was the ratty rug, replaced by deep rose paint and pale matting. The only clues to the room's occupant were the striped scarf across the bed, and the scribbled paper scattered across the desktop.

Sophie padded over to the desk to investigate, picked up an ivory pen, its gold nib crusted with dried ink. Beneath it was a half-written letter. She couldn't make head or tail of the scrawly handwriting, but the date was clear enough: *June 12, 1860.*

Sophie's hand shook a little.

The War Between the States was due to start in—Sophie thought for a moment—less than a year. She wondered whether she should warn her ancestors about it, decided she shouldn't risk changing the course of history by mistake and returning to the present to find out she hadn't been born. She might, however, let the slaves know that they'd be free in a few years— nothing too specific, just a hint, to give them something to look forward to.

But that was for when she'd actually met a slave. She put the letter back where she'd found it.

On the marble-topped nightstand, she found a white leather Bible and a copy of "Hiawatha" by Henry Wadsworth Longfellow, which had been used for pressing flowers. Inside the nightstand were a white porcelain pot and a faint stink that reminded her of a not-very-clean public bathroom. She shut the door quickly. Chamber pots were a part of the past she'd never thought much about.

Neither were corsets, which she found in the big mirrored armoire, hanging on hooks next to mysterious white cotton garments and pastel dresses with long, bulky skirts. She touched a flounce, wondering whether the Fairchild it belonged to was old or young, and if she might let Sophie try on her clothes.

Next, Sophie went to the window. In 1860, there was no window seat, just a square bay with a vanity table set it in to catch the light. A white gauze curtain framed the view she'd glimpsed by moonlight two nights before. Then, it had disappeared like smoke. This time, it wasn't going to go away.

Sophie caught sight of her reflection in the triple mirror on the vanity. She looked like she'd been dragged through a hedge backwards. There wasn't much she could do about the mud on her dress and arms, but she couldn't bear to meet her ancestors with her hair looking, yes, like a hooraw's nest. Sophie searched through the clutter of bottles and jars and ribbons, until she found a silver brush. It wasn't polite to use some else's brush without asking, but this was an emergency.

As she raised the bush to her hair, the door opened. Sophie spun around to see girl staring at her—a real Miss Lolabelle in a poufy white dress and a striped silk sash around her tiny waist. Her dark hair was bundled into a net and her skin was pink-and-white. With her eyes and mouth all round with surprise, she looked just like a doll a tourist would buy on Decatur Street.

The girl put one hand to her throat and gave a very Miss LolaBelle-like little scream. "Antigua!" she gasped. "Antigua! Come here!"

A Negro girl appeared at her shoulder. "Yes, Miss Liza."

A slave. A real, live slave. She was very pretty, with rosy-brown skin, and eyes the same Coca-Cola brown as Miss Lola—Miss Liza's. Sophie noted the bright yellow turban wrapped around the Negro girl's head and the little silver cross strung on a red thread around her throat and was surprised. She'd thought a slave would look more down-trodden.

"You put Miss Liza's brush down!" the slave girl said. "Right now, you hear?"

Sophie dropped the brush with a clatter.

"I do believe she was fixing to steal it!" Miss Liza's voice was a high-pitched whine, not nearly as pretty as her face. "Bring her along to the office, Antigua. Papa will know what to do." She disappeared in a flurry of white ruffles.

Antigua grabbed Sophie's arm and shook it. "You in trouble, girl! What you doing here, anyway?"

This was not how Sophie had imagined her adventure beginning. She licked her lips. "Um. I got here by magic."

Antigua gave her a vicious shake. "Magic? I never heard of no magic that put folks where they don't belong to be. You crazy, girl? Or just foolish?"

"It's the truth," Sophie protested.

"Crazy *and* foolish," Antigua said. "Listen here, now. You don't want more trouble than you already got, you best find some other tale to tell Dr. Charles. Magic! I never!"

The slave girl took a firm grip of Sophie's arm and dragged her out to the gallery and down the back steps. Sophie was too shocked to resist. Were slaves allowed to hustle white people around like that? Wasn't that the reason the old days were good? Because Negroes knew their place?

Antigua entered the house through a door that didn't exist in 1960, and hustled Sophie down the back hall to Aunt Enid's office—or what would be Aunt Enid's office, a hundred years in the future. When she'd knocked, she propelled Sophie across the room to the fireplace, where Miss Lolabelle was sitting by a lady on a sofa, carrying on while a tall gentleman patted her shoulder.

Antigua released Sophie and stepped back, leaving her staring at her illustrious ancestors.

The lady on the sofa was blond and pale and thin as a rail, and dressed in grey silk and a lacy cap with long side-pieces. Wool and knitting needles lay on the sofa beside her. The gentleman, got up in a stiff high collar that made Sophie's neck itch to look at, had a long, sad face and an aquiline nose. A Fairchild nose, in fact.

The gentleman seated himself in what looked exactly like Grandmama's big wing-chair. "My daughter says she discovered you in her room with her silver hair brush in your hand." His voice was firm, but not unfriendly. "I trust you have some reasonable explanation?"

Sophie was so astonished to hear someone talking just like a character in a Dickens novel that it took her a moment to realize he was actually talking to her. It took another moment to realize she was going to have to answer him.

The lady picked up her knitting. She was working on a sock. "Perhaps a whipping will loosen her tongue, Dr. Fairchild."

Sophie went cold all over. It occurred to her that adventures might not be as much fun to live through as to read about.

"I think we can get to the bottom of this without whipping, my dear," Dr. Fairchild said.

"I cannot agree. The wench is a thief. Even your mother believes in whipping thieves."

"Now, Lucy, we don't *know* she's a thief."

The lady raised her almost invisible brows scornfully. She had a good face for scorn, with ice-blue eyes and a thin mouth. She was knitting without looking at what she was doing. Sophie found her terrifying. "She's bold enough for one. You, girl. Didn't anybody ever teach you not to look at your betters?"

Hastily, Sophie dropped her eyes to her feet.

"You've nothing to be frightened of," Dr. Fairchild said. "If you're innocent. Now. What is your name and where you come from?"

"Sophie," she said, her voice shaking slightly. "I'm from New Orleans."

"There! We're making progress. Can you tell me, Sophie, how you got here from New Orleans?"

It was all too obvious neither of the Fairchilds would believe any story involving magical Creatures and time travel. Why didn't any of the books mention that adventures were like taking a test you hadn't studied for?

"You got here somehow," Dr. Fairchild prompted. "Did you come by boat?"

Sophie had had teachers who couldn't wait for an answer. If she just stood there looking dumb and scared, he'd probably just tell her what he wanted her to say.

"Yes, Sir," she answered eagerly. "A boat from New Orleans."

Mrs. Fairchild clicked her needles angrily. "That's a bare-faced lie, Dr. Fairchild. There hasn't been a steamboat by in weeks."

"They probably put her off at Doucette," he pointed out. "Saved themselves some time."

Miss Liza gave an impatient little bounce. "What does it matter where she came from? She was stealing my hairbrush, and she ought to be whipped!"

Mrs. Fairchild turned her icy glare on her daughter. "Your father is conducting this interrogation, Elizabeth. It does not become you to interrupt him."

Miss Liza scowled.

"The truth now, Sophie," Dr. Fairchild went on. "Did you get off the steamboat at Doucette?"

This might have been a trick question, coming from someone else. But Dr. Fairchild looked to be what Grandmama would call a Perfect Gentleman, and Perfect Gentlemen didn't lay traps. "Yes, Sir."

"Nonsense," Mrs. Fairchild said. "We're a good five miles from Doucette. Did someone drive you here?"

Mrs. Fairchild, on the other hand, was not a Perfect Lady. "No, ma'am," Sophie improvised. "I walked."

"Walked! Dr. Fairchild, I do believe this wench is a runaway as well as a thief. Just look at the state of her!"

"I disagree, my dear. She's not much more than a child. She couldn't have made the journey from New Orleans alone. It's more likely she lost her way between here and Doucette and fell into a ditch. She seems a little simple."

Mrs. Fairchild gave a laugh. "All slaves are simple when they're in trouble."

Sophie looked up, shocked. "But I'm not—"

Mrs. Fairchild laid her knitting aside and pulled something from her waistband—a leather strap, about an inch wide. Sophie looked down hastily, "—a runaway," she finished.

"If you want us to believe you," Dr. Fairchild said sternly, "you must tell us exactly who sent you here, and why."

Sophie hardly heard him. How could anybody think she was a slave? Slaves were Negroes. She was white. In 1960, white people were white and colored people were colored and nobody had any trouble telling them apart. It was true she was barefoot and she had a tan. Couldn't they tell the difference between tan and black? Hadn't they noticed her Fairchild nose?

The silence lengthened: Dr. Fairchild wasn't going to help her this time. Sophie was on the edge of panic when Mrs. Fairchild said, "If you look at her carefully, Dr. Fairchild, I think you'll see why she's reluctant to answer. Elizabeth, you may leave us."

"*Mama!*"

"Do as your mother says, puss," Dr. Fairchild said.

"But, Daddy!"

"Now, Liza."

Miss Liza flounced away. Dr. Fairchild took Sophie's chin in his large, warm hand and studied her carefully, just like Grandmama. Sophie felt her face heat uncomfortably.

"Well." Dr. Fairchild let her go. "Your master is Mr. Robert Fairchild, isn't he?"

Sophie nodded numbly.

"Robert always did spoil his servants," Mrs. Fairchild observed.

"My brother," Dr. Fairchild said, "treats his servants as he was taught to treat them."

"Which includes sending them on a long journey up-river without so much as a sack? And what about her traveling pass?"

"Very true, my dear. Do you have a traveling pass, Sophie?"

Sophie tensed. "I lost it?"

"You lost it." Dr. Fairchild made an impatient noise. "Don't you know how dangerous it is for a girl like you to be without a traveling pass? If the patrollers found you, they'd put you in chains and drag you back to your master, and that would be a lot of trouble for everybody."

Mrs. Fairchild said, "This is all very well, Dr. Fairchild, but it doesn't tell us what she was doing in Elizabeth's bedroom."

Dr. Fairchild sighed. "Very well, Lucy. Sophie. Why were you in Miss Liza's room? The truth, now."

Because it's my room, a hundred years from now. "I—got lost."

"A likely story! If you ask me, Dr. Fairchild, there's more to this girl than meets the eye. Have you ever seen anything like those spectacles?"

Sophie touched her glasses. They were just ordinary, blue plastic frames with little metal flowers on the temples. "My father gave them to me."

Mrs. Fairchild sent her a glare that could have stripped paint. "If you refer to Mr. Robert as your father again, I *will* have you whipped."

"Now, Lucy, the girl probably doesn't know any better. It's like Robert to have spoiled her, just as it's like him to send her without writing to warn us. Unless, perhaps, he wrote Mother. Or she might have a letter with her. Do you have a letter from your master, child?"

"I lost that, too." Sophie found it all too easy to sound pathetic. "I lost everything."

"Convenient. I don't mind telling you, Dr. Fairchild, I don't believe I've ever heard such a collection of untruths since the day I was born."

Dr. Fairchild sighed. "Well, she's a Fairchild—no question about that. I'll talk it over with Mother tonight and write Robert in the morning. In the meantime, we'll just presume she's a new addition to the family. Antigua?"

The slave girl had been standing by the door so quietly, Sophie had forgotten she was there. She acknowledged her name with a little curtsy. "Yes, Dr. Charles."

"Get this girl something to eat, then take her to Mammy."

Mrs. Fairchild took up her knitting again. "You, girl. How old are you?"

"Thirteen, ma'am."

"I thought you were younger. Thirteen is much too old to be running around with your legs showing. Get her something decent to wear, Antigua. As for you, girl, I can't even begin to imagine what you're used to in Mr. Robert's household. In my household, you will behave with proper humility, or you will be punished."

"Yes, ma'am. Thank you, ma'am."

Dizzy with relief, Sophie curtsied and followed Antigua out of the office. She thought she'd done pretty well, all things considered. A member of the family, Dr. Charles had said. Maybe things were going to work out after all.

CHAPTER 7

It had been raining in 1860, too. The sky was a patchy grey, and the wet grass clung to Sophie's legs as she followed Antigua around the back of Oak Cottage and along the edge of the garden.

A whiff of something good brought water to her mouth. "What's that?"

Antigua snorted. "You don't know roast chicken when you smells it? I thought you just acting simple so's Dr. Charles feel sorry for you. Maybe it ain't an act, huh?"

Sophie was stung. "I'm not simple."

"Then don't ask fool questions."

Sophie shut her mouth and wondered when the friends she'd wished for were going to show up.

They walked up to Aunt Enid's garden shed, looking bare and business-like without its blanket of vine. Sophie peered through the open door into a noisy, smoky room full of women in long dresses shelling beans, stirring pots, chopping vegetables, and kneading bread on Aunt Enid's potting table. The mammoth fireplace was all cluttered with pots on hooks and a long spit with chickens strung along it like beads on a string. The air was hot and sticky as boiling molasses and hummed with flies.

Sophie stepped back, hoping Antigua would bring her food outside.

"Well, looky there!" a voice exclaimed. "A stranger!"

Next thing she knew, Sophie was standing at the center of a semicircle of curious black faces asking questions faster than she could answer them.

"Where you from?"

"Ain't you light!"

"What-for them things setting on you nose?"

Sophie hadn't been this close to so many Negroes since she was eight and Mama had stopped her going to church with Lily. She'd liked Lily's church, where the singing was a lot more lively than at St. Martin's Episcopal and the ladies were all got up in Sunday dresses and fancy hats. These women, in their faded dresses and tightly wrapped headcloths, frightened her.

Sophie pushed her glasses up on her nose and smiled nervously.

"Well, Miss High-and-Mighty!" a short, round woman exclaimed. "Can't you answer a civil question?"

"Don't act more foolish than God made you, China. Can't you see the child's scared half to death?"

The woman who had spoken was tall—as tall as Papa, with reddish-brown skin and a blue headcloth. The other women moved aside to give her room.

Knowing authority when she saw it, Sophie held out her hand. "How do you do?"

"Well, I never," China said, and everybody laughed.

"Hush yourselves, now," the queenly woman said. "Ain't you never seen a body with manners before?" Her hand, hard and scaly with work, folded around Sophie's. "I'm Africa, Old Missy's cook."

Antigua appeared at Africa's elbow. "She belong to Mr. Robert. Or so she say."

A dozen pairs of eyes turned to Sophie with a new and intense interest. She felt her ears burn.

"Oh, she Mr. Robert's, sure enough," said a dark, skinny woman.

Someone else laughed. "And ain't it just like him, sending off his high-yellow girl for his mammy to raise up for him?"

Africa ignored them. "What's your name, child?"

"Sophie."

"Sophie." Africa's smile showed missing teeth. "And what're them things on your nose, Sophie?"

"Glasses."

Africa held Sophie's chin and lifted her glasses off her nose. The world disappeared into a multicolored blur. Sophie squeaked and made a blind grab.

"Don't fret, child. I'm just looking," said Africa.

"But I can't *see*! You don't understand!"

"I sure enough don't." Africa dangled the glasses by the earpiece. "Old Missy, she don't have spectacles like these. Dr. Fairchild, *he* don't have spectacles like these, and he's a medical man. How come you got them?"

"So I can see," Sophie almost wailed. "Give them back to me. Please!"

Africa held the glasses up to her eyes, yanked them away as though they'd bitten her. "Whoo-eee! You blind as sin, child!" She handed them back. "Better take good care of them. Oak River ain't New Orleans. If they get broke, you'll just have to do without."

"Not less you ask Mr. Robert to get you some more," said Antigua nastily. "What work you do at Mr. Robert's house, anyway?"

Sophie settled her glasses back on her nose. "Work?"

"Yes," Antigua sneered. "Work. You know—what black folk do and white folk don't?"

Sophie looked down at her feet, sun-darkened and streaked with dried mud. There was a scratch above one arch and a bug crawling on her big toe. The feet surrounding her were mostly darker, but two or three might have been as pale as hers under the dirt. She tried to imagine what would happen if she raised her head right now and announced that she was not a slave, but a genuine white Fairchild, brought into the past by magic.

They'd think she was crazy, just like Antigua had. And if she insisted, they'd probably tell Dr. Fairchild, who would think she was crazy, too. Maybe if she just went along, and was agreeable and polite, she could keep out of trouble until the Creature showed up to rescue her.

Africa clapped her hands sharply. "Y'all get back inside, and get on with dinner. Unless you're hankering to tell Mrs. Charles she ain't going to eat until three?"

"No, ma'am," said China with feeling. "I likes my black skin just fine on my back where it belong."

The other women laughed and went back into the kitchen. Africa looked down at Sophie. "I 'spect you wants a corn cake."

Sophie hesitated. That kitchen was probably as full of germs as it was of flies. And none of those slaves looked very clean. Still, she *was* hungry, and she loved corncakes. Lily used to make them, light and spongy and a little sweet. Besides, she was the heroine of this adventure, and heroines never got so much as a head cold.

"Please, ma'am. If it's not any trouble."

Africa led her through the flies and heat to a wooden bin full of flat, grayish things that looked like cardboard cookies. The corn cake tasted even more like cardboard than it looked, but Sophie was empty enough to choke it down anyway, and even remembered to thank Africa for it before going outside, where Antigua sitting on the bench waiting for her. "Come on, if you done stuffing you face. I gots work to do."

She got up and trotted purposefully away, Sophie at her heels.

As they came into the yard, Sophie was hit with a truly eye-watering stink. "What's *that*?"

"Soap boiling." Antigua pointed to where three Negro women with their sleeves rolled up were stirring a big iron pot over an open fire.

Sophie sneezed. "That's not what soap smells like."

"How else pig fat and lye supposed to smell? What you make your soap from in New Orleans? Manna?"

"I don't know. We buy our soap at a store."

Antigua rolled her eyes. "I 'spect everything better in New Orleans."

Sophie didn't bother to respond. It was obvious the slave girl was bound and determined to take everything she said as a slight and an insult. There'd been girls like that at school. The only thing to do was keep her mouth shut and hope Mammy was friendlier.

Antigua picked her way across the yard with her pink skirts held up out of the mud, with Sophie trailing behind, gaping at the busy slaves like a tourist on Bourbon Street. Each cabin was a workshop, and the work done there spilled out into the yard: barrel making, carpentry, leather-work, forging iron. They fetched up at a cabin where a woman sat in the door, stitching at a cloud of white stuff. A mysterious, rhythmical clacking came from inside.

"Afternoon, Asia," Antigua said. "This here is Sophie. Mr. Robert send her on a boat from New Orleans. Mrs. Charles say give her some decent clothes." Antigua wrinkled her nose. "Better wash her first. And be quick. I taking her to Mammy, and there ain't much time before dinner."

Asia bundled the white cloud into her arms. "She better come on in, then."

Sophie followed Asia into the cabin. The clacking came from a huge wooden loom worked by a shadowy figure, arms flying, flat, bare feet working the treadles like a giant spider.

Asia shook her head. "That Antigua. She so full of herself, she liable to bust like a bullfrog one fine day. This here's Sophie, Hepzibah. She need some decent clothes, right quick."

The clacking died away, and the weaving woman disentangled herself from the loom. When she stood up, Sophie saw she was thin, and would have been tall if her back hadn't been curled like a hoop. "Welcome, Sophie. That a mighty pretty dress you got there." Hepzibah took a fold of the blue gingham shirtwaist and rubbed it between her fingers. "I ain't never seen such fine weaving. Where this fabric come from?"

Sophie pulled away nervously. "New Orleans. My mama bought it for me."

"Then your mama ain't got good sense," Asia said. "That dress ain't seemly for a big girl like you. Make a nice Sunday dress for one of the child-rens, though."

"No!" Sophie crossed her arms tightly, panicked. What if changing her clothes meant she couldn't go home? What if she left her dress in the past and Mama was mad? "It's mine. You can't have it."

Hepzibah frowned. "It ain't Christian, keeping something ain't no use to you when there's a plenty other folks could use it."

Her expression told Sophie that Hepzibah wouldn't hesitate to remove the dress by force. Reluctantly, she took it off—and her bra, and her under-pants—and, miserably embarrassed, stood in a corner while Asia sponged her briskly with cold water out of a bucket. Hepzibah gave her a pair of coarse cotton drawers and a nightgown-like chemise, a long brown homespun dress and a sacking apron. When Sophie was dressed, Asia raked through her hair with her fingers and braided it in six tight plaits, tied a white cloth she called a "tignon" over them, and knotted the ends into rabbit ears.

"There," she said. "I 'spect you be getting something nicer directly. Light-skinned girl like you bound to end up in the Big House."

Sophie came out into the yard, feeling awkward and itchy and hot. Antigua sauntered away from the young stable hand she'd been teasing, and gave Sophie a contemptuous once-over. "Well, you clean," she said. "Ain't nothing ever going to make you decent."

Sophie spared a wistful thought for the Natterjack, whose magic made the time-traveling children fit in whenever they went. What with wondering what was going to happen to her and Antigua hustling her from pillar to post, she was much too worried to pay much attention to the scenery. She passed the maze without even thinking to look at it.

And then she saw Oak River Big House.

It stood on a rise surrounded by gardens and flowering trees, three stories of bright red brick, with a wide gallery, tall white columns, and a double stair that curved graceful arms around a marble fountain in which a stone nymph poured water out of an urn. It was splendid and proud and any Fairchild who entered it must be proud, too.

Sophie stood up straighter. She'd asked the Creature for an adventure, and adventures had to be full of misunderstandings and hardships, or what was the point? She was a Fairchild, and this was her ancestral home.

She followed Antigua around the fountain to a blue door that opened onto a long, stone-floored corridor. A young black man in a short blue jacket came out of a door carrying a glass on a silver tray. "Careful, Antigua," he said. "Young Missy send her a note, make her cross as two sticks."

Antigua shrugged and herded Sophie into a room furnished with a big desk and shelves full of papers.

"Mammy, this here's Sophie," she announced, curtseying. "She from New Orleans." And then she left.

Sophie, who'd been expecting someone fat and jolly and Aunt Jemima-ish, studied the Negro woman behind the desk with a sinking heart. She was thin as a rake, nunnishly dressed in black and white, and looked about as jolly as Mama in a temper.

The woman up from the note she was reading, adjusted her narrow steel spectacles, and fixed Sophie with a sharp gaze that reminded her uncomfortably of a particularly strict math teacher she'd had in fifth grade.

"Mrs. Charles has told me about you, Sophie. She says you are rude and spoiled and possibly a thief. I won't tolerate a thief and I won't tolerate uppity behavior, whatever color you are. The law doesn't care who your father is, and neither do I. If your mother was a slave, so are you. Do you hear me?"

Sophie gaped at her. "You can't talk to me like that!"

Mammy got up from her desk and slapped Sophie across the face.

Sophie put her hand to her stinging cheek. "You hit me!"

"If you don't keep your thoughts and your eyes to yourself, I'll do more than that." Mammy took Sophie's arm in a firm grip. "You need to learn your place, girl. You can sit in the linen room for a spell, think things over."

*　　*　　*

Locked in the linen room, Sophie had plenty of time to plan what she was going to say to the Creature when it showed up, about throwing her into an adventure and then just abandoning her. She tried to think what she might have said to the Fairchilds to persuade them she wasn't a slave, moved on to imagining how Mama would have handled Mammy, and spent some time worrying over whether Mama would think she'd run away and call the police.

If Mama even noticed.

Sophie closed her eyes, clicked her bare heels together, and repeated "There's no place like home" until she started to cry. When she was cried out, she wiped her face on her apron and distracted herself by poking through the sheets (heavy linen) and towels (heavier linen). She stood by the window and watched the shadow of the Big House creep slowly over the geometrical beds of the formal garden. Mid-afternoon, she saw a procession of slaves trotting into the house carrying big tin boxes slung on poles. She wondered what was in the boxes. She wondered if anybody was going to give her anything to eat.

Time passed. The shadows crawled. She wished she had something to read.

The slaves brought the boxes out again and carried them around the corner of the house and out of sight. The light faded, palmetto bugs whirred against the ceiling and shadows of hunting bats flitted silently across the sky. And then it was night, and a slave she hadn't seen before was at the door with a lantern, telling her to come along.

"Mammy, she say you sleep in the Quarters tonight, maybe it teach you to mind you manners."

As the slave girl led her through the fragrant, buggy darkness, Sophie leaned that her name was Sally, that she was a housemaid, and just about the nosiest person Sophie had ever met. Too tired to think of any answers to her questions about New Orleans and Sophie's mother and Mr. Robert, Sophie just shook her head, which brought on a furious speech about folks who thought they were better than other folks that kept Sally busy until they reached the oak grove.

"See this here?" Sally swung the lantern to illuminate the first few feet of a narrow path. "Just follow it on a ways, and you come to the Quarters. Africa say she take you in, the good Lord know why. First cabin to the right."

It's not easy to follow a path you can't see. Sophie groped her way forward step by step, jumping at every noise and stubbing her bare toes on every stick and stone. By the time she reached the end of the trees, she was jumpy as a cat. She also needed a bathroom.

In front of her, a double row of cabins glowed faintly in the moonlight, their doors open to catch whatever breeze should happen to chance along. Behind them, a field of young cane rustled sleepily to itself, and cicadas fiddled wildly.

Sophie climbed to the porch of the first cabin to the right and peeked cautiously through the uncurtained window. Firelight flickered on the face of the slave woman who'd given her the corncake, stirring an iron pot hung over the fire on a hook. On the floor, a child was playing with a baby, and three men sat around a rough table, their faces grim in the flickering light of a smoky candle.

Sophie's pulse stuttered nervously. The men looked just exactly like the kind of dirty, ragged Negroes Mama had warned her against, except they were all working. One was stuffing a sack with what looked like a tangle of black thread; the second was sewing another sack closed. The third man sat in the only chair in the room whittling with his head bent like he was too tired to hold it up. Around them, the walls were covered with clothes and tools hung on hooks; baskets and bunches of herbs dangled from the ceiling. The air was still and hot and thick with grease and sweat and small, biting insects.

If there'd been anywhere else to go, Sophie would have crept away again. As it was, she hesitated until the child looked up and saw her at the window. "Who that?"

Sophie moved shyly to the door. "Sophie."

The child scrambled to its feet. Sophie couldn't tell whether it was a girl or a boy, its hair trimmed like a lamb's wool close to his head, its bony body covered by a coarse brown shirt. "My name's Canada. You come to supper?" The child took Sophie's hand and pulled her forward. "This here's Sophie. She ain't borned here."

"She sure as shooting ain't," one of the men said. "Dr. Charles a good Christian gentleman. Ain't it just like Mr. Robert, though?"

Africa turned from the fire. "Hush, Flanders. Ain't her fault who her pa is. Come here, sugar."

Sophie edged around the table, clutching her skirt so she wouldn't touch anything.

"This here's my husband, Ned." Africa laid a gentle hand on the skinny man's shoulder. He raised his face, pale brown and deeply lined.

"Pleased to meet you, sir," Sophie said shyly.

Ned showed a graveyard of yellow teeth in a wide smile. "I pleased to meet you, too, child."

"The boys are Poland and Flanders," Africa said. "The baby's Saxony. Tote me some water, Canny girl. I'm making us some spoon-bread to welcome Sophie to Oak River."

By this time, Sophie was ready to burst. Not wanting to ask about a bathroom where the men could hear, she followed Canada outside. But she couldn't make her understand.

"I don't know 'bout no bathroom," the little girl said. "The water in the cistern here's for drinking. Sometimes we washes in a barrel, but in summer, mostly we swims."

"I don't have to wash," Sophie said. "I have to tinkle."

"Tinkle?"

Sophie was ready to die of embarrassment. "Pee."

Giggling, Canada led her to a little wooden house out in the field behind the cabins. It smelled foul, it was full of flies, and there wasn't any paper, only a basket of scratchy moss to clean up with. Sophie was past caring.

Supper was greens and a little chicken and the water they'd been boiled in—pot liquor, Africa called it—and a deliciously creamy spoon-bread, eaten more or less in silence, which suited Sophie just fine. She was tired and frightened, and hadn't the first idea what slaves liked to talk about.

As soon as the last crumb of spoon-bread disappeared, Canada and Africa cleared the table, Poland put the baby to bed in a basket, and all three men went out into the night—to hoe their vegetable-patch, Canada said. Sophie sat in Ned's chair, trying to keep out of the way and wondering where she was going to sleep.

A woman came to the door asking Africa to step round to the Big House, as Korea's baby was on the way. Africa bustled around pulling gourds and dried plants from the rafters and tying them in a sack, then left in a hurry.

Canada yawned. "Time we go to bed. Momi, she sometimes out all night when a baby come."

She took Sophie's hand and led her into a tiny back room. Sophie could just make out two ticking mattresses, covered with pieced quilts, taking up most of the floor space. Canada gestured to the smaller one. "This my bed," she said. "But you can share."

Sophie had never shared a bed in her life, and didn't want to start now. But there wasn't any place else to sleep. She began to cry helplessly.

"Aww," Canada said. "You homesick for you Momi?" She put her skinny arms around Sophie's waist and her head against her shoulder. "Don't you cry. She send you a message, I 'spect, next boat from New Orleans. You going to like it here. Folks is nice, mostly, and Old Missy and Dr. Charles, they don't believe in whipping 'less you do something real bad. Lie down now and go to sleep. Everything look better in daylight. You wait and see."

CHAPTER 8

An iron clanging woke Sophie while it was still dark.

"Morning bell," a child's voice informed her. "Momi say I supposed take you to Mammy. Can you watch Saxony while I do my chores?"

The mattress crackled as Canny scrambled away. Sophie sat up and rubbed her face. She felt grubby from sleeping in her clothes, hungry, and even more tired than she'd been when she lay down. The adventures of the day before hadn't been a dream after all. The Creature had really taken her back in time and her ancestors had really mistaken her for a slave. The magic hadn't ended at midnight or when she went to sleep. It looked like she was stuck in the past until the Creature took her home.

If it even intended to. Maybe, Sophie thought, the Creature was an evil spirit, whose treats were really tricks. Maybe it was laughing itself sick in whatever betwixt and between place it lived. She just hoped leaving her here until the war started wasn't its idea of a good joke.

She would have liked a real bathroom with running water and Cheerios for breakfast. What she got was an outhouse, a bucket to wash in, and a hunk of cold cornbread, just like everybody else.

The sky grew pearly with dawn. Africa and her men-folk left for work. Canada handed Saxony to Sophie, who held the dark little thing gingerly while Canada rolled up the mattresses and swept the floors with a straw broom nearly as big as she was. By the time everything was tidy, the sun had burned away the mist and Saxony was fussing.

Canada heaved the baby onto her hip. "I fetch Saxy here down to old Auntie Europe—she look out for the picanninies. Then I show you the bestest way to the Big House."

It had rained in the night, and the morning smelled clean and damp. Sophie waited for Canada on the front steps, scratching at some new bug bites on her leg and trying not to think about whether Mammy would slap her again or if Dr. Fairchild's Mama was as mean as his wife.

There was certainly plenty to distract her. Chickens scratched and squabbled in the dusty road between the cabins, ignoring scrawny dogs, who ignored them back. From the cabin next door, a tethered goat gazed with yellow, slitted eyes through the fence-slats at the rows of vegetables in Africa's garden. Birds sang from the oak grove and dipped and soared above the restless cane.

The Good Old Days were sure livelier than the present. Sophie thought she'd like them just fine, if she didn't have to be a slave.

Then Canada ran up, and it was time to go to the Big House.

Thinking it over, Sophie decided that Canada must be her official magical sidekick and guide. She certainly acted like one—pointing out the fastest shortcuts to the Big House and the yard, warning her what parts of the gardens were off-limits, telling her how to deal with Mammy.

"She bark like a mad dog," Canny said, "But she don't hardly ever bite 'less you sass her. You just bend real respectful, say yes'm and no'm and keep you eyes down, and she be happy as a goat in a briar patch."

Like Miss Ely, Sophie thought, remembering the strict math teacher. *It's just playacting. I don't really have to mean it.* She grinned at Canny, knocked on Mammy's door, went in, and bobbed politely.

"There you are," said Mammy. "That headcloth looks like a possum's been nesting in it."

Sophie glanced up, caught a fierce dark glare, and looked down again. "I'm sorry. I didn't have a mirror."

"Sass and excuses!" Mammy whipped off Sophie's tignon and refolded it. "If it were up to me, I'd send you right back to Mr. Robert. But Mrs. Fairchild's a kind, Christian lady and she takes her responsibilities seriously. Just you keep in mind that kind is not the same as weak. Mrs. Fairchild ran this plantation all alone when the Master passed and Dr. Charles was off North learning to be a doctor. She still runs it. She's not likely to be impressed by a mongrel slave-wench who thinks she's as good as white folks." Mammy yanked the tignon tight. "Follow me."

A few moments later, Sophie was on the gallery of the Big House, curtsying to her five-times great grandmother, Mrs. Charles Fairchild of Oak River Plantation with her eyes fixed on the spreading pool of her wide black skirts. She felt slightly sick.

"So you're Sophie," a sweet, slow voice said. "Look up, child. I want to see your face."

Shyly, Sophie lifted her gaze to a round, rosy face framed by a frilly white cap, a little rosebud mouth, a very unFairchild-like button nose, and clear blue eyes.

"What an adventure you've had!" Mrs. Fairchild said merrily. "And how like Mr. Robert not to tell us he was sending you. I've written to scold him. Now. What shall we do with you? I suppose you do fancy sewing?"

Sophie considered lying, decided it would lead to disaster. "No, ma'am."

"We shall have to teach you, then. Dr. Charles tells me you're well-spoken. What are your accomplishments?"

"Accomplishments, ma'am?"

"Can you dress hair, for instance? Starch and iron?"

What did slaves do, anyway? Sophie wracked her brain for some useful skill. "I like to read. And I won a prize once, for my handwriting."

"I declare!" Mrs. Fairchild produced a fat leather book from the folds of her dress. "Can you read this?"

The spine was stamped in gold: *Little Dorrit*, by Charles Dickens. Sophie opened the book eagerly. If there was one thing she was good at, it was reading aloud. Whenever teachers wanted something read in class, she was always the first to be called on. She found the first chapter and began: *"Thirty years ago, Marseilles lay burning in the sun, one day. A blazing sun upon a fierce August day was no greater rarity in southern France then, than at any other time, before or since.—"*

"You read very well, child." Mrs. Fairchild sounded surprised. "Isn't it just like Robert to have you taught! He never did give a snap of his fingers about the law. What do you think, Mammy?"

"I think she's next-door to useless. But she can fetch and carry and help Aunt Winney see after your things."

"You're right. Winney will be glad of the help, and there's no one better to train her up as a lady's maid." Mrs. Fairchild gave Sophie a friendly smile.

"It will be nice to have a bright young face around me. Not dressed like a yard hand, though. You ask Winney if she can find something in that armoire full of gowns Miss Charlotte left behind when she married."

*   *   *

Aunt Winney, it turned out, was Mrs. Fairchild's body servant. She was older and even stouter than her mistress, and couldn't go up and down stairs without puffing and groaning from the pain in her legs and back. She'd traveled from Virginia to Oak River with the former Miss Caroline Wilkes Berry when she was a bride, which was why, as she told Sophie, she had a Christian name instead of one of them heathenish Oak River names.

"You be grateful you ain't called New Guinea or Mexico," the old woman said. "MIssy Caro say old Massa's grandpappy begun it when he buy the firstest slaves for Oak River. He name them Asia, America, Africa, Europe, Australia, and England."

Aunt Winney reminded Sophie of the old ladies at St. Martin's, chatty and cozy and full of gossip and pats on the cheek. So what if she was leather-colored and had her hair tied up in a jaunty red-checked tignon? She was friendly and more than happy to answer Sophie's questions.

"England? The other names are continents. Why not South America or Antarctica?"

Aunt Winney chuckled. "You so sharp, you going cut youself. Old Massa's grandpappy come from England, that why-for. Now, lets us see what Miss Lotty got you might could wear."

By the time the bell rang at noon, Sophie was the proud possessor of two high-necked calico dresses, two petticoats, white calico stockings that tied at her knees with string, a crisp white apron, and a pair of scuffed brown boots with buttons up the side that were too big and had to be stuffed with rags to keep her feet from sliding.

Aunt Winney smiled. "You pretty as a picture, sugar."

Pretty? Sophie turned and stared in the mirror.

A stranger stared back at her with dark, surprised eyes. With her hair hidden by the white tignon and a shape created by layers of petticoat and a fitted top, she looked almost grown-up. But pretty? Mama certainly wouldn't have thought so.

Aunt Winney's dark, round face appeared over her shoulder. "Now don't you go running away with the notion that yaller skin make you better than other folks. You hear what I say?"

Why did people kept telling her to be humble? The girl in the mirror looked meek enough to Sophie. "Yes, ma'am."

"Good. Now, run on down to the kitchen and fetch me a bowl of mush. You can catch a bite while you down there, but no lollygagging."

The shortcut to Oak Cottage passed behind the maze. Sophie was tempted to run in to look for the Creature, remembered it was off-limits, decided she'd let it go. Being a slave wasn't as bad as she had feared, now she'd been assigned to the Big House. She liked her many-times-great grandmother, and it seemed like her grandmother liked her, too. Maybe they'd get to be friends, and Sophie could tell her about the present. That would make a good adventure.

When she reached the kitchen, Sophie asked a slave woman shelling lima beans on the bench outside for two bowls of mush. The woman glared at her. "Bowls is in the blue dresser and mush in the iron pot. Wait on your own self."

Sophie took two steps into what felt like a steam bath perfumed with pepper and onion and browning butter and her stomach turned over. She'd been feeling off all morning—nerves, she'd thought. Maybe it was just hunger. Careful to keep out of everybody's way, she found the blue dresser and the bowls. The iron pot hung at the side of hearth. Sophie looked in and saw yellow mush mixed with unidentifiable lumps that might be potatoes or yams or chunks of fatty meat. There were flies struggling on it—and probably in it, too.

Heat washed over Sophie like scalding water, her stomach clenched, and she threw up on the stone hearth.

First she thought she'd die of shame and then she just thought she'd die. Everything inside her seemed to be trying to get out and her head beat like a thousand drums. Shrill voices pierced her ears, pinching hands pulled at her as she was heaved up like a bundle of laundry and carried out into the air.

After that, Sophie was conscious of very little except how miserable she was. At some point, her fouled clothes were taken off. She felt water cooling her burning skin, then a coarse gown that rasped her like sand paper. Large, cool hands touched her rigid belly and her forehead. She heard a voice she knew was Dr. Charles's saying that Robert should never have sent a city girl to the swamp in fever season.

She dragged her eyes open, saw her arm stretched over a white basin. Dr. Charles was beside her, holding a knife as bright and painful to look at as a bolt of lightning.

The knife bit into the crook of her elbow, and she felt very weak and sleepy and Papa was squeezing her arm and telling her that he'd come to take her home.

"I miss my Punkin-Pie," he said, and opened his mouth wider and wider, swallowing her arm clear up to the elbow. Sophie was wondering, without real interest, whether he intended to eat her clear up when she noticed the Creature floating in the air beside her, its face all puckered like a baby about to cry. She opened her mouth to give it a piece of her mind, then got distracted by Papa turning into an old man with a tall hat like Abraham Lincoln's. But he couldn't be Abraham Lincoln because Lincoln was white and this old man was black as his hat, black as the crooked stick he carried, wound with red thread and white shells.

He waved the stick towards a door outlined with a thread of blinding light. As Sophie watched, the thread widened to a scarf, then a ribbon. The door was opening.

"Fetch Africa," a woman's voice said. "This girl going fast."

What girl? Sophie wondered. And where was she going?

"Papa Legba." She saw the Creature crouched at the old man's feet. "Can you save this-here white girl? I go to a lot of bother to get her, and there ain't another one will do as well."

The old man gave the Creature a look that could have skinned a mule. "Serve you right, duppy, if she do die. You can't just go dragging folks through time like it was a railway station!"

One amber eye peered up impudently. "Don't serve *her* right, though. Dead, she ain't worth nothing. Live, she might could do some good."

The old man studied the Creature, his face still as a carving. Suddenly he laughed. "That plan of yours, duppy, is like something Compair Lapin and Bouki might hatch when they been drinking corn likker. Going to be fun to watch. But you best remember all doorways belong to me. I choose when they open, where they lead, and who may pass through."

The Creature touched the old man's boot. "I remember."

Sophie was about to ask the old man if he could open a door and send her home when a dark blue void opened over her bed. She saw a light sparkling in the heart of it, crystal blue. The scent of salt water tickled her nose; the taste of molasses filled her mouth. The bed rocked under her, floating on a gently swelling sea. A wave leapt up, caressed her body coolly, withdrew. The void filled with a velvety voice singing a wordless song, and a queenly figure appeared, crowned with gold and veiled with strings of pearls.

"Yemaya," said the old man in the hat.

"Don't you know better than to lead a child through into this time with no preparation? The water and the food are poison to one who is not used to them. You play a dangerous game, Legba." The musical voice was stern.

"I *am* dangerous," said the old man silkily.

"And I am not?"

For a moment, the air around the two entities crackled and buzzed. Then the old man laughed. "You're barking up the wrong tree, Yemaya. This game belongs to the little trickster, who plots but never plans."

The Creature grinned sheepishly.

"You play with forces you do not understand," the woman told it, angry and amused. "Do not do so again."

"No, ma'am," the Creature said. "Not 'less I needs to. Can you fix her?"

"I can," the velvety voice said. "I will."

The door snicked shut, darkness fell, and Sophie was asleep.

*   *   *

After a dreamless, drifting time, Sophie woke to an unfamiliar room, the crimson glow of a fire, and a woman bent over a big-bellied pot like a witch in a fairy tale. She felt like she'd done three thousand sit-ups and run fifty miles in a desert, but she wasn't sick any more.

The woman turned. Without her glasses, Sophie couldn't see her face, but she was dressed in blue with yellow around her head, like Yemaya, and held herself like a queen.

"Bout time you woke up," the woman said. "I ain't got no root for sleeping-sickness."

It was a beautiful voice, but it was human, and Sophie recognized it. "You're Canada's mother. Africa."

"That's right, and I'm right glad you know it. You been clear off your head since Dr. Charles bled you yesterday." Africa put aside a curtain of gauzy fabric, slid an arm under Sophie's shoulders, and held a steaming cup to her lips.

The mixture was bitter and mossy and thick with bits of leaves. As Sophie choked it down, Africa said, "I don't know what to make of you, and that's the truth. The Master of the Crossroads, he goes his own way. That way sometimes bright and sometimes dark, but it ain't never what I'd call easy."

Sophie frowned. "Do you mean the old man, or the Creature?"

"What creature is that, sugar?"

"The one that brought me here. I have to find it, so I can go back home."

Africa smoothed her hair gently. "This your home now, sugar, less Mr. Robert change his mind. You rest."

*　　*　　*

Next time Sophie woke, Dr. Charles was taking her pulse.

"Strong and regular," he said. "Mrs. Fairchild will be pleased. A couple of days of rest, and you'll be as good as new."

Dr. Charles gave her hand a pat and moved away. Sophie found her glasses under the pillow and put them on. The room snapped into focus. Sophie looked around at four iron beds draped in gauze, and a cabinet full of jars and bottles beside a table where Dr. Charles sat unrolling a long strip of linen around a slave woman's arm. A second slave, an older woman in a big white apron, stood beside him with a jar.

Dr. Charles snipped off the bandage, tied the ends, and tucked them in neatly. "There, Rhodes. I don't want you back in the fields for another few days yet. I'll tell Mr. Akins to assign you something light."

The woman Rhodes thanked him and left. The older woman, whose name was Aunt Cissie, fetched in skinny man with a hacking cough, followed by a big man complaining of a griping in his guts, an old woman bent over with rheumatism, and three or four more. Sophie watched Dr. Charles examine them, peering into mouths and eyes, sounding chests, instructing Aunt Cissie to give them liniment or spoons-full of foul-smelling liquid, asking after the health of a brother, an aunt, a father, a wife, listening to the soft-voiced, respectful answers. When the last patient had left, he dismissed Aunt Cissie, pulled out a long black book, and started to write in it.

The pen scratched softly, the flies buzzed lazily against the ceiling. Sophie was on the edge of drifting off to sleep again when a clattering on the porch jerked her awake. The door flew open and a man stomped in. He was dirty and roughly dressed, and Sophie thought he was another field hand until she saw that he kept his broad-brimmed hat on his greasy curls and looked Dr. Charles straight in the eye.

"Devon Cut needs a new gang-driver," he said.

Dr. Charles kept on writing. "Give it to Old Guam."

"Guam? That pipe-sucker?" His voice was like a street car braking. "He ain't done an honest day's work since the day his mammy weaned him."

"Mrs. Fairchild has chosen Old Guam, and I agree." Dr. Charles laid down his pen. "By the way, Akins, I've had a letter from Chicago. The new evaporators are on their way to New Orleans and should be here, God willing, in a few weeks. Have you read those articles I gave you?"

Akins tipped his hat to the back of his head. "Yessir," he said. "That there evaporator's a fine machine, but I'm thinking it's a mite complicated for them niggers to run."

"Given that a black man invented the apparatus, I have no doubt black men can learn to operate it, given the proper training." Dr. Charles got up and put on a black frock coat. "Come along to the Big House, and we'll discuss it. Why, hello, Canada. Have you come to visit Sophie?"

Sophie saw Canada, looking very small and black and meek, standing in the door with a large covered basket on her arm. "Yessir." Her voice was so low Sophie could hardly hear her. "I brung her some broth."

Dr. Charles patted the little girl's head as he left. Atkins ignored her completely. As soon as they were out the door, Canada turned and stuck out her tongue.

"Who's that horrible man?" Sophie asked.

"That old Mist' Akins, the overseer. His Mama beat him with an ugly stick so hard, it gone straight on till his soul."

Sophie laughed. "You're funny, Canada."

"White folks calls me Canada." She pulled a canister from the basket. "You call me Canny."

Sophie pulled herself up against the thin pillow. There was so much she didn't know about living in the past. If she was going to be stuck here for a while, she'd better learn—preferably before she saw Mammy again. "Canny, will you tell me about Oak River?"

"Sure. What you want to know?"

"Everything, I guess. I never lived on a plantation before."

Canny giggled. "You surely ain't. Flandy like to bust himself laughing when he hear 'bout you asking for a bath-room!"

Sophie flushed. "I know I've got a lot to learn."

"What you want to know?"

"Well, how soap is made and what a gang-driver does and why there's a curtain over the bed, to start off with."

Canny nodded. "Well, a gang-driver, he watch the field hands so they don't slack off. The mosquito bar keep the mosquitoes from eating you all alive in the night. I don't know nothing 'bout soap-making 'cept it stink to Heaven, but I know lots 'bout doves. I takes care of all the doves in the pigeon house."

"Tell me about the doves, then," Sophie said. "But I also need to know about cooking and washing and ironing and—"

"Ain't nobody know all that," Canny said. "And if'n they did, they too busy to hang round here telling you about it." She thought a moment. "Tell you what. Tomorrow's Saturday. Everybody gots a plenty of chores, but I asks around some, see who can maybe come by for a spell. That suit you?"

"That suits me just fine," Sophie said. "Thank you."

Canny unscrewed the canister and poured a fragrant golden stream into a tin cup. "Momi say if this set well, she see bout trying you on boil chicken and white bread. You gots to drink, too—water, milk, sassafras tea."

"Your Mama sure knows a lot about sick people."

"Momi know everything there is about everything," said Canny. "Momi a two-headed woman."

"Huh?"

"A two-headed woman. Sometimes, when she bring the babies and tend to folks and make *gris-gris*, she not just herself, but the other one, too."

"The other one?" Sophie remembered the velvety face in her dream. "You mean Yemaya?"

"Shush—that name a special secret. Maybe Momi tell you about it by and by." She made a face. "Maybe she tell me, too. Now drink up you soup, and tell you a story. You ever heard how come snakes got poison in they mouth and nothing else ain't got it?"

"No," said Sophie.

"Don't they tell no stories in New Orleans?"

"They tell lots of stories. Just not that one."

Canny settled down cross-legged at the foot of the bed. "When God make the snake, he put him in the bushes to ornament the ground. But things didn't suit the snake, so one day he get on a ladder and go up to see God."

Sophie finished the fragrant chicken broth, took off her glasses, and listened sleepily as the snake complained to God about getting stomped on and God gave him poison to protect himself. Canny described how, when the snake got a little carried away with his gift, the other animals climbed the heavenly ladder to complain in their turn. Sophie's eyes grew heavier and heavier. About the time God was coming up with an answer to their complaints, she fell asleep.

THE SEA KING'S SECOND BRIDE

C. S. E. Cooney

2011 RHYSLING WINNER, LONG POEM CATEGORY

March is blowing wet and snowy when I stumble on the Sea King
He has washed up from the water—all his nakedness like heaven
With his hair so lank and heavy, green and black as
Sodden seaweed, with his harp of kelp and pearl
Cracked to pieces on his knee

"What ails you, my Sea King?" I ask this creature, laughing
I love him—how I love him, immediate and sudden
The way you love a rainstorm, the Milky Way, a leopard
That reckless love of wild things after years pent in a city

"My bride Agneta left me," says the Sea King like the thunder
Like the salt and surf and thunder
"She has left our seven children, and our castle made of coral
She has gone back to her father, to his bright and airy kingdom
Has maybe found a lover—some brawny freckled farmer
She left me for another."

"But tell me, pretty sea-thing," I tease the lonely Sea King
"What motivates this horror? Perhaps—because you beat her?
Or threatened sharks would eat her? Or treated her with seven sons
Got upon her one by one, and not a year between them?

That might just be a reason, if reason's what you're after.
It's a basis to be bitter . . ."

(And no wonder! Poor Agneta!)

His Majesty grows maudlin, how he glances
How he glistens! So cunning, yet so awkward
On these sands that bloat and bleach him, in this shape
Akin to man-shape, gills agape and fins aquiver
How the Sea King's skin is silver, like lightning under water!

"Agneta was my daybreak," mourns the Sea King on the seashore
"I never knew a morning 'til the morning that I met her
When I stole her from her father, leaving only dew behind us
I cried to her, *Come under! Come beneath and be my consort!*
She said she feared the drowning, but I covered her in lilies
A crown of purest lilies, white as beeswax, soft as velvet
I combed her hair with sea-shells, and fed her
From my fingers
Her slightest wish I granted with the mightiest of magic
I played this harp of pearl, and it swept away
Her memory.
She didn't mind forgetting.
I thought I made her happy."

The Sea King's eyes are dark and wide, like otters slick with oil spill
I poke his spiny ribcage and the silver fish that dance there
He jumps—perhaps it tickled? At least he can be tickled!

"Cheer up, my doughty Sea King!" I shout in manner bracing
"For I sicken of this city, of its traffic lights and taxes
Of the emails and the faxes, and the work and wage and worry
So, tell you what, my darling: you take me to your kingdom

And I'll romp with all your children, spin them stories by the daylight
Sing them lullabies at nighttime
And when they're sound and sleeping, I will creep
Into your bower, to your bed of bright anemone, where
I'll comb your hair with seashells, pour my palms in perfumed oil
By and by I'll take you deeper than ever Sea King ventured
We will scour off what's rotting, all these thoughts of sweet Agneta
Do you think we have a bargain?"

The Sea King does not answer:
But he shrugs his flashing shoulders
And I take this for a yes.

It wasn't like a marriage:
No broom or blood or bonfire
But he made a few adjustments for my sub-aquatic breathing
Taught his certain way of speaking, like a whale when it's singing
And a kind of seeing clearly through the brine and murk and current

And when I see him clearly, see my Sea King underwater
(He isn't much to look at—until he's underwater)
Then madder do I love him, love his glimmer in the gloaming
Like a tooth or moon or treasure
That you wish might be a knife-blade so to wed it with your flesh

Sure enough his children love me, seven princes crowned in lilies
We are happy in our frolics, and they giggle at my ragging
At my bad jokes and my chitchat, and the way I tease their father
At breakfast we are raucous, and at dinner most uncouth
At supper, always laughing—well, the kids and I are laughing
But the Sea King sits in silence and recalls his wife Agneta

"She heard the church bells ringing—and she left me, never caring
For my soreness or despairing
Forsaking all her children
Forgetting her beloved."

His wet blanket on our banquets
Somewhat dampens the hilarity, somewhat chisels at my charity
And the boys slink off for climates more conducive to their gaiety
And I tell their father gently, with what kindness I can muster
That our memories are fragile, that we cannot help forgetting
And that precious poor Agneta—please recall, my dearest Deep One—
Had been practically lobotomized by all his fell enchantments
So please strive for some compassion!

"Agneta!" cries the Sea King, "Agneta!" and "Agneta!"

And even though I love him, there are times I'd trade his kingdom
(Yes, his castle made of coral, and his princes crowned in lilies)
For a single good harpoon

By late April I am brooding
And by May I'm truly scheming
And in June I hatch a plan half-conceived in idle dreaming:

"Oh, the bells, the church bells ringing!"
I groan unto my Sea King, rending small strategic punctures
In my robes of pearl and seaweed

"The steeple bells that scream matins—the sound of papa weeping!
In waking or in sleeping, every night and noon I hear them
As if I stood just near them! Oh, the bells, the bells—I weaken
At their tintinnabulations!

Won't you let me, dearest Sea King, break to surface and behold them!
An hour, just an hour, but one hour I do beg you!"

Well, the Sea King doesn't like that.
Does not like that.
Not at all.

He is roused to indignation, which in turn ignites to fury
He is bright as any blizzard, he is cold and white and wondrous
And his bare feet stomp a tidal wave that would have swamped Atlantis
(If Atlantis weren't already swamped from when Agneta left him)
And he blusters and he thunders, and he coaxes and he wheedles:

Don't I like his coral castle with its turrets neat as needles?
And its grottos and its bowers and its gardens and its mazes?
Don't I love to love his children, am I not content to stay here
Like the lampreys and the stingrays and the sharks who come to play
     here?

How he sulks and how he scowls, how he pleads and how he howls!
But—"The bells! The bells!" I mutter, growing slack and wan and fainter
'Til he grants me what I ask for: "Just an hour, mind—ONE HOUR!"
And up he swims me, grimly
And he doesn't see I'm smiling

My father's at St. Agnes, where he's often found on Sundays
With his choir, and his piano, and the band that plays on Sundays
And I sit with the sopranos, and I join in at the descant
And my father smiles a little, even winks a droll good morning
He is busy with conducting and he's maybe even praying
Thus I stay the hour allotted me, through Eucharist and homily
But—all in all I'd rather be
Fathoms down beneath the sea, with magic and with mystery

My seven heathen darlings
And a very cranky Sea King

When the bells have ceased to ring, I kiss my father swiftly
He tells me that he's missed me
I let him know I'm happy
(even lacking crowns of lilies)
(even sopping wet and smelly)
I say I'm truly happy.
It's all he ever wanted.

When he sees me rushing toward him, arms out-flung and smile kindled
The Sea King looks astonished, quite bewildered and bedazzled
Like he's never seen my likeness

"Your hair is bright as goldfish! Your face is sweet as morning!"

Taking up his silver hand, I vow as how I've missed him
Missed his scales and his spackles and his webbed and clammy skin

"How choking is the incense! How blinding are the candles
After months spent in the darkness of your castle made of coral.
But it's nice to see my father! Let's go visit him this autumn!
We can introduce the children."

The Sea King's rapid smile is a dreadful shock of pleasure
Like a little boy's first mischief, like a damsel's foremost coyness
Like a man who's given manna when he begged for stale bread
He cocks his head and murmurs through the tousles and the tangles:
"I never brought you lilies."

My goblet runneth over, so I scold him, rather sternly:

"There is time enough for trinkets—
Time immortal, time forever, time for starfish in my bathtub
Time for flowers and a foot rub, time for tokens meant
For me alone—and not some ghostly maiden, be she
Ever pure and pious, be she pretty as a lily
For you see, my doughty Sea King, I am from a doting family
And I know that you've been lonely, and I know I'm no Agneta—
But I'm warm and I am willing
I can offer what I offer, but it will not come to begging
Do you want me for you lover? Or pine for one who left you?"

The Sea King pauses, pondering
(I almost punch his face in) then he smiles like a
dolphin, like a green wave clean and leaping, and he solemnly incants:

"Come down with me, come under!
Come beneath and be my consort
I will tell you all my secrets, I will let you take me deeper
Where no Sea King dared to venture, where Agneta never wandered
You will whisper your desires, and together we'll uncover
All the fire in the ocean."

Then I give my awkward Sea King
This small thing that I've been saving
For a moment like this moment when both he and I are ready
First a kiss and then a promise, then a topple and a tumble
It is frantic, it is frenzied, and we finish in a fever
Come unclasped in joyous moisture
And he leads me to the river
Where we hear the children singing.

THE MAN WHO BRIDGED THE MIST

Kij Johnson

Kit came to Nearside with two trunks and an oiled-cloth folio full of plans for the bridge across the mist. His trunks lay tumbled like stones at his feet where the mailcoach guard had dropped them. The folio he held close, away from the drying mud of yesterday's storm.

Nearside was small, especially to a man of the capital where buildings towered seven and eight stories tall, a city so large that even a vigorous walker could not cross in a day. Here hard-packed dirt roads threaded through irregular spaces scattered with structures and fences. Even the inn was plain, two stories of golden limestone and blue slate tiles with (he could smell) some sort of animals living behind it. On the sign overhead, a flat, pale blue fish very like a ray curvetted against a black background.

A brightly dressed woman stood by the inn's door. Her skin and eyes were pale, almost colorless. "Excuse me," Kit said. "Where can I find the ferry to take me across the mist?" He could feel himself being weighed, but amiably: a stranger, small and very dark, in gray—a man from the east.

The woman smiled. "Well, the ferries are both on this side, at the upper dock. But I expect what you really want is someone to oar the ferry, yes? Rasali Ferry came over from Farside last night. She's the one you'll want to talk to. She spends a lot of time at The Deer's Hart. But you wouldn't like The Hart, sir," she added. "It's not nearly as nice as The Fish here. Are you looking for a room?"

"I hope I'll be staying in Farside tonight," Kit said apologetically. He didn't want to seem arrogant. The invisible web of connections he would need for his work started here with this first impression, with all the first impressions of the next few days.

"That's what *you* think," the woman said. "I'm guessing it'll be a day or two—or more—before Rasali goes back. Valo Ferry might, but he doesn't cross so often."

"I could buy out the trip's fares, if that's why she's waiting."

"It's not that," the woman said. "She won't cross the mist 'til she's ready. Until she feels it's right, if you follow me. But you can ask, I suppose."

Kit didn't follow but he nodded anyway. "Where's The Deer's Hart?"

She pointed. "Left, then right, then down by the little boat yard."

"Thank you," Kit said. "May I leave my trunks here until I work things out with her?"

"We always stow for travelers." The woman grinned. "And cater to them too, when they find out there's no way across the mist today."

* * *

The Deer's Hart was smaller than The Fish, and livelier. At midday the oak-shaded tables in the beer garden beside the inn were clustered with light-skinned people in brilliant clothes, drinking and tossing comments over the low fence into the boat yard next door where, half lost in steam, a youth and two women bent planks to form the hull of a small flat-bellied boat. When Kit spoke to a man carrying two mugs of something that looked like mud and smelled of yeast, the man gestured at the yard with his chin. "Ferrys are over there. Rasali's the one in red," he said as he walked away.

"The one in red" was tall, her skin as pale as that of the rest of the locals, with a black braid so long that she had looped it around her neck to keep it out of the way. Her shoulders flexed in the sunlight as she and the youth forced a curved plank to take the skeletal hull's shape and clamped it in place. The other woman, slightly shorter, with the ash-blond hair so common here, forced an augur through the plank and into a rib, then hammered a peg into the hole she'd made. After three pegs the boatwrights straightened. The plank held. *Strong,* Kit thought. *I wonder if I can get them for the bridge?*

"Rasali!" a voice bellowed, almost in Kit's ear. "Man here's looking for you." Kit turned in time to see the man with the mugs gesturing, again with his chin. He sighed and walked to the waist-high fence. The boatwrights stopped to drink from blueware bowls before the one in red and the youth came over.

"I'm Rasali Ferry of Farside," the woman said. Her voice was softer and higher than he had expected of a woman as strong as she, with the fluid vowels of the local accent. She nodded to the boy beside her: "Valo Ferry of Farside, my brother's eldest." Valo was more a young man than a boy, lighter-haired than Rasali and slightly taller. They had the same heavy eyebrows and direct amber eyes.

"Kit Meinem of Atyar," Kit said.

Valo asked, "What sort of name is Meinem? It doesn't mean anything."

"In the capital, we take our names differently than you."

"Oh, like Jenner Ellar." Valo nodded. "I guessed you were from the capital—your clothes and your skin."

Rasali said, "What can we do for you, Kit Meinem of Atyar?"

"I need to get to Farside today," Kit said.

Rasali shook her head. "I can't take you. I just got here and it's too soon. Perhaps Valo?"

The youth tipped his head to one side, his expression suddenly abstract. He shook his head. "No, not today, I don't think."

"I can buy out the fares if that helps. It's Jenner Ellar I am here to see."

Valo looked interested but said, "No," to Rasali, and she added, "What's so important that it can't wait a few days?"

Better now than later, Kit thought. "I am replacing Teniant Planner as the lead engineer and architect for construction of the bridge over the mist. We start work again as soon as I've reviewed everything. And had a chance to talk to Jenner." He watched their faces.

Rasali said, "It's been a year since Teniant died. I was starting to think Empire had forgotten all about us and that your deliveries would be here 'til the iron rusted away."

Valo frowned. "Jenner Ellar's not taking over?"

"The new Department of Roads cartel is in my name," Kit said, "but I hope Jenner will remain as my second. You can see why I would like to meet him as soon as is possible, of course. He will—"

Valo burst out, "You're going to take over from Jenner after he's worked so hard on this? And what about us? What about *our* work?" His cheeks were flushed an angry red. *How do they conceal anything with skin like that?* Kit thought.

"Valo," Rasali said, a warning tone in her voice. Flushing darker still, the youth turned and strode away. Rasali snorted but said only: "Boys. He likes Jenner and he has problems with the bridge, anyway."

That was worth addressing. *Later.* "So what will it take to get you to carry me across the mist, Rasali Ferry of Farside? The project will pay anything reasonable."

"I cannot," she said. "Not today, not tomorrow. You'll have to wait."

"Why?" Kit asked, reasonably enough, he thought; but she eyed him for a long moment as though deciding whether to be annoyed.

"Have you gone across mist before?" she said at last.

"Of course," he said.

"But not the river," she said.

"Not the river," he agreed. "It's a quarter-mile across here, yes?"

"Yes." She smiled suddenly, white even teeth and warmth like sunlight in her eyes. "Let's go down and perhaps I can explain things better there." She jumped the fence with a single powerful motion, landing beside him to a chorus of cheers and shouts from the garden's patrons. She slapped hands with one, then gestured to Kit to follow her. She was well liked, clearly. Her opinion would matter.

The boat yard was heavily shaded by low-hanging oaks and chestnuts, and bounded on the east by an open-walled shelter filled with barrels and stacks of lumber. Rasali waved at the third boat maker, who was still putting her tools away. "Tilisk Boatwright of Nearside. My brother's wife," she said to Kit. "She makes skiffs with us but she won't ferry. She's not born to it as Valo and I are."

"Where's your brother?" Kit asked.

"Dead," Rasali said and lengthened her stride.

They walked a few streets over and then climbed a long even ridge perhaps eighty feet high, too regular to be natural. *A levee,* Kit thought, and distracted himself from the steep path by estimating the volume of earth and the labor that had been required to build it. Decades, perhaps, but how long ago? How many miles did it stretch? Which department had overseen it, or had it been the locals? The levee was treeless. The only feature was a slender wood tower hung with flags on the ridge, probably for signaling across the mist to Farside since it appeared too fragile for anything else. They had storms out here, Kit knew; there'd been one the night before. How often was the tower struck by lightning?

Rasali stopped. "There."

Kit had been watching his feet. He looked up and nearly cried out as light lanced his suddenly tearing eyes. He fell back a step and shielded his face. What had blinded him was an immense band of mist reflecting the morning sun.

Kit had never seen the mist river itself, though he bridged mist before this, two simple post-and-beam structures over narrow gorges closer to the capital. From his work in Atyar, he knew what was to be known. It was not water nor anything like. It formed somehow in the deep gorge of the great riverbed before him. It found its way some hundreds of miles north, upstream through a hundred narrowing mist creeks and streams before failing at last in shreds of drying foam that left bare patches of earth where they collected.

The mist stretched to the south as well, a deepening, thickening band that poured out at last from the river's mouth a thousand miles south, to form the mist ocean, which lay on the face of the salt-water ocean. Water had to follow the river's bed to run somewhere beneath or through the mist, but there was no way to prove this.

There was mist nowhere but this river and its streams and sea, but the mist split Empire in half.

After a moment, the pain in Kit's eyes grew less and he opened them again. The river was a quarter-mile across where they stood, a great gash of light between the levees. It seemed nearly featureless, blazing under the sun like a river of cream or of bleached silk, but as his eyes accustomed themselves, he saw the surface was not smooth but heaped and hollowed, and that it shifted slowly, almost indiscernibly, as he watched.

Rasali stepped forward and Kit started. "I'm sorry," he said with a laugh. "How long have I been staring? It's just—I had no idea."

"No one does," Rasali said. Her eyes when he met them were amused.

The east and west levees were nearly identical, each treeless and scrub-covered, with a signal tower. The levee on their side ran down to a narrow bare bank half a dozen yards wide. There was a wooden dock and a boat ramp, a rough switchback leading down to them. Two large boats had been pulled onto the bank. Another, smaller dock was visible a hundred yards downstream, attended by a clutter of boats, sheds and indeterminate piles covered in tarps.

"Let's go down." Rasali led the way, her words coming back to him over her shoulder. "The little ferry is Valo's. *Pearlfinder. The Tranquil Crossing's* mine." Her voice warmed when she said the name. "Eighteen feet long, eight wide. Mostly pine, but a purpleheart keel and pearwood headpiece. You can't see it from here, but the hull's sheathed in blue-dyed fishskin. I can carry three horses or a ton and a half of cartage or fifteen passengers. Or various combinations. I once carried twenty-four hunting dogs and two handlers. Never again."

Channeled by the levees, a steady light breeze eased down from the north. The air had a smell, not unpleasant but a little sour, wild. "How can you manage a boat like this alone? Are you that strong?"

"It's as big as I can handle," she said. "but Valo helps sometimes for really unwieldy loads. You don't paddle through mist. I mostly just coax the *Crossing* to where I want it to go. Anyway, the bigger the boat, the more likely that the Big Ones will notice it—though if you *do* run into a fish, the smaller the boat, the easier it is to swamp. Here we are."

They stood on the bank. The mist streams he had bridged had not prepared him for anything like this. Those were tidy little flows, more like fog collecting in hollows than this. From this angle, the river no longer seemed a smooth flow of creamy whiteness, nor even gently heaped clouds. The mist forced itself into hillocks and hollows, tight slopes perhaps twenty feet high that folded into one another. It had a surface but it was irregular, cracked in places and translucent in others. The boundary didn't seem as clearly defined as that between water and air.

"How can you move on this?" Kit said, fascinated. "Or even float?" The hillock immediately before them was flattening as he watched. Beyond it something like a vale stretched out for a few dozen yards before turning and becoming lost to his eyes.

"Well, I can't, not today," Rasali said. She sat on the gunwale of her boat, one leg swinging, watching him. "I can't push the *Crossing* up those slopes or find a safe path unless I feel it. If I went today, I know—I *know*—" she tapped her belly—"that I would find myself stranded on a pinnacle or lost in a hole. *That's* why I can't take you today, Kit Meinem of Atyar."

* * *

When Kit was a child, he had not been good with other people. He was small and easy to tease or ignore, and then he was sick for much of his seventh year and had to leave his crèche before the usual time, to convalesce in his mother's house. None of the children of the crèche came to visit him but he didn't mind that. He had books and puzzles, and whole quires of blank paper that his mother didn't mind him defacing.

The clock in the room in which he slept didn't work, so one day he used his penknife to take it apart. He arranged the wheels and cogs and springs in neat rows on the quilt in his room, by type and then by size; by materials; by weight; by shape. He liked holding the tiny pieces, thinking of how they might have been formed and how they worked together. The patterns they made were interesting but he knew the best pattern would be the working one, when they were all put back into their right places and the clock performed its task again. He had to think that the clock would be happier that way, too.

He tried to rebuild the clock before his mother came upstairs from her counting house at the end of the day, but when he had reassembled things, there remained a pile of unused parts and it still didn't work; so he shut the clock up and hoped she wouldn't notice that it wasn't ticking. Four days more of trying things during the day and concealing his failures at night, and on the fifth day the clock started again. One piece hadn't fit anywhere, a small brass cog. Kit still carried that cog in his pen case.

* * *

Late that afternoon, Kit returned to the river's edge. It was hotter and the mud had dried to cracked dust. The air smelled like old rags left too long in a pail. He saw no one at the ferry dock, but at the fisher's dock upstream people were gathering, a score or more of men and women with children running about.

The clutter looked even more disorganized as he approached. The fishing boats were fat coracles fashioned of leather stretched on frames, all tipped bottom up to the sun and looking like giant warts. The mist had dropped so that he could see a band of exposed rock below the bank. He could see the dock's pilings clearly. They were not vertical but had been set at an angle to make a cantilevered deck braced into the stone underlying the bank. The wooden pilings had been sheathed in metal.

He approached a silver-haired woman doing something with a treble hook as long as her hand. "What are you catching with that?" he said.

Her forehead was wrinkled when she looked up, but she smiled when she saw him. "Oh, you're a stranger. From Atyar, dressed like that. Am I right? We catch fish—" Still holding the hook, she extended her arms as far as they would stretch. "Bigger than that, some of them. Looks like more storms, so they're going to be biting tonight. I'm Meg Threehooks. Of Nearside, obviously."

"Kit Meinem of Atyar. I take it you can't find a bottom?" He pointed to the pilings.

Jen Threehooks followed his glance. "It's there somewhere, but it's a long way down and we can't sink pilings because the mist dissolves the wood. Oh, and fish eat it. Same thing with our ropes, the boats, us—anything but metal and rock, really." She knotted a line around the hook's eye. The cord was dark and didn't look heavy enough for anything Kit could imagine catching on hooks that size.

"What are these made of, then?" He squatted to look at the framing under one of the coracles.

"Careful, that one's mine," Meg said. "The hides—well, and all the ropes—are fishskin. Mist fish, not water-fish. Tanning takes off some of the slime so they don't last forever either, not if they're afloat." She made a face. "We have a saying: foul as fish-slime. That's pretty nasty, you'll see."

"I need to get to Farside," Kit said. "Could I hire you to carry me across?"

"In my boat?" She snorted. "No, fishers stay close to shore. Go see Rasali Ferry. Or Valo."

"I saw her," he said ruefully.

"Thought so. You must be the new architect—city folk are always so impatient. You're so eager to be dinner for a Big One? If Rasali doesn't want to go then don't go, stands to reason."

Kit was footsore and frustrated by the time he returned to The Fish. His trunks were already upstairs, in a small cheerful room overwhelmed by a table that nearly filled it, with a stiflingly hot cupboard bed. When Kit spoke to the woman he'd talked to earlier, Brana Keep, the owner of The Fish (its real name turned out to be The Big One's Delight) laughed. "Rasali's as hard to shift as bedrock," she said. "And truly, you would not be comfortable at The Hart."

* * *

By the next morning, when Kit came downstairs to break his fast on flatbread and pepper-rubbed water-fish, everyone appeared to know everything about him, especially his task. He had wondered whether there would be resistance to the project, but if there had been any it was gone now. There were a few complaints, mostly about slow payments—a universal issue for public works—but none at all about the labor or organization. Most in the taproom seemed not to mind the bridge, and the feeling everywhere he went in town was optimistic. He'd run into more resistance elsewhere, building smaller bridges.

"Well, why should we be concerned?" Brana Keep said to Kit. "You're bringing in people to work, yes? So we'll be selling room and board and clothes and beer to them. And you'll be hiring some of us and everyone will do well while you're building this bridge of yours. I plan to be wading ankle-deep through gold by the time this is done."

"And after," Kit said, "when the bridge is complete—think of it, the first real link between the east and west sides of Empire. The only place for three thousand miles where people and trade can cross the mist easily, safely, whenever they wish. You'll be the heart of Empire in ten years. Five." He laughed a little, embarrassed by the passion that shook his voice.

"Yes, well," Brana Keep said in the easy way of a woman who makes her living by not antagonizing customers, "we'll make that harness when the colt is born."

For the next six days, Kit explored the town and surrounding countryside.

He met the masons, a brother and sister that Teniant had selected before her death to oversee the pillar and anchorage construction on Nearside. They were quiet but competent and Kit was comfortable not replacing them.

Kit also spoke with the Nearside ropemakers, and performed tests on their fishskin ropes and cables, which turned out even stronger than he had hoped, with excellent resistance to rot and to catastrophic and slow failure. The makers told him that the rope stretched for its first two years in use, which made it ineligible to replace the immense chains that would bear the bridge's weight; but it could replace the thousands of vertical suspender chains that that would support the roadbed with a great saving in weight.

He spent much of his time watching the mist. It changed character unpredictably: a smooth rippled flow, hours later a badland of shredding foam, still later a field of steep dunes that joined and shifted as he watched. The river generally dropped in its bed each day under the sun and rose after dark, though it wasn't consistent.

The winds were more predictable. Hedged between the levees, they streamed southward each morning and northward each evening, growing stronger toward midday and dusk, and falling away entirely in the afternoons and at night. They did not seem to affect the mist much except for tearing off shreds that landed on the banks as dried foam.

The winds meant that there would be more dynamic load on the bridge than Teniant Planner had predicted. Kit would never criticize her work publicly and he gladly acknowledged her brilliant interpersonal skills, which had brought the town into cheerful collaboration, but he was grateful that her bridge had not been built as designed.

He examined the mist more closely, as well, by lifting a piece from the river's surface on the end of an oar. The mist was stiffer than it looked, and in bright light he thought he could see tiny shapes, perhaps creatures or plants or something altogether different. There were microscopes in Atyar, and people who studied these things; but he had never bothered to learn more, interested only in the structure that would bridge it. In any case, living things interested him less than structures.

Nights, Kit worked on the table in his room. Teniant's plans had to be revised. He opened the folios and cases she had left behind and read everything he found there. He wrote letters, wrote lists, wrote schedules, wrote duplicates of everything, sent to the capital for someone to do all the subsequent copying. His new plans for the bridge began to take shape. He started to glimpse the invisible architecture that was the management of the vast project.

He did not see Rasali Ferry except to ask each morning whether they might travel that day. The answer was always no.

*   *   *

One afternoon, when the clouds were heaping into anvils filled with rain, he walked up to the building site half a mile north of Nearside. For two years, off and on, carts had tracked south on the Hoic Mine road and the West River Road, leaving limestone blocks and iron bars here in untidy heaps. Huge dismantled shear-legs lay beside a caretaker's wattle-and-daub hut. There were thousands of large rectangular blocks.

Kit examined some of the blocks. Limestone was often too chossy for large-scale construction but this rock was sound, with no apparent flaws or fractures. There were not enough, of course, but undoubtedly more had been quarried. He had written to order resumption of deliveries and they would start arriving soon.

Delivered years too early, the iron trusses that would eventually support the roadbed were stacked neatly, painted black to protect them from moisture, covered in oiled tarps, and raised from the ground on planks. Sheep grazed the knee-high grass that grew everywhere. When one eyed him incuriously, Kit found himself bowing. "Forgive the intrusion," he said and laughed: too old to be talking to sheep.

The test pit was still open, with a ladder on the ground nearby. Weeds clung when he moved the ladder as though reluctant to release it. He descended.

The pasture had not been noisy but he was startled when he dropped below ground level and the insects and whispering grasses were suddenly silenced. The soil around him was striated shades of dun and dull yellow. Halfway down, he sliced a wedge free with his knife: lots of clay, good foundation soil as he had been informed. Some twenty feet down, the pit's bottom looked like the walls, but when he crouched to dig at the dirt between his feet with his knife, he hit rock almost immediately. It seemed to be shale. He wondered how far down the water table was. Did the Nearsiders find it difficult to dig wells? Did the mist ever backwash into one? There were people at University in Atyar who were trying to understand mist, but there was still so much that could not be examined or quantified.

He collected a rock to examine in better light and climbed from the pit in time to see a teamster approaching, leading four mules, her wagon groaning under the weight of the first new blocks. A handful of Nearsider men and women followed, rolling their shoulders and popping their joints. They called out greetings and he walked across to them.

When he got back to The Fish hours later, exhausted from helping unload the cart and soaked from the storm that had started while he did so, there was a message from Rasali. *Dusk* was all it said.

* * *

Kit was stiff and irritable when he left for *The Tranquil Crossing*. He had hired a carrier from The Fish to haul one of his trunks down to the dock but the others remained in his room, which he would probably keep until the bridge was done. He carried his folio of plans and paperwork himself. He was leaving duplicates of everything on Nearside, but after so much work it was hard to trust any of it to the hands of others.

The storm was over and the clouds were moving past, leaving the sky every shade between lavender and a rich purple-blue. The largest moon was a crescent in the west, the smaller a half circle immediately overhead. In the fading light, the mist was a dark, smoky streak. The air smelled fresh. Kit's mood lightened and he half-trotted down the final slope.

His fellow passengers were there before him: a prosperous-looking man with a litter of piglets in a woven wicker cage (Tengon whites, the man confided, the best bloodline in all Empire); a woman in the dark clothes fashionable in the capital, with brass-bound document cases and a folio very like Kit's; two traders with many cartons of powdered pigment; a mail courier with locked leather satchels and two guards. Nervous about their first crossing, Uni and Tom Mason greeted Kit when he arrived.

In the gathering darkness the mist formed tight-folded hills and coulees. Swifts darted just above the surface, using the wind flowing up the valley, searching for insects, he supposed. Once a sudden black shape, too quick to see clearly, appeared from below. Then it, and one of the birds, was gone.

The voices of the fishers at their dock carried to him. They launched their boats and he watched one and then another and then a gaggle of the little coracles push themselves up a slope of the mist. There were no lamps.

"Ready, everyone?" Kit had not heard Rasali approach. She swung down into the ferry. "Hand me your gear."

Stowing and embarkation were quick, though the piglets complained. Kit strained his eyes but the coracles could no longer be seen. When he noticed Rasali waiting for him, he apologized. "I guess the fish are biting."

Rasali glanced at the river as she stowed his trunk. "Small ones. A couple of feet long only. The fishers like them bigger, five or six feet, though they don't want them too big, either. But they're not fish, not what you think fish are. Hand me that."

He hesitated a moment, then gave her the folio before stepping into the ferry. *The Tranquil Crossing* sidled at his weight but sluggishly: a carthorse instead of a riding mare. His stomach lurched. "Oh!" he said.

"What?" one of the traders asked nervously. Rasali untied the rope holding them, pulled it into the boat.

Kit swallowed. "I had forgotten. The motion of the boat. It's not like water at all."

He did not mention his fear but there was no need. The others murmured assent. The courier, her dark face sharp-edged as a hawk, growled, "Every time I do this, it surprises me. I dislike it."

Rasali unshipped a scull and slid the great triangular blade into the mist, which parted reluctantly. "I've been on mist more than water but I remember the way water felt. Quick and jittery. This is better."

"Only to you, Rasali Ferry," Uni Mason said.

"Water's safer, anyway," the man with the piglets said.

Rasali leaned into the oar and the boat slid away from the dock. "Anything is safe until it kills you."

The mist absorbed the quiet sounds of shore almost immediately. One of Kit's first projects had been a stone single-arch bridge over water, far to the north in Eskje province. He had visited before construction started, and he was there for five days more than he had expected, caught by a snowstorm that left nearly two feet on the ground. This reminded him of those snowy moonless nights, the air as thick and silencing as a pillow on the ears.

Rasali did not scull so much as steer. It was hard to see far in any direction except up, but perhaps it was true that the mist spoke to her for she seemed to know where best to position the boat for the mist to carry it forward. She followed a small valley until it started to flatten and then mound up. The *Crossing* tipped slightly as it slid a few feet to port. The mail carrier made a noise and immediately stifled it.

Mist was a misnomer. It was denser than it seemed. Sometimes the boat seemed not to move through it so much as across its surface. Tonight it seemed like the dirty foam that strong winds could whip from Churash Lake's waves, near the western coast of Empire. Kit reached a hand over the boat's side. The mist piled against his hand, almost dry to the touch, sliding up his forearm with a sensation he could not immediately identify. When he realized it was prickling, he snatched his arm back in and rubbed it on a fold of his coat. The skin burned. Caustic, of course.

The man with the pigs whispered, "Will they come if we talk or make noise?"

"Not to talking or pigs' squealing," Rasali said. "They seem to like low noises. They'll rise to thunder sometimes."

One of the traders said, "What are they if they're not really fish? What do they look like?" Her voice shook. The mist was weighing on them all, all but Rasali.

"If you want to know you'll have to see one for yourself," Rasali said. "Or try to get a fisher to tell you. They gut and fillet them over the sides of their boats. No one else sees much but meat wrapped in paper or rolls of black skin for the ropemakers and tanners."

"*You've* seen them," Kit said.

"They're broad and flat. But ugly."

"And Big Ones?" Kit asked.

Her voice was harsh. "*Them* we don't talk about here."

No one spoke for a time. Mist—foam—heaped up at the boat's prow and parted, eased to the sides with an almost inaudible hissing. Once the mist off the port side heaved and something dark broke the surface for a moment, followed by other dark somethings, but they were not close enough to see well. One of the merchants cried without a sound or movement.

The Farside levee showed at last, a black mass that didn't get any closer for what felt like hours. Fighting his fear, Kit leaned over the side, keeping his face away from the surface. "It can't really be bottomless," he said half to himself. "What's under it?"

"You wouldn't hit the bottom, anyway," Rasali said.

The Tranquil Crossing eased up a long swell of mist and into a hollow. Rasali pointed the ferry along a crease. And then they were suddenly a stone's throw from the Farside dock and the light of its torches.

People on the dock moved as they approached. Just loudly enough to carry, a soft baritone voice called, "Rasali?"

She called back, "Ten this time, Pen."

"Anyone need carriers?" A different voice. Several passengers responded.

Rasali shipped the scull while the ferry was still some feet away from the dock, and allowed it to ease forward under its own momentum. She stepped to the prow and picked up a coiled rope there, tossing one end across the narrowing distance. Someone on the dock caught it and pulled the boat in, and in a very few moments the ferry was snug against the dock.

Disembarking and payment was quicker than embarkation had been. Kit was the last off and after a brief discussion he hired a carrier to haul his trunk to an inn in town. He turned to say farewell to Rasali. She and the man—Pen, Kit remembered—were untying the boat. "You're not going back already," he said.

"Oh, no." Her voice sounded loose, content, relaxed. Kit hadn't known how tense she was. "We're just going to tow the boat down to where the Twins will pull it out." She waved with one hand to the boat launch. A pair of white oxen gleamed in the night, at their heads a woman hardly darker.

"Wait," Kit said to Uni Mason and handed her his folio. "Please tell the innkeeper I'll be there soon." He turned back to Rasali. "May I help?"

In the darkness he felt more than saw her smile. "Always."

*   *   *

The Red Lurcher, more commonly called The Bitch, was a small but noisy inn five minutes' walk from the mist, ten (he was told) from the building site. His room was larger than at The Fish, with an uncomfortable bed and a window seat crammed with quires of ancient hand-written music. Jenner stayed here, Kit knew, but when he asked the owner (Widson Innkeep, a heavyset man with red hair turning silver), he had not seen him. "You'll be the new one, the architect," Widson said.

"Yes," Kit said. "When he gets in, please tell Jenner I am here."

Widson wrinkled his forehead. "I don't know, he's been out late most days recently, since—" He cut himself off, looking guilty.

"—since the signals informed him that I was here," Kit said. "I understand the impulse."

The innkeeper seemed to consider something for a moment, then said slowly, "We like Jenner here."

"Then we'll try to keep him," Kit said.

*   *   *

When the child Kit had recovered from his illness, he did not return to the crèche—which he would have been leaving in a year in any case—but went straight to his father. Davell Meinem was a slow-talking humorous man who nevertheless had a sharp tongue on the sites of his many projects. He brought Kit with him to his work places: best for the boy to get some experience in the trade.

Kit loved everything about his father's projects: the precisely drawn plans, the orderly progression of construction, the lines and curves of brick and iron and stone rising under the endlessly random sky.

For the first year or two, Kit imitated his father and the workers, building structures of tiny beams and bricks made by the woman set to mind him, a tiler who had lost a hand some years back. Davell collected the boy at the end of the day. "I'm here to inspect the construction," he said, and Kit demonstrated his bridge or tower, or the materials he had laid out in neat lines and stacks. Davell would discuss Kit's work with great seriousness until it grew too dark to see and they went back to the inn or rented rooms that passed for home near the sites.

Davell spent nights buried in the endless paperwork of his projects, and Kit found this interesting as well. The pattern that went into building something big was not just the architectural plans or the construction itself; it was also labor schedules and documentation and materials deliveries. He started to draw his own plans but he also made up endless correspondences with imaginary providers.

After a while, Kit noticed that a large part of the pattern that made a bridge or a tower was built of people.

*   *   *

The knock on Kit's door came very late that night, a preemptory rap. Kit put down the quill he was mending and rolled his shoulders to loosen them. "Yes," he said aloud as he stood.

The man who stormed through the door was as dark as Kit, though perhaps a few years younger. He wore mud-splashed riding clothes.

"I am Kit Meinem of Atyar," Kit said.

"Jenner Ellar of Atyar. Show it to me." Silently Kit handed the cartel to Jenner, who glared at it before tossing it onto the table. "It took long enough for them to pick a replacement."

Might as well deal with this right now, Kit thought. "You hoped it would be you."

Jenner eyed Kit for a moment. "Yes. I did."

"You think you're the most qualified to complete the project because you've been here for the last—what is it? Year?"

"I know the sites," Jenner said. "I worked with Teniant to make those plans. And then Empire sends—" He turned to face the empty hearth.

"—Empire sends someone new," Kit said to Jenner's back. "Someone with connections in the capital, influential friends but no experience with this site, this bridge. It should have been you, yes?"

Jenner was still.

"But it isn't," Kit said, and let the words hang for a moment. "I've built eight bridges in the past fifteen years. Four suspension bridges, two major spans. Two bridges over mist. You've done three, and the biggest span you've directed was three hundred and fifty feet, six stone arches over shallow water and shifting gravel on Mati River."

"I know," Jenner snapped.

"It's a good bridge." Kit poured two glasses of whiskey from a stoneware pitcher by the window. "I coached down to see it before I came here. It's well made and you were on budget and nearly on schedule in spite of the drought. Better, the locals still like you. Asked how you're doing these days. Here."

Jenner took the glass Kit offered. *Good.* Kit continued, "Meinems have built bridges—and roads and aqueducts and stadia, a hundred sorts of public structures—for Empire for a thousand years." Jenner turned to speak but Kit held up his hand. "This doesn't mean we're any better at it than Ellars. But Empire knows us—and we know Empire, how to do what we need to. If they'd given you this bridge, you'd be replaced within a year. But I can get this bridge built and I will." Kit sat and leaned forward, elbows on knees. "With you. You're talented. You know the site. You know the people. Help me make this bridge."

"It's real to you," Jenner said finally. Kit knew what he meant: *You care about this work. It's not just another tick on a list.*

"Yes," Kit said. "You'll be my second for this one. I'll show you how to deal with Atyar and I'll help you with contacts. And your next project will belong entirely to you. This is the first bridge but it isn't going to be the only one across the mist."

Together they drank. The whiskey bit at Kit's throat and made his eyes water. "Oh," he said, "that's *awful*."

Jenner laughed suddenly and met his eyes for the first time: a little wary still but willing to be convinced. "Farside whiskey is terrible. You drink much of this, you'll be running for Atyar in a month."

"Maybe we'll have something better ferried across," Kit said.

*   *   *

Preparations were not so far along on this side. The heaps of blocks at the construction site were not so massive and it was harder to find local workers. In discussions between Kit, Jenner and the Near—and Farside masons who would oversee construction of the pillars, final plans materialized. This would be unique, the largest structure of its kind ever attempted: a single-span chain suspension bridge a quarter of a mile long. The basic plan remained unchanged: the bridge would be supported by eyebar-and-bolt chains, four on each side, allowed to play independently to compensate for the slight shifts that would be caused by traffic on the roadbed. The huge eyebars and their bolts were being fashioned five hundred miles away and far to the north, where iron was common and the smelting and ironworking were the best in Empire. Kit had just written to the foundries to start the work again.

The pillar and anchorage on Nearside would be built of gold limestone anchored with pilings into the bedrock; on Farside they would be pink-gray granite with a funnel-shaped foundation. The towers' heights would be nearly four hundred feet. There were taller towers back in Atyar, but none had to stand against the compression of a bridge.

The initial tests with the fishskin rope had showed it to be nearly as strong as iron without the weight. When Kit asked the Farside tanners and ropemakers about its durability, he was taken a day's travel east to Feknai, to a waterwheel that used knotted belts of the material for its drive. The belts, he was told, were seventy-five years old and still sound. Fishskin wore like maple-wood so long as it wasn't left in mist, but it required regular maintenance.

He watched Feknai's little river for a time. There had been rain recently in the foothills and the water was quick and abrupt as light. *Water bridges are easy,* he thought a little wistfully, and then: *Anyone can bridge water.*

Kit revised the plans again to use the lighter material where they could. Jenner crossed the mist to Nearside to work with Daell and Stivvan Cabler on the expansion of their workshops and ropewalk.

Without Jenner (who was practically a local, as Kit was told again and again), Kit felt the difference in attitudes on the river's two banks more clearly. Most Farsiders shared the Nearsiders' attitudes—money is money and always welcome—and there was a sense of the excitement that comes of any great project, but there was more resistance here. Empire was effectively split by the river, and the lands to the east—starting with Nearside—had never seen their destinies as closely linked to Atyar in the west. They were overseen by the eastern capital, Triple, and their taxes went to building necessities on their own side of the mist. Empire's grasp on the eastern lands was loose and had never needed to be tighter.

The bridge would change things. Travel between Atyar and Triple would grow more common and perhaps Empire would no longer hold the eastern lands so gently. Triple's lack of enthusiasm for the project showed itself in delayed deliveries of stone and iron. Kit traveled five days along the Triple Road to the district seat to present his credentials to the governor, and wrote sharp letters to the Department of Roads in Triple. Things became a little easier.

It was midwinter before the design was finished. Kit avoided crossing the mist. Rasali Ferry crossed seventeen times. He managed to see her nearly every time, at least for as long as it took to drink a beer.

* * *

The second time Kit crossed, it was midmorning of an early spring day. The mist mirrored the overcast sky above: pale and flat, like a layer of fog in a dell. Rasali was loading the ferry at the upper dock when Kit arrived and to his surprise she smiled at him, her face suddenly beautiful. Kit nodded to the stranger watching Valo toss immense cloth-wrapped bales to Rasali, then greeted the Ferrys. Valo paused for a moment but did not return Kit's greeting, only bent again to his work. Valo had been avoiding him since the beginning of his time there. With a mental shrug, Kit turned from Valo to Rasali. She was catching and stacking the enormous bales easily.

"What's in those? You throw them as though they were—"

"—paper," she finished. "The very best Ibraric mulberry paper. Light as lambswool. You probably have a bunch of this stuff in that folio of yours."

Kit thought of the vellum he used for his plans, and the paper he used for everything else: made of cotton from the south, its surface buffed until it felt hard and smooth as enamelwork. Ibraric paper was only useful for certain kinds of printing. He said, "All the time."

Rasali piled on bales and more bales until the ferry was stacked three high. He added, "Is there going to be room for me in there?"

"Pilar Runner and Valo aren't coming with us," she said. "You'll have to sit on top of the bales, but there's room as long as you sit still and don't wobble."

As Rasali pushed away from the dock Kit asked, "Why isn't the trader coming with her paper?"

"Why would she? Pilar has a broker on the other side." Her hands busy, she tipped her head to one side in a gesture that somehow conveyed a shrug. "Mist is dangerous." Somewhere along the River a ferry was lost every few months: horses, people, cartage, all lost. Fishers stayed closer to shore and died less often. It was harder to calculate the impact to trade and communications of this barrier splitting Empire in half.

This journey—in daylight, alone with Rasali—was very different from Kit's earlier crossing: less frightening but somehow wilder, stranger. The cold wind down the river was cutting and brought bits of dried foam to rest on his skin, but they blew off quickly without pain and left no mark. The wind fell to a breeze and then to nothing as they navigated into the mist.

They moved through what looked like a layered maze of cirrus clouds. He watched the mist along the *Crossing*'s side until they passed over a small hole like a pockmark, straight down and no more than a foot across. For an instant he glimpsed open space below them. They were floating on a layer of mist above an air pocket deep enough to swallow the boat. He rolled onto his back to stare up at the sky until he stopped shaking; when he looked again, they were out of the maze, it seemed. The boat eased along a gently curving channel. He relaxed a little and moved to watch Rasali.

"How fares your bridge?" Rasali said at last, her voice muted in the muffled air. This had to be a courtesy—everyone in town seemed to know everything about the bridge's progress—but Kit was used to answering questions to which people already knew the answers. He had found patience to be a highly effective tool.

"Farside foundations are doing well. We have maybe six more months before the anchorage is done, but pilings for the pillar's foundation are in place and we can start building. Six weeks early," Kit said a little smugly, though this was a victory no one else would appreciate and in any case the weather was as much to be credited as any action on his part. "On Nearside, we've run into basalt that's too hard to drill easily so we sent for a specialist. The signal flags say she's arrived, and that's why I'm crossing."

She said nothing, seemingly intent on moving the great scull. He watched her for a time, content to see her shoulders flex, hear her breath forcing itself out in smooth waves. Over the faint yeast scent of the mist, he smelled her sweat, or thought he did. She frowned slightly but he could not tell whether it was due to her labor or something in the mist, or something else. Who was she, really? "May I ask a question, Rasali Ferry of Farside?"

Rasali nodded, eyes on the mist in front of the boat.

Actually, he had several things he wished to know: about her, about the river, about the people here. He picked one almost at random. "What is bothering Valo?"

"He's transparent, isn't he? He thinks you take something away from him," Rasali said. "He is too young to know what you take is unimportant."

Kit thought about it. "His work?"

"His work is unimportant?" She laughed, a sudden puff of an exhale as she pulled. "We have a lot of money, Ferrys. We own land and rent it out—The Deer's Hart belongs to my family; did you know that? But he's young and he wants what we all want at his age, a chance to test himself against the world and see if he measures up. And because he's a Ferry he wants be tested against adventures. Danger. The mist. Valo thinks you take that away from him."

"But he's not immortal," Kit said, "whatever he thinks. The river can kill him. It will, sooner or later. It—"

—*will kill you.* Kit caught himself, rolled onto his back again to look up at the sky.

In The Bitch's taproom one night, a local man had told him about Rasali's family: a history of deaths, of boats lost in a silent hissing of mist, or the rending of wood, or screams that might be human and might be a horse. "So everyone wears ash-color for a month or two, and then the next Ferry takes up the business. Rasali's still new, two years maybe. When she goes, it'll be Valo, then Valo's sister. Unless Rasali or Valo have kids by then.

"They're always beautiful," the man had added after some more porter, "the Ferrys. I suppose that's to make up for having such short lives."

Kit looked down from the paper bales at Rasali. "But you're different. You don't feel you're losing anything."

"You don't know what I feel, Kit Meinem of Atyar." Cool light moved along the muscles of her arms. Her voice came again, softer. "I am not young; I don't need to prove myself. But I will lose this. The mist, the silence."

Then tell me, he did not say. *Show me.*

She was silent for the rest of the trip. Kit thought perhaps she was angry, but when he invited her, she accompanied him to the building site.

*　　*　　*

The quiet pasture was gone. All that remained of the tall grass was struggling tufts and dirty straw. The air smelled of sweat and meat and the bitter scent of hot metal. There were more blocks here now, a lot more. The pits for the anchorage and the pillar were excavated to bedrock, overshadowed by mountains of dirt. One sheep remained, skinned and spitted, and greasy smoke rose as a boy turned it over a fire beside the temporary forge. Kit had considered the pasture a nuisance, but looking at the skewered sheep he felt a twinge of guilt.

The rest of the flock had been replaced by sturdy-looking women and men who were using rollers to shift stones down a dugout ramp into the hole for the anchorage foundation. Dust dulled their skin and muted the bright colors of their short kilts and breastbands. In spite of the cold, sweat had cleared tracks along their muscles.

One of the workers waved to Rasali and she waved back. Kit recalled his name: Mik Rounder, very strong but he needed direction. Had they been lovers? Relationships out here were tangled in ways Kit didn't understand. In the capital such things were more formal and often involved contracts.

Jenner and a small woman knelt conferring on the exposed stone floor of the larger pit. When Kit slid down the ladder to join them, the small woman bowed slightly. Her eyes and short hair and skin all seemed to be turning the same iron gray. "I am Liu Breaker of Hoic. Your specialist."

"Kit Meinem of Atyar. How shall we address this?"

"Your Jenner says you need some of this basalt cleared away, yes?"

Kit nodded.

Liu knelt to run her hand along the pit's floor. "See where the color and texture change along this line? Your Jenner was right: this upthrust of basalt is a problem. Here where the shale is, you can carve out most of the foundation the usual way with drills, picks. But the basalt is too hard to drill." She straightened and brushed dust from her knees. "Have you ever seen explosives used?"

Kit shook his head. "We haven't needed them for any of my projects. I've never been to the mines, either."

"Not much good anywhere else," Liu said, "but very useful for breaking up large amounts of rock. A lot of the blocks you have here were loosed using explosives." She grinned. "You'll like the noise."

"We can't afford to break the bedrock's integrity."

"I brought enough powder for a number of small charges. Comparatively small."

"How—"

Liu held up a weathered hand. "I don't need to understand bridges to walk across one. Yes?"

Kit laughed outright. "Yes."

*   *   *

Liu Breaker was right; Kit liked the noise very much. Liu would not allow anyone close to the pit but even from what she considered a safe distance, behind a huge pile of dirt, the explosion was an immense shattering thing, a crack of thunder that shook the earth. There was a second of echoing silence. After a collective gasp and some scattered screams, the workers cheered and stamped their feet. A small cloud of mingled smoke and rock dust eased over the pit's edge, sharp with the smell of saltpeter. The birds were not happy; with the explosion, they had burst from their trees and wheeled nervously.

Grinning, Liu climbed from her bunker near the pit, her face dust-caked everywhere but around her eyes, which had been protected by the wooden slit-goggles now hanging around her neck. "So far so good," she shouted over the ringing in Kit's ears. Seeing his face she laughed. "These are nothing—gnat sneezes. You should hear when we quarry granite up at Hoic."

Kit was going to speak more with her when he noticed Rasali striding away, toward the river. He had forgotten she was there. He followed her, half shouting to hear himself. "Some noise, yes?"

Rasali whirled. "What are you *thinking*?" She was shaking and her lips were white.

Taken aback, Kit answered, "We are blowing the foundations." *Rage? Fear?* He wished he could think a little more clearly but the sound seemed to have stunned his wits.

"And making the earth shake! The Big Ones come to thunder, Kit!"

"It wasn't thunder," he said.

"Tell me it wasn't worse!" Tears glittered in her eyes. Her voice was dulled by the drumming in his ears. "They will come, I *know* it."

He reached a hand out to her. "It's a tall levee, Rasali. Even if they do, they're not going to come over that." His heart in his chest thrummed. His head was hurting. It was so hard to hear her.

"*No one* knows what they'll do! They used to destroy whole towns, drifting inland on foggy nights. Why do you think they built the levees a thousand years ago? The Big Ones—"

She stopped shouting, listening. She mouthed something but Kit could not hear her over the beating in his ears, his heart, his head. He realized suddenly that these were not the after-effects of the explosion; the air itself was beating. He was aware at the edges of his vision of the other workers, every face turned toward the mist. There was nothing to see but the overcast sky. No one moved.

But the sky was moving.

Behind the levee the river mist was rising, a great boiling upheaval of dirty gray-gold against the steel-gray of the clouds, at least a hundred feet high, to be seen over the levee. The mist was seething, breaking open in great swirls and rifts, everything moving, changing. Kit had seen a great fire once when a warehouse of linen had burned in Atyar, where the smoke had poured upward and looked a little like this before bring torn apart by the wind.

Gaps opened in the mountain of mist and closed, and others opened, darker the deeper they were. And through those gaps, in the brown-black shadows at the heart of the mist, was movement.

The gaps closed. After an eternity the mist slowly smoothed and then settled back behind the levee and could no longer be seen. He wasn't really sure when the thrumming of the air blended back into the ringing of his ears.

"Gone," Rasali said with a sound like a sob.

A worker made one of the vivid jokes that come after fear; the others laughed, too loud. A woman ran up the levee and shouted down, "Farside levees are fine; ours are fine." More laughter: people jogged off to Nearside to check on their families.

The back of Kit's hand was burning. A flake of foam had settled and left an irregular mark. "I only saw mist," Kit said. "Was there a Big One?"

Rasali shook herself, stern now but no longer angry or afraid. Kit had learned this about the Ferrys, that their emotions coursed through them and then dissolved. "It was in there. I've seen the mist boil like that before but never so big. Nothing else could heave it up like that."

"On purpose?"

"Oh, who knows? They're a mystery, the Big Ones." She met his eyes. "I hope your bridge is very high, Kit Meinem of Atyar."

Kit looked to where the mist had been, but there was only sky. "The deck will be two hundred feet above the mist. High enough. I hope."

Liu Breaker walked up to them, rubbing her hands on her leather leggings. "So, *that's* not something that happens at Hoic. *Very* exciting. What do you call that? How do we prevent it next time?"

Rasali looked at the smaller woman for a moment. "I don't think you can. Big Ones come when they come."

Liu said, "They do not always come?"

Rasali shook her head.

"Well, cold comfort is better than no comfort, as my Da says."

Kit rubbed his temples. The headache remained. "We'll continue."

"Then you'll have to be careful," Rasali said, "or you will kill us all."

"The bridge will save many lives," Kit said. *Yours, eventually.*

Rasali turned on her heel.

Kit did not follow her, not that day. Whether it was because subsequent explosions were smaller ("As small as they can be and earn my fees," Liu Breaker said) or because they were doing other things, the Big Ones did not return, though fish were plentiful for the three months it took to plan and plant the charges, and break the bedrock.

*   *   *

There was also a Meinem tradition of metal working, and Meinem reeves, and many Meinems went into fields altogether different, but Kit had known from nearly the beginning that he would be one of the building Meinems. He loved the invisible architecture of construction, looking for a compromise between the vision in his head and the sites, the materials, and the people that would make them real. The challenge was to compromise as little as possible.

Architecture was studied at University. His tutor was a materials specialist, a woman who had directed construction on an incredible twenty-three bridges. Skossa Timt was so old that her skin and hair had faded together to the white of Gani marble, and she walked with a cane she had designed herself for efficiency. She taught him much. Materials had rules, patterns of behavior: they bent or crumbled or cracked or broke under quantifiable stresses. They augmented or destroyed one another. Even the best materials in the most stable combinations did not last forever—she tapped her own forehead with one gnarled finger and laughed—but if he did his work right, they could last a thousand years or more. "But not forever," Skossa said. "Do your best but don't forget this."

*   *   *

The anchorages and pillars grew. Workers came from towns up and down each bank, and locals were hired on the spot. The new people were generally welcome. They paid for rooms and food and goods of all sorts. The taverns settled into making double and then triple batches of everything, threw out new wings and stables. Nearside accepted the new people easily, the only fights late at night when people had been drinking and flirting more than they should. Farside had fist fights more frequently, though they decreased steadily as skeptics gave in to the money that flowed into Farside, or to the bridge itself, its pillars too solid to be denied.

Farmers and husbanders sold their fields and new buildings sprawled out from the towns' hearts. Some were made of wattle and daub, slapped together over stamped-earth floors that still smelled of sheep dung. Others, small but permanent, went up more slowly, as the bridge builders laid fieldstones and timber in their evenings and on rest days.

The new people and locals mixed together until it was hard to tell the one from the other, though the older townfolk kept scrupulous track of who truly belonged. For those who sought lovers and friends, the new people were an opportunity to meet someone other than the men and women they had known since childhood. Many took casual lovers, and several term-partnered with new people. There was even a Nearside wedding, between Kes Tiler and a black-eyed builder from far to the south called Jolite Deveren, whatever that meant.

Kit did not have lovers. Working every night until he fell asleep over his paperwork, he didn't miss it much, except late on certain nights when thunderstorms left him restless and unnaturally alert, as though lightning ran under his skin. Some nights he thought of Rasali, wondered whether she was sleeping with someone that night or alone, and wondered if the storm had awakened her, left her restless as well.

Kit saw a fair amount of Rasali when they were both on the same side of the mist. She was clever and calm and the only person who did not want to talk about the bridge all the time.

He did not forget what Rasali said about Valo. Kit had been a young man himself not so many years before, and he remembered the hunger that young men and women felt to prove themselves against the world. Kit didn't need Valo to accept the bridge—he was scarcely into adulthood and his only influence over the townspeople was based on his work—but Kit liked the youth, who had Rasali's eyes and her effortless way of moving.

Valo started asking questions, first of the other workers and then of Kit. His boat-building experience meant the questions were good ones. Kit passed on the first things he had learned as a child on his father's sites and showed him the manipulation of the immense blocks and the tricky balance of material and plan, the strength of will that allows a man to direct a thousand people toward a single vision. Valo was too honest not to recognize Kit's mastery and too competitive not to try and meet Kit on his own ground. He came more often to visit the construction sites.

After a season, Kit took him aside. "You could be a builder if you wished."

Valo flushed. "Build things? You mean bridges?"

"Or houses or granges or retaining walls. Or bridges. You could make peoples' lives better."

"Change peoples' lives?" He frowned suddenly. "No."

"Our lives change all the time whether we want them to or not," Kit said. "Valo Ferry of Farside, you are intelligent. You are good with people. You learn quickly. If you were interested, I could start teaching you myself or send you to Atyar to study there."

"Valo Builder . . ." he said, trying it out, then: "No." But after that, whenever he had time free from ferrying or building boats, he was always to be found on the site. Kit knew that the answer would be different the next time he asked. There was for everything a possibility, an invisible pattern that could be made manifest given work and the right materials. Kit wrote to an old friend or two, finding contacts that would help Valo when the time came. He would not be ashamed of this new protegé.

The pillars and anchorages grew. Winter came and summer, and a second winter. There were falls, a broken arm, two sets of cracked ribs. Someone on Farside had her toes crushed when one of the stones slipped from its rollers and she lost the foot. The bridge was on schedule even after the delay caused by the slow rock-breaking. There were no problems with payroll or the Department of Roads or Empire, and only minor, manageable issues with the occasionally disruptive representatives from Triple or the local governors.

Kit knew he was lucky.

*   *   *

The first death came during one of Valo's visits.

It was early in the second winter of the bridge, and Kit had been in Farside for three months. He had already learned that winter meant gray skies and rain and sometimes snow. Soon they would have to stop the heavy work for the season. Still, it had been a good day and the workers had lifted and placed most of a course of stones.

Valo had returned after three weeks at Nearside building a boat for Jenna Bluefish. Kit found him staring up at the slim tower through a rain so faint it felt like fog. Halfway up the pillar, the black opening of the roadway arch looked out of place.

Valo said, "You're a lot farther along since I was here last. How tall now?"

Kit got this question a lot. "A hundred and five feet, more or less. A little over a quarter finished."

Valo smiled, shook his head. "Hard to believe it'll stay up."

"There's a tower in Atyar, black basalt and iron, five hundred feet. Five times this tall."

"It just looks so delicate," Valo said. "I know what you said, that most of the stress on the pillar is compression, but it still looks as though it'll snap in half."

"After a while you'll have more experience with suspension bridges and it will seem less . . . unsettling. Would you like to see the progress?"

Valo's eyes brightened. "May I? I don't want to get in the way."

"I haven't been up yet today and they'll be finishing up soon. Scaffold or stairwell?"

Valo looked at the scaffolding against one face of the pillar, the ladders tied into place within it, and shivered. "I can't believe people go up that. Stairs."

Kit followed Valo. The steep internal stair was three feet wide and endlessly turning, five steps up and then a platform, turn to the left and then five more steps and turn. Eventually the stairs would be lit by lanterns set into alcoves at every third turning, but today Kit and Valo felt their way up, fingers trailing along the cold damp stone, a small lantern in Valo's hand. The stairwell smelled of water and earth and the thin smell of the burning lamp oil. Some of the workers hated the stairs and preferred the ladders outside, but Kit liked it here. For these few moments he was part of his bridge, a strong bone buried deep in flesh he had created.

They came out at the top and paused a moment to look around the unfinished course, and at the black silhouette of the crane against the dulling sky. The last few workers were breaking down a shear-leg that had been used to move blocks. A lantern hung from a pole jammed into one of the holes the laborers would fill with rods and molten iron. Kit nodded to them as Valo went to an edge to look down.

"It is wonderful," Valo said, smiling. "Being high like this—you can look right down into people's kitchen yards. Look, Teli Carpenter has a pig smoking."

"You don't need to see it to know that," Kit said dryly. "I've been smelling it for two days."

Valo snorted. "Can you see as far as White Peak yet?"

"On a clear day, yes," Kit said. "I was up here two—"

A heavy sliding sound and a scream. Kit whirled to see one of the workers on her back, one of the shear-leg's timbers across her chest. Loreh Tanner, a local. Kit ran the few steps to Loreh and dropped beside her. One man, the man who had been working with her, said, "It slipped—oh, Loreh, please hang on," but Kit could see already that it was futile. She was pinned against the pillar, chest flattened, one shoulder visibly dislocated, unconscious, breathing labored. Foam bloomed from her lips, black in the lantern's bad light.

Kit took her cold hand. "It's all right, Loreh. It's all right." It was a lie and in any case she could not hear him, but the others would. "Get Hall," one of the workers said and Kit nodded: Hall was a surgeon. And then, "And get Obal, someone. Get her husband." Footsteps ran down the stairs and were lost into the hiss of rain just beginning and someone's crying and Loreh's wet breathing.

Kit glanced up. His chest heaving, Valo stood staring. Kit said to him, "Help find Hall," and when the boy did not move he repeated it, his voice sharper. Valo said nothing, did not stop looking at Loreh until he spun and ran down the stairs. Kit heard shouting far below as the first messenger ran toward the town.

Loreh took a last shuddering breath and died.

Kit looked at the others around Loreh's body. The man holding Loreh's other hand pressed his face against it crying helplessly. The two other workers left here knelt at her feet, a man and a woman, huddled close though they were not a couple. "Tell me," he said.

"I tried to stop it from hitting her," the woman said. She cradled one arm: obviously broken though she did not seem to have noticed. "But it just kept falling."

"She was tired. She must have gotten careless," the man said, and the broken-armed woman said, "I don't want to think about that sound."

Words fell from them like blood from a cut. This was what they needed right now, to speak and to be heard. So he listened, and when the others came, Loreh's husband Obal, white-lipped and angry-eyed, the surgeon Hall, and six other workers, Kit listened to them as well, and gradually moved them down through the pillar and back toward the warm lights and comfort of Farside.

Kit had lost people before and it was always like this. There would be tears tonight, and anger at him and at his bridge, anger at fate for permitting this. There would be sadness and nightmares. And there would be lovemaking and the holding close of children and friends and dogs—affirmations of life in the cold wet night.

*　　*　　*

His tutor at University had said, during one of her frequent digressions from materials and the principles of architecture, "Things will go wrong."

It was winter, but in spite of the falling snow they walked slowly to the coffee house, as Skossa looked for purchase for her cane. She continued, "On long projects, you'll forget that you're not one of them. But if there's an accident? You're slapped in the face with it. Whatever you're feeling? Doesn't matter. Guilty, grieving, alone, worried about the schedule. None of it. What matters is *their* feelings. So listen to them. Respect what they're going through."

She paused then, tapped her cane against the ground thoughtfully. "No, I lie. It does matter but you will have to find your own strength, your own resources elsewhere."

"Friends?" Kit said doubtfully. He knew already that he wanted a career like his father's. He would not be in the same place for more than a few years at a time.

"Yes, friends." Snow collected on Skossa's hair but she didn't seem to notice. "Kit, I worry about you. You're good with people, I've seen it. You like them. But there's a limit for you." He opened his mouth to protest but she held up her hand to silence him. "I know. You do care. But inside the framework of a project. Right now it's your studies. Later it'll be roads and bridges. But people around you—their lives go on outside the framework. They're not just tools to your hand, even likable tools. Your life should go on, too. You should have more than roads to live for. Because if something does go wrong, you'll need what *you're* feeling to matter, to someone somewhere, anyway."

*   *   *

Kit walked through Farside toward The Bitch. Most people were home or in one of the taverns by now, a village turned inward; but he heard footsteps running behind him. He turned quickly. It was not unknown for people reeling from a loss to strike at whatever they blamed, and sometimes it was a person.

It was Valo. Though his fists were balled, Kit could tell immediately that he was angry but that he was not looking for a fight. For a moment Kit wished he didn't need to listen, that he could just go back to his rooms and sleep for a thousand hours, but there was a stricken look in Valo's eyes: Valo, who looked so much like Rasali. He hoped that Rasali and Loreh hadn't been close.

Kit said gently, "Why aren't you inside? It's cold." As he said it, he realized suddenly that it *was* cold. The rain had settled into a steady cold flood.

"I will. I was, I mean, but I came out because I thought maybe I could find you, because—" The boy was shivering.

"Where are your friends? Let's get you inside. It'll be better there."

"No," he said. "I have to know first. It's like this always? If I do this, build things, it'll happen for me? Someone will die?"

"It might. It probably will, eventually."

Valo said an unexpected thing: "I see. It's just that she had just gotten married."

The blood on Loreh's lips, the wet sound of her crushed chest as she took her last breaths— "Yes," Kit said. "She had."

"I just . . . I had to know if I need to ready for this. I guess I'll find out."

"I hope you don't have to." The rain was getting heavier. "You should be inside, Valo."

Valo nodded. "Rasali—I wish she were here. She could help maybe. You should go in too. You're shivering."

Kit watched him go. Valo had not invited him to accompany him back into the light and the warmth. He knew better than to expect that, but for a moment he had permitted himself to hope otherwise.

Kit slipped through the stables and through the back door at The Bitch.

Wisdon Innkeep, hands full of mugs for the taproom, saw him and nodded, face unsmiling but not hostile. That was good, Kit thought, as good as it would get tonight.

He entered his room and shut the door, leaned his back to it as if to hold the world out. Someone had already been in his room. A lamp had been lit against the darkness, a fire laid, and bread and cheese and a tankard of ale set by the window to stay cool. He began to cry.

*   *   *

The news went across the river by signal flags. No one worked on the bridge the next day or the day after that. Kit did all the right things, letting his grief and guilt overwhelm him only when he was alone, huddled in front of the fire in his room.

The third day, Rasali arrived from Nearside with a boat filled with crates of northland herbs on their way east. Kit was sitting in The Bitch's taproom, listening. People were coping, starting to look forward again. They should be able to get back to it soon, the next clear day. He would offer them something that would be an immediate, visible accomplishment, something different, perhaps guidelining the ramp.

He didn't see Rasali come into the taproom, only felt her hand on his shoulder and heard her voice in his ear. "Come with me," she murmured.

He looked up puzzled, as though she were a stranger. "Rasali Ferry, why are you here?"

She said only, "Come for a walk, Kit."

It was raining but he accompanied her anyway, pulling a scarf over his head when the first cold drops hit his face.

She said nothing as they splashed through Farside. She was leading him someplace but he didn't care where, grateful not to have to be the decisive one, the strong one. After a time she opened a door and led him through it into a small room filled with light and warmth.

"My house," she said. "And Valo's. He's still at the boatyard. Sit."

She pointed and Kit dropped onto the settle beside the fire. Rasali swiveled a pot hanging from a bracket out of the fire and ladled something into a mug. She handed it to him and sat. "So. Drink."

It was spiced porter and the warmth eased the tightness in his chest. "Thank you."

"Talk."

"This is such a loss for you all, I know," he said. "Did you know Loreh well?"

She shook her head. "This is not for me, this is for you. Tell me."

"I'm fine," he said, and when she didn't say anything, he repeated with a flicker of anger: "I'm *fine*, Rasali. I can handle this."

"Probably you can," Rasali said. "But you're not fine. She died and it was your bridge she died for. You don't feel responsible? I don't believe it."

"Of course I feel responsible," he snapped.

The fire cast gold light across her broad cheekbones when she turned her face to him, but she said nothing, only looked at him and waited.

"She's not the first," Kit said, surprising himself. "The first project I had sole charge of, a toll gate. Such a little project, such a silly little project to lose someone on. The wood frame for the passageway collapsed before we got the keystone in. The whole arch came down. Someone got killed." It had been a very young man, slim and tall with a limp. He was raising his little sister. She hadn't been more than ten. Running loose in the fields around the site, she had missed the collapse, the boy's death. Dafuen? Naus? He couldn't remember his name. And the girl—what had her name been? *I should remember. I owe that much to them.*

"Every time I lose someone," he said at last, "I remember the others. There've been twelve in seventeen years. Not so many, considering. Building's dangerous. My record's better than most."

"But it doesn't matter, does it?" she said. "You still feel you killed each one of them, as surely as if you'd thrown them off a bridge yourself."

"It's my responsibility. The first one, Duar—" *that* had been his name; there it was. The name loosened something in Kit. His face warmed: tears, hot tears running down his face.

"It's all right," she said. She held him until he stopped crying.

"How did you know?" he said finally.

"I am the eldest surviving member of the Ferry family," she said. "My father died. My mother. My aunt died seven years ago. And then I watched my brother leave to cross the mist, three years ago now. It was a perfect day, calm and sunny, but he never made it. He went instead of me because the river felt wrong to me that day. It could have been me. It should have, maybe. So I understand."

She stretched a little. "Not that most people don't. If Petro Housewright sends his daughter to select timber in the mountains and she doesn't come back—eaten by wolves, struck by lightning, I don't know—is Petro to blame? It's probably the wolves or the lightning. Maybe it's the daughter, if she did something stupid. And it *is* Petro, a little; she wouldn't have been there at all if he hadn't sent her. And it's her mother for being fearless and teaching that to her daughter, and Thom Green for wanting a new room to his house. Everyone except maybe the wolves feels responsible. This path leads nowhere. Loreh would have died sooner or later." Rasali added softly, "We all do."

"Can you accept death so readily?" he asked. "Yours even?"

She leaned back, her face suddenly weary. "What else can I do, Kit? Someone must ferry and I am better suited than most—and by more than my blood. I love the mist, its currents and the smell of it and the power in my body as I push us all through. Petro's daughter Cilar—she did not want to die when the wolves came, I'm sure, but she loved selecting timber."

"If it comes for you?" he said. "Would you be so sanguine then?"

She laughed and the pensiveness was gone. "No indeed. I will curse the stars and go down fighting. But it will still have been a wonderful thing, to cross the mist."

*   *   *

At University, Kit's relationships had all been casual. There were lectures that everyone attended, and he lived near streets and pubs crowded with students; but the physical students had a tradition of keeping to themselves that was rooted in the personal preferences of their predecessors and in their own. The only people who worked harder than the engineers were the ale-makers, the University joke went. Kit and the other physical students talked and drank and roomed and slept together.

In his third year, he met Domhu Canna at the arcade where he bought vellums and paper: a small woman with a heart-shaped face and hair in black clouds that she kept somewhat confined by gray ribbons. She was a philosophical student from a city two thousand miles to the east, on the coast.

He was fascinated. Her mind was abrupt and fish-quick and made connections he didn't understand. To her, everything was a metaphor, a symbol for something else. People, she said, could be better understood by comparing their lives to animals, to the seasons, to the structure of certain lyrical poems, to a gambling game.

This was another form of pattern-making, he saw. Perhaps people were like teamed oxen to be led, or like metals to be smelted and shaped to one's purpose, or like the stones for a dry-laid wall, which had to be carefully selected for shape and strength, sorted, and placed. This last suited him best. What held them together was not external mortar but their own weight and the planning and patience of the drystone builder. But it was an inadequate metaphor. People were this, but they were all the other things as well.

He never understood what Domhu found attractive in him. They never talked about regularizing their relationship. When her studies were done halfway through his final year, she returned to her city to help found a new university, and in any case her people did not enter into term marriages. They separated amicably and with a sense of loss on his part at least, but it did not occur to him until years later that things might have been different.

*   *   *

The winter was rainy but there were days they could work and they did. By spring, there had been other deaths unrelated to the bridge on both banks: a woman who died in childbirth, a child who had never breathed properly in his short life, two fishers lost when they capsized, several who died for the various reasons that old or sick people died.

Over the spring and summer they finished the anchorages, featureless masses of blocks and mortar anchored to the bedrock. They were buried so that only a few courses of stone showed above the ground. The anchoring bolts were each tall as a man, hidden behind the portals through which the chains would pass.

The Farside pillar was finished by midwinter of the third year, well before the Nearside tower. Jenner and Teniant Planner had perfected a signal system that allowed detailed technical information to pass between the banks, and Kit took full advantage of it. Documents traveled each time a ferry crossed. Rasali made thirty-eight trips. Though he spent much of his time with Kit, Valo made nineteen. Kit did not cross the mist at all unless the flags told him he must.

It was early spring and Kit was in Farside when the signals went up: *Message. Imperial seal.* He went to Rasali at once.

"I can't go," she said. "I just got here yesterday. The Big Ones—"

"I have to get across and Valo's at Nearside. There's news from the capital."

"News has always waited before."

"No it hasn't. News waited restlessly, pacing along the levee until we could pick it up."

"Use the flags," she said impatiently.

"The seals can't be broken by anyone but me or Jenner. He's over here. I'm sorry," he said, thinking of her brother, dead four years before.

"If you die no one can read it," she said, but they left just after dusk anyway. "If we must go, better then than earlier or later."

He met her at the upper dock at dusk. The sky was streaked with bright bands of green and gold, clouds catching the last of the sun so that they glowed but radiated no light. The current down the river was steady. The mist between the levees was already in shadow, smooth dunes twenty feet high.

Rasali waited silently, coiling and uncoiling a rope in her hands. Beside her stood two women, a man, and a dog: dealers in spices returning from the plantations of Gloth, the dog whining and restless. Kit was burdened with document cases filled with vellum and paper rolled tightly and wrapped in oilcloth. Rasali seated the merchants and their dog in the ferry's bow, their forty crates of cinnamon and nutmeg amidships, Kit in the back near her. In silence she untied and pushed away from the dock.

She stood at the stern, braced against the scull. For a moment he could pretend that this was water they moved on and he half expected to hear sloshing, but the big paddle made no noise. It was so quiet that he could hear her breath, the dog's nervous panting in front, and his own pulse, too fast. Then the *Crossing* slid up the long smooth slope of a dune and there was no possibility that this could be anything but mist.

He heard a soft sighing, like air entering a once-sealed room. It was hard to see so far, but the lingering light showed him mist heaving on the face of a neighboring dune, like a bubble coming to the surface of mud. The dome grew and then burst. There was a gasp from one of the women. A shape rolled away, too dark for Kit to see more than its length.

"What—" he said in wonder.

"Fish," Rasali breathed to Kit. "Not small ones. They are biting tonight. We should not have come."

It was night now. The first tiny moon appeared, followed by stars. Rasali oared gently through the dunes, face turned to the sky. At first he thought she was praying but she was navigating. There were more fish now: each time the sighing sound, the dark shape half seen. He heard someone singing, the voice carrying somehow, from far behind.

"The fishers," Rasali said. "They will stay close to the levees tonight. I wish. . . ."

But she left the wish unspoken. They were over the deep mist now. He could not say how he knew this. He had a sudden vision of the bridge overhead, a black span bisecting the star-spun sky, the parabolic arch of the chains perhaps visible, perhaps not. People would stride across the river an arrow's flight overhead, unaware of this place beneath. Perhaps they would stop and look over the bridge's railings but they would be too high to see the fish as any but small shadows—supposing they saw them at all, supposing they stopped at all. The Big Ones would be novelties, weird creatures that caused a safe shiver, like hearing a frightening story late at night.

Perhaps Rasali saw the same thing for she said suddenly, "Your bridge. It will change all this."

"It must. I am sorry," he said again. "We are not meant to be here on mist."

"We are not meant to cross this without passing through it. Kit—" Rasali said as though starting a sentence and then fell silent. After a moment she began to speak again, her voice low, as though she were speaking to herself. "The soul often hangs in a balance of some sort. Tonight do I lie down in the high fields with Dirna Tanner or not? At the fair, do I buy ribbons or wine? For the new ferry's headboard, do I use camphor or pearwood? Small things. A kiss, a ribbon, a grain that coaxes the knife this way or that. They are not, Kit Meinem of Atyar. Our souls wait for our answer because any answer changes us. This is why I wait to decide what I feel about your bridge. I'm waiting until I know how I will be changed."

"You never know how things will change you," Kit said.

"If you do not, you have not waited to find out." There was a popping noise barely a stone's throw to starboard. "Quiet."

On they moved. In daylight, Kit knew, the trip took less than an hour but now it seemed much longer. Perhaps it was. He looked up at the stars and thought they had moved but perhaps not.

His teeth were clenched, as were all his muscles. When he tried to relax them, he realized it was not fear that cramped him but something else, something outside him. Rasali's stroke faltered.

He recognized it now, the sound that was not a sound, like the deepest pipes on an organ, a drone too low to hear but which turned his bones to liquid and his muscles to flaked and rusting iron. His breath labored from his chest in grunts. His vision narrowed. Moving as though through honey, he strained his hands to his head, cradling it. He could not see Rasali except as a gloom against the slightly less gloom of the mist but he heard her pant, tiny pain-filled breaths like an injured dog.

The thrumming in his body pounded at his bones now, dissolving them. He wanted to cry out but there was no air left in his lungs. He realized suddenly that the mist beneath them was raising itself. It piled up along the boat's sides. *I never got to finish the bridge*, he thought. *And I never kissed her.* Did Rasali have any regrets?

The mound roiled and became a hill, which became a mountain obscuring part of the sky. The crest melted into curls and there was a shape inside, large and dark as night itself, that slid and followed the collapsing mist. It seemed not to move, but he knew that was only because of the size of the thing, that it took ages for its full length to pass. That was all he saw before his eyes slipped shut.

How long he lay there in the bottom of the boat, he didn't know. At some point he realized he was there. Some time later he found he could move again, his bones and muscles back to what they should be. The dog was barking. "Rasali?" he said shakily. "Are we sinking?"

"Kit." Her voice was a thread. "You're still alive. I thought we were dead."

"That was a Big One?"

"I don't know. No one has ever seen one. Maybe it was just a Fairly Large One."

The old joke. Kit choked on a weak laugh.

"Shit," Rasali said in the darkness. "I dropped the oar."

"Now what?" he said.

"I have smaller spares, but it's going to take longer and we'll land in the wrong place. We'll have to tie off and then walk up to get help."

I'm alive, he did not say. *I can walk a thousand miles tonight.*

It was nearly dawn before they got to Nearside. The two big moons rose just before they landed, a mile south of the dock. The spice traders and their dog went on ahead while Kit and Rasali secured the boat and walked up together. Halfway home, Valo came down at a dead run.

"I was waiting and you didn't come—" He was pale and panting. "But they told me, the other passengers, that you made it and—"

"Valo." Rasali hugged him and held him hard. "We're safe, little one. We're here. It's done."

"I thought. . . ." he said.

"I know," she said. "Valo, please, I am so tired. Can you get the *Crossing* up to the dock? I am going to my house and I will sleep for a day, and I don't care if the Empress herself is tapping her foot, it's going to wait." She released Valo, saluted Kit with a weary smile, and walked up the long flank of the levee. Kit watched her leave.

* * *

The "Imperial seal" was a letter from Atyar, some underling arrogating authority and asking for clarification on a set of numbers Kit had sent— scarcely worth the trip at any time, let alone across mist on a bad night. Kit cursed the capital, Empire, and the Department of Roads, and then sent the information along with a tautly worded paragraph about seals and their appropriate use.

Two days later, he got news that would have brought him across the mist in any case. The caravan carrying the first eyebars and bolts was twelve miles out on the Hoic Mine Road. Kit and his ironmaster Tandreve Smith rode out to meet the wagons as they crept southward and found them easing down a gradual slope near Oud village. The carts were long and built strong, their contents covered, each pulled by a team of tough-legged oxen with patient expressions. Their pace was slow and drivers walked beside them, singing something unfamiliar to Kit's city-bred ears.

"Ox-tunes. We used to sing these at my uncle's farm," Tandreve said, and sang:

> *"Remember last night's dream,*
> *the sweet cold grass, the lonely cows.*
> *You had your bollocks then."*

Tandreve chuckled, and Kit with her.

One of the drivers wandered over as Kit pulled his horse to a stop. Unattended, her team moved forward anyway. "Folks," she said and nodded. A taciturn woman.

Kit swung down from the saddle. "These are the chains?"

"You're from the bridge?"

"Kit Meinem of Atyar."

The woman nodded again. "Berallit Red-Ox of Ilver. Your smiths are sitting on the tail of the last wagon."

One of the smiths, a rangy man with singed eyebrows, loped forward to meet them and introduced himself as Jared Toss of Little Hoic. They walked beside the carts as they talked, and he threw aside a tarp to show Kit and

Tandreve what they carried: stacks of iron eyebars, each a rod ten feet long with eyes at either end. Tandreve walked sideways as she inspected them. She and Jared soon lost themselves in a technical discussion. Kit kept them company, leading Tandreve's forgotten horse and his own, content for the moment to let the masters talk it out. He moved a little forward until he was abreast of the oxen. *Remember last night's dream,* he thought and then: *I wonder what Rasali dreamt?*

* * *

After that night on the mist, Rasali seemed to have no bad days. She took people the day after they arrived, no matter what the weather or the mist's character. The tavern keepers grumbled at this but the decrease in time each visitor stayed was made up for by the increase in numbers of serious-eyed men and women sent by firms in Atyar to establish offices in the towns on the River's far side. It made things easier for the bridge as well, since Kit and others could move back and forth as needed. Kit remained reluctant, more so since the near-miss.

There was enough business for two boats. Valo volunteered to ferry more often but Rasali refused the help, allowing him to ferry only when she couldn't prevent it. "The Big Ones don't seem to care about me this winter," she said to him, "but I can't say they would feel the same about tender meat like you." With Kit she was more honest. "If he is to leave ferrying to go study in the capital, it's best sooner than later. Mist will be dangerous until the last ferry crosses it. And even then, even after your bridge is done."

It was only Rasali who seemed to have this protection. The fishing people had as many problems as in any year. Denis Redboat lost his coracle when it was rammed ("—by a Medium-Large One," he laughed in the tavern later: sometimes the oldest jokes really were the best), though he was fished out by a nearby boat before he sank too deep. The rash was only superficial but his hair grew back only in patches.

* * *

Kit sat in the crowded beer garden of The Deer's Hart watching Rasali and Valo cover with fishskin a little pinewood skiff in the boat yard next door. Valo had called out a greeting when Kit first sat down and Rasali turned her head to smile at him, but after that they ignored him. Some of the locals stopped by to greet him and the barman stayed for some time, telling him about the ominous yet unchanging ache in his back, but for most of the afternoon Kit was alone in the sun, drinking cellar-cool porter and watching the boat take shape.

In the midsummer of the fourth year, it was rare for Kit to have all the afternoon of a beautiful day to himself. The anchorages had been finished for some months. So had the rubble-filled ramps that led to the arched passages through each pillar. The pillars themselves had taken longer, and the granite saddles that would support the chains over the towers had only just been put in place.

They were only slightly behind on Kit's deadlines for most of the materials. More than a thousand of the eyebars and bolts for the chains were laid out in rows, the iron smelling of the linseed oil used to protect them during transit. More were expected in before winter. Close to the ramps were the many fishskin ropes and cables that would be needed to bring the first chain across the gap. They were irreplaceable—probably the most valuable thing on the work sites—and were treated accordingly, kept in closed tents that reeked.

Kit's high-work specialists were here, too: the men and women who would do the first perilous tasks, mostly experts who had worked on other big spans or the towers of Atyar.

Valo and Rasali were not alone in the boat yard. Rasali had sent to the ferry folk of Ubmie a hundred miles to the south, and they had arrived a few days before: a woman and her cousin, Chell and Lan Crosser. The strangers had the same massive shoulders and good looks the Ferrys had, but they shared a faraway expression of their own. The river was broader at Ubmie, deeper, so perhaps death was closer to them. Kit wondered what they thought of his task. The bridge would cut into ferry trade for many hundreds of miles on either side and Ubmie had been reviewed as a possible site for the bridge, but they must not have resented it or they would not be here.

Everything waited on the ferry folk. The next major task was to bring the lines across the river to connect the piers—fabricating the chains required temporary cables and catwalks be in place first—but this could not be rushed. Rasali, Valo, and the Crossers all needed to feel at the same time that it was safe to cross. Kit tried not to be impatient. In any case he had plenty to do—items to add to lists, formal reports and polite updates to send to the many interested parties in Atyar and Triple, instructions to pass on to the ropemakers, the masons, the road-builders, the exchequer. And Jenner: Kit had written to the capital, and the Department of Roads was offering Jenner the lead on the second bridge across the river, to be built a few hundred miles to the north. Kit was to deliver the cartel the next time they were on the same side, but he was grateful the officials had agreed to leave Jenner with him until the first chain on this bridge was in place. Things to do.

He pushed all this from his mind. *Later*, he said to the things, half-apologetically. *I'll deal with you later. For now just let me sit in the sun and watch other people work.*

The sun slanted peach-gold through the oak's leaves before Rasali and Valo finished for the day. The skiff was finished, an elegant tiny curve of pale wood, red-dyed fishskin, and fading sunlight. Kit leaned against the fence as they tossed a cup of water over its bow and then drew it into the shadows of the storage shed. Valo took off at a run—*so much energy, even after a long day;* ah, youth—as Rasali walked to the fence and leaned on it from her side.

"It's beautiful," he said.

She rolled her neck. "I know. We make good boats. Are you hungry? Your busy afternoon must have raised an appetite."

He had to laugh. "We laid the capstone this morning. I *am* hungry."

"Come on then. Thalla will feed us all."

Dinner was simple. The Deer's Hart was better known for its beer than its foods, but the stew Thalla served was savory with chervil and thick enough to stand a spoon in. Valo had friends to be with, so they ate with Chell and Lan, who turned out to be like Rasali, calm but light-hearted. At dusk, the Crossers left to explore the Nearside taverns, leaving Kit and Rasali to watch heat lightning in the west. The air was thick and warm, soft as wool.

"You never come up to the work sites on either side," Kit said suddenly after a comfortable, slightly drunken silence. He inspected his earthenware mug, empty now except for the smell of yeast.

Rasali had given up on the benches and sat instead on one of the garden tables. She leaned back until she lay supine, face toward the sky. "I've been busy, perhaps you noticed?"

"It's more than that. Everyone finds time here and there. And you used to."

"I did, didn't I? I just haven't seen the point lately. The bridge changes everything but I don't see yet how it changes me. So I wait until it's time. Perhaps it's like the mist."

"What about now?"

She rolled her head until her cheek lay against the rough wood of the tabletop: looking at him, he could tell, though her eyes were hidden in shadows. What did she see, he wondered. What was she hoping to see? It pleased him but made him nervous.

"Come to the tower now, tonight," he said. "Soon everything changes. We pull the ropes across and make the chains and hang the supports and lay the road. It stops being a project and becomes a bridge, a road. But tonight it's still just two towers and some plans. Rasali, climb it with me. I can't describe what it's like up there—the wind, the sky all around you, the river below." He flushed at the urgency in his voice. When she remained silent he added, "You change whether you wait for it or not."

"There's lightning," she said.

"It runs from cloud to cloud," he said. "Not to earth."

"Heat lightning." She sat up. "So show me this place."

*   *   *

The work site was abandoned. The sky overhead had filled with clouds lit from within by the lightning, which was worse than no light at all since it ruined their night vision. They staggered across the site, trying to plan their paths in the moments of light, doggedly moving through the darkness. "Shit," Rasali said suddenly in the darkness, then: "Tripped over something or other. Ghost sheep." Kit found himself laughing.

They took the internal stairs instead of the scaffold. Kit knew them thoroughly, knew every irregular turn and riser, so he counted them aloud to Rasali as he led her by the hand. They reached one hundred and ninety-four before they saw light from a flash of lightning overhead, two hundred and eighteen when they finally stepped onto the roof, panting for air.

They were not alone. A woman gasped; she and the man with her bolted down the stairs, laughing. Rasali said with satisfaction, "Sera Oakfield. I'd recognize that laugh anywhere. Then that was Erno Bridgeman with her."

"He took his name from the bridge?" Kit asked but Rasali said only, "Oh," in a child's voice. Silent lightning painted the sky over her head in sudden strokes of purple-white, shot through what seemed a dozen layers of cloud, an incomprehensible complexity of light and shadow.

"The sky is so much closer." She walked to the edge and looked down at Nearside. Dull gold light poured from doors open to the heavy air. Kit stayed where he was, content to watch her. The light—when there was light—was shadowless and her face looked young and full of wonder. After a time she came to him.

They said nothing, only kissed and then made love in a nest of their discarded clothes. Kit felt the stone of his bridge against his knees, his back. It was still warm as skin from the day's heat, but not as warm as Rasali. She was softer than the rocks and tasted sweet.

A feeling he could not have described cracked open his chest, his throat, his belly. It had been a long time since he had had sex, not met his own needs. He had nearly forgotten the delight of it, the sharp rising shock of his coming, the rocking ocean of hers. Even their awkwardness pleased him, because it held in it the possibility of doing this again, and better.

When they were done they talked. "You know my goal, to build this bridge." Kit looked down at her face, there and gone in the flickering of the lightning. "But I do not know yours."

Rasali laughed softly. "Yet you have seen me succeed a thousand times, and fail a few. I wish to live well."

"That's not a goal," Kit said.

"Why? Because it's not yours? Which is better, Kit Meinem of Atyar? A single great victory or a thousand small ones?" And then: "Tomorrow," Rasali said. "We will take the rope across tomorrow."

"You're sure?" Kit asked.

"That's a strange statement coming from you. The bridge is all about crossing being a certainty, yes? Like the sun coming up each morning? We agreed this afternoon. It's time."

*　　*　　*

Dawn came early with the innkeeper's rap on the door. Kit woke disoriented, tangled in the sheets of his little cupboard bed. After he and Rasali had come down from the pillar, Rasali to sleep and Kit to do everything that needed to happen before the rope was brought across, all in the few hours remaining to the night. His skin smelled of Rasali but he was stunned with lack of sleep, and had trouble believing the sex had been real. But there was stone dust ground into his palms. He smiled and, though it was high summer, sang a spring song from Atyar as he quickly washed and dressed. He drank a bowl filled with broth in the taproom. It was tangy, lukewarm. A single small perch stared up at him from a salted eye. Kit left the fish, and left the inn.

The clouds and the lightning were gone. Early as it was the sky was already pale and hot. The news was everywhere and the entire town, or so it seemed, drifted with Kit to the work site, flowed over the levee, and settled onto the bank.

The river was a blinding creamy ribbon, looking as it had the first time he had seen it; and for a minute he felt dislocated in time. High mist was seen as a good omen and though he did not believe in omens he was nevertheless glad. The signal towers' flags hung limp against the hot blue-white sky.

Kit walked down to Rasali's boat, nearly hidden in its own tight circle of people. As Kit approached, Valo called, "Hey, Kit!" Rasali looked up. Her smile was like welcome shade on a bright day. The circle opened to accept him.

"Greetings, Valo Ferry of Farside, Rasali Ferry of Farside," he said. When he was close enough, he clasped Rasali's hands in his own, loving their warmth despite the day's heat.

"Kit." She kissed his mouth to a handful of muffled hoots and cheers from the bystanders and a surprised noise from Valo. She tasted like chicory.

Daell Cabler nodded absently to Kit. She was the lead ropemaker. She, her husband Stivvan, and the journeymen and masters they had summoned were inspecting the hundreds of fathoms of twisted fishskin cord, loading them without kinks onto spools three feet across and loading those onto a wooden frame bolted to *The Tranquil Crossing*.

The rope was thin, not much more than a cord, narrower than Kit's smallest finger. It looked fragile, and nothing like strong enough to carry its own weight for a quarter of a mile. The tests said otherwise.

Several of the stronger people from the bridge handed down small heavy crates to Valo and Chell Crosser, in the bow. Silverwork from Hedeclin and copper in bricks: the ferry was to be weighted somewhat forward, which would make the first part of the crossing more difficult but should help by the end, as the cord paid out and took on weight from the mist.

"—We think, anyway," Valo had said, two months back when he and Rasali had discussed the plan with Kit. "But we don't know. No one's done this before." Kit had nodded and not for the first time wished that the river had been a little less broad. Upriver perhaps—but no, this had been the only option. He did write to an old classmate back in Atyar, a man who now taught the calculus, and presented their solution. His friend had written back to say that it looked as though it ought to work, but that he knew little of mist.

One end of the rope snaked along the ground and up the levee. No one touched the rope. They crowded close but left a narrow lane and stepped only carefully across it. Daell and Stivvan Cabler followed the lane back up and over the levee, to check the temporary anchor at the Nearside pillar's base.

There was a wait. People sat on the grass or walked back to watch the Cablers. Someone brought broth and small beer from the fishers' tavern. Valo and Rasali and the two Crossers were remote, focused already on what came next.

And for himself? Kit was wound up but it wouldn't do to show anything but a calm, confident front. He walked among the watchers and exchanged words or a smile with each of them. He knew them all by now, even the children.

It was nearly midmorning before Daell and Stivvan returned. The ferryfolk took their positions in the *Crossing*, two to each side, far enough apart that they could pull on different rhythms. Kit was useless freight until they got to the other side, so he sat at the bow where his weight might do some good. Uni stumbled as she was helped into the boat's stern: she would monitor the rope but, as she told them all, she was nervous: she had never crossed the mist. "I think I'll wait 'til the catwalks go up before I return," she added. "Stivvan can sleep without me 'til then."

"Ready, Kit?" Rasali called forward.

"Yes," he said.

"Daell? Lan? Chell? Valo?" Assent all around.

"A historic moment," Valo announced. "The day the mist was bridged."

"Make yourself useful, boy," Rasali said. "Prepare to scull."

"Right," Valo said.

"Push us off," she said to the people on the dock. A cheer went up.

*　　*　　*

The dock and all the noises behind them disappeared almost immediately. The ferryfolk had been right that it was a good day for such an undertaking. The mist was a smooth series of ripples no taller than a man, and so dense that the *Crossing* rode high despite the extra weight and drag. It was the gentlest he had ever seen the river.

Kit's eyes ached from the brightness. "It will work?" Kit said, meaning the rope and their trip across the mist and the bridge itself—a question rather than a statement: unable to help himself, even though he had worked the calculations himself and had Jenner and Daell and Stivvan and Valo and a specialist in Atyar all check them, even though it was a child's question. Isolated in the mist, even competence seemed insufficient.

"Yes," Daell Cabler said from aft.

The rowers said little. At one point Rasali murmured into the deadened air, "To the right," and Valo and Lan Crosser changed their stroke to avoid a gentle mound a few feet high directly in their path. Mostly the *Crossing* slid steadily across the regular swells. Unlike his other trips, Kit saw no dark shapes in the mist, large or small. From here they could not see the dock, but the levee ahead was scattered with Farsiders waiting for the work they would do when the ferry landed.

There was nothing he could do to help, so Kit watched Rasali scull in the blazing sun. The work got harder as the rope spooled out until she and the others panted. Shining with sweat, her skin was nearly as bright as the mist in the sunlight, and he wondered how she could bear the light without burning. Her face looked solemn, intent on the eastern shore. Her eyes were alight with reflections from the mist. Then he recognized her expression. It was joy.

How will she bear it, he thought suddenly, *when there is no more ferrying to be done?* He had known that she loved what she did but he had never realized just how much. He felt as though he had been kicked in the gut. What would it do to her? His bridge would destroy this thing that she loved, that gave her name. How could he not have thought of that? "Rasali," he said, unable to stay silent.

"Not now," she said. The rowers panted as they dug in.

"It's like . . . pulling through dirt," Valo gasped.

"Quiet," Rasali snapped and then they were silent except for their laboring breath. Kit's own muscles knotted sympathetically. Foot by foot the ferry heaved forward. At some point they were close enough to the Farside upper dock that someone threw a rope to Kit and at last he could do something, however inadequate. He took the rope and pulled. The rowers pushed for their final strokes. The boat slid up beside the dock. People swarmed aboard, securing the boat to the dock, the rope to a temporary anchor on the bank.

Released, the Ferrys and the Crossers embraced, laughing a little dizzily. They walked up the levee toward Farside town and did not look back.

Kit left the ferry to join Jenner Ellar.

* * *

It was hard work. The rope's end had to be brought over an oiled stone saddle on the levee and down to a temporary anchor and capstan at the Farside pillar's base, a task that involved driving a team of oxen through a temporary gap Jenner had cut into the levee: a risk but one that had to be taken.

More oxen were harnessed to the capstan. Daell Cabler was still pale and shaking from the crossing, but after a glass of something cool and dark, she and her Farside counterparts walked the rope to look for any new weak spots. They found none. Jenner stayed with the capstan. Daell and Kit returned to the temporary saddle in the levee, the notch polished like glass and gleaming with oil.

The rope was released from the dockside anchor. The rope over the saddle whined as it took the load and flattened, and there was a deep pinging noise as it swung out to make a single line down from the saddle, down into the mist. The oxen at the capstan dug in.

The next hours were the tensest of Kit's life. For a time, the rope did not appear to change. The capstan moaned and clicked, and at last the rope slid by inches, by feet, through the saddle. He could do nothing but watch and rework all the calculations yet again in his mind. He did not see Rasali, but Valo came up after a time to watch the progress. Answering his questions settled Kit's nerves. The calculations were correct. He had done this before. He was suddenly starved and voraciously ate the food that Valo had brought for him. How long had it been since the broth at The Fish? Hours. Most of a day.

The oxen puffed and grunted and were replaced with new teams. Even lubricated and with leather sleeves, the rope moved reluctantly across the saddle, but it did move. And then the pressure started to ease and the rope paid through the saddle faster. The sun was westering when at last the rope lifted free of the mist. By dusk, the rope was sixty feet above it, stretched humming-tight between the Farside and Nearside levees and the temporary anchors.

Just before dark, Kit saw the flags go up on the signal tower: *secure*.

*   *   *

Kit worked on and then seconded projects for five years after he left University. His father knew men and women at the higher levels in the Department of Roads, and his old tutor, Skossa Timt, knew more, so many were high-profile works, but he loved all of them, even his first lead, the little toll gate where the boy, Duar, had died.

All public work—drainage schemes, roadwork, amphitheaters, public squares, sewers, alleys and mews—was alchemy. It took the invisible patterns that people made as they lived, and turned them into stone and brick and wood and space. Kit built things that moved people through the intangible architecture that was his mind and his notion—and Empire's notion—of how their lives could be better.

The first major project he led was a replacement for a collapsed bridge in the Four Peaks region north of Atyar. The original had been a chain suspension bridge but much smaller than the mist bridge would be, crossing only a hundred yards, its pillars only forty feet high. With maintenance, it had survived heavy use for three centuries, shuddering under the carts that brought quicksilver ore down to the smelting village of Oncalion; but after the heavy snowfalls of what was subsequently called the Wolf Winter, one of the gorge's walls collapsed, taking the north pillar with it and leaving nowhere stable to rebuild. It was easier to start over, two hundred yards upstream.

The people of Oncalion were not genial. Hard work made for hard men and women. There was a grim, desperate edge to their willingness to labor on the bridge, because their livelihood and their lives were dependent on the mine. They had to be stopped at the end of each day or, dangerous as it was, they would work through moonlit nights.

But it was lonely work, even for Kit who did not mind solitude, and when the snows of the first winter brought a halt to construction, he returned with some relief to Atyar to stay with his father. Davell Meinem was old now. His memory was weakening though still strong enough. He spent his days overseeing construction of a vast and fabulous public maze of dry-laid stones brought from all over Empire: his final project, he said to Kit, an accurate prophecy. Skossa Timt had died during the Wolf Winter, but many of Kit's classmates were still in the capital. Kit spent evenings with them, attended lectures and concerts, entered for the season into a casual relationship with an architect who specialized in waterworks.

Kit returned to the site at Oncalion as soon as the roads cleared. In his absence, through the snows and melt-off, the people of Oncalion had continued to work in the bitter cold, laying course after course of stone. The work had to be redone.

The second summer, they worked every day and moonlit nights and Kit worked beside them.

Kit counted the bridge as a failure although it was coming in barely over budget and only a couple of months late, and no one had died. It was an ugly design; the people of Oncalion had worked hard but joylessly; and there was all his dissatisfaction and guilt about the work that had to be done anew.

Perhaps there was something in the tone of his letters to his father, for there came a day in early autumn that Davell Meinem arrived in Oncalion, riding a sturdy mountain horse and accompanied by a journeyman who vanished immediately into one of the village's three taverns. It was the middle of the afternoon.

"I want to see this bridge of yours," Davell said. He looked weary but straight-backed as ever. "Show it to me."

"We'll go tomorrow," Kit said. "You must be tired."

"Now," Davell said.

They walked up from the village together. It was a cool day and bright, though the road was overshadowed with pines and fir trees. Basalt outcroppings were stained dark green and black with lichens. His father moved slowly, pausing often for breath. They met a steady trickle of local people leading heavy-laden ponies. The roadbed across the bridge wasn't quite complete and could not take carts yet, but ponies could cross carrying ore in baskets. Oncalion was already smelting these first small loads.

At the bridge, Davell asked the same questions he had asked when Kit was a child playing on his work sites. Kit found himself responding as he had so many years before, eager to explain—or excuse—each decision; and always, always the ponies passing.

They walked down to the older site. The pillar had been gutted for stones so all that was left was rubble, but it gave them a good view of the new bridge: the boxy pillars, the curve of the main chains, the thick vertical suspender chains, the slight sprung arch of the bulky roadbed. It looked as clumsy as a suspension bridge could. Yet another pony crossed, led by a woman singing something in the local dialect.

"It's a good bridge," Davell said.

Kit shook his head. His father, who had been known for his sharp tongue on the work sites though never to his son, said, "A bridge is a means to an end. It only matters because of what it does. Leads from *here* to *there*. If you do your work right they won't notice it, any more than you notice where quicksilver comes from, most times. It's a good bridge because they are already using it. Stop feeling sorry for yourself, Kit."

*　　*　　*

It was a big party that night. The Farsiders (and, Kit knew, the Nearsiders) drank and danced under the shadow of their bridge-to-be. Torchlight and firelight touched the stones of the tower base and anchorage, giving them mass and meaning, but above their light the tower was a black outline, the absence of stars. Torches ringed the tower's parapet; they seemed no more than gold stars among the colder ones.

Kit walked among them. Everyone smiled or waved and offered to stand him drinks but no one spoke much with him. It was as though the lifting of the cable had separated him from them. The immense towers had not done this; he had still been one of them to some degree at least—the instigator of great labors but still, one of them. But now, for tonight anyway, he was the man who bridged the mist. He had not felt so lonely since his first day here. Even Loreh Tanner's death had not severed him so completely from their world.

On every project, there was a day like this. It was possible that the distance came from him, he realized suddenly. He came to a place and built something, passing through the lives of people for a few months or years. And then he left. A road through dangerous terrain or a bridge across mist saved lives and increased trade, but it changed the world as well. It was his job to make a thing and then leave to make the next one—but it was also his preference, not to remain and see what he had done. What would Nearside and Farside look like in ten years, in fifty? He had never returned to a previous site.

It was harder this time or perhaps just different. Perhaps *he* was different. He was staying longer this time because of the size of the project, and he had allowed himself to love the country on either side of the bridge. To have more was to have more to miss when he eventually left.

Rasali—what would her life look like?

Valo danced by, his arm around a woman half a head taller than he—Rica Bridger—and Kit caught his arm. "Where is Rasali?" he shouted, then knowing he could not be heard over the noise of drums and pipes, he mouthed *Rasali*. He didn't hear what Valo said but followed his pointing hand.

Rasali was alone, flat on her back on the river side of the levee, looking up. There were no moons, so the Sky Mist hung close overhead, a river of stars that poured east to west. Kit knelt a few feet away. "Rasali Ferry of Farside."

Her teeth flashed in the dark. "Kit Meinem of Atyar."

He lay beside her. The grass was like bad straw, coarse against his back and neck. Without looking at him she passed a jar of something. Its taste was strong as tar and Kit gasped for a moment.

"I did not mean. . . ." he started but trailed off, unsure how to continue.

"Yes," she said and he knew she had heard the words he didn't say. Her voice contained a shrug. "Many people born into a Ferry family never cross the mist."

"But you—" He stopped, felt carefully for his words. "Maybe others don't but you do. And I think maybe you must do so."

"Just as you must build," she said softly. "That's clever of you to realize that."

"And there will be no need after this, will there? Not on boats anyway. We'll still need fishskin, so the fishers will still go out, but they—"

"—stay close to shore," she said.

"And you?" he asked.

"I don't know, Kit. Days come, days go. I go onto the mist or I don't. I live or I don't. There is no certainty but there never is."

"It doesn't distress you?"

"Of course it does. I love and I hate this bridge of yours. I will pine for the mist, for the need to cross it. But I do not want to be part of a family that all die young without even a corpse for the burning. If I have a child she will not need to make the decision I did: to cross the mist and die, or to stay safe on one side of the world and never see the other. She will lose something. She will gain something else."

"Do you hate me?" he said finally, afraid of the answer, afraid of any answer she might give.

"No. Oh, no." She rolled over to him and kissed his mouth, and Kit could not say if the salt he tasted was from her tears or his own.

*   *   *

The autumn was spent getting the chains across the river. In the days after the crossing, the rope was linked to another and pulled back the way it had come, coupled now; and then there were two ropes in parallel courses. It was tricky work, requiring careful communications via the signal towers, but it was completed without event, and Kit could at last get a good night's sleep. To break the rope would have been to start anew with the long difficult crossing. Over the next days, each rope was replaced with fishskin cable strong enough to take the weight of the chains until they were secured.

The cables were hoisted to the tops of the pillars, to prefigure the path one of the eight chains would take: secured with heavy pins set in protected slots in the anchorages, making straight sharp lines to the saddles on the pillars and then, two hundred feet above the mist, the long perfect catenary. A catwalk was suspended from the cables. For the first time, people could cross the mist without the boats, though few chose to do so, except for the high workers from the capital and the coast: a hundred men and women so strong and graceful that they seemed another species and kept mostly to themselves. They were directed by a woman Kit had worked with before, Feinlin. The high-workers took no surnames. Something about Feinlin reminded him of Rasali.

The weather grew colder and the days shorter, and Kit pushed hard to have the first two chains across before the winter rains began. There would be no heavy work once the ground got too wet to give sturdy purchase to the teams. Calculations to the contrary, Kit could not quite trust that cables, even fishskin cables, would survive the weight of those immense arcs through an entire winter—or that a Big One would not take one down in the unthinking throes of some great storm.

The eyebars that would make up the chain were ten feet long and required considerable manhandling to be linked with bolts larger than a man's forearm. The links became a chain, even more cumbersome. Winches pulled the chain's end up to the saddles and out onto the catwalk.

After this, the work became even more difficult and painstaking. Feinlin and her people moved individual eyebars and pins out onto the catwalks and joined them in place; a backbreaking dangerous task that had to be exactly synchronized with the work on the other side of the river so that the cable would not be stressed.

Most nights Kit worked into the darkness. When the moons were bright enough, he, the high-workers, and the bridgewrights would work in shifts, day and night.

He crossed the mist six more times that fall. The high-workers disliked having people on the catwalks but he was the architect, after all, so he crossed once that way, struggling with vertigo. After that he preferred the ferries. When he crossed with Valo, they talked exclusively about the bridge—Valo had decided to stay until the bridge was complete and the ferries finished, though his mind was already full of the capital—but the other times, when it was Rasali, they were silent, listening to the hiss of the V-shaped scull moving in the mist. His fear of the mist decreased with each day they came closer to the bridge's completion, though he couldn't say why this was.

When Kit did not work through the night and Rasali was on the same side of the mist, they spent their nights together, sometimes making love, at other times content to share drinks or play ninepins in The Deer's Hart's garden. Kit's proficiency surprised everyone but himself—he had been famous for his accuracy, back in Atyar. He and Rasali did not talk again about what she would do when the bridge was complete, or what he would do, for that matter.

The hard work was worth it. It was still warm enough that the iron didn't freeze the high-worker's hands on the day they placed the final bolt. The first chain was complete.

Though work was slow through the winter, it was a mild one, and the second and third chains were in place by spring. The others were completed by the end of the summer.

* * *

With the heavy work done, some of the workers returned to their home-places. More than half had taken the name Bridger or something similar. "We have changed things," Kit said to Jenner on one of his Nearside visits, just before Jenner left for his new work. "No," Jenner said: "*You* have changed things." Kit did not respond but held this close and thought of it sometimes with mingled pride and fear.

The workers who remained were all high-workers, people who did not mind crawling about on the suspension chains securing the support ropes. For the past two years, the ropemakers for hundreds of miles up- and downstream had been twisting, cabling, looping, and reweaving the fishskin cables that would support the road deck. Crates, each marked with the suspender's position in the bridge, stood in carefully sorted towers in the old sheep field.

Kit's work was now all paperwork, it seemed—so many invoices, so many reports for the capital—but he managed every day to watch the high-workers. Sometimes he climbed to the tops of the pillars and looked down into the mist and saw Rasali's or Valo's ferry, a shape like an open eye half-hidden in tendrils of blazing white or pale gray.

Kit lost one more worker, Tommer Bullkeeper, who climbed onto the catwalk for a drunken bet and fell, with a maniacal cry that changed into unbalanced laughter as he vanished into the mist. His wife wept in mixed anger and grief, and the townspeople wore ash-color, and the bridge continued. Rasali held Kit when he cried in his room at The Bitch. "Never mind," she said. "Tommer was a good person: a drunk but good to his sons and his wife, careful with animals. People have always died. The bridge doesn't change that."

The towns changed shape as Kit watched. Commercial envoys from every direction gathered. Some stayed in inns and homes. Others built small houses, shops, and warehouses. Many used the ferries and it became common for these people to tip Rasali or Valo lavishly—"in hopes I never ride with you again," they would say. Valo laughed and spent this money buying beer for his friends. The letter had come from University and he would begin his studies with the winter term, so he had many farewells to make. Rasali told no one, not even Kit, what she planned to do with hers.

Beginning in the spring of the project's fifth year, they attached the road deck. Wood planks wide enough for oxen two abreast were nailed together with iron stabilizer struts. The bridge was made of several hundred sections constructed on the worksites and then hauled out by workers. Each segment had farther to go before being placed and secured. The two towns celebrated all night the first time a Nearsider shouted from her side of the bridge and was saluted by Farsider cheers. In the lengthening evenings, it became a pastime for people to walk onto the bridge and lie belly-down at its end, and look into the mist so far below them. Sometimes dark shapes moved within it but no one saw anything big enough to be a Big One. A few heedless locals dropped heavy stones from above to watch the mist twist away, opening holes into its depths, but their neighbors stopped them. "It's not respectful," one said; and, "Do you want to piss them off?" said another.

Kit asked her but Rasali never walked out with him. "I see enough from the river," she said.

*   *   *

Kit was Nearside, in his room in The Fish. He had lived in this room for five years and it looked it. Plans and timetables overlapped one another, pinned to the walls in the order he had needed them. The chair by the fire was heaped with clothes, books, a length of red silk he had seen at a fair and could not resist. It had been years since he sat there. The plans in his folio and on the oversized table had been replaced with waybills and receipts for materials, payrolls, and copies of correspondence between Kit and his sponsors in the government. The window was open and Kit sat on the cupboard bed, watching a bee feel its way through the sun-filled air. He'd left half a pear on the table. He was waiting to see if the bee would find it, and thinking about the little hexagonal cells of a beehive, whether they were stronger than squares and how he might test this.

Feet ran along the corridor. His door flew open. Rasali stood there blinking in the light, which was so golden that Kit didn't at first notice how pale she was, or the tears on her face. "What—" he said as he swung off his bed.

"Valo," she said. "*Pearlfinder.*"

He held her. The bee left, then the sun, and still he held her as she rocked silently on the bed. Only when the square of sky in the window faded to purple and the little moon's crescent eased across it, did she speak. "Ah," she said, a sigh like a gasp. "I am so tired." She fell asleep as quickly as that, with tears still wet on her face. Kit slipped from the room.

The taproom was crowded, filled with ash-gray clothes, with soft voices and occasional sobs. Kit wondered for a moment if everyone had a set of mourning clothes always at hand and what this meant about them.

Brana Keep saw Kit in the doorway and came from behind the bar to speak with him. "How is she?" she said.

"I think she's asleep right now," Kit said. "Can you give me some food for her, something to drink?"

Brana nodded, spoke to her daughter Lixa as she passed into the back, then returned. "How are *you* doing, Kit? You saw a fair amount of Valo yourself."

"Yes," Kit said. Valo chasing the children through the field of stones, Valo laughing at the top of a tower, Valo serious-eyed with a handbook of the calculus in the shade of a half-built fishing boat. "What happened? She hasn't said anything yet."

Brana spread her hands out. "What can be said? Signal flags said he was going to cross just after midday but he never came. When we signaled over they said he left when they signaled."

"Could he be alive?" Kit asked, remembering the night that he and Rasali had lost the big scull, the extra hours it had taken for the crossing. "He might have broken the scull, landed somewhere downriver."

"No," Brana said. She was crying, too. "I know, that's what we wanted to hope. But Asa, one of the strangers, the high-workers; she was working overhead and heard the boat capsize, heard him cry out. She couldn't see anything and didn't know what she had heard until we figured it out."

"Three more months," Kit said mostly to himself. He saw Brana looking at him so he clarified: "Three more months. The bridge would have been done. This wouldn't have happened."

"This was today," Brana said, "not three months from now. People die when they die. We grieve and move on, Kit. You've been with us long enough to understand how we see these things. Here's the tray."

*   *   *

When Kit returned, Rasali was asleep. He watched her in the dark room, unwilling to light more than the single lamp he'd carried up with him. *People die when they die.* But he could not stop thinking about the bridge, the nearly finished deck. *Another three months. Another month.*

When she awakened, there was a moment when she smiled at him, her face weary but calm. Then she remembered and her face tightened and she started crying again. After a while Kit got her to eat some bread and fish and cheese and drink some watered wine. She did so obediently, like a child. When she was finished she lay back against him. Her matted hair pushed up into his mouth.

"How can he be gone?"

"I'm so sorry," Kit said. "The bridge was so close to finished. Three more months, and this wouldn't have—"

She pulled away. "What? Wouldn't have happened? Wouldn't have *had* to happen?" She stood and faced him. "His death would have been unnecessary?"

"I—" Kit began but she interrupted him, new tears streaking her face.

"He *died*, Kit. It wasn't necessary, it wasn't irrelevant, it wasn't anything except the way things are. But he's gone and I'm not and *now* what do I do, Kit? I lost my father and my aunt and my sister and my brother and my brother's son, and now I lose the mist when the bridge is done and then what? What am I then? Who are the Ferry people then?"

Kit knew the answer. However she changed, she would still be Rasali. Her people would still be strong and clever and beautiful. The mist would still be there, and the Big Ones. But she wouldn't be able to hear these words, not yet, not for months maybe. So he held her and let his own tears slip down his face and tried not to think.

*   *   *

Five years after the Oncalion bridge was completed, Kit was two years into building an aqueduct planned across the Bakyar valley. There were problems. The first stones could not sustain both the weight of the aqueduct and the water it was meant to carry. His predecessor on the project had been either incompetent or corrupt, and Kit was still sorting through the mess she had left behind. They were a season behind schedule, but when he heard about Davell Meinem's death, he left immediately for Atyar. Some time would be required to put his father's affairs in order but mostly he did not wish to miss Twentieth-day, when Davell would be remembered. Kit had known that Davell's death would leave a hole in him, but he had known his father was dying for years. He hadn't expected this to hurt as much as it did.

The Grayfield was a little amphitheatre Davell had designed when he was young, matured now to a warm half-circle of white stone and grass, fringed with cherry trees. It was a warm day, brilliantly sunny. The air smelled of honey-cakes and the last of the cherry blossoms. Kit was Davell's only child, so he stood alone at the red-tasseled archway to greet those who came. He was not surprised at how many came to honor his father, more and more until the amphitheatre overflowed, the honey-cakes were all eaten, and the silver bowls were filled with flowers, one from each mourner. Davell Meinem had built seven bridges, three aqueducts, a forum, two provincial complexes, and innumerable smaller projects, and he had maintained contacts with old friends from each of them; many more people had liked him for his humor and his kindness.

What surprised Kit was all the people who had come for *his* sake: fellow students, tutors, old lovers and companions, even the man who ran the wine shop he frequented whenever he was in the city. Many of them had never even met his father. He had not known that he was part of their patterns.

Five months later, when he was back in the Bakyar valley, a letter arrived wrapped in dirty oiled paper and clearly from far away. It was from the miners of Oncalion. "We heard about your father from a trader when we were asking about you," the letter said. "We are sorry for your loss."

*   *   *

The fairs to celebrate the opening of the bridge started days before the official date of Midsummer. Representatives of Empire, from Atyar and Triple, from the regional governors and anyone else who could contrive an excuse all polished their speeches and waited impatiently in suites of tents erected on hurriedly cleaned-up fields near (but not too near) Nearside. The town had bled northward until it surrounded the west pillar of the bridge. The land that had once been sheep-pasture—Sheepfield, it was now—at the foot of the pillar was crowded with fair tents and temporary booths, cheek by jowl with more permanent shops of wood and stone that sold food and the sorts of products a traveler might find herself needing.

Kit was proud of the new streets. He had organized construction of the crosshatch of sturdy cobblestones as something to do while he waited through the bridge's final year. The new wells had been a project of Jenner's, planned from the very beginning, but Kit had seen them completed. Kit had just received a letter from Jenner with news of his new mist bridge up in the Keitche mountains: on schedule, a happy work site. It was gneiss bedrock, so he was using explosives and had hired Liu Breaker for it; she was there now and sent her greetings.

Kit walked alone through the fair which had climbed the levee and established itself along the ridge. A few people, townspeople and workers, greeted him but others only pointed him out to their friends (*the man who built the bridge; see there, that short dark man*); and still others ignored him completely, just another stranger in a crowd of strangers. When he had first come to build the bridge everyone in Nearside knew everyone else, local or visitor. He felt solitude settling around him again, the loneliness of coming to a strange place and building something and then leaving. The people of Nearside were moving forward into this new world he had built, the world of a bridge across the mist, but he was not going with them.

He wondered what Rasali was doing over in Farside, and wished he could see her. They had not spoken since the days after Valo's death except once for a few minutes when he had come upon her at The Bitch. She had been withdrawn though not hostile. He had felt unbalanced and not sought her out since.

Now, at the end of his great labor, he longed to see her. When would she cross next? He laughed. He of all people should know better: *ten minutes' walk.*

The bridge was not yet officially open but Kit was the architect. The guards at the toll booth only nodded when he asked to pass and lifted the gate for him. A few people noticed and gestured as he climbed. When Uni Mason (hands filled with fairings) shouted something he could not hear clearly, Kit smiled and waved and walked on.

He had crossed the bridge before this. The first stage of building the heavy oak frames that underlay the roadbed had been a narrow strip of planking that led from one shore to the other. Nearly every worker had found some excuse for crossing it at least once before Empire had sent people to the tollgates. Swallowing his fear of the height, Kit himself had crossed it nearly every day for the last two months.

This was different. It was no longer his bridge but belonged to Empire and to the people of Nearside and Farside. He saw it with the eyes of a stranger.

The stone ramp was a quarter of a mile long, inclined gradually for carts. Kit hiked up, and the noises dropped behind and below him. The barriers that would keep animals (and people) from seeing the drop-off to either side were not yet complete: there were always things left unfinished at a bridge's opening, afterthoughts and additions. Ahead of him, the bridge was a series of perfect dark lines and arcs.

The ramp widened as it approached the pillar, and offered enough space for a cart to carefully turn onto the bridge itself. The bed of the span was barely wide enough for a cart with two oxen abreast, so Nearside and Farside would have to take turns sending wagons across. *For now,* Kit thought. *Later we can widen it, or build another. They.* It would be someone else.

The sky was overcast with high clouds the color of tin, their metallic sheen reflected in the mist below Kit. There were no railings, only fishskin ropes strung between the suspension cables that led up to the chains. Oxen and horses wouldn't like that, or the hollow sound their feet would make on the boards. Kit watched the deck roll before him in the wind, which was constant from the southwest. The roll wasn't so bad in this wind but perhaps they should add an iron railing or more trusses to lessen the twisting and make crossing more comfortable. Empire had sent a new engineer to take care of any final projects: Jeje Tesanthe at Atyar. He would mention it to her.

Kit walked to one side so that he could look down. Sound dropped off behind him, deadened as it always was by the mist. He could almost imagine that he was alone. It was several hundred feet down, but there was nothing to give scale to the coiling field of hammered metal below him. Deep in the mist he saw shadows that might have been a Big One or something smaller or a thickening of the mist, and then, his eyes learning what to look for, he saw more of the shadows, as though a school of fish were down there. One separated and darkened as it rose in the mist until it exposed its back almost immediately below Kit.

It was dark and knobby, shiny with moisture, flat as a skate, and it went on forever—thirty feet long perhaps, or forty, twisting as it rose to expose its underside or what he thought might be its underside. As Kit watched, the mist curled back from a flexing scaled wing of sorts, and then a patch that might have been a single eye or a field of eyes or something altogether different, and then a mouth like the arc of the suspension chains. The mouth gaped open to show another arc, a curve of gum or cartilage. The creature rolled and then sank and became a shadow and then nothing as the mist closed back over it.

Kit had stopped walking when he saw it. He forced himself to move forward again. A Big One, or perhaps just a Medium-Large One. At this height it hadn't seemed so big or so frightening. Kit was surprised at the sadness he felt.

Farside was crammed with color and fairings as well, but Kit could not find Rasali anywhere. He bought a tankard of rye beer and went to find some place alone.

*   *   *

Once it became dark and the Imperial representatives were safely tucked away for the night, the guards relaxed the rules and let their friends—and then any of the locals—on the bridge to look around. People who had worked on the bridge had papers to cross without charge for the rest of their lives but many others had watched it grow, and now they charmed or bribed or begged their way onto their bridge. Covered lamps were permitted, though torches were forbidden because of the oil that protected the fishskin ropes. From his seat on the levee, Kit watched the lights move along the bridge, there and then hidden by the suspension cables and deck, dim and inconstant as fireflies.

"Kit Meinem of Atyar."

Kit stood and turned to the voice behind him. "Rasali Ferry of Farside." She wore blue and white, and her feet were bare. She had pulled back her dark hair with a ribbon and her pale shoulders gleamed. She glowed under the moonlight like mist. He thought of touching her, kissing her, but they had not spoken since just after Valo's death.

She stepped forward and took the mug from his hand, drank the lukewarm beer, and just like that the world righted itself. He closed his eyes and let the feeling wash over him.

He took her hand and they sat on the cold grass and looked out across the river. The bridge was a black net of arcs and lines. Behind it the mist glowed blue-white in the light of the moons. After a moment he asked, "Are you still Rasali Ferry, or will you take a new name?"

"I expect I'll take a new one." She half-turned in his arms so that he could see her face, her eyes. "And you? Are you still Kit Meinem, or do you become someone else? Kit Who Bridged the Mist? Kit Who Changed the World?"

"Names in the city do not mean the same thing," Kit said absently. "*Did* I change the world?" He knew the answer already.

She looked at him for a moment as though trying to gauge his feelings. "Yes," she said slowly after a moment. She turned her face up toward the loose strand of bobbing lights: "There's your proof, as permanent as stone and sky."

"'Permanent as stone and sky,'" Kit repeated. "This afternoon—it flexes a lot, the bridge. There has to be a way to control it but it's not engineered for that yet. Or lightning could strike it. There are a thousand things that could destroy it. It's going to come down, Rasali. This year, next year, a hundred years from now, five hundred." He ran his fingers through his hair. "All these people, they think it's forever."

"No, we don't," Rasali said. "Maybe Atyar does, but we know better here. Do you need to tell a Ferry that nothing will last? *These* cables will fail eventually, *these* stones will fall—but not the *dream* of crossing the mist, the dream of connection. Now that we know it can happen, it will always be here. My father died. My sister Rothiel. My brother Ster. Valo." She stopped, swallowed. "Ferrys die, but there is always a Ferry to cross the mist. Bridges and ferryfolk, they are not so different, Kit." She leaned forward, across the space between them, and they kissed.

* * *

"Are you off soon?"

Rasali and Kit had made love on the levee against the cold grass. They had crossed the bridge together under the sinking moons, walked back to The Deer's Hart and bought more beer, the crowds thinner now, people gone home with their families or friends or lovers—the strangers from out of town bedding down in spare rooms, tents, anywhere they could. But Kit was too restless to sleep and he and Rasali ended up back by the mist, down on the dock. Morning was only a few hours away and the smaller moon had set. It was darker now and the mist had dimmed.

"In a few days," Kit said, thinking of the trunks and bags packed tight and gathered in his room at The Fish: the portfolio, fatter now and stained with water, mist, dirt and sweat. Maybe it was time for a new one. "Back to the capital."

There were lights on the opposite bank, fishers preparing for their work despite the fair, the bridge. *Some things don't change.*

"Ah," she said. They both had known this. It was no surprise. "What will you do there?"

Kit rubbed his face and felt stubble under his fingers. "Sleep for a hundred years. Then there's another bridge they want, down at the mouth of the river, a place called Ulei. The mist's nearly a mile wide. I'll go down and look at the site and start working on a budget."

"A mile," Rasali said. "Can you do it?"

"I think so. I bridged this, didn't I?" His gesture took in the bridge and the woman beside him. "Ulei is on an alluvial plain. There are some low islands. That's the only reason it's possible. So maybe a series of flat stone arches, one to the next. You? You'll keep building boats?"

"No." She leaned her head back and he felt her face against his ear. She smelled sweet and salty. "I don't need to. I have a lot of money. The rest of the family can build boats but for me that was just what I did while I waited to cross the mist again."

"You'll miss it," Kit said. It was not a question.

Her strong hand laid over his. "Mmm," she said, a sound without implication.

"But it was the *crossing* that mattered to you," Kit said, realizing it. "Just as with me, but in a different way."

"Yes," she said and after a pause: "So now I'm wondering. How big do the Big Ones get in the Mist Ocean? And what's on the other side?"

"Nothing's on the other side," Kit said. "There's no crossing something without an end."

"Everything can be crossed. Of course it has an end. There's a river of water deep under the Mist River, yes? And that water runs somewhere. And all the other rivers, all the lakes—they all drain somewhere. There's a water ocean under the Mist Ocean and I wonder whether the mist ends somewhere out there, if it spreads out and vanishes and you find you are floating on water."

"It's a different element," Kit said, turning the problem over. "So you would need a boat that works through mist, light enough with that broad belly and fishskin sheathing; but it would have to be deep-keeled enough for water."

She nodded. "I want to take a coast-skimmer and refit it, find out what's out there. Islands, Kit. Big Ones. *Huge* Ones. Another whole world maybe. I think I would like to be Rasali Ocean."

"You will come to Ulei with me?" he said but he knew already. She *would* come, for a month or a season or a year or even longer, perhaps. They would sleep tumbled together in an inn very like The Fish or The Bitch, and when her boat was finished, she would sail across Ocean, and he would move on to the next bridge or road. Or he might return to the capital and a position at University. Or he might rest at last.

"I will come," she said. "For a bit."

Suddenly he felt a deep and powerful emotion in his chest: overwhelmed by everything that had happened or would happen in their lives, the changes to Nearside and Farside, the ferry's ending, Valo's death, the fact that she would leave him eventually or that he would leave her. "I'm sorry," he said.

"I'm not," she said and leaned across to kiss him, her mouth warm with sunlight and life. "It is worth it, all of it."

All those losses, but this one at least he could prevent.

"When the time comes," he said: "When you sail. I will come with you,"

A fo ben, bid bont. To be a leader, be a bridge.
Welsh proverb

2012 NEBULA AWARDS WINNERS, NOMINEES, AND HONOREES

NOVEL: WINNER

Among Others, Jo Walton (Tor)

NOVEL: NOMINEES

Embassytown, China Miéville (Macmillan UK; Del Rey; Subterranean Press)
Firebird, Jack McDevitt (Ace Books)
God's War, Kameron Hurley (Night Shade Books)
Mechanique: A Tale of the Circus Tresaulti, Genevieve Valentine (Prime Books)
The Kingdom of Gods, N. K. Jemisin (Orbit US; Orbit UK)

NOVELLA: WINNER

"The Man Who Bridged the Mist," Kij Johnson (*Asimov's Science Fiction*, October/November 2011)

NOVELLA: NOMINEES

"Kiss Me Twice," Mary Robinette Kowal (*Asimov's Science Fiction*, June 2011)

"Silently and Very Fast," Catherynne M. Valente (WSFA Press; *Clarkesworld Magazine*, October 2011)

"The Ice Owl," Carolyn Ives Gilman (*The Magazine of Fantasy and Science Fiction*, November/December 2011)

"The Man Who Ended History: A Documentary," Ken Liu (*Panverse Three*, Panverse Publishing)

"With Unclean Hands," Adam-Troy Castro (*Analog Science Fiction and Fact*, November 2011)

NOVELETTE: WINNER

"What We Found," Geoff Ryman (*The Magazine of Fantasy and Science Fiction*, September/October 2011)

NOVELETTE: NOMINEES

"Fields of Gold," Rachel Swirsky (*Eclipse 4*, Night Shade Books)

"Ray of Light," Brad R. Torgersen (*Analog Science Fiction and Fact*, December 2011)

"Sauerkraut Station," Ferrett Steinmetz (*GigaNotoSaurus*, November 2011)

"Six Months, Three Days," Charlie Jane Anders (*Tor.com*, June 2011)

"The Migratory Pattern of Dancers," Katherine Sparrow (*GigaNotoSaurus*, July 2011)

"The Old Equations," Jake Kerr (*Lightspeed Magazine*, July 2011)

SHORT STORY: WINNER

"The Paper Menagerie," Ken Liu (*The Magazine of Fantasy and Science Fiction*, March/April 2011)

SHORT STORY: NOMINEES

"Her Husband's Hands," Adam-Troy Castro (*Lightspeed Magazine*, October 2011)

"Mama, We Are Zhenya, Your Son," Tom Crosshill (*Lightspeed Magazine*, April 2011)

"Movement," Nancy Fulda (*Asimov's Science Fiction*, March 2011)

"Shipbirth," Aliette de Bodard (*Asimov's Science Fiction*, February 2011)

"The Axiom of Choice," David W. Goldman (*New Haven Review*, Winter 2011)

"The Cartographer Wasps and the Anarchist Bees," E. Lily Yu (*Clarkesworld Magazine*, April 2011)

ANDRE NORTON AWARD FOR YOUNG ADULT SCIENCE FICTION AND FANTASY BOOK: WINNER

The Freedom Maze, Delia Sherman (Big Mouth House)

NORTON NOMINEES:

Akata Witch, Nnedi Okorafor (Viking Juvenile)

Chime, Franny Billingsley (Dial Books; Bloomsbury)

Daughter of Smoke and Bone, Laini Taylor (Little, Brown Books for Young Readers; Hodder & Stoughton)

Everybody Sees the Ants, A. S. King (Little, Brown Books for Young Readers)
The Boy at the End of the World, Greg van Eekhout (Bloomsbury Children's Books)
The Girl of Fire and Thorns, Rae Carson (Greenwillow Books)
Ultraviolet, R. J. Anderson (Orchard Books; Carolrhoda Lab)

RAY BRADBURY AWARD FOR OUTSTANDING DRAMATIC PRESENTATION: WINNER

Doctor Who: "The Doctor's Wife," Neil Gaiman (writer), Richard Clark (director) (BBC Wales)

BRADBURY: NOMINEES

Attack the Block, Joe Cornish (writer/director) (Optimum Releasing; Screen Gems)
Captain America: The First Avenger, Christopher Markus and Stephen McFeely (writers), Joe Johnston (director) (Paramount)
Hugo, John Logan (writer), Martin Scorsese (director) (Paramount)
Midnight in Paris, Woody Allen (writer/director) (Sony)
Source Code, Ben Ripley (writer), Duncan Jones (director) (Summit)
The Adjustment Bureau, George Nolfi (writer/director) (Universal)

2011 Damon Knight Grand Master Award: Connie Willis
Solstice Award: Octavia Butler (posthumous) and John Clute
SFWA Service Award: Bud Webster

PAST NEBULA AWARDS WINNERS

1965

Novel: *Dune* by Frank Herbert

Novella: "He Who Shapes" by Roger Zelazny and "The Saliva Tree" by Brian Aldiss (tie)

Novelette: "The Doors of His Face, the Lamps of His Mouth" by Roger Zelazny

Short Story: "'Repent, Harlequin!' Said the Ticktockman" by Harlan Ellison

1966

Novel: *Babel-17* by Samuel R. Delany and *Flowers for Algernon* by Daniel Keyes (tie)

Novella: "The Last Castle" by Jack Vance

Novelette: "Call Him Lord" by Gordon R. Dickson

Short Story: "The Secret Place" by Richard McKenna

1967

Novel: *The Einstein Intersection* by Samuel R. Delany

Novella: "Behold the Man" by Michael Moorcock

Novelette: "Gonna Roll the Bones" by Fritz Leiber

Short Story: "Aye, and Gomorrah" by Samuel R. Delany

1968

Novel: *Rite of Passage* by Alexei Panshin
Novella: "Dragonrider" by Anne McCaffrey
Novelette: "Mother to the World" by Richard Wilson
Short Story: "The Planners" by Kate Wilhelm

1969

Novel: *The Left Hand of Darkness* by Ursula K. Le Guin
Novella: "A Boy and His Dog" by Harlan Ellison
Novelette: "Time Considered as a Helix of Semi-Precious Stones" by Samuel R. Delany
Short Story: "Passengers" by Robert Silverberg

1970

Novel: *Ringworld* by Larry Niven
Novella: "Ill Met in Lankhmar" by Fritz Leiber
Novelette: "Slow Sculpture" by Theodore Sturgeon
Short Story: No Award

1971

Novel: *A Time of Changes* by Robert Silverberg
Novella: "The Missing Man" by Katherine MacLean
Novelette: "The Queen of Air and Darkness" by Poul Anderson
Short Story: "Good News from the Vatican" by Robert Silverberg

1972

Novel: *The Gods Themselves* by Isaac Asimov
Novella: "A Meeting with Medusa" by Arthur C. Clarke
Novelette: "Goat Song" by Poul Anderson
Short Story: "When It Changed" by Joanna Russ

1973

Novel: *Rendezvous with Rama* by Arthur C. Clarke
Novella: "The Death of Doctor Island" by Gene Wolfe
Novelette: "Of Mist, and Grass, and Sand" by Vonda N. McIntyre
Short Story: "Love Is the Plan, the Plan Is Death" by James Tiptree Jr.
Dramatic Presentation: *Soylent Green*

1974

Novel: *The Dispossessed* by Ursula K. Le Guin
Novella: "Born with the Dead" by Robert Silverberg
Novelette: "If the Stars Are Gods" by Gordon Eklund and Gregory Benford
Short Story: "The Day before the Revolution" by Ursula K. Le Guin
Dramatic Presentation: *Sleeper* by Woody Allen
Grand Master: Robert Heinlein

1975

Novel: *The Forever War* by Joe Haldeman
Novella: "Home Is the Hangman" by Roger Zelazny
Novelette: "San Diego Lightfoot Sue" by Tom Reamy

Short Story: "Catch That Zeppelin" by Fritz Leiber
Dramatic Presentation: *Young Frankenstein* by Mel Brooks and Gene Wilder
Grand Master: Jack Williamson

1976

Novel: *Man Plus* by Frederik Pohl
Novella: "Houston, Houston, Do You Read?" by James Tiptree Jr.
Novelette: "The Bicentennial Man" by Isaac Asimov
Short Story: "A Crowd of Shadows" by C. L. Grant
Grand Master: Clifford D. Simak

1977

Novel: *Gateway* by Frederik Pohl
Novella: "Stardance" by Spider and Jeanne Robinson
Novelette: "The Screwfly Solution" by Racoona Sheldon
Short Story: "Jeffty Is Five" by Harlan Ellison

1978

Novel: *Dreamsnake* by Vonda N. McIntyre
Novella: "The Persistence of Vision" by John Varley
Novelette: "A Glow of Candles, A Unicorn's Eye" by C. L. Grant
Short Story: "Stone" by Edward Bryant
Grand Master: L. Sprague de Camp

1979

Novel: *The Fountains of Paradise* by Arthur C. Clarke
Novella: "Enemy Mine" by Barry B. Longyear
Novelette: "Sandkings" by George R. R. Martin
Short Story: "GiANTS" by Edward Bryant

1980

Novel: *Timescape* by Gregory Benford
Novella: "Unicorn Tapestry" by Suzy McKee Charnas
Novelette: "The Ugly Chickens" by Howard Waldrop
Short Story: "Grotto of the Dancing Deer" by Clifford D. Simak
Grand Master: Fritz Leiber

1981

Novel: *The Claw of the Conciliator* by Gene Wolfe
Novella: "The Saturn Game" by Poul Anderson
Novelette: "The Quickening" by Michael Bishop
Short Story: "The Bone Flute" by Lisa Tuttle [declined by author]

1982

Novel: *No Enemy but Time* by Michael Bishop
Novella: "Another Orphan" by John Kessel
Novelette: "Fire Watch" by Connie Willis
Short Story: "A Letter from the Clearys" by Connie Willis

1983

Novel: *Startide Rising* by David Brin
Novella: "Hardfought" by Greg Bear
Novelette: "Blood Music" by Greg Bear
Short Story: "The Peacemaker" by Gardner Dozois
Grand Master: Andre Norton

1984

Novel: *Neuromancer* by William Gibson
Novella: "Press Enter []" by John Varley
Novelette: "Blood Child" by Octavia Butler
Short Story: "Morning Child" by Gardner Dozois

1985

Novel: *Ender's Game* by Orson Scott Card
Novella: "Sailing to Byzantium" by Robert Silverberg
Novelette: "Portraits of His Children" by George R. R. Martin
Short Story: "Out of All Them Bright Stars" by Nancy Kress
Grand Master: Arthur C. Clarke

1986

Novel: *Speaker for the Dead* by Orson Scott Card
Novella: "R&R" by Lucius Shepard
Novelette: "The Girl Who Fell into the Sky" by Kate Wilhelm
Short Story: "Tangents" by Greg Bear
Grand Master: Isaac Asimov

1987

Novel: *The Falling Woman* by Pat Murphy
Novella: "The Blind Geometer" by Kim Stanley Robinson
Novelette: "Rachel in Love" by Pat Murphy
Short Story: "Forever Yours, Anna" by Kate Wilhelm
Grand Master: Alfred Bester

1988

Novel: *Falling Free* by Lois McMaster Bujold
Novella: "The Last of the Winnebagos" by Connie Willis
Novelette: "Schrödinger's Kitten" by George Alec Effinger
Short Story: "Bible Stories for Adults, No. 17: The Deluge" by James Morrow
Grand Master: Ray Bradbury

1989

Novel: *The Healer's War* by Elizabeth Ann Scarborough
Novella: "The Mountains of Mourning" by Lois McMaster Bujold
Novelette: "At the Rialto" by Connie Willis
Short Story: "Ripples in the Dirac Sea" by Geoffrey A. Landis

1990

Novel: *Tehanu: The Last Book of Earthsea* by Ursula K. Le Guin
Novella: "The Hemingway Hoax" by Joe Haldeman
Novelette: "Tower of Babylon" by Ted Chiang
Short Story: "Bears Discover Fire" by Terry Bisson
Grand Master: Lester del Rey

1991

Novel: *Stations of the Tide* by Michael Swanwick
Novella: "Beggars in Spain" by Nancy Kress
Novelette: "Guide Dog" by Mike Conner
Short Story: "Ma Qui" by Alan Brennert

1992

Novel: *Doomsday Book* by Connie Willis
Novella: "City Of Truth" by James Morrow
Novelette: "Danny Goes to Mars" by Pamela Sargent
Short Story: "Even the Queen" by Connie Willis
Grand Master: Fred Pohl

1993

Novel: *Red Mars* by Kim Stanley Robinson
Novella: "The Night We Buried Road Dog" by Jack Cady
Novelette: "Georgia on My Mind" by Charles Sheffield
Short Story: "Graves" by Joe Haldeman

1994

The 1994 Nebulas were awarded at a ceremony in New York City in late April 1995.

Novel: *Moving Mars* by Greg Bear
Novella: "Seven Views of Olduvai Gorge" by Mike Resnick
Novelette: "The Martian Child" by David Gerrold

Short Story: "A Defense of the Social Contracts" by Martha Soukup
Grand Master: Damon Knight
Author Emeritus: Emil Petaja

1995

Novel: *The Terminal Experiment* by Robert J. Sawyer
Novella: "Last Summer at Mars Hill" by Elizabeth Hand
Novelette: "Solitude" by Ursula K. Le Guin
Short Story: "Death and the Librarian" by Esther M. Friesner
Grand Master: A. E. van Vogt
Author Emeritus: Wilson "Bob" Tucker

1996

Novel: *Slow River* by Nicola Griffith
Novella: "Da Vinci Rising" by Jack Dann
Novelette: "Lifeboat on a Burning Sea" by Bruce Holland Rogers
Short Story: "A Birthday" by Esther M. Friesner
Grand Master: Jack Vance
Author Emeritus: Judith Merril

1997

Novel: *The Moon and the Sun* by Vonda N. McIntyre
Novella: "Abandon in Place" by Jerry Oltion
Novelette: "Flowers of Aulit Prison" by Nancy Kress
Short Story: "Sister Emily's Lightship" by Jane Yolen
Grand Master: Poul Anderson
Author Emeritus: Nelson Slade Bond

1998

Novel: *Forever Peace* by Joe Haldeman
Novella: "Reading the Bones" by Sheila Finch
Novelette: "Lost Girls" by Jane Yolen
Short Story: "Thirteen Ways to Water" by Bruce Holland Rogers
Grand Master: Hal Clement (Harry Stubbs)
Author Emeritus: William Tenn (Philip Klass)

1999

Novel: *Parable of the Talents* by Octavia E. Butler
Novella: "Story of Your Life" by Ted Chiang
Novelette: "Mars Is No Place for Children" by Mary A. Turzillo
Short Story: "The Cost of Doing Business" by Leslie What
Script: *The Sixth Sense* by M. Night Shyamalan
Grand Master: Brian W. Aldiss
Author Emeritus: Daniel Keyes

2000

Novel: *Darwin's Radio* by Greg Bear
Novella: "Goddesses" by Linda Nagata
Novelette: "Daddy's World" by Walter Jon Williams
Short Story: "macs" by Terry Bisson
Script: *Galaxy Quest* by Robert Gordon and David Howard
Ray Bradbury Award: Yuri Rasovsky and Harlan Ellison
Grand Master: Philip José Farmer
Author Emeritus: Robert Sheckley

2001

Novel: *The Quantum Rose* by Catherine Asaro
Novella: "The Ultimate Earth" by Jack Williamson
Novelette: "Louise's Ghost" by Kelly Link
Short Story: "The Cure for Everything" by Severna Park
Script: *Crouching Tiger, Hidden Dragon* by James Schamus, Kuo Jung Tsai, and Hui-Ling Wang
President's Award: Betty Ballantine

2002

Novel: *American Gods* by Neil Gaiman
Novella: "Bronte's Egg" by Richard Chwedyk
Novelette: "Hell Is the Absence of God" by Ted Chiang
Short Story: "Creature" by Carol Emshwiller
Script: *Lord of the Rings: The Fellowship of the Ring* by Frances Walsh, Phillipa Boyens, and Peter Jackson
Grand Master: Ursula K. Le Guin
Author Emeritus: Katherine MacLean

2003

Novel: *Speed of Dark* by Elizabeth Moon
Novella: "Coraline" by Neil Gaiman
Novelette: "The Empire of Ice Cream" by Jeffrey Ford
Short Story: "What I Didn't See" by Karen Joy Fowler
Script: *Lord of the Rings: The Two Towers* by Frances Walsh, Phillipa Boyens, Stephen Sinclair, and Peter Jackson
Grand Master: Robert Silverberg
Author Emeritus: Charles L. Harness

2004

Novel: *Paladin of Souls* by Lois McMaster Bujold
Novella: "The Green Leopard Plague" by Walter Jon Williams
Novelette: "Basement Magic" by Ellen Klages
Short Story: "Coming to Terms" by Eileen Gunn
Script: *Lord of the Rings: Return of the King* by Frances Walsh, Phillipa Boyens, and Peter Jackson
Grand Master: Anne McCaffrey

2005

Novel: *Camouflage* by Joe Haldeman
Novella: "Magic for Beginners" by Kelly Link
Novelette: "The Faery Handbag" by Kelly Link
Short Story: "I Live with You" by Carol Emshwiller
Script: *Serenity* by Joss Whedon
Grand Master: Harlan Ellison
Author Emeritus: William F. Nolan

2006

Novel: *Seeker* by Jack McDevitt
Novella: "Burn" by James Patrick Kelly
Novelette: "Two Hearts" by Peter S. Beagle
Short Story: "Echo" by Elizabeth Hand
Script: *Howl's Moving Castle* by Hayao Miyazaki, Cindy Davis Hewitt, and Donald H. Hewitt
Andre Norton Award: *Magic or Madness* by Justine Larbalestier
Grand Master: James Gunn
Author Emeritus: D. G. Compton

2007

Novel: *The Yiddish Policemen's Union* by Michael Chabon
Novella: "Fountain of Age" by Nancy Kress
Novelette: "The Merchant and the Alchemist's Gate" by Ted Chiang
Short Story: "Always" by Karen Joy Fowler
Script: *Pan's Labyrinth* by Guillermo del Toro
Andre Norton Award for Young Adult Science Fiction and Fantasy: *Harry Potter and the Deathly Hallows* by J. K. Rowling
Grand Master: Michael Moorcock
Author Emeritus: Ardath Mayhar
SFWA Service Awards: Melisa Michaels and Graham P. Collins

2008

Novel: *Powers* by Ursula K. Le Guin
Novella: "The Spacetime Pool" by Catherine Asaro
Novelette: "Pride and Prometheus" by John Kessel
Short Story: "Trophy Wives" by Nina Kiriki Hoffman
Script: *WALL-E* by Andrew Stanton and Jim Reardon. Original story by Andrew Stanton and Pete Docter
Andre Norton Award: *Flora's Dare: How a Girl of Spirit Gambles All to Expand Her Vocabulary, Confront a Bouncing Boy Terror, and Try to Save Califa from a Shaky Doom (Despite Being Confined to Her Room)* by Ysabeau S. Wilce
Grand Master: Harry Harrison
Author Emeritus: M. J. Engh
Solstice Award: Kate Wilhelm, Martin H. Greenberg, and the late Algis Budrys
SFWA Service Award: Victoria Strauss

2009

Novel: *The Windup Girl* by Paolo Bacigalupi
Novella: "The Women of Nell Gwynne's" by Kage Baker
Novelette: "Sinner, Baker, Fabulist, Priest; Red Mask, Black Mask, Gentleman, Beast" by Eugie Foster
Short Story: "Spar" by Kij Johnson
Ray Bradbury Award: *District 9* by Neill Blomkamp and Terri Tatchell
Andre Norton Award: *The Girl Who Circumnavigated Fairyland in a Ship of Her Own Making* by Catherynne M. Valente
Grand Master: Joe Haldeman
Author Emeritus: Neal Barrett Jr.
Solstice Award: Tom Doherty, Terri Windling, and the late Donald A. Wollheim
SFWA Service Awards: Vonda N. McIntyre and Keith Stokes

2010

Novel: *Blackout/All Clear* by Connie Willis
Novella: "The Lady Who Plucked Red Flowers beneath the Queen's Window" by Rachel Swirsky
Novelette: "That Leviathan Whom Thou Hast Made" by Eric James Stone
Short Story: "Ponies" by Kij Johnson and "How Interesting: A Tiny Man" by Harlan Ellison (tie)
Ray Bradbury Award: *Inception* by Christopher Nolan
Andre Norton Award: *I Shall Wear Midnight*, by Terry Pratchett

2011

Novel: *Among Others*, Jo Walton
Novella: "The Man Who Bridged the Mist," Kij Johnson

Novelette: "What We Found," Geoff Ryman

Short Story: "The Paper Menagerie," Ken Liu

Ray Bradbury Award: *Doctor Who*: "The Doctor's Wife," Neil Gaiman (writer), Richard Clark (director)

Andre Norton Award: *The Freedom Maze*, Delia Sherman

Damon Knight Grand Master Award: Connie Willis

Solstice Award: Octavia Butler (posthumous) and John Clute

SFWA Service Award: Bud Webster

ABOUT THE COVER ARTIST

Julie Dillon is a freelance illustrator living and working in Northern California. She received a bachelor of fine arts from California State University, Sacramento, in 2005, with continued education at the Academy of Art University in San Francisco and Watts Atelier of the Arts. She has won numerous honors for her work, including the 2010 Chesley Award in the Best Color Work, Unpublished category for *Planetary Alignment* and the Best Cover Illustration in Orson Scott Card's Intergalactic Medicine Show for her piece used for Jason Sanford's short story "The Never Never Wizard of Apalachicola." At the ArmadilloCon Art Show in 2012, she won Best in Show, Best Artist, and Best Color Work. Her work has also received nominations for World Fantasy and Chesley Awards, and she has had pieces in *Spectrum 17*, *Spectrum 18*, and *Spectrum 19*. Her painting *Artificial Dreams* was featured as the cover art for the twentieth-anniversary can of Corel™ Painter 12. She has done pieces for numerous clients, including Tor Books, Wizards of the Coast, and Fantasy Flight Games.

ABOUT THE EDITOR

Propped against the bookcase in Catherine Asaro's home office is the framed diploma of her Harvard doctoral degree in chemical physics. Nearby, dangling from the doorknob, is a bag stuffed with the workout clothes she wears for dance classes when she pulls herself away from her writing. A former professional dancer, this California native has little time for the ballet barre these days. The author of more than twenty-five books, her work includes science fiction, fantasy, and near-future thrillers. She has twice won a Nebula® Award, once for the novel *The Quantum Rose* and again for the novella "The Spacetime Pool." Among her many other distinctions, she is a multiple winner of the AnLab Readers' Choice Award from *Analog* and a three-time recipient of the *RT* Award for Best Science Fiction Novel. Her most recent books are the anthology *Aurora in Four Voices* and the novel *Lightning Strike, Book One*, and *Lightning Strike, Book Two*.

When she isn't writing, Catherine teaches in the Physics Department at the University of Maryland, Baltimore County. She has also coached secondary school students in math competitions, including the nationally ranked Howard Area Homeschoolers and Chesapeake ARML team. Her students have placed at the top levels in numerous competitions, such as the USA Math Olympiad and USA Math Talent Search. In addition, she is a member of SIGMA, a think tank of speculative writers that advises the government as to future trends affecting national security. She also served two terms as president of Science Fiction and Fantasy Writers of America.

As a dancer and musician, Catherine has performed with troupes and in musicals on both coasts and in Ohio. She founded and served as artistic director for two groups at Harvard: the Mainly Jazz Dance Company and the Harvard University Ballet. After she graduated, her undergraduates took over Mainly Jazz and made it into a college club. She has released two music CDs and is working on her third. Her first CD, *Diamond Star*, is the soundtrack for her novel of the same name. She appears as a vocalist at cons, clubs, and other venues in the United States and abroad, including as the guest of honor at the Denmark and New Zealand National Science Fiction Conventions. Visit her at www.facebook.com/Catherine.Asaro.